HAPPY JACK, THE ROVER.

"You jes speak up sharp, and tell me where my young Massa Jack is," replied the undaunted nigger, bringing his gingham to the front in preparation for another charge.

HAPPY JACK, THE ROVER,

With "PETER THE GREAT" and "HANNIBAL,"

HIS

TWO INIMITABLE NIGGER WARRIORS.

"What have they been doing to you, my poor Peter?" said Jack.

London:

ALDINE PUBLISHING COMPANY, 9, RED LION COURT, FLEET STREET, E.C.,

And of all Booksellers throughout the world.

CONTENTS.

CONTENTS—*continued.*

HAPPY JACK,
THE ROVER.

"LIFE's like a ship, in constant motion,
  Sometimes high, and sometimes low,
Where every one must brave the ocean,
  Whatsoever wind may blow ;
If unassail'd by squall or show'r,
  Wafted by the gentle gales,
Let's not lose the fav'ring hour,
  While success attends the sails.

" Or, if wayward winds should bluster,
  Let us not give way to fear ;
But let us all our patience muster,
  And learn from Reason how to steer.
Let judgment keep you ever steady,
  'Tis a ballast never fails ;
Should danger rise, be ever ready
  To manage well the swelling sails."

OLD SONG, 1798

CHAPTER I.

THE MISSING MEN.

"SOMETHING wrong ashore, sir."

A young middy touched his cap to his captain as he uttered these words, and stood in a respectful attitude waiting for a reply. Captain Cursley of H.M.S. "Thunderbolt" looked at him sneeringly, and turned upon his heel without a word.

"Something wrong ashore, sir," said the boy again. "I can hear firing."

He was a handsome lad, and the cool treatment of the captain had brought a deep flush to his face, which made him look more handsome still. The large, full eyes glistened, and the fine mouth quivered as he spoke for the second time ; and as the captain walked up the quarter-deck, he followed him with a determined air, which showed he was not to be put down by the treatment he had received.

"Something wrong ashore, sir," he said, for the third time.

"It seems to me, Mr. Scarborough," said the captain, turning savagely upon him, "that you are always finding some mare's-nest or the other. I hear no firing, and there is nothing wrong."

"Pray pardon me, sir," persisted the boy, "but I have very quick ears, and I am sure I can hear firing in the wood."

"You talk nonsense, sir," returned the captain, his face pale with fury. "In the first place, there are no inhabitants on this coast ; and if there were, they would carry no arms."

"But Mr. Warren has several marines with him, sir."

"Then Mr. Warren has disobeyed orders, and as soon as he returns I will place him under arrest."

"He would not have taken the marines with him, sir, but just before starting he saw some natives on the beach, armed with bows and spears. There is the firing again, sir."

"Hold your tongue, sir."

"I cannot, while my friend is in trouble," replied the boy, boldly ; "perhaps being murdered. May I beg of you, Captain Cursly, to allow me to take the long-boat and go ashore ? "

"There is no need, sir."

"I assure you there is, sir."

"This is rank mutiny!" cried the captain. "Mr. Dorning !"

The first lieutenant, who had been listening to their colloquy with an anxious face, came forward and touched his hat.

"Place Mr. Scarborough under arrest."

The first lieutenant touched his hat again, and summoned a corporal of marines and two men. The middy took off his cutlass, and surrendered it with a bow ; then, with another salute to the captain, he followed the men to the lower deck. Then, like a flash from the electric wire, the news passed over the ship that Happy Jack and the captain had come to an open rupture at last.

No surprises were expressed at this, for it had long been looked for. Since the boy joined—some two years before—the captain had been, to use the sailors' phrase, "down upon him ;" and the only reason which could be found for it was that the boy was the very antipodes of his superior officer. Jack Scarborough was handsome, brave, generous, and cheerful, and loved by all the men; while Captain Cursly had the face of an Indian idol, was as mean as a man can be, and having upon more than one occasion shown strong symptoms of the white feather, had secured the cordial hatred and contempt of every man under his command.

As soon as the boy was gone, the captain turned to the first lieutenant and asked him if he had heard any firing.

"I think, sir, that Mr. Scarborough was right," replied Mr. Dorning.

"I did not ask you whether Mr. Scarborough was right or wrong," returned the captain, furiously. "Did you hear any firing, sir?"

"I did, sir."

"Can you hear any now?"

"No, sir."

"Can you see any signs of the returning boat?"

"I cannot, sir."

"Then take the long-boat and go in search of her."

Mr. Dorning touched his hat, and then bade the boatswain pipe hands to the long-boat, and as soon as it was lowered he took his seat, and the men bent to their oars.

The captain, with a sullen brow, paced the quarter-deck, watching the boat as it skimmed over the waves. He felt that he had done wrong—for he had heard the firing from the first, and would have sent help at once but for the unfortunate anxiety of Jack Scarborough, whose most intimate friend, Tom Warren, was in command of the cutter. It was only because Jack had been the first to speak of the danger, that the captain had refused to recognise it.

Several officers and men were within hearing of the words which had passed between the middy and the captain, and although none dare express their sentiments upon the subject, their looks showed the way their sympathies were bent, and if scorn could have withered up Captain Cursly, he would have been turned at once to ashes.

He knew the feeling, and read it, for he was no fool; but as such looks were not entered upon the list of offences, he could take no cognisance of them. Nevertheless, he recorded several names in his memory for future punishment, whenever an opportunity offered.

In such a man evil is ever dominant—nothing can mould the cold, hard clay of his nature, nothing break through that wall of self which shuts out all that is just and noble. If Captain Cursly could have been touched, the scene around would have softened him.

Above, a sky of deep blue; below, an ocean rippling in the sunlight; before, a stretch of land, rich with the graceful foliage of the tropics, with a narrow belt of silver sand dividing the wood from the sea.

The "Thunderbolt" was anchored about two miles from the beach, just far enough to soften the outlines of the trees, without mingling their graceful outlines into a haze of indefinite beauty.

The tints of that forest, too, were innumerable—red, copper-colour, and all shades of green—and from its depths, softened by distance, there came the shrill whistle of birds, whose gorgeous plumage flashed often in the sunlight as they flitted to and fro.

No ill-built town, no meagre pier, jutting like a pole into the sea, no structure of man's making was there to mar the beauty of the scene.

Even Jim Swaby, the boatswain, who had a remarkable wooden expression of countenance, was impressed by it; and as he, too, followed the long-boat with his eye, and marked the flashing of the oars involuntarily gave vent to his feelings in words.

"I'm shivered," he said, "if it ain't better than a picter in the R'yal 'Cadlemy."

"What is the 'Cadlemy, Mr. Swaby?" asked one of the men near him.

"The 'Cadlemy," replied the boatswain, "is a house in London where a lot of chaps hang their picters on the walls for those who can't paint to look at."

"It's werry kind on 'em, Mr. Swaby."

"And it would be kinder on 'em if they didn't charge a bob for it," said Mr. Swaby. "But let that pass. I went to see the picters, and I enjoyed 'em well, considering; but the picter I went to see disappointed me."

"What was that, Mr. Swaby?"

"The 'Death o' Nelson,' and you never seed sich a thing. Nelson, clean and spick and span, as if turned out for a fancy ball, and lying in an attitude as if he rather enjoyed dying than otherwise, and the officers and men standing round quite reg'lar, making believe to look sorrowful, but anybody could see that every man in that picter was gammoning, although the real men as stood round Nelson felt it sore enough. There was one chap wiping his eyes with a white pocket-handkercher, and I never saw a man looking more like an ass. I'd a good mind to put my fist through it, but I thought the hartist might feel a little hurt if I did, so I sheered off, and took a look at the landskips, which were every one on 'em more than nat'ral."

"Here's the long-boat coming back, Mr. Swaby."

"And without the cutter: that looks bad."

Ten minutes more watching, and the long-boat touched the side.

Mr. Dorning stepped upon the deck and saluted the captain.

"Found the cutter, sir?"

"No, sir. Mr. Warren and the men gone, signs of a fight, and blood upon the sand."

"Any trace of the way they have gone?"

"Very little, sir. Wood very thick, but signs here and there of bodies dragged through gaps in the undergrowth."

"Then you think they are all murdered?"

"I am afraid so, sir."

"This comes of sending ashore for fruit. The men in future will have to do without."

"There is much sickness on board, and we had need of limes, sir," the first lieutenant ventured to suggest; "and if—"

"I have nothing more to say upon the subject," said the captain, turning away.

"One moment, Captain Cursly," said Mr. Dorning, stepping forward a pace. "Shall I take a couple of boats' crews and search the wood?"

"You cannot search all Africa," was the reply. "It was a fool's errand from the first. Who suggested it?"

"Mr. Warren, sir."

"Then Mr. Warren has met with the reward of his folly," returned Captain Cursly.

"And is Mr. Scarborough to be kept under arrest?"

"Certainly, and on arrival home he will be tried by court-martial for disobedience."

The first-lieutenant said no more.

Any demurring would only have brought trouble upon himself, without helping our hero, and half an hour afterwards the "Thunderbolt" was standing out to sea with all sails set, leaving Africa and the lost men behind her.

———

CHAPTER II.

THE TWIN NIGGERS.

THERE was much discontent on board the ship when it was found that Happy Jack was to be kept under arrest,

and curses deep, if not loud, were heard fore and aft.

Jim Swaby, the boatswain, sought, as in duty bound, to quell the mutinous mutterings he heard on every side.

"You must put a stopper on your jawing-tackle," he said, "or I shall have to interduce some of you to Aunt Sarah. Can't you *think*, you beggars, and not talk?"

The men did think, and the more they thought, the less they liked their captain, and whenever he set foot on deck, there was nothing but sullen silence, and sullen looks around him.

A little more fuel, a little more fanning, and the fire would break out.

Jim Swaby, with "Aunt Sally"—a stiff piece of knotted rope—in his hand, walked about in a thoughtful manner, prepared to check the very first signs of an outburst.

There were two causes of discontent—the first, the imprisonment of their favourite young officer; the second, the undoubted wanton and wilful abandonment of the lost men to their fate.

At the very least, Captain Cursly ought to have devoted a week to a thorough search of the shore and wood.

If dead, there would be no harm done; but if any were still alive, they might be saved.

The officers saw the lowering looks, and knowing what they portended, did their best to pacify the men, and in a great measure succeeded; but the state of the ship was far from being satisfactory, and the sight of the Channel Waters, at the end of two months, was hailed with joy by those in command.

During this time, our hero suffered nothing worse than the monotony of confinement. Had he dared, Captain Cursly would have liked to put the lad in irons, but that was a step he could not venture upon, mutiny would immediately have followed.

The "Thunderbolt" passed through the Needles, and anchored at Spithead, where the flagship of Admiral Savenay was lying.

As soon as the anchor was down, Captain Cursly, in "full rig," went away in the cutter to report himself.

While he was gone, Mr. Dorning, the first lieutenant, visited our hero, whom he found cheerfully and contentedly seated upon a locker, chatting with the boatswain, Jim Swaby.

"I've come, Scarborough," he said, "to chat a little with you about the coming trial. Perhaps, Mr. Swaby, you will not mind leaving us together?"

"Sartainly not," replied Mr. Swaby; "but I wish to say this much, sir—that if you are goin' to pitch into the cap'n, you needn't be afeard o' me. I'll stand up anywhere ashore and tell him he's a black-hearted willain!"

"Hush, Mr. Swaby!" said the other; "you forget where you are, and whom you are speaking to. It is my duty to report such language."

"I ax your honour's pardon," said the boatswain; "but for the minute I did forget. But, Lor', sir! I knows I'm all right with *you*, and thanking you kindly, I'll take my leave."

When the boatswain was gone, Mr. Dorning took a seat beside our hero, and speaking in a low tone, revealed the subject he came to speak upon.

"Now, Scarborough, tell me about your friends. Where can they be found, for you have need of all their help?"

"I have no friend but one uncle."

"And where is he?"

"At Clifton Grange, about seven miles from Portsmouth."

"You had better communicate with him at once."

"But surely this trial will never end seriously."

"I cannot say how it will end," replied the lieutenant, cautiously; "so much depends upon the nature of the charges, and—the frame of mind of the court."

"I see—I see," said Jack, smiling, contemptuously. "The court being composed of commanders, it will go hard with the middy. But I will fight them to the end. My uncle is rich, and he will spare nothing to save the honour of our name. I will write to him at once."

"And I will post the letter when I go ashore."

"Thank you, Mr. Dorning—you are very kind."

Jack then sat down and wrote the following letter—

"MY DEAR UNCLE,—Your own Jack is in trouble, having run against the skipper, who always has his fur the wrong way, and won't stand rubbing. You will find me on board the 'Thunderbolt,' lying off Spithead.—Believe me, my dear uncle, your own JACK."

Mr. Dorning took the letter, and went on shore, where he faithfully posted it.

This act of kindness showed his sagacity and true appreciation of Captain Cursly's spirit, who, on his return that evening, looked over the post-bag of the ship with the deliberate intention of stopping all letters written by our hero.

The next morning Jack received notice that he was to take his trial for insubordination and mutinous conduct in seven days, and that he was to hold himself in readiness to answer several charges made by his superior officer, Captain Cursly.

Jack at once wrote to the admiral, politely intimating that he should be most happy to attend at the time specified, and that he believed he should be able to confound his accuser and enemy.

In the evening, Mr. Dorning brought Jack a letter, and although he did not tell our hero that he had been watching for the bag for more than an hour, so as to secure it, such was, nevertheless, the fact, and it was by this that he saved the letter from falling into the clutches of the captain.

This was the contents of the missive, which Jack read aloud—

"Clifton Grange, Monday Morning.

"MY OWN DEAR BOY,—Your letter found me in bed, and without waiting to get up I hasten to answer it. Stand to your guns, and let the blackguard have it. I will see you through it, whatever it may cost. Look for me to-morrow.—Your affectionate uncle,

"CARTON SCARBOROUGH."

"Just like him!" cried Jack, enthusiastically. "What's this? A postscript. 'I shall bring Peter the Great with me.' I'm jolly glad of that!"

"Who is Peter the Great?" asked Mr. Dorning, opening his eyes.

"Peter is the funniest fellow you ever knew," replied Jack, laughing heartily. "He is a nigger, and such a nigger. Uncle bought him and his twin brother in America, and gave them their freedom. Hannibal is the brother's name.

"Do they live with Mr. Scarborough?"

"Both. Peter in the house, where he attends upon my uncle; Hannibal works in the garden, and he is stronger than any two men about the place. But Peter is the greatest fun—wait until you see him."

"I shall look forward to his arrival as a great treat."

"You may, sir," returned Jack.

Accordingly, Mr. Dorning kept a sharp look-out, and the next day he saw a boat approaching the ship with a living freight of four men.

One was rowing, and he was white; a second was sitting in the stern, and he was white; the others were in the bow, and they were black.

"Friends of Scarborough, I think," said the lieutenant to his captain, who was standing near.

Captain Cursly immediately turned his back, resolved to ignore all connection of the prisoner; but in this he most signally failed, for speedily a certain nigger named Peter the Great appeared upon the summit of the gangway, and proceeded to look about him.

Peter was indeed a humorous-looking fellow, and his attire alone would have done credit to any professional.

A tall, stiff, shiny hat, long-tailed coat, high collar, in itself a curiosity in the way of linen, and a very fat umbrella tucked under his arm.

The first lieutenant had walked away, and there was no member of the ship's company, save the captain, near Peter the Great, and to him Peter addressed himself.

"You seen my massa, sar?"

The captain never moved, but kept his back towards the speaker, pretending to look steadily out to sea.

Settling his neck in his collar, and grasping the handle of his umbrella, Peter advanced.

"You seen my young Massa Jack, sar?"

No answer.

Then the wrath of Peter the Great arose, and with a mighty thwack he brought his umbrella against the calves of the captain's legs.

"Now, sar, have you seen my Massa Jack?"

Pen cannot describe the wrath of Captain Cursly, as he turned round and glared at Peter the Great.

Accustomed to command and be obeyed, a little lord in his own domain, he expected to see the vile intruder fall upon his knees and implore pardon, at the very least.

But his assailant, in the first place, did not know who he was, and if he had, it is very problematical if he would have cared.

"Why—you—you—" gasped the infuriated captain; and then, entirely at a loss for words, he shook his fist, in impotent fury.

"You jest speak up sharp, and tell me where my young Massa Jack is," replied the undaunted nigger, bringing his gingham to the front in preparation for another charge.

There were several spectators to this scene, Mr. Dorning among them, and the faces of one and all were convulsed with laughter, and it was only by a powerful effort that the first lieutenant managed to compose his features and step forward to interfere.

"Put that—that inkpot rascal into irons!" roared Captain Cursly. "I'll have him strung up at the yard-arm!"

"What's all this disturbance about?" said a genial voice, and a fine, handsome old gentleman of about fifty-five years, stepped upon the deck, followed by another negro, who was clad simply in a striped linen shirt and trousers.

"Is this brute a servant of yours?" demanded Captain Cursly.

"He is my servant, and he is not a brute," was the quiet reply. "I sent him up to learn if my nephew is still confined on board this craft."

"You, I suppose, are the uncle of my prisoner, the mutinous John Scarborough?" said Captain Cursly.

"John Scarborough *is* my nephew," returned the other, "and he is not your prisoner, but the prisoner of the State, and whether he has been mutinous or not, remains to be proved. You needn't glare at me, sir! I am not under your petty control, and pray remember this—no man is fit to command others until he has learnt to command himself."

A low murmur of applause escaped the lips of the seamen who were assembled near, and the furious commander turned round and bade them go to their posts.

He would have liked to have put the whole of them in irons, but that would have been a little too much to undertake just then.

"Now, sir," said Mr. Carton Scarborough, "can I see my nephew?"

"Mr. Dorning," said the captain, "will you call the prisoner to see his friends?"

"You may have occasion to regret this pert insolence," said Jack's uncle. "I have brought down better birds than you, before to-day."

He then, after a word of caution to the two negroes not to commit themselves, followed the first lieutenant below, where Jack was anxiously expecting him.

The meeting was a warm one, for uncle and nephew loved each other, and as soon as the first greeting was over, they set about arranging the defence, assisted by Mr. Dorning, whose love of justice mastered his prudence, and led him to support the weaker side.

In the meantime, Peter the Great, maintained his dignity on deck by taking up a very imposing attitude, in which his favourite gingham played a very striking part, and Hannibal, his brother, whose muscular development was gigantic, leaned, easily, against the side of the vessel, and grinned until every tooth in his head could be seen.

Captain Cursly retired to his cabin, and in about half an hour Mr. Scarborough reappeared, followed by Mr. Dorning, who saw him over the side.

"I shall expect you at my hotel, remember," said Mr. Scarborough. "We can talk much better over dinner. Come, you niggers. You shall see Jack another time."

"I accept your invitation with pleasure," replied the lieutenant, and then they shook hands and parted.

The twin negro brothers stepped into the boat, and the man pushed off.

"Hannibal, ole boy," whispered Peter the Great.

"What am it, Peter?" asked the other.

"Dis gingham berry good ting," said Peter.

"Berry good," said Hannibal, and then the two chuckled and wriggled like eels, and they were chuckling and wriggling when the boat grated upon the beach.

CHAPTER III.

CONFUSION.

THE morning appointed for the trial broke bright and clear, and, when the warning gun sounded, Jack drew in his belt and stood ready to move.

A few moments later, Mr. Scarborough appeared, and with him came Peter the Great and Hannibal, who, forgetting all but their love for our hero, rushed upon him and fairly hugged him.

"Oh! Massa Jack, Massa Jack!" bellowed Peter the Great, "dis a great shame; but—"

Peter did not finish the sentence, but he flourished his mighty umbrella and rolled his eyes.

Hannibal doubled his arm, and the muscles stood out like ropes, and although he said nothing, that action showed that he was ready and willing to do his share of the defence.

Let us now go to the flag-ship, where all is prepared—the president and members of the court-martial, the marines drawn up, the table covered with papers and books, and Captain Cursly ready to take the oath and swear away the good name of the boy he hated without cause.

Jack entered the room, bowed to the court, and took his stand at the head of the table.

Behind him came his uncle, accompanied by Peter the Great and Hannibal, Peter making a very great display of both hat and umbrella, having one under each arm.

Mr. Scarborough bowed to the court; and the president, Admiral Sir Charles Codrington, rose from his seat, and shook him heartily by the hand.

Captain Cursly turned pale, and he felt the ground, which, half an hour before, had felt so secure, slipping beneath his feet.

However, there he was, and the case must be gone through with, and bracing himself up, he told his story.

In substance, it was this—

That, from the hour he joined, the prisoner, John Scarborough, had shown a frivolous disregard of the rules of his service, had neglected his duties, been late upon his watch, and when remonstrated with, had shown a tendency to open defiance; and furthermore, had invariably anticipated orders in matters which did not concern him.

In winding up, the captain gave a gross exaggeration of the scene which had taken place on the coast of Africa, and left the case in the hands of the court.

The court did not seem to be much impressed, for half its members were dozing, and the admiral was positively smiling.

When Captain Cursly concluded, he asked the prisoner if he had any question to put.

"I have," said Jack.

"Then do it, and make them as much to the point as possible."

"Hannibal," whispered Peter the Great.

"What am it?" asked Hannibal.

"Shall I give him one now?"

Peter touched his gingham, and looked at Captain Cursly significantly, from which it was plain that a plan of assault had been laid between the sable twins.

"I think not, jest yet, Peter. Wait until I can ketch hold ob him collar, and hold him down."

It was a very fortunate thing that Hannibal decided upon this course, for the result of "cobbing" Captain Cursly in such a place would have been most disastrous to the youth they wished to protect.

Jack proceeded to put his questions.

"You say, Captain Cursly, that I was very impertinent, and insisted upon telling you what was your duty."

"You did."

"Was there not great need for me to speak?"

"No."

"Was not the cutter ashore with Mr. Warren and eight men for fresh water and fruit?"

"It was."

"Were they not away some hours?"

"I believe so—I was not on deck when the boat left."

"Was there not firing on shore?"

"Yes."

"Did you hear it?"

"Not at first."

"And did I not hear it, and was not that the reason I gave for speaking?"

"I do not remember."

"Surely, Captain Cursly, you can remember that?" said the president.

Captain Cursly paused a moment, and then replied—

"I cannot."

"Was it not afterwards known that there had been firing?" continued Jack.

"Yes."

"And were not all hands lost for want of help?"

"They were lost, but I do not think that help could have been given."

"Was not help sent too late?"

"Help was sent."

"After my arrest?"

"Yes."

"I have no more questions to ask," said Jack.

"Is that your defence, prisoner?" asked the court.

"It is," replied Jack.

"Clear the court," cried the president; and the prisoner, followed by his friends, was marshalled out.

Jack was perfectly at his ease, but his uncle was afraid that he had not made enough of his case. Peter the Great and Hannibal were very doubtful, too.

"You should have gone into every detail of his petty oppression," said his uncle; "the fellow is a tyrant and a coward."

"I think you would act as I have done," said Jack, "if you knew naval officers as well as I do. Petty oppression is everywhere where a ship floats, and a court-martial is better without being bothered with a lot of petty detail. I am content to leave my case as it is."

"And dis chile, Hannibal, not come up," said Peter.

"Come up where?" asked Jack.

"He say to me dis morning—" Peter began.

"No; you say to me," interposed Hannibal.

"No; you say to me," repeated Peter the Great, "'I say, Peter,' you say, 'when we git into dat court, I take him by de collar, while you gib him goss wid dat umblerella ob your'n.'"

"Give who? Give what?" asked Mr. Scarborough.

"Gib dat Cap'n Cursy one wid de gingham," said Peter.

"Why, confound you for a pair of fools," said Mr. Scarborough: "that would have made a pretty mess of it."

"Jes' what I tole you," said Peter, to his brother.

"You tole me!" cried Hannibal, his black eyes rolling with fury. "If dis chile eber heard such big lie from morshall lips! Who stop you in de court? Who say to you—"

"Quiet there, will you!" cried the officer of marines; and the twins shut their mouths and glared at each other.

Jack winked at his uncle, and turned aside to laugh.

"The court is open," cried a voice; and once more the prisoner was ushered in.

The sentence was an immediate and prompt acquittal of all the charges, and Jack's cutlass and other insignia of his office were returned to him. Then Mr. Scarborough stepped forward.

"Jack," he said, "send in your resignation at once—here. A navy which admits of the possibility of such charges is not fit for you to serve in."

"Don't be hasty, Scarborough," whispered the president.

"I am not hasty," replied the other, in the same tone. "But I cannot subject my boy to the possibility of disgrace and punishment, even if he had been guilty of the offence."

"Once he leaves the service, he cannot return."

"Will you punish Captain Cursly?"

"I do not see my way to that," replied the president. "He will be privately censured, of course; but that is all we can do. He is very well connected."

"Bother his connection!" said Mr. Scarborough. "It is not fair to let such a man loose again to serve. He ought to be dismissed the service."

"That is more than can be done," said the admiral.

"Then my boy gives in his resignation."

The admiral shrugged his shoulders, and took a pinch of snuff. As a civilian, he felt Mr. Scarborough was right; but from a naval point of view he was decidedly wrong. If the case had been his own, he might have done the same.

"But he shall not live an idle life," said Mr. Scarborough. "If Captain Cursly has neglected his duty, my nephew shall do it for him. I will fit him out a vessel—I am rich enough to do it—and he shall bring back to England the true story of poor Warren and his men; and, if alive, he shall bring them home, and put that heartless man to shame."

"You have grown romantic in your old days," said the admiral, with a smile.

"Perhaps so," was the reply; "but it shall be done."

Their conversation was now interrupted by a little confusion at the entrance of the court, which arose from Peter the Great having aimed a blow at Captain Cursly as he was leaving, and having taken too wild an aim, had bonnetted the officer of the marines in his place.

Such an act might have got him into trouble but for Hannibal, his brother, who seized him round the waist, and carried him straight away to the boat in waiting, where he put him into the stern, covered him up with a rug, and sat upon him.

Shortly afterwards, Jack and his uncle came over the side, and the boat put off for the shore.

CHAPTER IV.

THE "SWALLOW."

JUST about the time of our hero's retirement from the navy, the Government of Great Britain were selling a number of vessels which had been declared unfit for service.

Many of these craft were of the brig class, well built, and fitted up in every way, and all were to be sold as they floated, with this exception, that the guns were removed and put to other uses.

Now, this sort of thing was nothing new.

Our Government is always selling out what it is pleased to call useless stock, and very often it happens that the very article sold is afterwards bought back again, leaving a wide margin of profit for the happy dealer, and many a ship declared one year to be unfit for use, is found within twelve months to be the very article required.

The sales I have alluded to went on briskly.

Most of the brigs were turned into the merchant service, but one was bought by Mr. Carton Scarborough for a very different object, which our readers understand.

It was destined for Jack's life at sea, and as soon as it was in Mr. Scarborough's possession, it was sent to Plymouth to be fitted out with every requirement for a cruise of several years.

There were no guns on board, and the port-holes were blocked for the time, and in this condition the brig looked as peaceable as you please, and those employed upon her thought that Mr. Scarborough was going to use her like a yacht—an idea that gentleman, from prudential motives, did not contradict.

In the meantime, the "Thunderbolt" was paid off, and Mr. Dorning, tired of the service, tendered his resignation.

It was accepted, and having commuted his pension, he went straight to Plymouth, and joined the brig, which had been named the "Swallow;" and the very next day, Jim Swaby, late boatswain of H.M.S. "Thunderbolt," came on board, too, and set to work putting things in order as naturally as possible.

Immediately after their arrival, sundry heavy packages came down from various parts of the country, and were got on board at once, and carefully put away in the hold.

Many of the men employed to get them on board wondered what they were, but as nobody relieved their curiosity, they were left to work out the problem in their own mind, which every man of them failed to do.

As soon as these packages were stowed away, the brig was ready for sea, and then, one morning early, Jack and his uncle, accompanied by Peter the Great and Hannibal, appeared on board the "Swallow," and were received with great cordiality by Mr. Dorning and Jim Swaby.

"So all is ready," said Mr. Scarborough.

"All is ready," replied Mr. Dorning. "The men came on board last night, and we have only to spread the canvas, and sheer off."

"You have got good men?"

"If I picked the navy, I could not find better."

"That is well; but are you contented to sail under such a captain?"

"Contented!" said Mr. Dorning, with a smile. "I will follow him through the wide world, and I am sure those are the sentiments of Jim Swaby."

"I'd die for the lad," said Jim; "and so would every man on board. We all know Happy Jack, sir. That's the name we gave him, sir, and that's the name he'll bear with us."

"He is a noble fellow," said Mr. Scarborough, looking with pride at Jack, who was taking stock of the brig with eyes brimful of pleasure; "but a little too bold. I hope to see him again when the cruise is over."

"You will see him again, never fear."

"And you think that he can sail a craft like this?"

"He was the smartest lad in the service," said Mr. Dorning. "But there, I've said enough. You may wonder that I should give up the post I held; but I am a man without patronage, and I should never have got my ship. The Admiralty would have kept me as a lieutenant until my head was white, and as I have still some love of fun in me, I prefer roaming with Jack to hanging about the Channel and stifling in dockyards. Your two servants go with us?"

"Yes," said Mr. Scarborough; nothing else would content them. They always loved the boy, and no dog could be more faithful than Peter and his brother. Goodbye!"

Mr. Dorning shook him heartily by the hand, and Jim Swaby "took a grip."

Then Mr. Scarborough and Jack went below to take their leave in private.

It was brief, and when the old man came up alone, his eyes were full of tears.

Silently he stepped into the boat, and without one look back, and with his head bent down, he was borne to the shore.

Then Jack appeared.

"We will sail at once," he said. "All hands there."

One after the other the broad canvas sheets filled out before the wind, and the "Swallow" gracefully heeled over, and dashed the spray right and left with her bows.

"She's a beauty!" cried Jack, enthusiastically. "Hurrah for a roving life!"

"Hurrah!" cried the others, and Peter the Great, led away by his ecstacy, dashed down his umbrella, and turned a wheel with such energy that he shot down the hatchway like a sack of coals.

"He's broken his neck!" cried Mr. Dorning.

"Not at all," replied Jack, laughing. "You don't know Peter. Here he is."

And as he spoke, Peter came forth, brushing his hat with his coat-sleeve.

"Dat de worst ob being on board ship," he said. "All de conflounded doors am in de floor. Whar my rumblerella?"

It was given to him, and then, without having apparently received even a contusion by his fall, Peter the Great strutted the deck with a majesty which excited the admiration of all beholders.

Away before the wind went the gallant little ship, leaping joyously over the waves like a thing with life; now plunging like a steed, now gliding like a swan, leaving behind her a track of white foam to mark her course.

About ten miles down the Channel a frigate hove in sight, and at once bore down upon them.

"That's the 'War Eagle,'" said Jim Swaby. "I knows her figure-head as well as I do my own phiz."

"Captain Cursly has been appointed to her," said Jack, quietly.

"And if he knows this is your craft, he may give you some trouble," said Mr. Dorning.

"I am upon a peaceable errand," returned Jack, "but I will not be snubbed by that fellow."

"There goes his signal for us to pull up."

"I shall do nothing of the sort. Out with the royals there."

The royals were let loose, and the "Swallow" dashed forward at an increased speed, for a stiff breeze was blowing, and the tops of the waves were white with foam.

"He knows us," said Mr. Dorning, who had been looking at the "War Eagle" through a glass. "There's his signal gone."

"Has he any authority to stop me?" asked Jack.

"None that I know of. But it depends upon his commission. I only heard that the 'War Eagle' was going on a foreign cruise."

"Authority or not, he shall not stay me," cried Jack. "Up with a gun there!"

"What would you do?" asked Mr. Dorning.

"Give him his answer. I'll give him just what he sent me—blank powder. If he gives me more, I'll return it."

"Think of your peril."

"I care not. How long can we keep clear of his shot?"

"He cannot reach us, going as we are, within two hours."

"Time to rig one of my guns," said Jack. "You need not take part in it unless you wish, nor any of my men. Pipe them aft, and I will say a few words to them."

Jim Swaby, with a fixed expression of face, piped a tune, and the men came running aft to hear what Jack had to say.

In a few words, he told the situation, and concluded thus—

"He has no right to stop me here. This is free water, and it is only done in spite. If he fires into us, shall we return it?"

"We will! Hurrah!" cried the men.

"I know that this craft is no match for the one behind us," continued Jack; "but the captain never yet faced shot, and he will funk the first fire. So up with the run, my men! You have two hours before you!"

"Hurrah for Happy Jack!" cried the tars, who, in their reckless way, looked upon the whole thing as a bit of fun, and soon several of the packages were taken from the hold, and placed upon the deck.

The coverings were stripped off, and a gun, with the various parts of the carriage, were revealed.

Mr. Dorning stood by, looking at these proceedings with a very doubtful face; but the energy of Jack and his men became infectious, and with a "confound the consequences!" he pulled off his coat, and went to work with the rest.

As the signal gun failed to bring up the brig, the frigate fired no more, but came on with a cloud of canvas gracefully spread out before the wind.

"I say, Hannibal," said Peter the Great.

"What am it, Peter?" asked Hannibal.

"I guess I like to gib dat ship one—old Cursem de cap'n."

"You leab him to Massa Jack," said Hannibal, confidently. "You see how he gib him goss."

The twin brothers were leaning off the stern while speaking, watching the frigate, which was slowly but surely overhauling them.

Night was far away, and escape by flight was impossible.

This even the darkies knew, and there was only two things to do—to fight in the end, or give in.

The latter Jack was resolved not to do, as a matter of pride.

"The fellow knows who commands here," he said, "and he only wants to overhaul me as an annoyance, and as I have had quite enough of Captain Cursly, I don't mean to give way."

The "Swallow" was built for eight guns, and all she required were in the hold.

Jack heartily wished that every one was in its place, so as to bite well when he did show his teeth; but twenty-four hours, at

least, were required to get his ship into real fighting trim, and he was obliged to rest content.

"Dat big hunk's coming nearer," said Peter the Great.

"And Massa Jack's gun quite ready," returned Hannibal, quietly.

The gun was now fixed amidships in the starboard side, and Jim Swaby, who was at the wheel, obeying a sign from Jack's hand, brought the "Swallow" round a bit, so as to show the mouth of the gun to the enemy.

Mr. Dorning seized a glass, and stood ready to report the movements on board the "War Eagle."

"Another blank shot coming," he cried.

"Boom!" came the sound of the gun, echoing far away to the very horizon.

"Ready, there!" cried Jack.

"Aye, aye, sir."

"Answer him."

Peter the Great and Hannibal were standing by the gun, and just as the word was given, Peter stooped down, and looked along the gun as the sailors had done.

Peter had not the slightest idea of gunnery, but imitation being a great qualification of the nigger, he could not refrain from imitating the movement.

The tar in charge of the touch-hole pulled the string.

Out flashed the flame, and the gun, recoiling, sent Peter, with his hat, collar, and umbrella, flying.

"Golly!" shrieked Hannibal. "Poor Peter's got bashed by dat 'ere gun. Peter, my brudder, look up, and open dat eye ob your'n!"

But Peter either would not or could not, and lay like a log upon the deck, without a sign of life.

———

CHAPTER V.

THE WHITE FEATHER.

MANY anxious friends immediately gathered round the prostrate Peter, and Hannibal, with the assistance of a sailor, put the injured one upon a barrel close by.

"Is he killed?" asked Mr. Dorning, anxiously.

"Killed!" said Jack, laughing. "The vagabond is not hurt a bit. He was only taken by surprise."

"Oh, that's it?"

Peter, who now began to show signs of animation, was, indeed, rolling about in a very wonderful manner, and although his

Silently Jack's uncle, his eyes full of tears, stepped into the boat, and without one
look back, and with his head bent down, was borne to the shore.

eyes were not fairly open, he showed a deal of white, and opened his mouth in a series of gasps, which would have done credit to a stranded codfish.

"A lilly drop ob rum," he gasped

One of the men gave him a little, but he only gasped the more.

"Another lilly drop," groaned Peter the Great.

"You no berrer, Peter?" asked Hannibal, in whose eyes there suddenly beamed a sarcastic gleam.

"No berrer," groaned Peter.

"Me bring him round," said Hannibal, quietly looking round.

There was a piece of boarding, part of one of the packing cases close by, and taking it in his hand, Hannibal took up a position behind his brother.

"You sure you no berrer, Peter?" he said.

"No berrer," moaned Peter.

Peter lay in a convenient position, with his coat-tails spread out on either side, and, with a terrific smack, the board descended on that portion of his frame usually associated with a chair, and like one suddenly galvanised, Peter the Great sprang up.

With a growl which was half a shriek, he pounced upon his umbrella, and turned upon his brother. What might have ensued we cannot say, for all consequences were checked by the sound of another gun from the frigate, and a shot came skipping over the sea.

It struck the bulwarks of the "Swallow," scattering a thousand splinters right and left, and slightly wounding one of the men.

"Ready there!" cried Jack.

"Pause one moment," said Mr. Dorning.

"I cannot pause now," returned Jack. "I will take the consequences. You can be exonerated if we are captured."

"In all things I stand by you," said Mr. Dorning.

"Ready there!" cried Jack.

"Aye, aye, sir!"

"Fire!"

The gun was well aimed, and two of the yards of the frigate came crashing down, and falling over the side, hung there.

"That has stopped her for half-an-hour," cried Jack. "Hurrah for the 'Swallow,' boys!"

"Hurrah for Happy Jack!" cried the men, and the shout they gave reached the frigate.

In all sailors there is an instinctive love of adventure, and, as a rule, a blue jacket rather enjoys risking his life and liberty, just as a countryman is fond of poaching because it is unlawful, and brings with it a certain risk.

Happy Jack's defiance was, therefore, very popular with his men, and, full of glee, they loaded the gun again, and waited for orders to fire once more.

Mr. Dorning, by means of the glass, was enabled to see what was going on on board the "War Eagle," and as he took in the various incidents, proceeded to report them.

"Officers running to and fro," he said. "Men busy cutting the wreck away. Another shot."

"Badly aimed!" said Jack, as the iron missive bounded away a full hundred yards across the bows. "Give them another, lads!"

"This will end with some of us up at the yard-arm," muttered Mr. Dorning.

Jack overheard him, and his big blue eyes twinkled with merriment.

"Don't be funky," he said.

"I am not," was the reply; "but this is about the most daring thing I ever heard of."

"He broke the law first," said Jack. "Well hit!"

The second shot from the "Swallow" struck the "War Eagle" in the bows, and a cloud of splinters sprang in every direction.

An officer was seen to leap upon the bulwarks and shake his fist at their little foe.

"Is that Captain Cursly?" asked Jack.

"No," replied Mr. Dorning. "He is nowhere to be seen."

"He has shown the white feather, and gone down below."

"Most likely."

"It was an old dodge of his whenever we had a little beat up with the savages."

"I remember it."

"Went below to examine the chart! Ha! ha!"

"Ha! ha!" laughed Mr. Dorning in concert, and Peter the Great joined in the chorus, without knowing why, with a bellow that would have done credit to a bull, and finished off by lying on his back and kicking his heels in the air."

"Peter has great spirits," said Mr. Dorning.

"Peter is the greatest fun I know of," replied Jack. "Nothing hurts him, nothing makes him melancholy, and nothing will induce him to change that style of dress He would not part with either hat, collar, or umbrella for the world."

"The 'War Eagle' has cut away her wreck."

"Then the chase begins again."

"I am not so sure of that," said Mr. Dorning, fixing his telescope. "Captain Cursly has come on deck."

"Screwed his courage up."

"No, by Jove! He means to turn tail. He is quarrelling with his officers. They turn from him in disgust, and now he crosses to the man at the wheel. He shows the white feather."

"Impossible!" cried Jack.

"It is true. Look at the cur. Take the glass, and look at him standing by the man at the wheel, to force him to his work. See how unwillingly the man obeys him. There she goes!"

"The fellow will be dismissed."

"Not he. He will find a dozen excuses for his cowardly conduct. Found it impossible to overtake us, and thought it better to return to the flag-ship for orders."

"Out with the bunting fore and aft!" cried Jack. "Let us leave him with all colours flying. Send another shot across his bows, and give three cheers for the gallant 'Swallow!'"

In a minute a dozen flags fluttered in the wind, and the first gun of the "Swallow" sent a third shot skipping over the sea, and with a cheer which reached the frigate, the gallant little craft sped upon her course.

"Hooroar for Massa Jack!" cried Hannibal.

"Hooroar!—Hooroar for Massa Jack for eber!" cried Peter the Great. "Hannibal, 'ole boy, hold my rumblerella, and let me show dese chaps how de nigger dance!"

Hannibal took possession of the precious gingham, and then, having secured all eyes, Peter began a dance of such wild proportions and agile movement that whole chapters would fail to describe it, and so we leave it to the imagination of our readers.

As they went down Channel, they passed several ships, homeward bound, and many a glass was turned upon the brig, with canvas set, and colours flying, and many a sailor wondered at this unwonted spectacle so near the shores of Old England, for she looked like a craft dressed out for a gala, and not like a ship that was outward bound.

"There's mischief in the looks of that craft," said more than one skipper. "I'll bet we shall hear more of her before the world is two years older."

And they were right.

Britain's shores were destined, ere long,

to ring with the fame of the "Swallow" and her gallant young commander—Happy Jack.

———

CHAPTER VI.

KACHVU, THE NEGRO CHIEF.

WE must now leap over a gap of two months in our story, and come to the time when the "Swallow" safely rounded the point, and anchored in the bay where, a year or so before, the men of the cutter of the "Thunderbolt" had disappeared.

The spot is as beautiful as ever, for this is the land of endless summer; the sky is the same deep blue; the sea the same gold-like, glittering water, and the foliage and birds are as rich in colour as before, and on the land there is the same stillness which speaks of the absence of man.

The "Swallow" drops her anchor and swings easily round with the tide, and as she does so, she shows four guns to the shore, for now all is ready—every gun is in its place to do battle in the hour of need.

A boat swings over the side and drops lightly into the water.

Then Happy Jack, still in the old, easy costume of a middy, steps into it, and Hannibal, Peter the Great, and a dozen men follow him.

Jim Swaby and Mr. Dorning look over and wave an adieu.

Then the boat speeds towards the shore.

"Dis berry much like Africa," said Peter the Great, breaking the silence.

"It is Africa," replied Jack. "I did not tell you we were coming here. I wanted to surprise you with the sight of your native land. You don't seem to be much overcome."

"Me no like him much," returned Peter. "Peter and Hannibal no t'ink well ob him."

"Why not?"

"Bad place—bad man. Mudder die and leab farder wif two lilly children. Bad farder—sell two lilly children for bottle ob rum and red cloth coat."

"White man gib the rum, but only promise de coat," put in Hannibal.

"Dat de white man's fault," said Peter. "We sell for a bottle ob rum and red coat."

"Is it possible that your father could be so heartless?" said Jack.

"It am a great big fack," replied Peter.

"Hannibal and I two lilly niggers rolling on de sand—up come farder and white man. 'Dere are my lilly kids,' say farder. Den white man bring out bottle ob rum and say, 'Bring de coat to-morrer.' Den he put us in a boat and row away. Farder lay down on his back and drink de rum right orf. He berry drunk before we get to de ship."

"What a heartless brute!" said Jack.

"Him not a bad farder *in his way*," explained Peter. "Him stand out for a good price for his lilly boys. Some farders sell dem for few beads. We fetch big bottle ob rum and red coat."

"Promised," said Jack.

"Dat so," assented Hannibal.

"Life on board ship berry bad," pursued Peter. "Bad hold—all stink—full ob niggers all in bad way. Some die, and den we frow 'em out—white man only get half home—oders all die. Hannibal and dis chile got sent to de plantation in Ameliky, where we work all day, and get goss from de oberseer's stick all night. We run away an hide in dear ole Massa Scarborough's house, who buy Hannibal and his brudder, and bring dem to England. Me die for Massa Scarborough and Massa Jack."

"Better live for me," replied Jack, laughing. "But there, you need not, either of you, kiss my hand. *I* didn't buy you."

"But Massa Jack berry kind," said Peter.

"Him de jolliest lilly man in all de world!" said Hannibal.

At this moment the boat grated upon the beach, and the sailors, leaping out, pulled it up high and dry. Jack and his faithful followers then put foot on *terra firma*.

All were armed with cutlass and pistols, except Peter the Great, who had his favourite gingham and a cutlass, but no pistols; but the gingham, we know, was a host in itself, and we may, therefore, consider him to have been as well armed as the rest.

"The sun burns like a furnace," said Jack. "Peter, why don't you open your umbrella?"

"Him no open again," replied Peter. "All de bones broken."

"And no wonder," returned Jack. "What a magnificent country this is!"

Well might Jack feel a thrill of pleasure as he looked upon the glorious scene.

Mangrove, cocoa, cotton, palm, and laurel trees, mingled together in harmonious profusion, with others bearing oranges, lemons, bananas, figs, pumpkins, water-melons, yams, prickly-pears, and white plums growing thick'y between, with such a profusion of fruit that a nation would not have languished for want of a supply.

Signs of man there were none, but birds were not wanting.

Pigeons, parrots, and guinea-hens were flying about in every direction, with a few of a strange species known as ox-eyes, all of gorgeous plumage, which gathered additional charms from the fierce rays of a noonday sun.

So entrancing was the scene, that our hero for the moment forgot the real object of his coming; but quickly arousing himself, he walked up the beach, and climbed to the summit of a knoll, where he took a long and earnest look around.

No signs of man—save those with him.

Naught but the sea, the sky, the wood, and the screeching birds.

"Poor Tom!" he sighed. "I am afraid I have come upon a fruitless errand. Some savage, perhaps cannibal tribe must have fallen upon you and your unfortunate men, and if they did not kill you, must have carried you away. Carried away! But whither?"

He turned towards the boat, which lay about half a mile away.

The crew, in obedience to orders, were lying on the shady side, waiting his return.

Peter the Great and Hannibal, in obedience to orders, too, were wandering about in search of signs of man.

The instinct of the negro is quite equal. if not superior, to that of the North American Indian, and take him on the whole, he is by far the better man.

The negro accepts civilisation—the American Indian will not.

The negro often develops into a very pleasant, serviceable, faithful friend; but the Indian is cold, cruel, and treacherous to the end.

Too much has been written in favour of the American tribes, and too little has been said about his darker brethren on the African coast.

The name of negro has been always associated with stupidity, and it is time for the world to be thoroughly undeceived.

Peter the Great and Hannibal were two fair representatives of their nation—Peter, with his love of fun and grotesque antics: Hannibal, with his dauntless courage, fidelity, and mighty muscular power.

In good hands, they were excellent fellows—in bad hands, they might have been something different, for the negro needs guiding, and he will freely follow whither you may lead him.

Some such thoughts as these flitted through our hero's mind as he stood upon the knoll, and he was still pondering upon the good qualities of his attendants as he descended.

On reaching the beach, he lay down to wait the report of Peter and his brother, who were industriously examining the borders of the wood.

Let us join them for awhile.

"Dere nobody here, Hannibal," said Peter, as they paused for a moment under the shade of a mangrove-tree.

Hannibal shook his head.

"None," he said. "I t'ink Massa Jack come to de wrong spot."

"What dat?" whispered Peter, stooping quickly down.

Hannibal stooped, too, and for a moment both were motionless.

"You hear?" whispered Peter.

"Me hear," said Hannibal, "big foot splosh among de leabes."

"Where Massa Jack?" said Peter.

"Ober dere; lying on de sand."

"Him asleep?"

"Me t'ink so."

"You stop here, Hannibal, and listen," said Peter. "Me go and stand by Massa Jack—cubber him face wif palm-leaf, so him no get sunstroke."

Hannibal nodded and Peter the Great moved away as silently as a shadow, his tall hat, which he kept perfectly brushed, shining with dazzling brilliancy.

The position of the various parties now were as follows—

The boat with the sleeping seamen was a quarter of a mile to the left of Peter, and Jack lay about the same distance to the right, and the wood which Peter stood by was about three hundred yards from the sea, running along the beach in an almost perfect straight line, rising here and there with the swelling ground.

Peter, with his umbrella under his arm, and his hat very much on the back of his head, struck out towards our hero; but ere he had walked fifty yards, he suddenly paused, and listened again.

An inexperienced ear would have heard nothing but the gentle murmur of the sea, and the screeching of the birds, but on the ears of the quick negro there fell a sound which, to him, was full of danger.

He heard footsteps in the wood.

Footsteps so light that a burglar might have envied the pedestrians, but unmistakably defined to the listener.

And they were the footsteps of many.

With his dark eyes rolling, Peter hastened on.

Crying out he felt would be folly, for Jack might not hear him, and if the foe were numerous, it might only bring on a premature attack.

To arouse Jack quietly, and get him to the boat, was the first thing to do.

The seamen were there, and they were safe; and Hannibal he knew could take care of himself.

"Dey stop now," muttered Peter, breathing a little more freely. "Me get up to Massa Jack now."

He had taken but one step more, when, from the very thickest part of the wood, and just opposite our hero, there glided out the form of a savage, with his eyes fixed upon the sleeping boy.

"Kachvu! Kachvu!" muttered Peter, as a look of horror spread over his face. "Kachvu berry, berry cruel! Me come, Massa Jack — berry quiet, and berry quick!"

CHAPTER VII.

FRIEND OR FOE.

THE man issuing from the wood was a magnificent specimen of the African —tall, well-shaped, and muscular.

Over his right shoulder hung a mantle of grass cloth, which reached to his knee; around his neck were several strings of beads of various sizes, and an ornament composed of the same things, woven in with some material, hanging from his hips, and covering his loins.

At his back was a bow and quiver.

In his hand he carried a long spear.

There is always an air in those accustomed to command which cannot be mistaken, and anyone looking at this savage would have recognised in him a leader of his people.

The nose was flat, and the lips thick; but his eyes were large and lustrous, and the features were harmonious, which, after all, is the secret of real beauty.

He saw the sleeping boy alone, for his eyes turned neither to the right nor the left; and after the first pause, he, with his spear lightly poised, advanced.

Step by step, with his eyes fixed, and nostrils dilated, as if he longed for blood, the savage chief whom Peter had called Kachvu drew nearer to our hero, who lay quietly sleeping, with cutlass drawn ready in his hand, an instinctive precaution

Jack had taken when he lay down to rest.

Step by step, with murder upon his dark face, he advanced until within a few feet of Jack; then the arm uplifted.

It might have been the rustle of the mantle, or the touch of some guardian spirit hand that roused Jack from his sleep—which, we cannot say—but at that instant he opened his eyes, and took in his danger at a glance.

With a cry of execration, he closed his hand upon his cutlass, and made an effort to rise to his feet; but it was too late, and Jack's mortal course would have ended then but for Peter.

Urged on by fear and fury, he had come upon the foe behind with the swiftness of the wind, and, forgetful of his cutlass, he raised his umbrella in the air, and brought it down upon Kachvu's head with a mighty crash.

The blow was irresistible, and the savage reeled, and fell upon his back, where he lay blinking in a very bewildered manner.

In a twinkling, Jack had cut the thong which held the quiver to his back, and removed the bow and arrows, and taken away the spear.

"Now, Massa Jack," said Peter, "let me hab another bash at him."

"Let him be," said Jack, laughing, "he is perfectly harmless now. If he attempts to run away, I know how to call him back."

Jack took a pistol from his belt, and pointed at the muzzle significantly.

"I am not likely to miss my aim," he said.

"But do let me hab anoder bash at him," pleaded Peter the Great, twirling his umbrella in a very scientific manner.

"Not now," said Jack. "You must be quiet, Peter."

Thereupon, Peter gave up his attitude, but stood ready to renew the assault, in case the savage became obstreperous; and Jack, with his pistol ready for use, quietly waited for the savage to come round.

Kachvu was more bewildered than hurt, and he soon recovered.

His first act was to feel for his bow, and finding it was gone, he drew up his legs close to his body, and bowed his head, as if ready to receive the death stroke.

"Get up," said Jack. "I am not going to kill you."

Kachvu raised his head, and looked intently into our hero's face.

"No kill?" he said.

"I will not kill you, if you obey me," said Jack. "Do you understand me?"

"Me un'rstan' little," said Kachvu.

"Dat big t'ef understand eberyt'ing," put in Peter the Great. "Him berry cleber."

The savage chief, now made aware of Peter's presence for the first time, honoured him with a look.

Peter took up a very dignified attitude, and the savage was impressed.

He bowed three times, overcome with the magnificence of Peter's apparel.

"You bad Kachvu," said Peter. "No bow to me. Here come Hannibal. I say, ole boy, you know dis t'ief?"

"Kachvu!" cried Hannibal, in surprise.

Kachvu, who knew neither of them, but fancied that they must be great potentates, bowed very reverentially again, and put some dust upon his head as a sign of his total submission.

"You know that man?" said Jack.

"Me know him," replied Hannibal, shaking his head; "me know him berry bad."

"Not bad *now*," said Kachvu, with emphasis.

"You attempted my life," returned Jack.

"No, 'tempt life," replied the savage; "me only stand with spear *so*. Kachvu good friend."

Of course Jack did not credit this, but he was at a loss to know what to do.

He did not care to kill the man in cold blood, nor did he desire to be bothered with him as a prisoner. What, then, was he to do?

"Your name is Kachvu," he said.

Kachvu bowed thrice.

"I want you to answer a few questions," continued our hero. "About a year ago, nine white men were lost about here. Do you know anything about them?"

There was the slightest possible pause ere Kachvu replied, and then he spoke with apparent frankness.

"Kachvu," he said, "know the whitee men."

"Are they alive?" said Jack, eagerly.

"All," said Kachvu.

Jack's heart leapt within him with pleasure.

This was great and good news, indeed.

"Do you know where they are?" was his next question.

"Dey live with Kachvu and his people," replied the savage.

"Live with you?"

"So—and they love Kachvu."

As the chief spoke, he rose to his feet and touched himself lightly upon the breast to express love.

Jack thought he was going to run away, and cocked his pistol.

"Kachvu not run away," said the other; "he stay long time."

"Where are your people?" asked Jack.

"Long off, far away," replied the chief.

"Then you are alone?"

"Kachvu quite alone," was the calm reply.

"Dat one big lie," said Peter the Great; "lot ob your men in de wood."

"Have you seen them?" said Jack.

"No; me hear dem."

"But you may have been mistaken?"

"No mistake," said Hannibal; "me hear dem, too."

During these utterances, Katchvu stood quite still, with the calm look upon his face of one compelled to listen to a falsehood.

His look was that of majestic indifference to the calumnious attack of a lower order of beings.

Jack was taken in.

"I think, Peter," he said, "that you are mistaken."

"I'll forfeit this 'ere rumblerella, if I am," said Peter; but, notwithstanding this most mighty offer, Jack still thought that he must be in error.

"Kachvu," he said.

Kachvu became all humility and attention.

"You say that my white friends are with your people?"

"It is so."

"Will you bring them here?"

"Kachvu bring them quick—swift as the bird."

"Go, then. I will trust you," said Jack. "If you keep your promise, you will be rewarded. If you fail, I will hunt you like a dog!"

"No let him go!" cried Peter the Great, thrusting out his gingham. "Kachvu one great lie all ober."

"No let him go," said Hannibal, putting his huge frame in the path of the the savage.

"I can do no good by keeping him," said Jack. "I will trust him. Let him pass."

The twin brothers drew aside with very dubious looks, and Kachvu strode one step forward, and then turned.

"Katchvu hab long way to go," he said. "He must hunt and kill. Let him hab bow and arrow."

"No," said Jack; "you have all you need for keep, in the way of fruit. I will trust you no further. Go, and keep your word."

A sullen flash passed over the savage's face, but in an instant it was gone.

Then he strode away, and went straight to the borders of the wood.

There he paused again, and looked around.

How changed he was.

The humility, the deference, all gone, and his form dilated with insolent triumph.

"Kachvu," he cried, "come again—soon!"

Then he put a hand on each side of his mouth, and gave a shrill whoop.

In a moment the wood seemed to be alive with men—fierce, dark, savage faces cropping up among the bushes, and peering from every tree.

"Oh, Massa Jack!" cried Hannibal, "you done it now."

"Back to the boat!" cried Jack; "and keep your face to the foe!"

CHAPTER VIII.

A RUNNING FIGHT, AND A VERY GREAT LOSS.

THE shrill whoop which came from the lips of Kachvu performed two things.

It brought his own men to the wood, and roused the sleeping sailors on the shore.

The tars saw what was amiss, and, leaving two in charge of the boat, came running forward to render to our hero what assistance they could give.

And he was in great need of it.

After one discharge of arrows, the blacks came pouring forth from the wood, with Kachvu, newly armed, at their head.

Each man bore a spear and bow, and many of them carried a shield, about two feet long and one broad, upon their left arm.

It was plain that they needed urging on for instead of advancing in a body, they showed a tendency to scatter about; but this Kachvu railed against, and made them keep close together, and attack at once.

The sailors were ready to meet them—in fact, they were eager to open the ball, and when Jack gave the word to charge, the compact body rushed up the sands with as much glee as schoolboys at play.

"It is our only chance to make ground," thought Jack. "If once we get them into the wood, we may make good our retreat!"

These words flashed through his mind as he rushed on at the head of his men, with Hannibal on one side, and Peter the Great on the other, his handsome face lighted up with enthusiasm.

"One round from the pistols," he said, "then the cutlass!"

"Hurrah!" cried the men.

The savages sent a flight of arrows, but their aim was very wild, and all fell harmless, with the exception of one, which went straight through the hat of Peter the Great, carrying away two or three locks of his most valuable wool. An inch lower down, and Peter would, there and then, have breathed his last.

After this discharge, the natives showed a disposition to turn tail, but Kachvu roared and foamed, and, as they evidently held him in great fear, the majority stood their ground.

Jack went straight for Kachvu, but that warrior, however brave, was wary, and skilfully put one of his men between himself and our hero.

The unhappy black received Jack's cutlass in the chest, and fell without a moan.

Kachvu made a rush at Jack, but Hannibal, who was was fighting with his right hand against two men, dashed out his left, and sent the chief to the earth like a log.

At this juncture, a cloud of savages rushed over the spot, and, for an instant, the gallant little band was driven back; but, in a moment, Jack rallied his men, and, with additional ardour they renewed the fight.

The natives numbered, at least, some hundreds, and, though at least twenty of their body had kissed the dust, and a large number had beaten a judicious retreat, they did not seem to diminish.

Jack's cutlass flashed right and left, dealing death with every stroke, and Hannibal's heavy sabre—a weapon formerly used by a giant guardsman—lopped off heads, arms, and legs, as if they had been straws.

Each sailor, too, fought bravely, and every cutlass waved by them told a terrible story of wounds and death.

Above the shrieks and cries of the wounded, and the shouts of the combatants, arose the voice of Kachvu, urging on his men in their own language, and, although Jack could not interpret the words, he knew their meaning pretty well by the tone.

Kachvu was urging on his followers to capture the whites—to rend, to tear them, or beware his vengeance.

Our hero and his men had each reserved a pistol for a final shot, in case of great emergency. Like all sailors, they preferred the cutlass to the pistol, and, although each moment getting more hard pressed, no man changed steel for powder.

Two of the men had fallen, thrust through the body with spears, and one was already dead.

One of the others stooped down to help him.

"Never mind me," he said. "Give it to the niggers hot."

His comrades obeyed him, and the savages began to fall like wheat before the scythe.

Still numbers threatened to carry the day, and just as the arms of many began to tire, a shout was heard in the rear, and twenty blue-jackets, headed by Jim Swaby, dashed in.

The fray had been seen from the deck of the "Swallow," and Mr. Dorning had despatched the old boatswain and the men to the rescue.

This addition to their force settled the question in favour of the whites.

The natives only waited long enough to lose about twenty more men, and then, with a whoop, the whole body plunged into the wood.

"Welcome, indeed, old friend," said Jack, as he held out his hand. "Upon my word, you just came in time."

Jack was hot, dusty, and tired, and leant upon his sword as he spoke.

There was blood upon him, too; but it was the blood of foes, and not his own.

"I heerd the wampires," said Jim. "Anybody hurt?"

"Two," replied Jack, "and poor Smith is dead; nobody else. Why—why, where's Peter?"

"Me see him in de fight," returned Hannibal, looking round bewildered; "but me no see him now."

Peter was gone!

There was no time to be lost, if Peter was to be saved.

That he was not slain, Jack was fully convinced, for his body would have been left behind by his enemies, and calling the men together, he asked who would volunteer for the service.

Exhausted as they were, every man held up his hand at once.

Jack would not take them all, and leave the ship unprotected, so he chose Hannibal, Jim Swaby, and a dozen men, most of whom had shown conspicuous bravery in the fight.

The rest he sent back, desiring them to

have a boat near the shore, and to keep a good look-out.

"And tell Mr. Dorning," he added, "that if I am not back in a few days, he is to act as he thinks best. Search for us will probably be useless, and he had better carry the news of our misfortune home."

Drawing his belt a little tighter, the brave lad then led his men into the wood, with Hannibal and Jim Swaby close behind.

Hannibal's face was a study.

He looked like a bloodhound on the scent—eyes wild, nostrils dilated.

His thick lips were compressed so tightly that the blood was driven back, and half their colour was gone.

"Come to my side," said Jack to him. "You must be our guide."

"Me find him," was Hannibal's answer.

And slightly bending his giant form, he led the way, in company with his master.

The savages, though very numerous, had left but little trace of the road they had taken.

They seemed to have the feet of cats, and Jack's eyes, although tolerably sharp, failed to perceive any signs of the direction they had taken.

But Hannibal had no doubt.

He saw distinctly the way they had gone, as if sign-posts had been set up, and walked on at a swift pace, but, at the same time, as lightly as the savages themselves.

The wood was magnificent.

Some of the trees were prodigious in size, their trunks rising bare at least a hundred feet, and then spreading out mighty branches, so thick with foliage that the sky could only be seen in small star-like patches.

Cedars and palms abounded, and innumerable plants of rare beauty and size grew between.

"A nice bit of plantation this," said one of the men.

"No talkee, now," muttered Hannibal.

"Silence, there!" said Jack.

And, like grim spectres, they marched on.

Their progress was very rapid, for the ground was fairly open, although the plants were so numerous, and very few serious obstacles were presented.

If anything was really in the way, such as a creeper or cactus, Hannibal, with a swift stroke of his cutlass, severed it, and tossed it aside with the hand of an expert; and as the earth was covered with a thick carpet, formed by the fallen leaves of ages,

their footsteps gave forth no sound, and the silence remained unbroken.

By-and-bye, the forest broke for a moment, and they came upon an open glade, the most strange and wonderful sight Jack and his men had ever seen.

A complete circle of rocks, cast up from the earth ages before, enclosed a basin of the purest water, so clear that they could see to the bottom, although the depth must have been at least a hundred feet.

Fish, large and small, gorgeous in colour, darted to and fro, like shafts of fire, sparkling up from the depths, and guanas and large lizards skimmed about the surface, waiting for the fish to rise, when they would become their prey.

Great branches of trees overhung the water, and upon these a multitude of birds rested, screaming out a deafening chorus.

"Glorious!" said Jack, carried away by the beauty of the scene.

"Talkee now," said Hannibal. No man make out what you say now—de birds scream."

Jim Swaby took advantage of this liberty to ask one of the men what he meant by kicking his heels as they came along.

The man said that he was anxious to get in front, in case of a turn-up with the land sharks.

Mr. Swaby said it was like his cursed "himpudence to try to take a rise out of his s'periors," and hinted that if he didn't keep a little more in the offing, that he would lop off a toe or two with his cutlass.

"All them chaps are regular envious," he said to Jack. "They can't let a man get the first knock on the head without howling at him. Goin' for'ard, sir?"

"Hannibal seems to be rather puzzled," said Jack.

"Me not at fault," said Hannibal, who had been looking intently at a rock, so close that he almost rubbed his nose against it; "me see where Peter lie down on him back."

"Where?" asked Jack.

"Dere," replied Hannibal, pointing to a rock which was as smooth as a paving-stone.

Jim Swaby looked at the rock with both eyes, then with each eye by itself, but could see nothing.

"If you can see anything there—" he began, when Hannibal interrupted him.

"Hannibal," he said, "got whole eye, you got half-eye. Me see where Peter lay him down, an' de brass buttons in him back mark de stone."

"Lying down!" said Jack; "then he may be dead."

"No," said Hannibal, confidently; "him make one, two marks—Peter wriggle. Go on now, Massa Jack."

They moved forward, skirting the huge basin, and plunged into the wood again.

The deeper they got, the more signs of animal life appeared.

First one monkey, then another, came down to the end of a branch, and hung by the tip of his tail, to get a good look at them; and by-and-by a whole troop of these lively creatures crossed their path in a mighty hurry, as if flying from some pursuer.

"Can I speak, Hannibal?" asked Jack.

"Talkee as much as you like," answered Hannibal.

"My——"

"Black nigger with Peter gone on quick —long way in front."

"I am sorry to hear that. Was it them who disturbed the monkeys?"

"No, Massa Jack. Dem monkeys show dere tails to black tiger—him come sneaking along soon—dere!"

He seized Jack's arm, and pulled him back for a moment, pointing ahead.

There, sure enough, was a black-looking brute following upon the trail of the monkeys as intent upon pursuing as they were escaping—so intent that, like them, he did not perceive the party in the wood.

Jack would have liked to have had a shot at him, but Hannibal said it was not good to shoot yet, and when the tiger had disappeared they moved on.

CHAPTER IX.

PETER'S TRIBULALION.

HALF-AN-HOUR'S walking brought them no nearer to the foe, and as the night was near, Jack felt inclined to despair.

"If darkness comes," he said, "we can do nothing."

"Rest little while," replied Hannibal, "then we go on."

"In the dark? Impossible!"

"Great light here at night—by firefly, Massa Jack. Such lubly little lantern on him tail."

"But not strong enough to give us light."

"Enough for Hannibal," replied the black; "me see de way to go."

This was no vain boast on the black's part, for when darkness came on, and the wood around them became illuminated with the wonderful fireflies, Hannibal only waited a short time to give the weary party a rest, and time to eat a little of the food they had prudently brought, and then moved on again.

* * * * *

Our friend Peter was not dead; he had been only captured.

In the heat of the fray, Kachvu's eyes had fallen upon him, and thirsting to possess Peter's clothes, had, with about twenty men, suddenly fallen upon him and carried him away.

Under ordinary circumstances, Peter would have been slain at once; but, fortunately for him, Kachvu had a superstitious dread of a dead man's clothes, more especially the clothes of a man whom he had murdered.

Not that the savage had much compunction in the matter of blood-spilling, for he was as merciless as a tiger at most times, and among his men, and such of the tribes who had the misfortune to live near him, he was looked upon as something a little above the average in ferocity.

He spared Peter from no other motive than that of getting his apparel in a way which would not disturb his conscience.

So Peter was gagged and carried away like a log through the wood to the basin where Hannibal saw signs of his presence.

Tired for the moment, the bearers had laid Peter down, and Peter, knowing that in all probability his brother would be put upon his track, had, as Hannibal declared. wriggled about so as to leave some signs of his presence.

Kachvu's men were as ferocious-looking savages as one would care to see; but to Peter they had no terrors.

He had lived long enough in savage land to know the value of hideous paint and ghastly bones hung about the body, and as far as these went, he did not care a rush; but what he did think about was his ultimate fate.

What would they do with him?

Roast, or toast, or boil, or skin him?

Any of these things he knew they might do, and something like fear took possession of him.

Still, he knew that his Master Jack would not desert him, and he had another comforter in the form of his umbrella, which he had clung to so tightly that the savages, in their hurry, had been obliged to bind it with his body, and there it was, with the handle sticking into his ribs, and the nozzle reclining lovingly upon his knee, embracing him, as it were, and comforting him in the hour of distress.

Kachvu, with his prisoner, travelled all night, and the next morning arrived at a spot which, for the present, he had made his home.

There were no signs of habitation except the long, low huts, one of which was guarded by a number of savages, who squatted around it with their arms ready to their hands, as bloodthirsty a lot of rascals as ever trod the earth.

As their chief appeared, they sprang to their feet, and hailed him with shouts.

Kachvu received their acknowledgments graciously, but singling out one, he had him secured and bound immediately.

What this man had done was not quite clear, but he paid the penalty of his crimes with his head, which Kachvu struck off himself, after two bungling attempts, with a heavy knife, which one of his men brought from the above-mentioned hut.

The others looked coolly upon the execution, and when it was over, tossed the body into the bushes. Half an hour later, Peter the Great saw a host of carrion crows hard at work feasting upon it.

"Me neber t'ink how bad black man was afore," he said, sadly. "Him better be white man's slabe."

King Kachvu, as his people called him, spent half an hour in private in the hut with a guard, which seemed to be his royal residence, and then came forth to take from Peter his lawful possessions.

Kachvu had a great notion of having things *given* to him, and he resolved to try persuasion with Peter; so, having removed the gag, he proceeded to interrogate him.

"You gib Kachvu coat?" he said.

No answer from Peter.

"Gib coat?" demanded Kachvu, frowning.

"Me gib you suffin', sare," replied Peter, glaring. "Take off dese bonds, and stan' up."

"You no gib coat?" said Kachvu.

"No!" said Peter, adding something very forcible, but very rude, to the effect that he would see him everything but blessed first.

"Den me make you," said Kachvu.

He signed to some of his men, and taking Peter up again, they carried him a short way from the huts to an open glade and laid him down.

King Kachvu took a seat upon the stump of a tree, and his men, with rude implements of wood—something like spades—proceeded to dig a deep hole.

"Wurra dat for?" demanded Peter, as a horrible thought burst upon him.

His enemy smiled sardonically, but he gave him no answer.

Peter's blood ran cold.

Was he to be buried alive?

"I tell you one ting, you cussed nigger," said Peter, "and dat is you soon hab Massa Jack here, and he make you hop like de little flea dat got into de fryin'-pan. Hab you heard dat story?"

Kachvu said nothing, and Peter went on—

"Me not tell such 'fernal nigger as you anyt'ing. You bury me alibe, sare?"

"Me will," said Kachvu, briefly, "if you no gib coat."

"You big rascal, and bury me *when* you got de coat," said Peter, "so Peter be bury wif him. Why you not murder dis chile and take de coat? Yah! Kachvu big coward. Him afraid of de lilly white ghose ob Peter comin' to him in de night.

"Peter not die if him gib up coat," said Kachvu.

But Peter did not believe him, and firmly impressed with the idea that all was over with him, he resolved to foil the chief of his prize.

The superstition of Kachvu and his people was well known to him.

By this time the hole was ready, and Peter was lifted by the men and carried to it.

Upon the chance of friends being near, he uttered a most dismal howl, which made even Kachvu jump up as if he had been pricked with a pin.

The next instant, Peter was gagged with a bit of wood and a withy, and put into the hole.

He expected to be laid out and covered at once, but no such thing.

They stood him upright, and filling the hole up to his shoulders, stamped the earth firmly around him.

Bound hand and foot, and pressed on all sides by the earth, Peter was perfectly helpless.

He could only glare upon his tormentors.

Kachvu made a sign to his men, and they disappeared.

Then squatting on the ground within half a dozen feet of Peter, he told him what he had to expect.

"You no gib coat," he said, "no gib coat to-day, but to-morrow, perhaps, you gib coat—eh?"

Peter could not answer except with his eyes, which spoke volumes of wrath.

Kachvu laughed gleefully, and playfully touched Peter's nose.

"Night come," he said. "All dark 'cept firefly. Lizard crawl about him face, whip-snake get round him throat— so, den, p'r'aps, you gib coat. If snake kill, Kachvu not kill. Him *find* Peter with eyes shut, and dead. Yah! den no ghost come."

Kachvu, you see, with all his ferocity, had his weaknesses, and the one fear of his life was the spectres of the dead.

It was the weak joint in his armour, and it saved Peter's life.

After taunting him a little more, Kachvu went away, and Peter was left alone.

CHAPTER X.

A DOUBLE RESCUE.

PETER THE GREAT was a very meditative nigger.

At home, in the peace and plenty of Mr. Scarborough's house, he had been celebrated for his ruminations, and now, as soon as Kachvu left him, the floodgates of his mind were opened, and he thought as follows:—

"Dis anyt'ink but comfor'ble—head berry warm, feet berry cold, and a sort ob ticklin' 'bout de legs, as if dem beetles was getting up dese trousers ob mine. Golly! what dat which wriggle so? Dat a worm, as sure as de name ob dis chile am Peter. Not ready for you yet, ole boy, although Peter soon die, and you make lots ob little holes in him. Dis gag hurt my simpermetrical mouf berry much."

After one or two efforts, Peter the Great got the withy between his teeth, and bit it through.

Then he spat it out, and was once more free to shout at will.

But it was no use bellowing, as far as he could see, so he remained quiet, and pursued his ruminations.

"I 'speck berry much dat if I get out ob dis, dat my coat will be sp'iled, and as for dat rumblerella, I shan't be able to take him into 'spectable society ag'in. Kachvu berry big villain, to be sure. Get away, sare, and leab dis chile's nose alone!"

This remark was addressed to a most pertinacious dragon-fly, which showed a tendency to settle on our friend's nose.

It seemed to be aware of his helpless condition, and buzzed within an inch of his face, as if laughing at and deriding his misery.

Peter the Great hissed, blew, and spat at it, but the pertinacious insect only enjoyed his misery the more, and finally settling down, deliberately stung him.

"Murder! Golly! dis nose ob mine hab got its beauty ruined. Yah! you villain! Get away, sare! You lubberly coward!—sting a man when him stuck into de earf like a wooden stick. Get away, sare!"

The dragon-fly betook himself away, as if satisfied with his work, and Peter occupied the next ten minutes in watching the rising of his nose, which swelled with amazing rapidity, until it was, at least, three times its usual size.

In repose, Peter's nose was a very fair-sized organ, but it was now something beyond the nasal ornament of man, and in addition to the swelling, it now began to itch tremendously.

"I gib de whole world just to rub him one moment," Peter muttered, as he rolled his head to and fro. "Oh, golly and brandysmash! dis is de mose scrutinating t'ing I eber know. Murder! Oh—Hark! What dat?"

A firing of pistols close by, followed by a series of most unearthly screams, and shouts from the savages, fell upon his ears.

"Massa Jack!" roared Peter, in an ecstacy of delight. "Hooroar for Massa Jack! Cut up de whole lot, and gib dat rascal, Kachvu, goss! Hooroar for Massa Jack!—and dat's Hannibal's lubly voice, I swar. Oh, Hannibal, my brudder, I neber lub you so much as now!"

The firing was continued, and above the cries of the savages was heard the shouts which can only spring from honest throats.

The clash of sabres, too, broke in upon the listener's ears.

"Dat de sort ob music," cried Peter, shaking himself like a madman. "Oh, for one lilly go in wif dis rumblerella! I'm here, Massa Jack! Your own lubly, faithful Peter the Great am dis way!"

A savage, all bloody, and covered with perspiration, now sprang into the open glade.

He threw his spear at Peter, but fortunately, missed him, and fled on.

"Tank you for dat," said Peter. "If eber we meet ag'in, I fetch you such a bash as make you fling your legs ober your head! I hear you make good fight,

Massa Jack! Hooroar! Massa Jack, dis way for de faithful Peter!"

But at present, Jack and his men seemed fully occupied, and, by the sound, the fight waxed fast and furious.

The screams of the wounded savages were awful, and the yells of the survivors were more like the howls of wild beasts than the utterances of men.

It was all over in a few minutes, however, and then there came a moment's lull.

Peter was wondering who had been victorious, when a great shout came rolling towards him, and he knew that Kachvu was beaten.

"Massa Jack, gib him goss!" bellowed Peter, wriggling so violently in his excitement, that he loosened the earth around him. "Dis way for ole Peter de Great, Massa Jack, dis way!"

A crash of underwood was now heard, and Jack, followed by Hannibal, leaped into the open ground.

"What have they been doing to you, my poor old Peter?" said Jack, who was ready to split at the spectacle his faithful follower presented.

"I'be been burried alibe, Massa Jack," replied Peter the Great. "Help me out, Hannibal, my lubly brudder!"

Hannibal took him by the arms, and drew him out like a cork; but, in the process, Peter's short Wellington boots were left behind.

"Dat jes' like you, Hannibal!" said Peter, furiously, forgetting all his love and gratitude for the moment. "Dat de way wif all cussed old hunks like you. What you care for your only brudder's boots?"

Hannibal made no reply, but clearing away the loose earth with his cutlass, he rescued the boots from their untimely grave, and, shaking the dirt out, handed them to Peter who melted in a moment.

"Hannibal," he said, "you am de best cherip in de wide world!"

Then, Peter's bonds being cut, they embraced with a fervour which threatened to break in their respective ribs, and really did squeeze every bit of breath out of their bodies.

"Now, are you ready?" asked Jack, who had been highly amused.

"Yes," replied Peter; "but dat am de way wif Hannibal—he always keep Massa Jack waiting!"

"I've great news for you, Peter."

"What am it, Massa Jack?"

"I have found Tom Warren."

"Dat so, Massa Jack? Hooroar for you!"

"And six of the men."

"Hooroar ag'in!"

"Hold your tongue, Peter! How can I talk to you if you keep bellowing like a bull? It seems that they were suddenly fallen upon, and two of their number killed outright. The rest—— Am I talking too quick for you, Peter?"

"No, Massa Jack. I jest a lilly bit stiff, and I t'ink dat a stag-beetle got into—— Jes' one minnit, Massa Jack, and me take him out!"

Peter drew aside, and, turning up his trousers, revealed a fine stag-beetle, which had fixed itself upon his shin.

Putting it on the ground, he brought down his foot upon it, and then, with a smile of triumph, moved on again.

"All right now, Peter?"

"All right, Massa Jack, 'cept a few lilly beggars ob some sort down my back. But I can see to dem by-and-by!"

"The rest, as I was saying," pursued Jack, "were overpowered by numbers, and carried away captive. They have been kept in a hut, and most cruelly treated. These savages must be monsters, indeed!"

"If black man bad, him berry bad!" said Peter.

"But if him good, him berry good!" put in Hannibal.

"You are right," said Jack. "Here we are, Tom. This is the missing Peter!"

Peter, conscious of what was due to respectable society, took off his hat, and made a very low bow. Tom Warren, a youth in tattered middy's attire, and pale and wan with recent suffering, but a very smart-looking fellow withal, held out his hand.

"I am glad to make your acquaintance, Peter," he said.

"And dis am de mose comfumbrious moment of my life," replied Peter.

Tom Warren would have laughed, but Jack winked to intimate that such a thing would hurt the feelings of Peter the Great.

So he refrained, and having been introduced to Hannibal, who had not his brother's command of language, and simply said, "Over mighty glad to see you, sare," he placed himself under Jack's orders, who was getting the men ready to return.

The two huts of King Kachvu were fired, and the score or so of dead savages who had been slain were left upon the ground.

Peter looked for his particular friend.

Kachvu, but he was nowhere to be seen.

"Kachvu no killed," he said to Jack.

"No," replied our hero. "He fought well at first, but when he found we were too much for him, he turned tail. Fall in, there! March! Take my arm, Tom. You are very weak."

"So are the other poor fellows."

"Who are already being helped by their comrades," said Jack. "Upon my word, you are all, indeed, translated. Who would think that any one of you had ever been on board a man-of-war?"

CHAPTER XI.

BRANDED.

THE party reached the shore without any mishap, and getting on board the "Swallow," she was soon under weigh.

Tom Warren and his men got a change of dress, and the men were enrolled as part of the crew.

"My work is soon done," said Jack, as he sat with Tom Warren at the dinner-table. "I can put Captain Cursly to shame by taking you home."

"He is a cowardly cur!" returned Tom Warren; "and nothing will give me greater pleasure than to show him up in his true colours."

"A sail in the offing," said Mr. Dorning, putting his head in at the door.

"What is she like?" asked Jack.

"A trader. She is signalling for help of some sort."

"Run up and see what it is," said our hero.

Shortly after, he and Tom went on deck, and found the stranger so near that she had shortened sail and was lowering a boat.

The master and some of the crew got into her, and pulled alongside the "Swallow," and the master stepped upon the deck.

Until that moment he had not seen the guns of the "Swallow," and when he caught sight of her equipment, he turned deadly pale.

He thought he had made a mistake, and put his head into the lion's mouth.

"I—I had no idea—" he stammered.

"What is the matter?" asked Jack, quietly.

"I—I took you for a peaceable trader," returned the merchant captain. "I—had—no—no idea——"

"What?"

"That you were—ahem!—I——"

"Scarcely know what to say," said Jack, laughing. "Come, man, don't stand stuttering and stammering there. What do you want?"

"I have some sick people on board, and we are out of lime-juice and quinine."

"Then I will give you some. Mr. Dorning, send some forward here."

The merchant captain looked more puzzled than ever, and it was plain that in the first instance he had given himself up for lost, and even Jack's good humour and kindness did not fairly restore him

Mr Dorning brought the quinine and lime-juice, and the merchantman received them with many expressions of thanks.

As he was about to go over the side, he turned and asked Jack to favour him with a word or two in private.

They drew aside, and the merchant captain, after a prefatory cough, said—

"This is the 'Swallow,' ain't it, sir?"

"Yes."

"I thought so. And whither are you bound?"

"Homeward," said Jack.

The visitor coughed again, and shuffled about on his feet.

"Home?" he said.

"Yes," said Jack.

"To England?"

Jack nodded.

"Then take my advice," said the skipper. "and don't go!"

He sank his voice to a whisper as he uttered these words, and drew a step back. as if he had said something which would bring down vengeance upon his own head.

Jack could not help smiling, but he was extremely puzzled.

"Why should I not go home?" he asked.

"Because—— But I can't tell you." said the skipper. "You see these two bits of paper?"

"Yes; they look like handbills."

"They are handbills," replied the man. "Now, I am going to give you them on one condition."

"What is it?" asked Jack, who thought the man was mad.

"That you don't read 'em until I am hull down, at least."

"I will promise you not to read them at all, if you like."

"Better read 'em," said the man, as he passed the papers into Jack's hands : " and now, good-bye."

After this, he was in a mighty hurry to go, and Jack, leaning over the side, saw him urging his men to pull for their lives.

They seemed to partake of his spirit of fright, and pulled like demons.

As soon as they got on board, every inch of canvas was spread, and the merchantman was soon out of sight.

Jack then told Tom Warren of the interview he had with the man, and to his surprise, Tom did not laugh.

"Don't read the papers here," he said. "Come down below. I am afraid there is mischief in the wind."

They went below, and Jack, opening the first, read as follows:—

"DESERTERS FROM THE NAVY.

"WHEREAS, twenty-two men having deserted from H.M.S. 'Thunderbolt,' as it is believed for the banding together for a felonious purpose,

TWENTY POUNDS REWARD

will be given for the capture and conviction of each and all of the missing men, who may be known by the following marks."

Here followed a detailed description of the twenty-two men, whom Jack had no difficulty in recognising as members of his crew.

Up to this time, he had no idea that they were deserters, and he saw the fix he was placed in.

"So that is how Cursly strikes," he said. "As if men were not deserting every day, and as if every merchant craft had not one or more of the men who had broken their word to escape tyranny."

"I thought the papers meant mischief," said Tom, quietly. "Read the other Jack."

Our hero spread the other out, and the moment his eyes fell upon the first lines, a look of anger sprang into his face.

It deepened as he read on, and when he finished, his indignation found vent in words.

"The pitiful cowards and asses!" he said. "What do you think they have done, Tom?"

"Read, and tell me," said Tom; "but I think I can guess."

Jack spread out the paper angrily, and read aloud—

"PIRACY ON THE HIGH SEAS.

"WHEREAS, it having come to the knowledge of H.M. Government that a brig has been fitted out in an English port for the purpose of piracy, and that the said brig is the property of and commanded by

JOHN SCARBOROUGH,

late midshipman of H.M.S. 'Thunderbolt,' the sum of

FIVE HUNDRED POUNDS

will be paid to any person who shall give such information as shall lead to his discovery—half to be paid on *apprehension*, and half on the *conviction* of the offender—and all loyal subjects are hereby desired to lend their aid in furthering the ends of justice."

Then followed a description of Jack and the brig, so minute that any man with half a sailor's eye could never mistake her.

No pains, it was evident, had been spared to bring about Jack's ruin.

"Was there ever such pitiful villainy?" said Jack. "It is all Cursly's work."

"No doubt," said Tom; "but what will you do? Go back to England?"

"No," replied Jack, his face flushing. "Not until I have shown how little of the traitor there is in me. England is at war, and her enemies are strong. I will fight such as I meet—aye, and fight English ships, too, if they fire upon me! Come on deck, Tom."

He ran up the companion in a fever of haste, and called aloud for Jim Swaby.

The boatswain appeared at once.

"Pipe all hands aft!" cried Jack.

The whistle sounded cheerily, and the men came tumbling up, and crowded round their captain.

Jack then read the two handbills, and made a few comments not at all complimentary to Captain Cursly, or those who aided and abetted him.

He concluded as follows—

"They have branded me as a felon, and would hang me, if I returned home: so, for the present, there is nothing left for me but a life upon the sea. Will you stand by me? Will you trust me, and be guided by my will or not? Who says yes?"

Up went a little forest of hands, crowned by Peter's gingham, and a general shout rang out.

"Who says no?"

A dead silence, and every hand down.

"That is well," said Jack. "Run up a white flag, and keep it at the masthead. That shall be *my* colour until my country gives me a better. Hannibal!"

Like an avalanche they broke upon the Privateer's deck, and drove back the howling mass.

"Yes, Massa Jack," said the mighty black, elbowing his way to the front.

"Are you with us?"

"I guess I am," said Hannibal.

"And you," Peter?"

Peter made no immediate reply, but stooping, smote the deck a mighty blow with his favourite weapon.

The action was sufficient, and there only remained to speak to Mr. Dorning, who was below.

Jack went down to him, and told him what had happened.

Mr. Dorning was palpably confused, and certainly did not like the turn events had taken.

"I did not expect this," he said. "Piracy is a serious matter."

"But we are not pirates," said Jack.

"It is all one, whether you are or not," returned Mr. Dorning. "If they catch us, every man will hang from the yard-arm."

"Pardon me," said Jack, "it does matter whether we are pirates or not. They may hang us, but they cannot make us blood-thirsty thieves. An honest man never need fear to die."

"But all honest men have a wish to live."

"I see," said Jack, "that you are not with us."

"Indeed I am not," said Mr. Dorning, after a pause. "You are young and some-what rash, and I think that if you, instead of running about the sea, were to put in at some foreign port, and communicate with the Government—"

Jack lay back, and laughed outright.

"Communicate with the Government!" he cried, "and get a frigate for an answer! No, Mr. Dorning, I shall do nothing of the sort just yet. When I *do* communicate with Government, I shall be in a position to demand a favourable answer. You need not join us."

"Indeed, I would rather not."

"Very well, Mr. Dorning. In a few hours we shall be in sight of Narau—a calling station for some of the trading vessels. You will easily get a passage home."

Mr. Dorning bit his lips, and looked as if he was ashamed of his desertion; but he was getting into years, and the fire of youth having died in him, the proposed roving was not suited to his palate; so he put his kit together, and Narau heaving in sight, a boat was lowered.

Jack took a kindly leave of him, and thanked him for all the interest he had shown, and also charged him with a message to his uncle and home.

"Tell him," he said, "that I will never show my face in England until I can put my enemies to the blush, and wipe away the stain upon my name."

Jack was very sorry to part with him; but taking all things into consideration, he thought that the absence of the ex-lieutenant would leave him a freer agent —in fact, the presence of one who had so long been his superior officer had acted as a check upon our hero, and he had never, up to the time of Mr. Dorning's depar-ture, felt quite like the commander of his own ship.

Now he was free; and with naught but friends and congenial spirits on board, he set sail in search of adventure upon the deep blue sea.

CHAPTER XII.

AN ENEMY AND A SLIGHT MISTAKE.

IT was night upon the sea, and darkness lay upon the face of the waters.

Clouds overspread the sky like a pall; but there was no storm, and scarcely a breath of wind—only just enough to bowl the "Swallow" along in a lazy manner, just as one walks who has no real purpose in view in the quiet field or lane.

It was Jim Swaby's watch on deck, and Peter the Great was with him.

The men sat about the forecastle quietly smoking, for Jack gave them many liber-ties, such as they had never known on board a man-of-war—liberties they very much appreciated.

Jim Swaby was a man who never forgot his duty, and although he was almost cer-tain that no other vessel was within fifty miles of them, he nevertheless kept a good look-out.

Peter, with his chin resting on the taff-rail, was, in his own way, keeping watch too.

"I say, Massa Swaby," said Peter the Great, after a long silence.

"What's the row, my Hemperor?" asked Jim, who had taken a great fancy to Peter, and heaped endearing names upon him.

"Dis a berry dark night."

"Uncommonly," said Jim. "A man can't see two feet from the tip of his nose."

"White can't," returned Peter: "black man *can*. Him see through a big brick wall. Yah!"

"If you say so, my noble Rooshian,"

said Jim, "I am bound to believe you; but when I get's you ashore, I'll play you a trick with a deal board ag'in your nose, and if you tell me how many fingers I hold up, I'll eat my grandmother's tabby tom-cat."

"Berry likely you hab to eat him," said Peter the Great, putting his umbrella down and craning his neck over the side. "Come here, Massa Swaby."

"I'm on your lee, my hancient markiss," said Jim.

"Can you see not'ing dere, Massy Swaby?"

"Where?"

"Perhaps dis rumblerella guide you," said Peter, taking it up and holding it in a line with Jim's eye. "You see not'ing near him nozzle?"

"Nothing. What do you see?"

"Ship, Massa Swaby."

"You think you do, my am'able barrow-night."

"I see him plain," said Peter the Great, emphatically. "Long ship—low hull—tall sticks and no sail. Where dat Hannibal?"

"I saw him asleep on a locker as I came up."

"Jes' you fetch him, Massa Swaby."

Jim crossed the deck and went below.

In a few moments he returned with Hannibal, who was stretching his long arms and yawning.

Peter, who could see him very distinctly, smote him smartly in the rear.

"Wake up, you lazy Hannibal!" he said, in a low tone. "What you see ober dere?"

Hannibal followed the direction of his brother's finger, and almost immediately replied—

"Big ship—low hull—tall sticks and no sail."

"I'm darned," exclaimed Jim Swaby, "if there ain't something in it! Why, what a fool I've been! A curious-looking craft crossed our course to-day, and we didn't take no notice of her. She crept up arter us. Peter, my King of the Cannibal Islands, go down and fetch the skipper and Mister Warren!"

In a very short time, Jack and Tom were on deck, and the fact of something being wrong having got afloat about the ship, the men were lively too, but everything was very quiet.

Jack heard the story, but, like Jim Swaby, he could see nothing.

He, however, knew that his faithful blacks had the eyes of hawks, and he believed what he heard.

A dead calm had now set in, and the "Swallow" rocked idly upon the sea.

"Speak low, all of you!" Jack said, in a soft tone. "There is something wrong in that craft. I thought so as she passed us this morning. Now, which of you two has the best ears?"

He addressed Peter the Great and Hannibal, both of whom instead of speaking of their own qualifications, promptly assailed that of his brother.

"Hannibal's ears stopped up wif putty," said Peter. "Him no hear a gun fired wif de barrel ag'in him nose!"

"Peter's ears come off a wooden image," said Hannibal. "Him hear not'ing, 'cept dinner-bell!"

"Dat's a brudderly way ob speaking to your brudder," said Peter, with an injured air. "But Hannibal hain't got no feeling. His heart am a cocoa-nut?"

"Peter's am—"

"Silence you two!" interposed Jack. "Both of you listen!"

The two negroes bent their heads down, and listened intently for a few seconds.

"What dat, Hannibal—two boats?"

"Two boats," said Hannibal, for a wonder agreeing with him.

"Cloth round de oars," Hannibal!"

"Dat right, Peter."

"Muffled oars!" said Jack. "Then we need no longer be dumb. Get the men quickly together, Tom; and you, Swaby, get the bow-gun ready. They take us for a merchantman, but they will find out their mistake! Lie quiet here, men. Is the gun ready?"

"Aye, aye, sir?"

"Now, Peter, are the boats near?"

"Dey halted, jes' one moment," replied Hannibal, speaking for his brother.

"Confound you!" said Peter, getting very wrathful. "Jes' like you—allers putting your ugly nose in your brudder's face!"

"Do be quiet," said Jack. "Now, Peter, come with me. Hannibal, you remain here with Mr. Warren. I think those fellows will come over the bows. When I cry 'Forward,' come to our help."

"All right, Jack."

"You, Swaby, come with me."

Jack, Peter, and Jim Swaby then took charge of the bow-gun, which was drawn back so as to leave a clear space between it and the bowsprit.

It was loaded to the muzzle with grape and canister.

"Now, Peter, report their movements," said Jack; "and speak low."

" Boat coming berry slow, Massa Jack," whispered Peter.

" Which way ? "

" For de bows."

" As I thought," muttered Jack. " When I nudge you, Jim, let fly."

" All right, sir."

" Boats along de side," whispered Peter.

" Quiet, now," said Jack, and then there came over the bows about a score of men, who gathered like shadows.

A moment's lull, and others, doubtless from the other boat, began to join them, and Jack nudged Jim Swaby.

With a roar as if the earth had been rent asunder, the long gun cast forth its deadly load, and the bows were swept almost clear.

The air was now filled with shrieks, and from the ship lying away iu the darkness there came a shout of surpise and dismay.

" Forward ! " cried Jack, and his gallant men leaped up.

About a dozen startled wretches were left, too dismayed to make any real stand in defence, and like sheep they were driven into the sea, where their shrieks were soon stifled by the heaving waters, which closed over their heads and bore them into eternity.

" That's made a clean sweep of them," said Jim Swaby.

" More boats coming, Massa Jack," said Peter the Great, and the words were barely uttered before a number of howling wretches came swarming over the sides.

" Burn a light there ! " cried Jack, and a lurid flame burst forth instantly, revealing all that were upon the deck.

He could see that his assailants were half naked, swarthy men, whose faces were demoniacal in their fury.

They might have been demons by their looks, but he was not daunted, and with a cheer, urged on his men to resist.

Both sides were desperate.

Defeat meant destruction, they knew, and it was a fight for dear life.

Jack hurriedly bade one of the men keep the light burning, and then dashed into the front of the fray, his gleaming cutlass dealing death and wounds at every stroke.

Hannibal, true to his master, kept at his side, and wherever the long arms of the black swept, there lay a silent or shrieking pirate to attest his prowess.

Peter was near, too, but having had his cutlass shivered at the very opening of the fight could only dodge about, and hurl defiance at the foe.

Blue burnt the light, giving a weird aspect to the ghastly scene.

High rose the shouts and shrieks of the combatants, and deeply moaned the dying.

" Down with the murderers ! " cried Jack, and, just then, he stood face to face with the pirate leader—a giant as big as Hannibal himself.

Hannibal was busy with two men, and could give no aid.

It would have gone hard with Jack, whose boyish strength was not yet a match for the mighty monster like the pirate, and he would have succumbed, but for the energy of Peter.

Jack parried the first blow of the pirate, and slashed him across the chest witb his cutlass.

The blood gushed out, but the wound did nothing more than add fury to the savage, and rushing in, he seized Jack's cutlass by the hilt, and raised his sword to cleave him down.

Our hero could have left hold of his cutlass, and fled, but he scorned to yield to such a foe, and he held fast.

Death stared him in the face, when a friendly hand intervened.

It was Peter the Great's.

That worthy had seen his young master's danger, and having nothing better than his gingham to give aid to Jack, thrust it forward, and put the ferule in the pirate's eye.

The rascal howled, but he struck, nevertheless, and the blow descended with mighty force upon—Peter's gingham, inflicting a severe wound upon the dingy green covering.

The next moment, Tom Warren cut the pirate down.

With the fall of their leader fell the hopes of the sea-robbers ; but feeling that no quarter would be given, they fought like desperate men.

Hitherto they had fought in a body, but now they suddenly scattered, and ran all over the deck, followed by the sailors, who levelled them one after the other, until not one of them could be seen erect.

Just then, the clouds parted, and a faint ray of light from the stars broke upon the scene.

The blue light died away, and the scene of fury and turmoil was over.

CHAPTER XIII.

JACK'S ISLAND HOME.

JACK was leaning upon his cutlass, worn out with his exertions, and close by sat Jim Swaby, binding up his leg, the calf of which had been rather heavily slashed by one of his assailants.

Hannibal, with Peter the Great, was examining the damage done to the "rumblerella," and Tom Warren, with the uninjured men, were gathering up the wounded.

This was the scene the stars first looked upon—a ghastly scene in the main, although there was something ludicrous in the anxiety of Hannibal and his brother.

Hannibal was affected by Peter, who was shedding tears.

"Right across the best bone ob him back," he said. "Oh, Hannibal! dis chile neber get ober de blow!"

"Oh, nonsense!" said Jack. "Put it down and we will try to doctor it presently. Give a hand with the wounded."

Peter carefully stowed his treasure away, and did as he was bidden. The wounded numbered about half-a-dozen, but only one was killed outright, one of the men who had been a captive in Kachvu's hut.

The pirate ship could now be seen lying about a mile away, and feeble efforts were now being made by the few men left on board to hoist sail. A gentle breeze was springing up, and the "Swallow," catching it first, bore down upon her.

Putting a man at the helm, Jack ordered the ports of the starboard guns to be opened and loaded with round shot.

When this was done, the light of morning broke in upon the scene.

They could now see the pirate plainly, with her mainsail set, and making clumsy efforts to get her top-gallants out before the breeze.

The "Swallow" neared her rapidly, and there was no chance of escape.

The scene on board the "Swallow" was ghastly enough, but there was no time to think of that. Jack was bent on making the other craft his prize.

"Heave to, you villains!" he cried, as the "Swallow" came within a hundred yards of its enemy.

The answer was a shot from a brass gun, which crashed through the rigging, cutting a stay of the mizzen, and bringing a mass of cordage upon the deck.

"Give him a broadside, lads!" cried Jack, and four guns returned the fire with deadly precision.

"Ready with the grappling-irons, Tom!" cried Jack.

"Aye, aye!" said Tom Warren, and the two crafts closing, the seamen poured upon the pirate's deck.

There was no more fighting, however, for the few men left did not number a dozen, and impelled by fear, they one and all leaped into the sea.

They struck out silently, keeping their dogged faces turned towards the foe, and Jack's heart melted as he saw them making this hopeless struggle for life.

"Out with a boat there!" he cried, and the boat dropped into the sea.

The seamen pulled out; but the pirates, merciless men in every way, and with no faith in others, refused to be saved. Each man, as the boat neared him, tossed up his arms with a defiant yell, and sank.

"They have no lack of courage," said Jack, as the boat returned. "What a pity that men like them should be so brutal!"

"Tyrants, bullies, and murderers are not always cowards," said Tom Warren.

"No rule, without an exception, Tom. Pipe all hands to clear the deck, Swaby!"

A month has elapsed since the fight with the pirate, and Jack has found a lone island, which is, for the time, to be his home.

It was a gem of Nature yet undiscovered by man, lying in the sea, where it gleamed in the light of the sun like a jewel, rich and ripe with Nature's gifts.

I have said that it was unknown to man; perhaps I ought to have said that it was on no map or chart, and that it was without inhabitants.

It is possible that some hardy wanderer like Francis Drake had alighted on it before, but he had kept his secret; and it was only by chance that our hero, cruising about with his prize, came upon it.

It was evening when he arrived, with the pirate craft, manned by a dozen men, and commanded by Tom Warren, in his wake.

Ordering out the boat, Jack, attended by his dark followers, and half-a-dozen seamen, went ashore.

Soon a magnificent scene, dim in outline from the ship, burst upon his view.

A giant rock, with magnificent trees springing from the crevices, their gnarled trunks and twisted branches almost touching the water, first greeted him.

A million dragonflies hung over the smooth entrance to a narrow creek, which seemed to terminate about a hundred yards inland, and the air was full of the cries of birds, and the chirp of grasshoppers.

But as the boat entered, an abrupt bend in the creek came in view, and two high, precipitous rocks rose on either side.

Another bend, and then the waters opened again, and a lovely creek, about half a mile in length, and a quarter wide, was seen.

Words cannot describe the beauty of this place.

The men rested on their oars, and gazed like beings enchanted.

Jack's pulse beat quickly, and even Peter the Great and Hannibal were hushed into silence.

On one side was a fine, sandy shore, leading up to a rich forest, where the mango and palm grew luxuriantly, and on the other side rose up piles of rocks, covered with every form of luxurious vegetation, and crowned on the summit with magnificent trees.

The water was so deep and still that everything was reflected in it like a mirror —rocks, trees, and sky—and it seemed a desecration to break the even surface with the oars.

"Oh, glorious!" cried Jack, breaking out at last. "Here is a home fit for a king! Here shall the 'Swallow' rest, and here shall be my home when I return from wandering o'er the sea. Shout, and let them know that we are here!"

The men shouted, and the rocks gave back a hundred echoes, bandying the "Hurrah!" from side to side, until the sound gradually died away.

Then came a faint answer from those on board the "Swallow" and the captive slaver.

Jack returned on board, and after dinner the two vessels were turned into their haven, as snug a retreat as ever was chosen by a rover of the seas.

When the anchors were dropped, the water was found too deep for their chains —indeed, they found no bottom, a most astounding and startling phenomenon in such a small piece of water.

"I knew it must be deep," said Jim Swaby. "You never see shallow water reflect like that."

"P'raps it got no bottom," suggested Hannibal.

"Perhaps you are a fool," growled Jim.

"P'raps he ain't," said Peter the Great, championing his brother. "Dat jes' like you white chaps. Who saw the slabe ship? Who— Yah! Wurra dat?"

"Me," said Jack. "I don't want any wrangling just now, Peter. If Hannibal is right, he is right; if he isn't, he isn't."

Peter scratched his head, not quite understanding, and Jack turned to consult Tom Warren as to how to secure the vessels in some kind of mooring. They decided upon anchoring to the rocks, as the sandy beach was partly open to the sea.

"I don't care to hide and skulk," said Jack; "but my enemies are strong, and a little caution is necessary. This shall be my stronghold, my fortress, and my castle. The entrance by water we can easily defend. All the ships of the navy could not force their way through there if we chose to keep it."

"The only weak point is the open beach there," said Tom.

"Which we will defend, Tom, in case of need."

"How?"

"We must get a couple of guns upon the rocks—I have two in the hold for spare purposes—and that will make my position on the beach—at least, that part which faces this creek—untenable."

"But the guns can be assailed behind, Jack."

"I have thought of that," replied our hero. "There is plenty of wood ready to hand, and I think we can make a stockade around our guns such as would defy all assaults."

"They could bring a nine-pounder or two ashore, and make mincemeat of it, Jack."

"A *ninety*-pounder would not touch such a stockade as I propose to make."

"Give me your notion, Jack."

"First, I will level a number of trees, trim them, and build a hut for the guns, leaving only two portholes, or embrasures —as I suppose they ought to be called—to fire through. In front of this place I will pile all the branches and leaves, and in turn, cover them with earth. This would stop any shot, as you know."

"But where will you get your earth?"

"From behind, where a deep trench shall be dug quite round my little fortress, and the earth not required for the front shall be used the same way in the rear, only I will make it stronger there."

"But suppose the enemy takes you in the rear, you will have no means of stopping his work, and he may take his time to unearth you?"

"Let him try," said Jack, confidently. "I shall be ready for him."

"I do not see how."

"Oh, Tom, what a dunce you are! Is it not easy to have a mine under this ditch, or more than one? And if it comes to a push, then up goes your assaulting party. Besides, I am sure that the road to the rocks is very difficult, if not quite inaccessible."

"How, then, will you get your guns up?"

"We can scale the face of the rock, and Jim Swaby will soon rig us some tackle to bring up the gun, I warrant you. But first, I must explore the country. To-morrow we will begin, as night is close at hand. Serve out rations of grog to the men, and tell them they may make a merry night of it."

"I will; and in the morning we start."

"Yes; you and I can go ashore. I shall put Jim Swaby to work, getting the tackle ready."

"What a jolly life, Jack, if it only lasts!"

"Aye! that is, Tom, if it only lasts."

And then they went down to dinner, and spent a very merry evening, talking over the prospect of the life ahead.

So it is with all.

We talk of this and that, and what we will do, and what we won't do, as if the Wheel of Life was in our own hands; and every man who thus lays out his course finds himself soon drifting into the opposite tack.

Is it not so, my readers?

And are we not, every hour of our lives, waking out from one dream or another of the hopeful past?

———

CHAPTER XIV.

PETER'S LITTLE DIFFICULTY.—SIGNS UPON THE ROCK.

"I SAY, Hannibal."

"What am it, Peter?"

"Massa Jack and Tom goin' out to-day."

"Wurra for?"

"'Sploring de isle."

"Golly, dat good! We hab some jolly fun, Peter."

"No, we don't, Hannibal," said Peter, mournfully. "Massa Jack say he don't want to be boddered wif us."

"Massa Jack say dat?" said Hannibal, incredulously.

"Yes," said Peter. "I hear dis morning dat he goin' out, and I say, Massa, you take Peter—'"

"Jes' like you, sticking yourself forrard," interposed Hannibal.

"I say to Massa Jack," repeated Peter, with emphasis, "I say to him, 'you take Peter *and* Hannibal, him cantankerous brudder,' and Massa Jack say, 'No. You two fellers stop at home and help Jim Swaby.'"

"Help him to do what?"

"Help him to cut down de tree up dere."

"Yah! Dat berry hard work; but if Massa Jack say so, den we must do it."

"Dat right, Hannibal," said Peter, approvingly, ignoring the fact that he had contemplated rebellion. "You allers take de right view ob t'ings. We help ole Swaby! Oh, yes, we help him!" and then they both winked.

This conversation took place over their breakfast, under the lee of the forecastle, and shortly after our hero and his friend went ashore.

Jim Swaby then piped up the men, and told them what work he had in hand.

It was very much to the taste of the sailors, and they were soon swarming like cats up the face of the rock, some with axes, others with ropes, and other things necessary for the felling of trees.

As soon as they were all up, Jim Swaby counted the men, and found all there but Hannibal and his brother, Peter the Great.

Going to the edge of the rock, he looked over, and saw them lying under the shadow of an awning spread between the masts, apparently fast asleep.

"Hallo, there, you lubbers!" he shouted.

No answer.

"Hallo! Hallo!" cried Jim. "Here, give me a handful of that clay. I'll wake 'em up."

A well-directed pellet, about the size of an egg, caught Peter in the pit of his stomach, and brought him into a sitting posture in a great hurry.

"Who dat killing dis chile?" he roared. "Yah! Dat you, Hannibal?"

"Me sleep faster," murmured Hannibal, as Peter, thinking that he was mistaken, lay down again.

A second pellet now descended, and struck the deck between the brothers.

They comprehended the nature of the assault at once.

"Dat ole Swaby," said Peter. "Him getting waxy. Stop a minute; I open a lilly bit of my eye, and look at him. I see ole Swaby making up lumps ob ground, jes' as de boys in Ole England make snow-balls."

"Hallo, there!" roared Jim. "Wake up, you lazy rascals!"

"Here come anoder shot," muttered Peter. "Look out, Hannibal!"

Down came the pellet straight at Peter again, just missing his head by a few inches, and spattering his face with clay.

"Berry good shot," said Peter, coolly, covering his face with his hat. "No wakee yet, Massa Swaby."

Jim, now really savage, sent another flying with such a perfect aim that it struck Peter's hat upon the crown, and drove it on his nose and chin.

"Murder!" he roared.

"Come up here, you lubbers!" cried out Jim, "or I'll shy one of these lumps of rock at you!"

All subterfuge was now at end, and so Hannibal arose, and stood beside his brother.

Peter elected himself as spokesman.

"What dat you want?" he asked, innocently.

"Why, to give a hand here!" roared Jim. "Don't you know that?"

"You know dat, Hannibal?" asked Peter.

"No," answered Hannibal.

"Nor me know it," said Peter. "No, Massa Swaby, we not know it."

"But the skipper said you were to——"

"De skipper is Massa Jack."

"Yes, you lubbers!"

"Massa Jack say so."

"Yes."

"You hear Massa Jack say so, Hannibal?"

"No," replied Hannibal.

"Hannibal no hear Massa Jack say so," said Peter, leaving himself out. "We t'ink dat you must be mistaken."

"I'm not mistaken, you lubbers!"

"We t'ink you are," replied Peter, "and so we will go and ask Massa Jack!"

Then the two brothers coolly got into a boat, and proceeded to pull towards the shore.

"Stop, there!" roared Jim. "Here! give me some lumps, and some of you help! Shy away!"

A perfect storm of missiles were thrown at the two grinning niggers, but they were soon out of reach, and running the boat upon the shore, got out.

Then Peter, taking off his hat, made a most elaborate bow to Jim Swaby, whose wrath was now at boiling point, and Hannibal cut a caper something like the fag end of a Spanish fandango, and then they ran away into the woods.

Although very angry, Jim soon got over it, and joined in the laughter of his men, who had been much amused by the artfulness of the two niggers. In the men, such conduct would have been rank mutiny, but Hannibal and Peter the Great were not amenable to the ordinary law of the ship. They were the servants of Jack, his private attendants, and were therefore in a position to take certain liberties.

"But I'm darned," said Jim Swaby, "if I don't lay a bit of rope about the Hemperor. He's at the bottom of the scamping."

The men made up for the absence of the niggers, and by the afternoon a pile of trees were lying ready to be cut up for the stockade. By that time, Jack and Tom joined them.

"Phew!" said Tom, as he advanced wiping his face. "It's a rough road."

"Yes," said Jack. "No fear of a very numerous enemy that way."

"Glad to hear it, skipper," returned Jim Swaby. "Rough road, sir?"

"Yes. Broken rocks, gulleys, waterfalls, and innumerable little streams," said Jack. "Such a break-neck country I never set out in before. Where's Peter?"

Jim Swaby then detailed, with a very solemn visage, the infamous conduct of the brothers, and how they had taken to the base subterfuge of seeking their master to know whether he wished them to work, when all they wanted to do was to escape it. Jim had not much idea of jokes in general, and he was still disposed to regard their conduct as open mutiny, but Jack and Tom seemed to be highly amused.

"The rascals are not much use at this sort of work," said our hero, "and I do think that you are better without them. They would have only got in the way, and done all sorts of things to check your progress."

"That's true," srid Jim. "I never made much out of a nigger yet, 'specially pet niggers."

"Both Hannibal and Peter fight well," returned Jack, "so we must overlook their faults. The men can now knock off."

"It's only early afternoon, sir."

"I know it, but I do not want to make their lives one round of toil. We can take a little ease here. How do we get down here?"

"I've got nothing but a knotted rope

at present, sir," said Jim; "but I'll have a rope ladder to-morrow."

"The very thing," said Jack, as he swung himself over the rock; "and, by-the-way, Swaby."

"Yes, sir."

"When Peter and Hannibal return, send them to me."

"Aye, aye, sir."

"Ain't he good 'un!" muttered the old boatswain, as Jack disappeared with Tom. "This is something like a service, ain't it, lads? Knock off at four bells, and take it easy. I wonder what some of the old wooden beggars at home would say to it?"

The men, released from their labours, went roaming gleefully about with all the frolicsome joy of sailors. A true salt makes himself happy on the slightest provocation, and, like the bee, gathers sweets from the most unpromising flowers.

Our hero had just finished his dinner, and was lighting a cigarette, when Jim Swaby ushered in the two culprits, Hannibal and Peter, brimful of repentance, Peter especially coming out strong, rolling his eyes in a ghastly way, and exhibiting unlimited contrition in his knees, which shook visibly.

Tom Warren turned his back, and looked the other way; but Jack, settling his face into a faint resemblance of sternness, asked them what they meant by their conduct.

Hannibal looked aloft, and lifted up one of his legs like an old hen roosting. Peter, instead of replying to Jack, addressed his brother.

"Hannibal," he said, "what do you mean by goin' on in dis way."

This unlooked-for attack so confused Hannibal that he turned upon his leg, still keeping the other up, and stared with angry eyes at the traitor, Peter.

"*Me* mean!" he said.

"Yes, you mean!" said Peter, undaunted. "Who led his brudder away?"

"*Me* lead you!" said Hannibal, aghast. "Didn't you say—"

"No, me didn't," replied Peter, without waiting to hear what had been said. "Massa Jack know I didn't."

"I know nothing of the sort," said Jack.

"Den Massa Tom do," insinuated Peter.

"I have nothing whatever to do with it," said Tom.

"Dat de way, when people get into trouble," said Peter, with an injured air. "Nobody gib de fallen man de help.

Eben Hannibal, my brudder—bone ob my flesh—turn him back upon me."

Hannibal was about to burst forth into indignant expostulation, when Jack interrupted him.

"The fact is," he said, "you are both in the wrong, and I hope when next I leave you anything to do that you will do it. Now, where have you been?"

"You say," said Hannibal, to Peter; "but tell de trufe."

"Dat come well from you," returned Peter, indignantly, "who neber spoke it but once, and den you make a mistake. Massa Jack, we been all ober de isle."

"Not all over it, surely," said Jack.

"Ober as much as we could in de time," said Peter the Great, "and we find big riber."

"A big river?"

"Yes, Massa Jack, big riber; cut de island in two, I t'ink."

"Then it is no river."

"I t'ink, Massa Jack, dat dis island bigger dan you t'ink. It go right ober dere, and dere no end. Hannibal climb up de hill, and look."

"You saw no end to the land?"

"No, Massa Jack. It berry big place, and de river big. Hannibal say de water salt; I say no; so I put my rumblerella in to stir him up before I taste, den up come a big hipplepotamus."

"A hippopotamus?"

"Yes, Massa Jack; and him lay hold ob my rumblerella. I say to Hannibal——"

"You howl," put in Hannibal.

"I *say* to Hannibal," pursued Peter, "come here and gib a hand. Hannibal slash him ober de nose, and den we go. So if the hipplepotamus dere, Massa Jack, dis a berry big riber."

"Yes. Well, go on."

"Den we walk about, and listen to de mocking bird and de hiss ob snake and udder t'ings, and den we come back until we come to a fire."

"A fire?"

"Yes, Massa Jack. Him out long ago, many munfs; but him out, and leabe de ashes. Fire berry big, too, and bones near him. Dat sign of many men."

"So it is, Peter," said Jack, a little troubled. "Where is it?"

"Close by. Jes' behind de rock."

"Strange that we did not see it," said Jack. "But go—you must be hungry—and get your supper."

Glad to get away, the dark brothers hastened out of the cabin. On the deck they met Jim Swaby.

"Well, my Hemperor," said he, "what did the skipper say to you?"

"He say dis much," replied Peter, "dat if eber you frow lumps of clay at me and my brodder ag'in, dat he will cut off dat pigtail ob yourn, and gib you one long licking all round de ship—didn't he, Hannibal?"

"Him did," said Hannibal, and then they went to supper arm-in-arm, leaving Jim Swaby astounded by their impudence.

CHAPTER XV.

INTRUDERS.

THE information derived from Peter the Great and Hannibal was not by any means satisfactory. The island not being in the charts, both Jack and Tom Warren had hoped and believed that it was entirely unknown to man until they had the good fortune to light upon it.

But it was plain that such was not the case.

Peter was not likely to be mistaken. The keen instincts of his race had been too often shown in his acts that there could be no doubt, and when, on the morrow, our hero visited the spot, the confirmation, if any were needed, was given.

Under the shelter of a high rock a fire had been.

Not much record of it was left—a few charred pieces of stick, rotted by the periodical rains, and a slightly scorched look at the bottom of the rock.

But these were all sufficient.

Men had been there, and the next question was—what class of men they were?

Peter and Hannibal at once declared that they were civilised men, or men who knew something of civilised life, and gave as a reason for their conclusion the fact that the wood burned was cut from the tree with a saw, a tool quite unknown to the wild tribes.

Then arose another question, and another—were the men still upon the isle, and if not, would they return?

Tom was inclined to think that the men had been shipwrecked, and either died, or were taken off by some vessel; but Jack pointed out that in case of shipwreck, some records of it must have been upon the shore.

"Suppose they came in a boat?" said Tom. "All sorts of accidents happen at sea. Ships spring leaks, catch fire, and get lost in fifty other ways."

"In case of such, I don't think men stay to put tools into the boat," said Jack. "Their chief thoughts are always directed to water and provisions."

"True: so it is no use conjecturing, Jack. We will not meet an evil half way."

"But we can take every precaution. I will get Swaby to fix a boom across the passage in the lake, and watch must be kept night and day."

"And in the meantime, Jack, we had better explore the isle a bit."

"Agreed."

This was begun at once.

Jack, Tom, and the two faithful blacks went back for a little provisions, and having given Jim Swaby all the instructions he required, started off.

Just before going, Jack told the old boatswain not to be alarmed if they were absent for a day or two, as he intended, if possible, to explore the island thoroughly.

"That is," he said, "if it is no larger than I think."

"But hadn't you better take a few men, sir?"

"No," said Jack. "You will want them all here. Keep a good look out, and if anything goes wrong, run a bit of red bunting to the mast-head."

"All right, sir."

"Now we will be off," said Jack. "You two fellows lead the way through the wood."

The two fellows—Peter and Hannibal—promptly started off, as full of glee as children released from school.

In the woods they were at home, and after the long imprisonment on board ship, they hailed the prospect of a few days in the forest with unqualified delight.

"Hannibal," said Peter.

"What dat?" asked Hannibal.

"Gib your brodder a back."

Hannibal ran forward a few paces, and stooped his head.

Peter rushed at him, and leaped over with such energy that he pitched straight upon his scull.

"Good heaven!" cried Tom, "the fool has killed himself!"

"Dat not de trufe," said Peter, springing up. "Peter berry sorry if him head not better dan de white man's. White man's skull no better dan de egg-shell. Take a back, Hannibal."

Hannibal took a back, and desirous of avoiding his brother's errors, dropped down a little short, coming heavily upon Peter's neck, and the two rolled upon the ground together.

"Did you eber see de like ob dat, Massa Jack?" said Peter, sitting up in a very rumpled condition. "Ain't it a confliction to hab a brodder like dat? Hannibal, you big fool, get up at once, sare."

Hannibal was lying upon his back, kicking up his long legs with delight.

Peter brought him to his senses with a mighty thwack from his gingham, and then they moved on.

"Children at play—lions when aroused," said Tom.

"You have hit it," replied Jack. "Steady there, you two. We shall not get on, if you two keep up this horse-play."

"Hannibal," said Peter, who had just tripped his brother up by putting the all-pervading gingham between his legs, "conduct yourself like a genelman. Jes' tink whar you are. Massa Jack hate to see a great hunks like you make a fool ob himself."

"Dat come well from Peter," said Hannibal, and then they moved on quickly for awhile.

In half an hour they came to the river where the hippopotamus had shown his nose the day before, and Peter pointed to the spot where he had struggled for the possession of his private property.

"And dere am de villain," he said, pointing to what appeared to be a log of wood, floating in the stream. "Dere he am, wif him lilly eye close, and fast asleep."

"Dis chile wake him up," said Hannibal, looking about for a stone.

He found one about the size of a man's head, and poising it for a moment, hurled it with terrific force at the sleeping brute.

It struck the hippopotamus' side, and bounded off without apparently hurting him.

The monster, however, turned over, and raising his head, peered at them with sleepy indifference.

Then he opened his jaws, and gave a species of yawn.

This act afforded Peter an opportunity he most desired.

Quickly seizing a stone, he hurled it with great precision straight between the monster's jaws.

The result was very edifying.

Up rose the brute, and beating the water ferociously, it uttered a terrible roar.

Peter and Hannibal wriggled about in an ecstacy of delight.

Jack and Tom got their pistols and cutlasses ready in case of assault.

But the hippopotamus had no such intention, and having dashed about for a minute or so, he sank out of sight.

"Dat a good pill for de hipplepotamus," said Peter. "T'ink he be much better after dat."

"No doubt, if he swallowed it," said Jack. "Was it the same you saw yesterday."

"Yes, Massa Jack; hipplepotamus allers lib in one place. Him no move about, like sensible people, to get a change of air."

They moved on, following the course of the stream, which ran through the thick forest.

The banks were high, so there was no swampy ground to impede their progress.

The signs of animal life were innumerable.

Hares, and a large species of rat, often started from almost under their feet; squirrels sprang from branch to branch, and the hiss of the snake was almost incessant.

They saw several varieties, most of them harmless—so the blacks declared; but a small, black, viperish-looking thing, coiled up in the fork of a tree, Peter killed immediately.

"Him no bite twice," he said. "One bite, and Massa Jack neber open him eye again."

"That is the whip-snake," said Tom. "I have seen many of them before."

"Hush! Massa Tom!" said Hannibal, pulling up suddenly. "You hear dat?"

A low growl, like that of far-off thunder, came upon their ears, and slowly died away.

"A storm, Hannibal."

"No, Massa Jack, dat de lion."

"A lion!"

"Yes. Me hear him—not far away."

"Him bery strong," said Peter, rolling up his sleeves. "Hannibal, you catch him by de tail while I put this rumblerella down him froat."

"If dat lion comes dis way," replied Hannibal, drawing his cutlas, "dat joke ob yours will go ober to de oder side ob your mouth, Peter."

"Hippopotami—snakes—lions?" said Jack. "Surely, Tom, this cannot be an island."

"I begin to think we are out of our reckoning, Jack. We have got upon the mainland, somehow. At all events, we can't be far from it. Look at Hannibal!"

The gigantic black was crouching down behind a tree, staring straight ahead, and looking very much like a beast of prey himself.

Peter was behind a tree, rolling up the affs of his coat.

The two young fellows drew near him.

"I guess, Massa Jack," said Peter, "dat a big fight jes' about comin' on."

It was no laughing matter, but Jack could not help smiling at the attitude Peter assumed.

Hannibal, without turning his head, held up his hand for silence.

Soon the crackling of branches was heard, and then another roar—deeper, because nearer.

It was, indeed, a dreadful sound, especially to those who hear it for the first time.

Jack felt his blood tingle with excitement, and Tom Warren, although pale, was calm.

"Him no chicken," whispered Peter, meaning the lion. "Golly, here him come!"

A crash of underwood followed, and a huge lion, his mane bristling with rage, sprang into sight.

It was no time to pause, and as if actuated by one impulse, the four adventurers fell upon him.

Jack first met his eye, and with a roar of rage, he leaped at him.

Our hero sprang aside, and Peter, being the next in line, got the benefit of the embrace.

The huge paw closed upon him and with a scream of agony he fell.

He gave himself up for lost.

The joke had, indeed, turned into something serious.

He felt the deadly claws pierce his flesh; but the report of a pistol rang out, hot blood gushed over him, and the king of the forest fell.

Shaken and half-dead with the momentary agony Peter sprang up just in time to see our hero draw his cutlass from the heart of the lion.

"Oh, Massa Jack! Massa Jack!" he said, "you berry brave."

"Don't give me all the thanks," replied Jack, laughing. "Tom Warren shot him in the head at the same moment."

"And I t'ank Massa Warren berry much," said Peter.

Then turning to his brother, he asked, with an injured air—

"And whar was you, Massa Hannibal?"

CHAPTER XVI.

A GUN.

"ME behind," replied Hannibal. "I cut at de brute when him go by, but de debil too quick."

So you do not'ing, sare?"

"Yes; me cut off him tail," replied Hannibal, producing the lion's caudal appendage.

"Gib me dat instrelment," said Peter.

And Hannibal handed it over to him.

"I keep dis," said Peter, curling it up, and stowing it away in his pocket, "and when Massa Swaby come any ob his nonsense wid dat rope ob his, I jes' bring out dis, and make him strip."

They could laugh now, although the late adventure had been no laughing matter.

The struggle, though brief, had been fraught with much danger. Another moment, and Peter's life would have been torn out of him.

The presence of mind displayed by the others had saved him.

The lion indeed was a noble beast, and looked grand as he lay stretched upon the earth in the stillness of death, his filmy eyes yet staring with the last agony.

"What a pity such creatures cannot be tamed like dogs," said Jack. "Fancy a few of these noble creatures wandering about the parks of dear old England! We must have his skin as a trophy."

Hannibal performed the operation, and folding it up, bound it over his shoulders, leaving the dressing until their return to the "Swallow."

As the party moved away, a number of carrion crows came through the trees, and settled on the carcase.

"That's what I can't make out," said Tom. "Look at those beggars. We saw nothing of them five minutes ago, and now here they come by swarms!"

"It's no use speculating," replied Jack. "No man ever made such problems of life. They are beyond his ken!"

All that day they moved on amidst the varied scene of forest life, and at night camped under a huge tree.

Peter and Hannibal, with a little rotten tinder, and two bits of wood, made a fire.

The knowledge of the blacks of these matters stood the party in good stead, for both Jack and Tom had forgotten to bring with them the means of procuring a light.

There was a deal of ugly buzzing and

roaring about them during the dark hours, but fear not being a ruling power within any of them, they slept tolerably well, and at early dawn, after a rude breakfast, they moved on again.

An hour's walk brought them to a change of scene.

Right in the centre of this wood rose a precipice like a wall.

At first the idea of scaling it seemed to be idle; but by following its course they came to a part where the surface was broken, and offered what sailors consider to be a very fair foothold.

Those hardy gentlemen who go for a month upon the Continent, and, with the aid of some score or so of guides, manage to reach the summit of a well-traversed Swiss mountain, would have found in this cliff a test of their courage: but, fortunately, our wandering friends were made of sterner stuff, and, in consequence, not likely to be turned back even by a real danger.

Jack, whose climbing powers had long made him famous among those who knew him, led the way, and Tom followed.

Peter came third, and Hannibal brought up the rear.

So up they went, sometimes with no better foothold than what a mere fragment of rock afforded; at another time crawling along a ledge so narrow that they had to worm their way along, sometimes clinging to shrubs which had chosen a hole in the rock for their resting-place, and sometimes springing to gain a hold at all.

They went slowly up a wall at least three hundred feet in height, until the summit was reached.

"Dat a stiff job," said Peter the Great. "Golly! Hannibal, stop him!"

Him was the umbrella, which Peter had bound around his waist with his sash, and now, slipping from its bonds, went bowling over the cliff.

Hannibal made a clutch at it and nearly followed, but he missed his mark, and Peter, lying upon his stomach, had the pleasure of seeing his favourite weapon bound from rock to rock and finally land in the midst of a group of ferns.

"Marcy on dis chile!" he muttered. "What a job. Massa Jack, I go and fetch him."

"You cannot do anything of the sort," replied Jack. "Climbing up was bad enough; to get down is impossible, unless you go head first."

"Dat de best rumblerella Massa Scarborough could get for money," mourned Peter, rocking himself to and fro. "Dere never was a chile wif such a broken heart."

"Perhaps there is a better road further on," suggested Tom.

"You can go and see, Peter," said Jack; "but remember this, you are not to risk your life to get it. I value you more than all the umbrellas in the world."

"Massa Jack berry kind to say so," replied Peter, "so I take care. Hannibal, you come wif me."

Hannibal shook his head.

"Not to get *dat* rumblerella?" urged Peter.

"Blow de rumblerella!" growled Hannibal. "Me stop wif Massa Jack."

"And dat a man who call hisself a brudder!" muttered Peter, as he walked away. "Hannibal, you not de man I take you for."

Hannibal said nothing, but squatted on the ground with an indifferent air.

Jack and Tom proceeded to look about them.

The scene was magnificent.

Far away over the tops of the trees they could see the blue water running in a line from north to south, and just peeping between an opening in the wood rose the masts of the "Swallow" and the "Dolt," as they had christened the pirate ship, on account of its having been so foolish as to run into the lion's jaws.

On the other side, as far as the eye could reach, was land.

Just beyond it was a faint blue haze, which might have been water; but this they could not determine, as it was indefinable; but the land between that haze and where they stood was a glorious panorama of natural beauty.

Woods, hills, slopes, and deep valleys, all rich with the prodigal gifts of the creation; palms, mangoes, cedars, and trees the names of which they did not know, with rich patches of flowers growing between streams, and brooklets, and waterfalls, all tending towards the great river, which could be traced from the blue haze far away, and through the forest, in sparkling fragments here and there, down towards the sea.

It was such a scene as neither of the lads had seen before, and they stood in silence, drinking in deep draughts of the pure air, and elate with an ecstacy of admiration, until the silence was broken by Hannibal.

"Massa Jack," he said, "dat riber berry dangerous."

"So I have been inclined to think,"

said Tom. "Ships and boats can come up there freely."

"You forget that the river is at least four miles away from our creek," returned Jack. "Boats, if they are coming, are welcome there. They cannot hurt us."

"But it would afford an enemy a deal of help."

"It would enable him to land guns and ammunition," said Jack; "but there is no danger at present. Look at those beautiful white birds, Tom."

"Magnificent!"

"Now they swoop down to the river. Tom, what do you say? Shall we track the river to the sea? The mouth may be impassable."

"As you will; but I doubt if it is not open."

"We shall see. Hannibal, you wait here for Peter."

"Yes, Massa Jack," said Hannibal, stretching himself out at full length; "but I t'ink you better take Hannibal wif you."

"No; we will go alone. We shall keep upon this cliff."

The summit of the high land was tolerably smooth, and followed the stream in an imperfect parallel line for some distance, and then suddenly the stream, instead of keeping towards the sea, swept round and passed into a cavern under the cliff, and disappeared.

This discovery, startling in itself, was made more so by the fact that nowhere was there any signs of its reappearing, and the stillness of the blue sea, which was now near them, forbade the supposition that the river emptied itself near the spot.

"Now, what may this mean, Tom?"

"It's a phenomenon, Jack; but nothing is to be wondered at in this world of infinite variety. Hark! I hear the waters thunder along the cavern!"

"It sounds like giants fighting and shouting. Hear that crash, as if a huge rock had tumbled into the sea."

"I begin to think, Jack, that we have fallen upon some enchanted isle, or perhaps we are dreaming."

"Keep quiet, and I will wake you up with this pin."

"Thank you, no, Jack. I do not require that sort of rousing."

"Well, Tom, nothing more is to be done with the river to-day. I do not think we have anything to fear in that direction. Let us return."

They walked back to the spot where they had left Hannibal.

The faithful fellow was there, but reclining no longer.

Standing on the very edge of the cliff, he was making signs to some one below, whom our friends judged rightly to be Peter the Great.

"Anything wrong with that confounded umbrella?" asked Tom.

"No, Massa Tom," replied Hannibal. "Peter found him, and he t'ink him hear a gun."

"A gun!"

"Yes, Massa Jack. Peter coming up now to 'splain."

In a few seconds, the nozzle of the umbrella appeared above the cliff, and Peter followed it, with a very anxious expression upon his face.

"What's this about a gun, Peter?" asked Jack.

"Me hear him," said that worthy, "jes' as me stoop to pick up dis t'ing ob mine."

"But we must have heard it, too."

"No, Massa Jack. Him only lilly gun."

"Pistol?"

"Yes, Massa Jack; and de wood stop de sound for white man."

"That is, our ears are not good enough. Have you heard any noise?"

"Me hear him now!" cried Peter, leaping up in his excitement.

"Me hear him, too!" said Hannibal, more quietly.

"Something's wrong," said Jack. "Come, we will get back to the 'Swallow.'"

"But how?" asked Tom.

"By following the course of the cliff until we can get down."

"Good place down dere," said Peter, pointing in the direction he had taken. "Massa Jack, follow me."

CHAPTER XVII.

THE FRENCH PRIVATEER.

PROUD of being able to put Hannibal's nose out of joint for once, Peter the Great led the way to the "good place" which proved to be a part of the cliff somewhat less precipitous than the rest, but still sufficiently perilous to give full employment for cool heads and strong legs and arms.

The descent was safely accomplished, and the party struck through the wood on their road home, the two blacks taking up the return trail as easily as if an ordinary highway lay before them.

No more shots were heard, nor, indee

did they expect to hear them, for the woods were so dense in parts, that a pistol-shot a hundred yards away would not have been noticed by ordinary ears; and how Peter had heard the sounds in the first instance was a great puzzle to Jack and Tom.

They reached the spot where the lion had been left on the previous day about noon, and found the bones as bare as a horse after the knackers have done with him, and Jack, desirous of a memento of the event, took away the skull.

Halting only for a little food and rest, they pushed on, and came within sight of the creek just as the night was falling.

Jack was about to walk out of the wood, when Peter held him back, and Hannibal performed the same office for Tom.

"Big ship," muttered Peter.

Our hero looked out to sea in the direction of Peter's finger, and saw a long, rakish-looking vessel about half a mile from shore, with bare poles.

"What can that be?" he muttered.

"She is French—I can see that much," replied Tom, "and I bet that she's a privateer."

"I can see her plainly now," returned Jack. "She is French built, certainly. I suppose Swaby knows of her coming."

"Of course he does. That was his pistol-shot to warn us."

"A foolish thing to do, if for no other purpose. But come, let us go forward."

"Me go," said Hannibal. "Something wrong wif de 'Swallow.' No light—all quiet—and big boat going back to de ship."

Yes, there was a big boat going slowly back to the strange vessel, *with only four hands in her.*

She was in no hurry.

The men were pulling leisurely, without any signs of affright—nothing about them like men who were in a hurry.

She was built to carry at least thirty men.

Where were the rest?

"I like this even less," said Jack.

"If Swaby has neglected his duty——" said Tom.

"Don't hint at it, Tom," cried Jack, as a dreadful fear came over him. "I cannot bear to think that I have lost the 'Swallow,' and all those brave men who were with me."

"They would have fired more than one or two shots in her defence."

"Peter may have heard only the end of the fight," said Jack. "Oh! this is dreadful doubt!—and here comes the darkness to hide all!"

"There will be a moon in an hour."

"The darkness suits me best," said Jack. "We will go down to the creek and see what has been going on. I told Swaby to burn a white light if all was well."

Silently, like four spectres, they crept over the ground down to the water's edge, and looked towards the "Swallow."

There was no light burning!

"Oh, heavens!" whispered Jack, "what is the meaning of this?"

"Shall we shout?"

"No. That would be to run too great a risk."

"But how shall we know what has been going on?"

"Stand here; I will see. Hold my cutlass and jacket."

"What are you going to do, Jack?"

"Swim to the 'Swallow' and see for myself."

"You will never do it."

"I will, Tom. I have always been a good hand in the water. Here are my shoes, and now good-bye."

"Don't risk it, Jack."

"I must and will."

"The lake is awfully deep—we found no bottom, you know."

"I remember," said Jack, with a shudder; "but do not stop me. I am resolved upon it, and the moon will soon be here. Then, perhaps, it will be too late."

"Better wait for it. Swaby and his men may be only resting."

"This silence means more than common resting," replied Jack. "They would have been fiddling and dancing at this hour. No more words, Tom—I am resolved to go!"

"Let me go with you."

"And have a drowning man to save. No Tom."

"Den me, Massa Tom," said Peter.

"Or dis chile," said Hannibal.

"No," replied Jack, firmly, "I go alone."

And then the brave lad, having touched their hands in case of its being a final adieu, slipped into the water and disappeared.

It was a weary time for the trio that waited in the darkness on the shores of the silent lake.

The night was calm, and the sea just fell with a gentle murmuring sound upon the beach.

The forest was still as death, the silence

"There's blood on your face, Massa Jack!" groaned Peter. "Come down, and let some ob dese ugly gosses down below take dat wheel!"

broken only by the occasional cry of some far-off night bird, and the stealthy rustling of some beast crawling on its way.

Time walked with leaden feet just then, and half an hour was turned into an age.

Hope bade the three watchers listen for a shout, but none came—the "Swallow" lay in gloom, and gave forth no sign.

"Hush! What is that?" whispered Tom. "People moving on the deck?"

"No, Massa Tom," replied Peter, sadly, "it am rotten branches fallin' in de wood."

"Where is poor Jack?"

"Me no hear him."

"You have lost your ears, Peter," said a quiet voice, as Jack crept out of the water; "and we have need of everything now."

"Is the 'Swallow' safe?"

"It is, Tom; but such of the crew as are left are battened down. The French privateers are on board!"

CHAPTER XVIII.

DARING DEEDS.

FOR a moment there was no answer given to this terrible announcement; but a low wail broke from Tom's lips, and crossing his hands he burst into tears.

There was nothing womanish or childish in such sorrow—for no greater bereavement could have befallen the adventurers —and Jack, although he uttered no sound, was weeping too.

Peter and Hannibal, overcome with the magnitude of the disaster, sat like two savage idols, fixed and motionless.

"But this is no time to weep," said Jack, rousing himself. "Let us act; and speedily too."

"What can be done?" muttered Tom.

"Much," replied our hero, "with strong hands and willing hearts. We can but die once, and die we shall if the 'Swallow' is lost to us."

"But what do you propose?"

"There are about twenty privateersmen on board," said Jack, "as far as I could see; and judging by appearances, I should say that they boarded her when our men were *all* below, and there and then battened them down. The boat has probably gone back for reinforcements. If they return, we can do nothing."

"Your plan, Jack—what is it?"

"Can you swim, Tom?"

"Yes."

"Really, now, can you get to the 'Swallow'?"

"I am sure I can; but I could not get back."

"And you, Peter and Hannibal?"

"Both swim, Massa Jack."

"Then all is not lost," said Jack, brightening up. "I think I can get my ship back again. We can creep on deck, and suddenly open the hatches in the dark, and Swaby and his men—who are on the watch, no doubt—will rush out like so many furies."

"A wild plan, Jack; but it is better than nothing."

"We can but try it. Off with your boots and coats, and carry nothing but your cutlasses."

Hannibal had nothing to take off, and as he was he plunged, or rather quietly dropped, into the water. The others followed, and Jack, striking out to the head of the party, led the way.

It was a stiff bit of work, when all in the darkness, and in that mysterious water which appeared to be unfathomable; but each of these four hearts was screwed to the sticking-point.

It was a journey for life or death.

Soon the black hulls of the "Swallow" and the "Dolt" were faintly seen, and a few strong strokes brought them to her side.

A rope hung from the bowsprit, and Jack, with the agility of a sprite, climbed up and crawled upon the deck.

Tom came next, and then Peter and Hannibal, and the four crouched down behind some barrels to look about them.

It was terribly dark, and Jack could see very little; but Peter made out a number of men lying quietly, as if asleep, and the regular breathing of the men showed that they had lain down to rest without any sense of fear.

"Hannibal!" whispered Jack.

"Yes, Massa Jack."

"You are the strongest—will you throw open the hatch-way?"

"Yes, Massa Jack."

"Quick, now—and remember we are near."

"Hush!"

One of the privateersmen now turned over and raised his head.

"*Qui va là?*" he said.

Not receiving an answer, he muttered a curse and lay down again.

Jack and the others, who held their breath, breathed freely again.

A pause, and then they moved on again.

Silently, slowly, they crept along till the hatchway was reached.

Jack bent down his ear, and heard a slight murmuring below.

"They are on the alert," thought Jack. "Now, Hannibal, up with the hatchway!"

The strong arms of the black tossed them aside, and Jack cried out—

"Come on men! Jack to the rescue!"

"Happy Jack to the rescue!" shouted twenty voices below, and the men came pouring upon the deck.

"A light here!" cried Jack, as the privateersmen awoke from their slumbers with a yell. "Stand, you dogs, and surrender!"

Accustomed to good discipline and order, the men of the "Swallow," by this time, had a light burning; and the privateersmen saw that their fate was sealed.

Scattered in every direction, they could do nothing; but, like beasts at bay, they showed fight.

The struggle was brief.

A dozen were quickly slain, and the rest gave in, submitting quietly to be bound.

Just as this work was over, the moon peeped above the sea, and shed a light upon the scene.

There was no longer any need for artificial flame, and one of the men by Jack's order, extinguished it.

We in this colder clime know nothing of moonlight as it is seen in the tropics, where the rays of the luminary are often bright enough to enable people to read the smallest print.

This was the light that now fell upon the "Swallow," revealing the ghastly dead and the sullen living men of the privateer.

So sudden had been the rescue, so prompt the action of Jack's men, that all was over ere one could conceive that it had well begun.

A few slashes of the cutlass, a few shrieks of defiance or pain, and all was over.

Not a shot had been fired.

The men crowded round Jack, and wanted to cheer him, but he bade them be still.

"We may have more work to do yet, my men," he said. "Where is Swaby?"

The old boatswain, who had been hanging about the rear, now stood forward with his head down.

"Swaby," said Jack, quietly, "I left the 'Swallow' in charge of you."

"Yes, sir," replied Jim; "but don't think I've done wrong—leastwise, I didn't mean to. There are, I think, extinervating circumstantials."

"You mean extenuating circumstances," said Jack. "Tell me what they are."

"We had finished the arternoon's work," said Jim, "and all hands were below 'cept the watch and Bob Williams, who was aloft, covering up the guns, which we have got into position. I called to him to make haste, and, coming down in a hurry, his foot slipped over, and he fell upon the deck."

"Poor fellow! Was he killed?"

"At first we thought he was; but he seemed to breathe a bit, and I got the watch to carry him down, and as there was only three on 'em, I lent a hand, and so we left the deck clear for a moment or two. Jest then, sir——"

"Ah! I see. These fellows had been watching you, and pulling up——"

"Climbed aboard, and battened us down. That's the truth. The boom weren't fixed, or the beggars——"

"Enough Swaby," said Jack, holding out his hand. "I exonerate you entirely: say no more. Matters are not a tittle so bad as I expected."

"It's werry kind o' yer, Master Jack," said Jim, brushing his hand across his eyes. "I've been mighty down in the mouth since it happened. Me and my mates thought a deal about you, for we knowed if you dropped into the hands of these wretches that it was all up with you."

"No doubt, Jim; but how was it that they have spared you?"

"I think they came on us unexpected, and although strong enough to batten us down, they daresn't let us up again."

"So they sent off boats for reinforcements."

"That's it, Master Jack. We could hear 'em talking, but who can understand their gibberish? It ain't a language, take it how you like."

"It has been a very narrow escape," returned Jack, "and it must be a lesson to us in the future."

"We got quite desperate thinking of you," said Jim, "and we was making preparations to blow up the 'Swaller' and all aboard when you opened the hatches.

"Indeed!"

"Yes, Master Jack; and in two more minutes it would have been done."

"Then you were wrong, Jim: and the next time you get into trouble, don't take your life into your own hands. You did not give it to yourself, and you have no right to take it away."

"That's right, Master Jack; but we had growed quite desperate."

"And now, as we may expect more friends," said Jack, "let us prepare for them. First, let us take a good look at the prisoners."

There was no need for a lantern, as the moon was now shining brilliantly.

Jack scanned the faces, and saw that the men were what he suspected them to be—Mexicans, half-breeds.

At the time of our story, the seas were infested with a number of privateering vessels, called the Mexican Navy, ostensibly put afloat to fight the Argentine Republic, but in reality their work was nothing more nor less than piracy.

They took anything and everything they could lay their hands upon.

A precious lot of rascals at the best.

"Mercy would be thrown away," said Jack; "they would give us none. Load the starboard guns with grape, and bring them to bear upon the entrance to the creek. Gag all the prisoners, and if one of them even so much as shuffles his feet, knock his head off. Here, Jones, Martin, and Grey!—take charge of them, will you?"

The three men named stepped out from the others, and promptly gagged the prisoners.

Then Jack, in French, told them what they might expect if they were not perfectly quiet.

They glared at him like wild beasts, but made not the slightest movement in reply.

The guns were loaded, and every man took up his post, waiting the return of the privateer's boat.

"Lie down, every man!" said Jack, "and silence for your lives, until I give the word! Then fire!"

CHAPTER XIX.

HARD WORK WITH THE PRIVATEER.

NOTHING could be more impressive than the scene now upon the deck of the "Swallow."

The prisoners, bound and gagged, listening for the approach of their comrades with emotions springing from hope and fear combined; the watch set upon them, ready, with drawn cutlass, to do their duty; the sailors lying by their guns;

Jack, with his most intimate associates, keeping a good look out; and the glorious moonlight shining upon all.

The quietude was perfect.

The beauty of every object around was totally at variance with the work of death and slaughter about to be enacted.

The small lake was like a mirror, and the rocks, bearing upon their surface the silvery light of the moon, with the elegant foliage resting in quietude, were literally enthralling in their beauty.

To the right lay the one open spot, looking out upon the beach, and the magnificent forest, from whence the cries of wild and nocturnal beasts came forth with the subdued harmony which distance gives to all sounds alike.

Jack had eyes and ears for these, and at another time he could have revelled in such a scene; but now, murderers and villains were near, and it was necessary that he should stand up and defend his life against them.

Hark! what sound is that?

A faint click, growing stronger each moment, and then a splashing of oars.

It is the enemy approaching.

"All ready there?" whispers Jack.

"Aye, aye, sir!" is the reply.

Nearer and nearer, growing stronger and stronger, comes the sound, and then there is a pause.

They are floating slowly into the mouth of the creek.

Again the splash of oars, and then a boat turns the corner, and comes into sight, the moon shining upon a number of men crowded into her.

"*Tout va bien?*" comes the question.

"Fire!" cries Jack, in answer, and the storm of grape sweeps away both boat and men.

So sudden, and so swift, and so terrific was the fire, that the boat was smashed to matchwood, and nine-tenths of the men were slain.

The few left, with gasping cries, struggled in the water for their lives.

It was pitiable to see them strive to clamber out; but the smooth surface of the rock offered neither foot nor handhold, and one by one they sank back despairing, until only two were left, and these struck out for the ship.

"Keep off!" cried Jack. "You peril your lives by coming here!"

"In mercy spare us!" cried one of the men. "We are English!"

"English and with those wretches?" said Jack. "Impossible!"

"It is true, sir," said the man. "Shoot

us if you will, but you will not regret sparing our lives. We were forced into this work."

"Throw them a rope," said Jack.

Jim Swaby cast out a life-belt, and the two men clutched at it with the strength of despair, and were hauled on board.

"Now," said Jack, "put down your arms and let me have a look at you."

The men drew their cutlasses and pistols and threw them upon the deck.

Jack signed to Hannibal and Peter to stand by them, and proceeded to take stock of their appearance.

They were English in face, certainly, but they wore the dress of the Mexican sailor.

They hung their heads, as if ashamed to stand in sight of honest men.

"What are your names?"

"Richard Moody," said one.

"Arthur Guy," replied the other.

"How came you with those privateers?"

"Shipwrecked, and got pressed into the service."

How long have you been in it?"

"Three months."

"Not long enough to make them thoroughly bad," mused Jack. "Now, answer all my questions honestly. What is the name of that vessel?"

"The 'Viper.'"

"How many guns?"

"Sixteen."

"How many hands are there left on board?"

"At least a hundred."

"All Mexicans?"

"Some of all sorts—the bad of every nation."

"Why did they come here?"

"This is a spot the captain knows, and he comes here sometimes to rest, and carry on his infamous games."

"Who is the captain?"

"Captain San Remano."

"Do you think he will attack us again?"

"Sure to. He is a desperate man."

"A hundred men, Tom," said Jack. "Heavy odds."

"All the better. It will give us some smart work. Look out, Jack!"

A rocket, evidently from the privateer, rose high in the air, and mingled its fires with the radiance of the moon.

"A signal!" said Jack. "We will answer it presently. Up with the anchor, there. Quick!"

"What are you going to do?"

"Go out and fight the fellow, of course. Why should I wait for him?"

This reply was just the thing to please the sailors, and with a shout they went to work.

The anchor, which had been fastened to the rock, was heaved in, the jolly boat lowered, and a dozen strong arms proceeded to tow out the "Swallow" to cope with its foe.

As they came in sight of the mouth of the creek, two boats coming from the privateer hastily put back, and got out of reach, but not before the bow gun of the "Swallow" had had one shot at them, and cut a gap through the midst of the hindmost.

The rest then got on board, and the privateer spread her sails.

Jack got his canvas out, and although there was little or no breeze, he had the tide in his favour, and slowly approached the craft so fittingly named the "Viper."

The moon showed her "teeth," that is, the guns, and the number of men crowding her deck, far outnumbering those Jack had under his command; but—

"Thrice is he armed who hath his quarrel just,"

and our hero did not quail.

In a quarter of an hour the privateer was within shot, and the "Swallow" opened fire.

"Aim at the rigging, men!" cried Jack. "Cripple him, and then we can do as we like with the beggar."

The privateer returned the fire, and the shot struck the hull of the "Swallow" about midships, going clean between the decks, and damaging her on the other side.

"He's got good guns," said Jim Swaby. "Steady, now. Bravo! there goes some of his timber!"

A mass of the privateer's rigging—topsails, spars, and ropes of the mainmast—now came thundering down upon the deck, burying a number of the men under it.

A yell of fury burst from the others, and their guns blazed fast and furiously.

"If we keep at this distance, he will sink us," said Jack. Up with the helm, and get across his stern. That's it! Never mind his fire. Steady, men! Now give him a broadside! Out with the grappling irons! Steady men—no hurry! I will lead you! Peter, where are you?"

"Here, and Hannibal, too."

"That's all right. Forward here!" cried Jack.

The two ships locked, and a hundred devilish faces glared at him; but, undaunted, the brave lad led the assault.

His men were men no longer—they were raging furies.

Like an avalanche they broke upon the privateer's deck, and drove back the howling mass.

With almost superhuman energy, the gallant fellows cut their way into the midst of the pirates, who had stripped themselves almost naked, and were cursing in the most horrible manner.

But everything was against them.

In the first place, their very numbers, too great for the deck, impeded their movements; and in the second, they had a bad cause, and not half the real courage of their assailants, who mowed them down like grass.

To add to their dismay, Jim Swaby, who had remained on board the "Swallow," with a few men, brought one of the guns to bear upon the pirates, and with deadly aim he sent a driving mass of grape through their midst, and when the smoke cleared away, Jack could see that the ship had become a very shambles.

The remaining pirates now made a desperate effort, and, headed by their captain, boarded the "Swallow," and sought to cut loose the grapnels.

Now was Jim Swaby's turn to exhibit courage, and right manfully he did it.

Parrying the first thrust of the pirate captain, he clove him through the lower lip and chin—a most frightful wound.

But this only served to infuriate the pirate leader yet the more, and making a furious onslaught, he rushed upon Jim, who slipped and fell.

Death looked into the face of the old boatswain, and he gave himself up for lost, but at that moment the cheery voice of Jack was heard, urging his men on—

"Forward, my noble 'Swallows,' and cut them down! Spare none of the villains!"

The infuriated pirate captain, as if resolved to do as much mischief as possible ere he succumbed, turned upon Jack, and their weapons met.

Cut and parry, parry and cut, swift and deadly in aim, their swords sending forth sparks of fire, the two unequally matched combatants trod the deck, all others around them being engaged in a battle of life and death.

The blood rushed from the pirate's mouth, and fell in ugly patches upon the deck.

The horrible, ghastly wound, and the fearful change it made in his face, half unnerved Jack; but it was no time to relax, and screwing himself up for a rush, he dashed in for a final blow.

His cutlass shivered in his hand, and all seemed lost; but, on the inspiration of the moment, he dived, and grasping the hilt of the other's weapon, wrenched it from his hand.

"Yield!" he cried.

"Never!" cried the pirate. "San Remano yields to no man!"

He drew a pistol as he spoke, and levelled it.

With a quick blow, Jack severed his hand from the arm at the wrist, and the fingers and palm fell upon the deck.

Don San Remano uttered no sound, but with his left hand drew another weapon.

Fortunately it was not cocked, and with a yell of despair, he cast it into the sea, and sprang after it.

Still the fight was not over.

Some of the pirates still lived and fought.

They were desperate, and desperation gives courage to the meanest brutes, and they fought well.

Several ran up the rigging, and crouched in the cross-trees, hopeless and despairing.

Jack paused, and rested, his eye taking in the scene.

He saw Hannibal mowing down the enemy right and left, and Peter dancing among them, with a cutlass in his right hand, and the never-failing umbrella in the other, both doing wonderful execution.

Peter might well revere his gingham for surely never did so feeble a weapon cause such confusion to an enemy.

They could not make it out.

If their cuts with a cutlass had been parried by a cutlass, they could have understood it; but to have that blessed bundle of rag and whalebone constantly thrust under their noses, without taking into consideration the nozzle, which was ever digging at their ribs, was exceedingly annoying and embarrassing.

Peter's language, too, was not complimentary.

"Call dat fightin'?" he said to one man, who had cut at Peter's throat, and been cut down in his turn. "You not know how to strike. Dat de sort ob blow! Ha, you sare! Anoder man cut at this chile behind. Take dat!"

Bang went the gingham across another's face, and before he had recovered the confusion engendered by this mode of attack, the cutlass had pierced his ribs, and he fell, with a quick, short gasp, which spoke of death.

Hannibal was silent, but he was deadly,

and soon the pirates began to shrink as he advanced, supported by Tom Warren, who was a regular young lion that night; and although bleeding from half a dozen little wounds, he kept to the front.

Another lull, and then Jack came forward again, and the struggle was soon over.

Those who did not die by the sword, took refuge, as usual, in the sea, preferring that death to the one they most righteously deserved; and as they went down, more than one shrieked a last defiance to their foe, who had proved to be the better and the stronger.

"Sharp work, Jack!" said Tom Warren, seating himself upon a gun-carriage. "I am quite worn out."

"You are wounded?" said Jack.

"A scratch or two, nothing more; and you have blood upon your sleeve!"

"It is mostly that of other men, although I think some fellow gave me a prick. But, as I cannot tell hardly where it is, it cannot be very serious."

"I hope not; but some of our poor fellows are hurt."

"I must see to them at once. Jim is a good rough surgeon, but he cannot do everything."

"Let me help you?"

"Certainly. And Hannibal! Peter! Come and bear a hand with the sick!"

The twin brothers, who had been comparing notes, came at once, and on the muster-roll being called, it was found that three of Jack's men were dead, and seven wounded, more or less seriously.

This was a heavy casualty to such a limited crew, and Jack resolved to return to the creek, and rest for a week, to give the men a chance of getting round.

———

CHAPTER XX.

SOMEBODY ALOFT.

IN consideration of their recent exertions, Jack resolved to give the crew a rest for the remainder of the night, and ordered the anchor of the " Swallow" to be dropped, and then his second great prize moored alongside.

As the wind had now entirely dropped, and the sky was perfectly clear, the canvas was not furled. A watch for an hour was told off, then Jack, and those who were at liberty, sought repose.

Before this was done, however, every want of the wounded was attended to; and no case tending towards a fatal ending, there was no need for any additional attendance.

In the first watch were both Peter and Hannibal. They had volunteered their services because neither felt the want of sleep very much, and as they could be trusted when they volunteered, although a little shaky when pressed, their services were gladly accepted.

Jack had just tumbled into his first sleep, and was well on the road to the land of dreams, when a hand was laid upon him, and, opening his eyes, he saw Peter with a lantern in his hand.

The buoyant negro was now so much changed that Jack scarcely knew him. He shook, he trembled, he quivered, and his black face positively looked blue.

"Oh! Oh! Massa Jack," he said, "here such a bad job!"

"What has happened now?" asked Jack, springing out of his hammock, seriously alarmed.

"Oh, Massa Jack, de debil come on board!"

"The devil?"

"Yes, Massa Jack; him come on board!"

"Truly, he might have been an hour ago," said Jack, looking about for his cutlass; "but why he should visit us when the work is done, and none but men who fight for right left, I cannot tell. What is he like?"

"Berry black, Massa Jack."

"Why, that's nothing—so are you."

"Him got eyes ob fire."

"So has a cat if a light is near her. Where is he?"

"In de rigging ob de maintop, Massa Jack."

"I'll come up and look."

Jack lost no time, for he could not understand this strange visitant, and, not being particularly superstitious, he was anxious to put an end to the mystery.

On arriving upon deck, he found Hannibal and the seamen of the watch standing at the foot of the mainmast with drawn cutlasses, but looking rather scared, nevertheless.

"Where is his Satanic Majesty?" asked Jack.

"Dere him be," said Hannibal, pointing aloft.

Jack looked, and there, sure enough, was a dark figure clinging to the crosstrees, and looking down upon them with eyes that reflected the light of the moon.

"Have you spoken to it?" he asked.

"Speak to de debil?" said Peter. "Not dis chile."

"Bosh!" returned Jack. "Hallo! there!"

"What you want, sare?" asked a feeble voice, of unmistakable origin.

"Why, I'm blowed," said one of the men, "if it ain't another nigger!"

"Of course it is," said Jack. "Now, then, aloft, come down with you!"

"Me do no harm, sare," returned the same voice. "Me only de ship's cook—not'ing to do wif dam pirate."

"Come down, and don't use bad language," said Jack. "Be quick, or I will help you!"

With many haltings and tremblings, a thin, emaciated specimen of the African race came tumbling down, and as soon as he reached the deck he prostrated himself in the most abject state of submission.

He was really and truly a nigger of the true blood, for he was many shades darker than anything Jack had ever seen, and he seemed to have been most cruelly treated. Jack's heart quite melted towards him.

"Get up," said Jack "and here, Peter, take your devil, and give him something to eat. What made you run up there?"

"Me berry much afraid," replied the nigger. "Great fight, and much blood. Ugh!"

"Are there any more aloft?" asked our hero.

"No more niggers," was the reply; "but two pirates."

"Two pirates! Now, then, come down, you fellows!"

Two men showed their heads and slowly descended. As soon as they reached the deck they threw down their weapons and folded their arms.

"Who are you?" asked Jack.

"Americans," was the reply.

"How came you pirates?"

"Driven to it by want."

"Will you join my service?"

The men looked up, startled by this unexpected kindness.

"Do you mean it, sir?" they said.

"Most assuredly. I think I can trust you."

"Oh, Heaven! forgive us our sins!" said one. "That is a mercy I never expected!"

"I do not kill in cold blood," replied Jack; "but you must take the oath of allegiance to me. If you break it, and afterwards fall in my powers, you shall die!"

The men eagerly protested that they would serve him to the end, and took a solemn oath to that effect, and one of the watch was sent to see to their hammocks, and arrange their numbers in the mess.

"What I am to do with you, I don't know!" said Jack, addressing the nigger. "You are not fit for seamanship, and as for cooking, we have a man already."

"Massa Jack," said Peter the Great, "me got a good idea!"

"Then let us have it, Peter."

"You often say, sare, dat Peter was a genelman."

"So you are, Peter."

"Then it quite true, sare?"

"Quite."

"Now, Massa Jack, ebery genelman hab a serbant. Dat true—ain't it?"

"Certainly."

"Den I hab dis chap for *my* serbant!"

"And mine!" put in Hannibal.

"Bash your imperence!" said Peter. "You put your ugly nose inter eberyt,ing. What good am a serbant to you? What dress hab you? Shirt and trousers. You wear not'ing—I quite ashamed ob you! You not fit for 'spectable society!"

"Berry good," said Hannibal, independently; "keep de cuss to yourself. Him more like a whip-snake dan a man!"

"You forget," said Jack, "that it rests with me!"

"Jes' like Hannibal," said Peter. "He allers take de words out ob Massa Jack's mouf! But, Massa Jack, gib me dis nigger?"

"I suppose I must; but be kind to him."

"Massa Jack, I foller you in all t'ings!"

Jack then went below, and Peter was left above with his prize.

He scanned him up and down, much as men do the first horse they happen to possess.

"You my serbant, sare?" he said.

"Your berry good serbant," replied the other.

"You know my name?"

"No, massa, I don't."

"My name, den, is Massa Peter de Great King ob—ob—de Isle ob Wight—you remember dat?"

"Yes, Massa Peter de Gate."

"Peter de Great, sare."

"Peter de Gate," repeated the negro.

"Debilish bad English dese poor niggers speak," said Peter, turning to Hannibal.

Hannibal scorned to make a reply.

"Now, sare," said Peter, "what your name?"

"Not got one, Massa Peter de Gate."

"Den I gib you one. I call you Pitchpot, because you so debilish dark. You hear, Pitchpot?"

"Yes, massa."

"Now come and hab somet'ing to eat, den I tell you what to do."

"And dis chile tell him what *not* to do " muttered Hannibal, as they walked away. "Peter ain't goin' to crample me to de earf. If he gib me much cheek, I'll bash him hat ober him eyes, and—and—steal dat gingham!"

Having given vent to his wrath in the foregoing fearful threats, Hannibal turned away, and our hero paced the deck to and fro.

Suddenly a burst of merriment came from the forecastle.

"They are spinning yarns," Jack muttered, smiling. "Well, they have work enough, and want recreation."

He came upon a group of men grinning from ear to ear, and Swaby in the centre.

"It's a fact," Swaby said. "We were hauled afore that tough old craft called Neptune.

"'Hullo! what's all this?' ses he."

"Ah! what indeed?" Jack broke in, and Swaby coloured, and looked rather sheepish.

"Well, the fact is, sir," one of the men said, "Swaby's been spinning a yarn—how he ran away with a mermaid, and lived under the sea with her, until he was found out, and taken before Neptune."

"I will hear the story myself," Jack said, moving away. "I have ordered a double allowance of grog. Enjoy yourselves, for you have tough work in store."

CHAPTER XXI.

IN THE CREEK.—A FEW DIFFICULTIES WITH A SERVANT.

THE number of wounded on board the "Swallow" was soon lessened.

A few days' rest in the genial climate quickly restored those whose wounds were not very serious, and the very worst soon began to progress favourably.

As none of the men had been hit by the heavy shot of the guns, there was not a single case of amputation—in fact, if such a thing had been needed, it could not have been performed, for there was no surgeon on board. Jim Swaby had a rough idea of how to treat wounds, and Jack and Tom knew a little about it, but nothing more. There was a goodly store of drugs on board, with directions how to use them, which had been provided by the fore-thought of Mr. Scarborough, for which the sick and wounded had now ample reason to be thankful.

The adventurers spent a week or two in happiness and peace. Under a most genial sun, and in a land where Nature had been prodigal with her gifts, it could not be otherwise, and the only embarrassment under which Jack laboured was the presence of the prisoners—those first secured on board the "Swallow."

These men, as our readers know, had been left in charge when the hatchway was battened down, and had been secured first when the hatchway was reopened. They were mostly half-castes—fierce, savage-looking fellows, who had evidently led a lawless life, and looked upon dark and desperate deeds as the natural work of man.

Still they were men, and the wildest and most lawless are amenable to kindness. Hitherto it had been their lot to know nothing more than the right of might— the strongest to the fore, and the weakest to the wall. If death had been dealt out to them, they would have accepted it as a matter of course, but getting kindness instead, they were fairly dumbfounded and puzzled.

Jack put them ashore by the creek and although he gave them no arms, he yet afforded them hatchets and saws to erect habitations, and wire to snare animals for food, at the same time telling them that they were to keep within certain boundaries, and not to attempt to board the vessels on pain of death.

Jim Swaby and many of the men were inclined to think that this mercy was a mistake, and would bring forth bad fruit; but it was not so. One day the men came down to the creek in a body, and made signs that they wished to speak with our hero.

In spite of the remonstrances of his friends, he went ashore, attended only by two men, and, as he expected, received no violence. Instead of it, the men tendered their services, and volunteered to serve him whithersoever they might go.

There was no mistaking their earnestness.

These wild, lawless wretches, who had never known better leaders that the blood-thirsty and the remorseless, had been subdued by his manly kindness, and were as much his slaves as ever man was in this world.

The act was wise, and proved beneficial to both.

Jack got a good supply of men and they

learnt a little of the advantages and merits of civilisation.

They might lack the full amount of courage shown at all times by the British tars, but they were undoubtedly devoted to the service they had entered upon.

At first, the tars disliked the society of these men; but as they became better acquainted, the gallant sailors showed the true generosity of their dispositions, and accepted them as comrades.

Altogether, the crew was very happy and united.

There was, however, one discordant element on board, which, however trivial, served to keep everybody alive, and that was the unhappy Pitchpot, who had undertaken to serve Peter the Great, and never did it.

A nigger is a nigger all the world over, and although some of them do voluntary work with freedom and goodwill, yet all do their best to shirk enforced labour.

Thus it was with Pitchpot.

Peter had desired a servant, and he had got one.

He had raised a Frankenstein unto himself, and the consequences were very severe, the more particularly as he now put his own work upon the shoulders of his servitor, who, in his turn, left the work to perform itself.

Let us take a case—an event of one morning.

"Peter," cried out Jack, "where's my sword I gave you to clean?"

"Bring him d'rectly, sare," replied Peter. "Him nearly done."

"Make haste, for I'm going ashore."

"Yes, sare."

Peter rushed up on deck, and encountered Hannibal.

"You see dat Pitchpot?" he asked.

Hannibal, in a scornful tone, replied—

"Him not *my* serbant. Neber trouble my head 'bout him."

"Pitchpot, you will'in!" roared out Peter.

No Pitchpot in sight, and no voice of Pitchpot in reply.

"You see dat Pitchpot?" asked Peter, of Jim Swaby.

"I saw the lubber below a few minutes ago, replied Jim.

Down rushed Peter, and found some of the men cleaning the guns, but no Pitchpot.

"Hab you seen dat cussed nigger ob mine?" asked Peter, getting into a fever of impatience and fear. "Massa Jack waitin' for him."

"Now, then, where are you?" cried Jack, from above. "Where is my sword?"

"Comin', sare. Jes' rubbin' up de hilt. Hab you seen dat 'farnal nigger, Pitchpot?"

The men pause and think. One says that he saw him half-an-hour ago sleeping in a tarpaulin upon the deck; but another says that the boatswain kicked him out of it. A third, however, remembers seeing the fellow outside the magazine, curled up and snoring beautiful.

Down to the magazine rushed Peter, and there, sure enough, was Pitchpot lying in a heap.

"Pitchpot! you nigger skunk!" roared Peter the Great, giving him a blow with the ever-present gingham. "Wake up, you dark beggar!"

Pitchpot declined to wake up, and continued to snore.

Peter suddenly remembered the caudal appendage of the lion which he carried in his pocket, and, bringing it out, gave Pitchpot a wipe with it that made him skip to his feet.

"Golly! Murder!" roared Pitchpot. "Who dat?"

"You hab de cheek ob de debil," replied Peter the Great, aiming another blow at him with such energy that he nearly fell upon his nose. Pitchpot skipped out of the way with the agility of an ape. "You eat, and drink, and stuff, and sleep, bash you! Where Massa Jack's sword?"

"Massa Jack sword?" asked Pitchpot, with an innocent look. "What dat?"

"Him dat I gib you to clean." said Peter the Great. "Golly! let me git anoder bash at you!"

"You gib me dat sword?" pursued Pitchpot, evading a direct answer as only a nigger can.

"I gib you him an hour ago, you black son ob a long legged ostrich," said Peter.

"Peter! Peter! where are you?" cried Jack, from above.

"Me comin' dis minute," said Peter, in an agony, and, pouncing upon Pitchpot, he held that unhappy nigger by the throat. "Now, you sare, you stuffed himage of a crokledile, where dat sword, or I shake de life out ob you."

"Me lose him," replied Pitchpot, driven into a corner at last.

"Lose him! Where?"

"Somewhere round about de ship."

This answer, so vague and exasperating, nearly drove Peter mad, and he shook the wretched Pitchpot until his teeth rattled again.

"Oh! murder, Massa!" he roared.

"Peter! Peter!" cried the voice of Jack

Peter dashed down Pitchpot, and rushed away in search of the missing sword. In five minutes he had inquired everywhere, and received the same answer—"The sword has not been seen."

Then, as there was no escape, he resolved to see Jack, and face it out with some story of having put it down for a moment and some men on board having hidden it away.

He found our hero waiting, with Tom and Hannibal, and two men in a boat, ready to pull them ashore.

"Now," said Jack, "where is my sword?"

"Dere some big t'ief on board dis ship," replied Peter.

"Have you lost it?"

"No, Massa Jack; but some big rascal stole him."

This reply, so characteristic of the dark race, brought a smile to Jack's face, and Tom Warren turned the other way. Hannibal stood quiescent, and smiled sardonically.

"Now, Peter," said Jack, "tell the truth."

"I do, Massa Jack. De sword am lost."

"But where did you put it?"

Peter the Great rolled his eyes in a reflective manner, as if solving some knotty problem. Jack saw the lie upon his lips, and checked him.

"That sword, Peter," he said, "you gave to Pitchpot."

"Dere never was such a cuss as dat Pitchpot!" replied Peter, falling heavily upon his follower and henchman. "Yesserday I gib him my collar to starch, and de beggar forgot what it was, and clean de sarspan wif it; and he brush dis hat de wrong way, so dat de fluff stand up like hair on de cat's back."

"You can give him what you like of your own," said Jack, "but in future give him nothing of mine. See, here is my sword, found in the biscuit-bin by Hannibal, who has cleaned it."

"Dat de berry sword," said Peter, as if called upon to give confirmation to an assertion. "I know him berry well."

It was impossible to be angry with him, so Jack turned away and entered the boat.

Peter was about to follow him, when Jack bade him summon Pitchpot and bring him too."

"He will be all the better for a little training," said Jack. "The poor fellow's head is half-addled."

The unfortunate Pitchpot was, after a little trouble, discovered by Peter, who ordered him to the boat, and accelerated his movements with a little taste of the tail.

Then the boat pushed off, and the party landed on the beach.

———

CHAPTER XXII.

FOR LIFE.

JACK'S stay there was not many hours, and was simply a little exploring party of pleasure. He returned in the afternoon, and held a council as to their future proceedings.

The wounded were, most of them, now in condition to work again, and as an idle life did not suit the purpose of our hero, he wanted to be moving once more.

He had done much for his reputation. The capture of the two privateers would have gone a great way towards redeeming his character, but not enough, and in addition to the necessity of performing other feats to show to his countrymen that he was neither a pirate nor a coward, there was the thirst for glory which burns in all breasts with more or less power.

England was at war, and there was much to be done with its enemies, and, in addition to those, the seas were infested with innumerable piratical craft, which sailed under one flag or the other, just as it happened to serve their turn.

The council consisted of Tom Warren, Jim Swaby, and our hero, with Hannibal and Peter the Great for listeners and lookers-on, and these worthies showed their impartiality by agreeing with everything that Jack said, and scouting all that fell from the lips of the others.

Jack was the hero of their hearts, and in their eyes he was infallible.

The end was, that the "Swallow" was to sail in the morning, and take whatever turned up. To fight everything they came across, unless it carried the British flag.

"I will never strike a blow at my country," said Jack, "for the blood of, say, that of any nation, if it is on my head, would give me no peace. I fight for right, and if I run, it will not be because I have any fear than the fear of doing wrong!"

"Dat Massa Jack all ober," whispered Peter to Hannibal. "Lilly boy at home ask him to fight, Massa Jack say 'No.' Big boy laugh, and Massa Jack gib him such a licking. Golly! you see him eye!"

Jack's resolution met with the general approval of the men, who had no disposition to rebel against their country; but most of them made a reservation, and that was to the effect "that they would like to have a turn with white-feather, Cursly." A great many of Jack's crew had, as our readers know, served under that funky commander, and knew how to value him.

"I'd like to have a turn with him singe-handed," said one, "and many might give him a cutlass, and lick him with a rope's-end. Lor'! wouldn't I make him dance!"

The idea of "cobbing old Cursly" was most uproariously received, and a variety of modes of administration, in case he ever fell into their hands, were proposed and adopted, the men little thinking how soon they might have an opportunity of carrying it into execution.

A few days later, the "Swallow" was turned out, and anchored off-shore. Then the opening of the creek was stopped by two trees which were felled on the rocks above. These were planted about midway, just at the first bend, and earth was strewn upon them, and creepers planted, so as to give the place the appearance of the entering of the creek, and so well was it carried out, that the most practised eye might have been deceived.

The masts of the captured vessel were taken down, and both were stowed as much out of sight as possible, and everybody landed upon the coast. Earth was piled upon the deck nearest to view, and ivy and other things planted to grow over the side. In a month they would be completely hidden.

All was secure, therefore, and the arrangements were perfect. Jack was going upon a long cruise, and it might be years before he returned to take the captured vessels home.

"Dat a berry good idea, Massa Jack," said Hannibal, who had watched all these proceedings with great interest, "and de creek stopped up well. No boat get t'rough dat. But how do you get back again?"

"Any casual visitor," replied Jack, "will take it for granted that the creek stops there; but I shall know better, and with a pound of gunpowder I will clear all the rubbish away."

"Ob course," said Peter, who had been a little more puzzled than his brother;

"Any fool see dat a pound ob gunpowder quite enough."

"More dan enough," put in Pitchpot, who happened to be near.

"Get away, you cussed black nigger!" roared Peter, feeling in his coat-tail pocket. "Poking your nose in among genelmen! Whar am dat lion tail? You got him, Hannibal?"

"Neber carry such rubbish wif me," replied Hannibal.

Pitchpot grinned all over his face.

"Lion tail berry good to eat," he said. "Make good soup."

"What dat?" roared Peter.

"Me find him, and me cook him," said Pitchpot, dodging away; "and Massa Peter eat him last night for supper."

"Golly smash!" said Peter, in a fury. "Was dat the soup?"

Pitchpot, in an agony of enjoyment, rolled upon the deck, and Hannibal roared like a bull.

Jack, with a laughing face, left them to fight it out.

Pitchpot's ecstacy was put an end to by a blow from the gingham, but ere a second could be delivered, he was dodging behind the mast, Peter, on the other side, vainly endeavouring to get another shot at him.

"I'll make pumpkin sarse ob you, Nigger Pitchpot!" he said. "I bash ebery bone in your body, and make soup ob you! Come out ob dat, you black-looking t'ief!"

"De tail in Massa Peter's coat when I brush him," urged Pitchpot, "and de tail goin' berry bad—a little more, and him too strong for soup. Pitchpot t'ink it a pity to waste him."

"Catch him by de scruff ob de neck, Hannibal!" said Peter.

"Not dis chile," replied Hannibal.

Without aid it was impossible to catch Pitchpot, who was as nimble as a cat, so Peter, after working himself into a lather, by his vain attempts, gave it up, and retired with great dignity, making mental resolves for the benefit of Pitchpot.

The "Swallow" shortly after left, and with her head to south, sailed for two days without sighting a vessel.

They left the land behind them, but on the morning of the third day they sighted a group of small islands, giving promise of great beauty, and Jack, who was passionately fond of the charms of Nature, ran his vessel between them, and anchored.

Here they spent a day or two, shooting, and amusing themselves in various ways;

but an idle life it was at best, and on the fourth day the anchor was weighed.

As they were slowly working their way in and out of the various openings between the islands, the man at the masthead cried out—

"A sail!"

"Where?" cried Jack, seizing his glass.

"On the weather bow, sir."

In a moment all was excitement, and all hands were piped to quarters.

"What is she like, sir?" asked Jim Swaby.

"Man-of-war, I think. Yes, there is a puff of white smoke. What can it mean?"

"Signal to a vessel not yet in sight, sir."

"Perhaps. We must make all sail," said Jack. "Starboard! Let her walk through it! Set the main gaff topsail! See how my 'Swallow' walks through the water! Listen to the swish, swish against her sides, Tom!"

"Another gun, Jack."

"That's nothing to us. She doesn't see us yet. She works too close in that isle there."

"Now she tacks!" roared Jim Swaby. "She's after us, Master Jack!"

"Is she?" said Jack, calmly. "Ah! you are right, Jim; and now I know her. It's the 'War Eagle!'"

"Old Cursly's Floating Hell, by this time," muttered Jim. "Another gun, sir. There goes the flags to the fore. She is signalling us."

"Run up the Union Jack and the white flag under it," replied Jack. "That's my answer."

"And you'll get back a shot in return," muttered Jim. "No; the signal ain't for us, sir. It's for another craft."

"Another sail right ahead!" sang out the man at the head.

"We are in for it!" said Jim, smiting his leg. "It's all up with us, Master Jack!"

"I do not think so," replied Jack. "We cannot fight them, of course. One broadside would sink us; but I will have a run for it. Out with all the canvas there! Jim, take the wheel!"

CHAPTER XXIV.

A DARING RUN.

WELL might there be a feeling of anxiety on board, for the danger was now imminent. The "War Eagle" was coming up with great strides, and the other vessel was so well to windward, that escape seemed impossible; but Jack's only chance was to try it.

After seeing his gallant little craft under jib-mainsail and foresail, and as much other canvas as she could carry, and everything right and tight, he ordered his men below, and then took the helm himself.

There was some demurring at this. Tom, Peter, Hannibal, and Jim all begged to be allowed to remain with him; but Jack was firm. He would be there alone.

"It is my wish—my choice," he said. "There is not much risk, and if one life is sacrificed, it had better be mine."

In vain they entreated, until he became peremptory, and ordered them all into the run.

"I cannot afford to lose valuable lives," he said. "Standing on deck will not help us—the enemy is too big—so get into the run every man of you."

The sailors then bundled downstairs, laughing, joking, and chatting, as if there was no imminent peril of their being sent to the bottom of the sea during the next half-hour; but sailors are strange beings, and it takes a deal to knock the fun out of them.

Just then the "War Eagle" luffed up in the wind, and her foresail lifted. A column of white smoke spurted over the bows, and was blown back by the wind. The report reached the "Swallow," and the shot fell close behind her.

"Not badly aimed," said Jack, coolly, giving the wheel a turn; "but nothing done yet."

Another succeeded, and this time struck the vessel upon the quarter. A shower of splinters flew about Jack's head, but he never moved a muscle.

At this moment a dark head appeared above the hatchway, and Hannibal's voice was heard.

"Massa Jack! Massa Jack!"

"What do you want, Hannibal?"

"Let dis chile come up, sare."

"Go below at once, and don't let me see your face again."

"Perhaps Massa Jack like mine better," said Peter, popping up as Hannibal disappeared.

Boom! and whirr! came a shot, striking the deck near the hatchway, and Peter disappeared as if by magic.

Jack thought he was killed.

"Poor fellow!" he muttered. "I could better have spared a better man."

"Dat berry near, Massa Jack!" cried

Peter, popping his bare head up. "Look at dis hat!"

A splinter, pointed like a tip-cat, and as thick as a rolling-pin, stood upright in the crown of Peter's *chapeau*—a very ugly-looking thing at the best.

"Get down," was all Jack said, and Peter, finding that he was indeed in earnest now, disappeared.

The other vessel—a corvette—had now hauled to the wind, and it seemed impossible for the "Swallow" to escape her broadside; but she was careering on gallantly, and Jack, who knew her sailing powers, was not without hope.

Her jib-boom was now bending like a lancewood bow, and the topmasts whipping about like fishing-rods, as she rushed through the water, scattering the spray high above her deck.

The "War Eagle" was drawing up, and her shot flying about on every side.

Tacking was out of the question, and bearing up was equally hopeless.

As the corvette was going free, the only chance was to stand on and try and weather it.

The corvette, now about two miles away, braced up sharp on the opposite tack, was evidently aware of Jack's object.

A shot from the corvette came bounding over the sea, but wide of the "Swallow," just as a hint to heave to.

The attempt to escape seemed madness. But Jack held on.

He was now so near that through the port-holes he could see the men standing at their guns, and a dozen glasses at least were pointed towards him.

The lone boy was evidently a puzzle to them, and the officers on the quarter-deck gathered together, and engaged in animated conversation.

When it concluded, one of them came forward, and the next instant a puff of white smoke was seen.

Then came the whirr of a round shot, and, grazing the mast, it cut through the main-sail.

Then followed a shower of grape, which peppered the little "Swallow" amid-ships.

Now, there is nothing so appalling as grape-shot. Round-shot, even in broadsides, is, in comparison, a thing to wink at. Musketry is a joke to it. But a shower of iron bullets, each about the size of a peach, is rather a serious thing, and if Jack did shut his eyes for a moment, there was nothing in the act to wonder at.

But it was only for a moment, and the same dauntless courage he had hitherto shown returned, and he shifted the wheel with an unflinching nerve.

Just then up popped Peter's head again.

"Massa Jack! Massa Jack!" he whispered.

"Am I to be obeyed, or not?" was Jack's reply without a turn of his head.

"There's blood on your face, Massa Jack!" groaned Peter. "Come down, and let some ob dese ugly gosses down below take dat wheel!"

"I am not hurt much, Peter," returned Jack. "A splinter, or shot—I know not which—just grazed me, that's all! This is my post! Go down!"

"Oh, Massa Jack, let me come up to you?"

"Hannibal!" cried Jack, still with his eyes ahead.

"Yes, Massa Jack!" roared out Hannibal from just behind his brother.

"Have the goodness to go down below, and take Peter with you!"

"Come out, you reflactory nigger!" said Hannibal to his brother.

"I'm b'iled if I do!" said Peter, clutching at the deck.

Hannibal went down a step or two and took hold of Peter's ankles:

"Will you come down, sare?" he asked

"Hannibal! you had better deflect afore you hab any nonsense wif me!" said Peter, in a solemn tone.

"I ax you once more," said Hannibal. "Will you come down?"

"*No!*" roared Peter, and Hannibal, throwing all his weight into the effort, gave his brother a most tremendous jerk.

Peter had but very little hold upon the deck, and down he went like a Jack-in-the-box, with such impetus that he drove Hannibal down to the bottom, where Jim Swaby and Tom Warren were standing, both of whom were knocked down upon their backs.

For a minute, there was a mighty amount of kicking and struggling, and, perhaps, a little bad language; but Jim Swaby and Tom succeeded in extricating themselves, and each grasping a rope's end, proceeded to belabour the brothers, who were still clasped in each other's arms, and heaping very questionable compliments upon each other.

"You take Hannibal, sir," said Jim Swaby, "and I'll let the other blacking-pot have it. Here's at 'em! Keep time, sir. One, two, three!"

This systematic attack speedily cooled

the energy of the twin niggers, who relaxed their hold upon each other, and took up a sitting position upon the deck.

"Dis a pretty game ob yours, Massa Swaby," said Peter; "hit a man when him down."

———

CHAPTER XXV.

A CLOSE SHAVE.

"HE no hit him when he get up," said Hannibal, rising, with a significant air.

"There, get away with you," said Tom, giving them a good-humoured push. "You were disobeying orders, Peter, or you would not have got into trouble."

"Massa Tom," said Peter, with a dignity which so well became him, "I take my orders from Massa Happy Jack, and when any oder man consume to come de s'perior ober me, I turn my back on him and march orf dis way."

Unfortunately for Peter, the turning was not quite so majestic as he intended it to be, for Pitchpot, his own sable attendant, being anxious to know what was going on, had crept up behind, and Peter, confused by the late struggle, fell over him.

What would have been done by Peter the Great it is impossible to say, for vengeance was driven out of his head by a mighty crash above, and a rattling sound, as if the clouds were raining stones upon the deck.

*   *   *

"Keep below, there!" cried Jack. "It is only a topmast. Will you keep down?"

These words were addressed to the four heads of Jim Swaby, Tom Warren, Peter, and his brother, who all appeared at the hatchway at the same time.

"What is the good of your coming here?" continued Jack. "I do not care to fight against my countrymen, and all depends upon the steering. I can do that without, as well as with, you."

"I am tired of being cooped up below," said Tom, stepping upon the deck.

"So am I," said Jim Swaby, following his example.

"So am Hannibal," added Peter, as he came forward. "Don't be hard on us, Massa Jack. We must lib and die wif you."

"As you will," said Jack, with a cheery smile; "but look out for squalls."

There was need to look out, for the corvette was now close upon their quarter, not more than three hundred yards away, and bowling along with the wind, and the green sea hissing and foaming around her.

The waves surged against her sides, throwing up foam like snow into her ports.

The press of canvas laid her over until her copper, gleaming like a mirror, was seen nearly through her whole length.

And there were her ports above, through which the good English guns were grinning, ugly, and open-mouthed, not at all the sort of gentlemen a nervous man would care to stare at in the face.

The men were at quarters, ready for boarding, and a more determined-looking lot of men those on board the "Swallow" had never seen.

"If they knew what we are, Jack, not a man on board that craft would touch us," said Tom.

"But they *don't* know," replied Jack, quietly; "and, as they take us for pirates, I have no doubt they mean to give it to us pretty stiff—if they can catch us."

"Which they are pretty nigh sartain to do," put in Jim Swaby.

"There's many a slip 'twixt the cup and the lip," said Jack, calmly. "For instance, that shot from their bow-gun is one of them."

The shot in question passed between him and Tom Warren as he spoke, and the wind of it fanned their cheeks.

Tom whistled, and felt his head, as if he were afraid of its being gone.

High above the mast of the corvette, flew the flag of Old England, which has braved a thousand years, and been planted in wider lands and in more seas than any flag of any known nation.

It was impossible to look upon it without emotion, for the hearts of all were, perforce, British to the core, and all their sympathies were with the men who treated them as foes.

"I would like to run up my Union Jack alone," said our hero; "but those who are after us would only call me a liar and a knave. Another shot. Very near you, Peter, that time."

"Berry near, Massa Jack," replied Peter, wriggling his head about. "It take de starch out ob my collar."

The second vessel in pursuit was now far behind, having lost the breeze, and was already far away in the horizon. The great battle, if such there was to be, would take place between the corvette and the "Swallow."

Tacking now became the order of the

The savage paused, and then stood up in his boat. A curious craft in its way, made of the bark of trees, covered with untanned skins of beasts.

day on the part of the corvette, but there was no hailing and trumpetting, although Jack heard a voice now and then sing out an imperative command, and every few minutes a cannon sent forth its missile, and the white, feathery smoke floated away upon the breeze.

Two round-shot now tore right through the deck of the "Swallow," and she trembled again, but not a man upon her decks quailed.

It was a run for life, and if that life was to end, then they were ready.

What had they to fear?

They were not pirates and murderers running from the grasp of justice, but honest men *misunderstood*, and he who commanded them had been driven by the cowardly conduct of Captain Cursly from his nation's service.

Had he been a deserter, he might have dreaded his impending fate; but being naught but a free, gallant, and honest young sailor, he had no cause to fear anything.

Suddenly the breeze began to fall, and then the superior powers of the "Swallow" became apparent. A light breeze was sufficient for her, but not for the craft in pursuit, and, foot by foot, the sea widened between them.

Then came frantic shouts from the corvette, and gun after gun was fired, some striking the "Swallow," but others flying far away.

Foot by foot, the gap widened, and within half an hour the iron hail began to fall short.

"All hands on deck, there!" cried Jack.

The men, who had been waiting all-impatient below, now came tumbling upon the deck, the last being Pitchpot, who put a respectful distance between himself and his lord and master, Peter the Great.

"Shout, lads!" cried Jack. "Three cheers for the 'Swallow'!'"

The hearty "hurrah" from the "Swallow" found no response from the corvette.

There all was anger and dismay, and, like a dog turned from the scent, she put about, and returned, slowly and sullenly, in the direction of her consort.

It was now about seven in the evening, and although the breeze continued to gradually fall, the "Swallow" kept on until the corvette was hull down; and the other craft out of sight.

An hour later, a headland arose in the horizon, and the "Swallow," by command of Happy Jack, was turned towards it."

"We are free," he said; "and now for more adventures. Tom, are you hungry?"

"As a wolf."

"Come down and dine, then; but, phew! it has been a narrow escape."

"Very," said Tom.

And they went down together.

"Hannibal," said Peter.

"Yes, my brudder," returned Hannibal.

"Am you hungry?"

"Berry."

"Den come down, and hab what Massa Jack and Tom can't eat. But fust let me settle wif dat nigger, Pitchpot."

Pitchpot was, however, out of sight, and as a licking for him could wait rather than a very strong appetite, Peter and Hannibal went below, and helped to wait at our hero's table.

They were so assiduous in their attentions that Jack complimented them, until he found that they were more anxious to remove dishes than to put them on, and when a wrangle outside between the two brothers over a knuckle-bone of ham took place, he perfectly understood their assiduity, and appreciated it accordingly.

CHAPTER XXVI.

THE WILD FISHERMEN.

THE damage done to the "Swallow" was repaired with remarkable promptitude.

The men, whose hearts were in their work, knotted and spliced the rigging, mended and shifted the sails, fixed the sprung and wounded spars, stopped up the shot-holes, and put all taut and square before the moon had been up two hours.

By this time, the breeze had dropped, and all hands were piped for grog and a merry evening. Jim Swaby had orders to serve out double rations, and being no mean hand at the fiddle, played the first hornpipe for the men to dance to.

A true-hearted Jack Tar is as loyal to his horn pipe as to his country, and a very amusing competition took place between the men of the "Swallow," and the way they cut and capered was a credit to the service.

Our hero remained below with Tom, and therefore the men had it all their own way, and being joined by the twins, Peter and Hannibal, they spent a most joyous evening.

It would require a mighty pen to give a

full, true, and particular account of Peter's performance that night, as he excelled in the dance.

He knew every step of the British hornpipe, and as he put in a few original movements of his own, it must be reckoned that he carried off the palm in that respect.

But the great hit of the evening was when he and Hannibal stood up together to show the tars what a native dance was like.

Shall I describe it?

No, I will not, for a description of it is beyond my powers; but if sixteen ordinary legs had attempted a like amount of capering, they would utterly have failed. Such twists, such turns, and heels so high in the air had never been seen before, and when they gave in, both were utterly exhausted.

As they lay panting upon the deck, complacently accepting the rounds of applause from the spectators, Pitchpot, for the first time, put in his appearance having calculated, with wondrous ingenuity, that he might now approach his master with perfect safety.

"You want me, Massa Peter?" he said.

Peter was breathless to answer, but he remembered his wrongs, and glared.

"Me understand dat you look about for me," grinned Pitchpot, who thought he might cut a joke with impunity.

But, alas! for human calculation; he was like many a wiser man before him—a little out.

Peter was very much done up, but like a dying horse, he still had a kick in him, and he gave Pitchpot one upon the shin, and as that wretched nigger stooped down to rub the afflicted part, the mighty gingham was brought down upon his head.

"Dat's quits!" gasped Peter.

And then he lay down at rest, and Pitchpot sneaked away into the cook's galley, where he devoted half an hour to rubbing his shin with some cold mutton fat.

At twelve o'clock, all hands but the watch were piped to rest, for Jack did not allow indiscriminate revelry, although he gave a vast amount of freedom, and after that, all was still for the night.

The sun rose upon a cloudless sky, and cast its rays upon a sea of glass.

The great waters were so transparent that thousands of fish could be seen below, revelling in their element, and going in and out the shadows of a pile of ugly-looking rocks about five fathoms down.

It was a pretty sight enough for those on board to while away an hour or two, but there was something of deeper interest not far away.

A rugged coast, with forests inland, lay not two miles from the "Swallow," and upon a promontory were several rude-looking huts, built in a very savage fashion.

Near them were half a dozen boats, drawn up high and dry.

This was interesting, but this was not all, for a solitary boat, propelled by a solitary man, was approaching, and presently came within hail.

Happy Jack and all hands were on deck, and Jack shouted out—

"Hallo, there! who are you?"

The man paused, resting upon his oars, and then stood up in his boat. A curious craft in its way, made of the bark of trees, covered with untanned skins of beasts.

He was a rough-looking fellow, in a shirt made of some blue-looking material, and round about his loins was a belt of skin, like that which covered the boat.

In it was a long knife, but no other weapon visible. Below his knees he had no dress, and his brown bare legs shone in the sunlight.

Who are you?" cried Jack.

The man made a sign, but returned no verbal answer. It was plain that he did not understand the question.

Then Jack tried him in French and Spanish with the same result.

"You try him, Peter, with your tongue," he said.

Peter shouted out a few words of his native tongue, but the man made the same sign as before.

"As if any darned critter could understand that gibberish!" muttered Jim Swaby.

Peter pulled up his collar, and glared contemptuously at Jim; but he said nothing, as it was neither the time nor place for wrangling.

Jack now made friendly signs, and the man pulled under the lee of the "Swallow," and climbed on board.

Thinking it best to be friendly, our hero held out his hand, but there seemed to be some offence in this, for, in a moment, the man was overboard again, and pulling hastily towards the shore.

"Got the blue funk!" said Jim Swaby.

"He cerainly went off very unceremoniously," said Jack. "How that fellow pulls—he has reached the shore already! Pass the glass, Tom. Thank you."

Our hero took a long and earnest look, then, closing the telescope, said—

"He has aroused his comrades, and they are all coming off in a body to attack, I suppose. Poor wretches! One discharge of grape would blow them clean out of the water!"

"Their pluck is the offspring of ignorance." said Tom Warren.

"You are quite right, sir," put in Jim Swaby. "They are so darned cheeky because they don't know better."

"I shall be sorry to hurt them," said Jack; "but if they give me any trouble, I shall make very short work of them. Load one of the guns with grape!"

The fleet of savage craft now drew near, and the men, each and every one of them, as wild as men could be, pulled up at about the same distance as the first, who came, and tossed up their oars.

"What signal is that?" asked Jack.

"Dey berry friendly," replied Peter the Great. "Dat a sign dey wish to trade."

Jack held up his hand, and instructed those around him to do the same.

The strangers then sat down again, and, paddling up to the ship's side, came readily on board.

There was a remarkable absence of fear in these men, and although they inspected the guns with great curiosity, there was none of the superstitious terror usually betrayed by savages.

They spoke to each other in an unknown tongue with great vivacity, and for a time, they were allowed to roam about at will.

It was only when one of them sought to draw a seaman's cutlass that Jack stopped their perambulations.

If they could not understand his language, they could his signs, and drawing together in a knot, they backed to the side of the ship as if anticipating an aggressive movement; but Jack held up his hand again, and they went no further.

Then one, evidently their leader, although his garb was as rude as the rest, signed an invitation to go ashore, and after a brief consultation, Jack ordered the long-boat to be lowered, and, in company with Swaby, Peter, and Hannibal, and a dozen seamen, prepared to accompany the strangers.

With a wild shout of joy, the savages dashed into their canoes in such a reckless fashion that two of them went clean over the other side into the sea.

Their friends, however, righted them and their boats with remarkable promptitude, and then the procession set out for the shore.

The canoes went first, and the long-boat brought up the rear, and as they skimmed over the intervening water, Jack took stock of the men into whose company he had fallen.

They were very fair for inhabitants of that latitude, and the regularity of their features bespoke European descent.

They were handsome, and well-shaped, and muscular, and bent to their oars in a way that would have done credit to the best seamen of our navy.

The boats touched land, and the party got out.

Then, for the first time, Jack saw a number of women and children peeping out timidly from the doors of the huts, both as wild and savagely-handsome as the men.

The country looked richer on a nearer approach, and as they walked up the slope, a serpent slid from under Jack's feet, and hissing, wriggled away under the long grass.

"That's a cobra," said Jack. "His bite is fatal."

"Him no bite black man," returned Peter the Great. "Black man and de snake berry good friends."

"Berry good," said Hannibal, gruffly.

"I should not like to see you make each other's acquaintance," returned Jack, laughing.

"Me show you presently," said Peter.

An opportunity for the exhibition presently offered.

The leader of the savages pointed to an open space in the ground, and by signs bade them sit down, and intimated that he and his comrades would hasten and get something to eat.

They went away, and as the sailors had kept by the long-boat in obedience to orders, Jack and his two faithful negroes were now left together.

Peter then selected a reed, and rapidly trimmed it into the form of a whistle.

"Now," he said, "you keep berry quiet, Massa Jack; and you, Hannibal, don't lift dat nose ob yours anoder inch higher! I'm goin' to show Massa Jack how much berry good friends de cobra and Peter is."

Then, taking up an imposing attitude, he began to play.

The first notes were very musical, and surprised Jack, who was not prepared for anything so rich and mellow from the rough instrument fashioned by Peter's hands.

CHAPTER XXVII.

SNAKE CHARMING.

AT first the efforts of the performer bore no fruit, and it seemed as if the only persons likely to be charmed were the performer and those who listened to him. But, after a brief delay, a small green snake came out slowly from the shelter of the bushes, and coiled itself up at Peter's feet.

It was not a cobra, but Jack knew it well by sight as a reptile whose venom was almost as deadly, and instinctively he drew his legs up.

The act was a natural one; but the next moment he felt ashamed of it, and stretched his feet out as before.

"Massa Jack no need to fear," whispered Hannibal.

The whisper was low, but it broke the charm, and the little wretch, raising its head, hissed in an ominous manner.

Peter, turning his eyes reproachfully upon his brother, played fast and furiously, and the snake, after two or three threatening turns of its neck, subsided into repose again.

Then Peter paused in his playing, and murmuring with his lips, stooped down and stroked the reptile upon the neck.

It coiled round his arm, and slowly worked its way up, and nestled in his bosom.

"Him safe now," said Peter; "but confound you, Hannibal! Wurra you open dat big, ugly mouth ob your'n for?"

"To tell Massa Jack not to be afraid."

"Thank you for nothing," returned Jack, drily. "I was not afraid."

"Nodody but a chunk like Hannibal t'ink dat Massa Jack afraid," said Peter, indignantly. "Now you see, sare, dat de snake and black man berry good friends."

"I see it perfectly well," replied Jack.

"But me show you more," said Peter the Great, putting the instrument to his lips again, and renewing the wild and melancholy, yet pleasing music.

In a few minutes, another snake—a splendid specimen of the deadly cobra—came out, and rising upon the tip of its tail, or nearly to the tip, commenced to dance graceful, fascinating movements, and Peter, now thoroughly excited, blew and fingered away like a mad piper.

Soon the dance was joined by another —and another—and another—until half-a-dozen, all of the same poisonous species, were going through a series of marvellous contortions in response to the music.

It was truly wonderful to see how they were subdued and led away by the sweet sounds, and the sight so novel to Jack quite charmed him.

Then, as before, Peter stopped playing, and uttering the monotonous droning he had employed before, he lured them, one by one, up his arms, into his bosom, until all lay nestled there.

"Now, Massa Jack," he exclaimed triumphantly, "are not de snakes and Peter berry much friends?"

"I must confess, Peter," said Jack, "that you have shown a wonderful power; but how is it that I have never heard of it before?"

"Massa Jack," said Peter, assuming the attitude which always accompanied his efforts at oratory, "de black man am a wonderful man, and Peter de most wonderful ob black men. Him no do all at once, but come out little and little, as long as Massa Jack libs."

"Have you this power?" asked Jack, addressing Hannibal.

Hannibal shook his head.

"Me no hab it," he said. "It berry rare. Peter's fader hab it, him grand-fader hab it, and Peter got it, but Hannibal not hab it."

"And yet you are twins?"

"Born at the same time," explained Peter, "and ob de same mudder, but *not* twins. Peter de best by seberal chalks!"

"You are a wonder, Peter. But, tell me, Peter, what you will do with them now?"

"Keep 'em here, and hab fun on board de 'Swallow,' Massa Jack."

"I doubt if they will be very welcome there. Such an addition to the mess would be rather dangerous."

"No danger, Massa Jack; dey not hurt anybody dat Peter tell 'em not to. Dey Peter's friends, and lub him berry much."

"You are quite sure?"

"Massa Jack, you hab de word ob honour from a real black genelman dat dey hurt nobody!"

On this assurance our hero was obliged to rest content, but it must be admitted that he had some doubts as to the issue of Peter's work.

The bite of a cobra he knew to be fatal, and however pacific they might be with Peter, there was a chance of their cutting up rough with other people.

He made one more effort to dissuade that sable gentleman from keeping his newly-acquired pets, but as Peter had evidently set his heart upon astonishing and amusing the men of the "Swallow," he did not press the subject.

The wild men whom they had fallen in with were seen to be returning, some of them towards our hero, and the rest bearing down upon the seamen, and all laden with fish and a rough kind of bread, so dark and unwholesome in its appearance that a pauper would have turned up his nose at it.

The leader presented some to Jack, who, knowing that most people of the earth were fond of breaking bread with strangers, and looked upon it as a sort of bond between them and their guests, did not scruple to partake of it.

Peter the Great and Hannibal, being very peckish indeed, and not being over particular, in a gastronomical sense, fell upon the food at once.

The others ate a little fish, but *no bread*.

"I suppose this is an especial dish prepared in our honour," thought Jack; "and it won't do to refuse it, so here goes."

He bit out a piece of it, and swallowed the morsel, which was as bitter as gall.

Then he took another, and by a mighty effort, got that down, the strangers watching him closely.

"Massa Jack," cried Peter, suddenly, "eat no more ob him. Dis bread poisoned!"

Jack cast away the loaf, but it was too late.

A numbed feeling came over him, and he sank back helpless.

At the same moment, Peter and Hannibal rolled over, and lay perfectly still.

———

CHAPTER XXVIII.

STRANGE FRIENDS IN THE HOUR OF NEED.

ALTHOUGH deprived of motion, Jack could yet see and hear.

The poisonous drug, whatever it was, still left him all his powers of observation.

This was not the case with Peter the Great and Hannibal, who—having eaten, at least, four times the quantity of bread partaken of by our hero—were quite overcome, and it was probably owing to the small quantity the latter had swallowed that his brain had not been overcome as well as his body.

The wild fishermen stood quietly watching the progress of their work, and as soon as Peter and Hannibal sank into insensibility, advanced towards them with the too apparent intention of cutting their throats, and robbing them of their arms.

The mind is very active in moments of great peril, and Jack took in the position in a flash.

It was this.

He was bound and helpless, in the power of savages, who were, without doubt, merciless and bloodthirsty wretches.

The only aid that could come promptly was from the seamen down by the boat, but these had, doubtless, by this time, fallen in the same trap.

The "Swallow" was too far away to lend assistance, even if those on board comprehended his peril, which, to say the least, was very doubtful.

All this in a moment crossed his mind, while the foremost savage was raising his knife to stab Peter the Great to the heart.

But a strange friend was at hand.

With a rapidity truly marvellous, one of the cobras uncoiled itself from Peter's bosom, and with an unerring aim sprang up and fastened itself upon the arm of the savage.

The deadly forked tongue was thrust out, and with a shriek of agony he fell.

The rest stepped back, shrieking.

They evidently held the poisonous serpent in deadly fear.

Jack, although helpless, was exultant, and he could have shouted for joy, but that his voice was lost to him

"Peter was right," he thought. "The cobra is a friend to the savage!"

Now ensued an amusing scene.

The cobra returned to Peter, and coiled itself *outside* his waistcoat, waiting for another attack to make another spring, and the wounded savage, shrieking fell.

His cries brought the rest of his people —men, women, and children—to the spot, who stood around him in a fear-stricken circle, while those who had witnessed the attack gave an account of it in wild and frenzied language.

What they said, Jack could not understand, but he could make out, from their actions, that they gave not only Peter credit for having protecting serpents in his breast, but all the rest—himself, Hannibal, and the men.

The idea of dying from the bite of the cobra seemed to be peculiarly abhorrent to them, for after a rapid exchange of words, they scattered, drew apart from the dying man, and took up stones.

Every man, woman, and child of these

savage people took part in the awful work.

Masses of rock, great and small, were poured upon him, and the blood ran out in streams from his bruised and tortured body.

The horrible work was soon done, and the wretched man, mangled and torn, lay still.

Then the rest, with wild shouts, ran away into the woods, and disappeared.

This commotion did not fail to attract the attention of Tom Warren, who, with a couple of boats and thirty men, hastened towards the shore, where, as he afterwards remarked, " a pretty kettle of fish awaited him."

At first, he thought all were dead, but a quick examination revealed the true state of things, and Jack, who was now recovering a little, was able to sit up, and gasp out a few words of explanation.

Tom Warren at once prescribed for him —a dose of salt water, which speedily removed the offending drug from his stomach, and restored him so far that he felt nothing worse than a little weakness and giddiness.

Hannibal was the next operated upon, and restored as quickly as Jack; but when they were going to Peter the Great, our hero remembered the late scene, and sounded a warning note.

The cobra had, prior to this, returned to its hiding-place, and there was nothing beyond voices to tell Tom of his danger.

In a few words, he told the story, and Tom involuntarily shuddered as he thought of his narrow escape.

The bite of the cobra was a thing too terrible even to think of.

Some of the seamen were despatched to restore those by the boat, and Tom, Jack, and Hannibal remained by Peter.

"What is to be done with him?" said Jack, with a puzzled air. " He is sleeping the sleep of the dead!"

" Suppose we carry him on board?" suggested Tom.

"A good idea, Tom," returned Jack, smiling; "but who will touch him first?"

"What an ass I am! I forget those cobras," replied Tom. " What can we do?"

" We cannot leave him here."

" Certainly not."

" Then we must watch by him."

"And a pretty good watch it will be," said Tom, dubiously. " I reckon that he

is in for a good twenty hours of it, if he ever recovers."

" Do you think he will die?"

" I cannot say."

" Can you tell me, Hannibal?" asked Jack, anxiously.

"Massa Jack," replied the negro, with a very solemn air, " dat sleep poor Peter neber get out ob, unless we wake him!"

Here was a nice predicament, and all sorts of plans were proposed for the getting out of it.

Jim Swaby proposed that one of them should advance, and when the cobras came out to attack, the others should seize them round the neck, and strangle them.

Not a bad proposal in its way, but who was to carry it out?

"They move like flashes of light," said Jack, " and a miss, if only the distance of an inch, would be fatal. Peter is in no immediate danger. Let us take time to consider."

Then Tom Warren proposed that Hannibal should try his hand at snake charming, but Hannibal said it would be no use, as Peter held the power alone.

"I think them critters are charmed by music," struck in Jim Swaby.

"They are," said Tom.

"Then I'm darned if my fiddle won't fix 'em, if the cap'n will give me leave to go aboard, and fetch it!"

Leave was, of course, given at once, and Jim took half a dozen men to pull him on board, and a quarter of an hour sufficed to take him there, and another to bring him back.

The precious instrument was taken out of its case, and Jim, lightly touching the strings to see that they were in tune, struck up the British horn-pipe.

Before half a dozen bars had been performed, the cobras came forth, and performed a number of evolutions very pleasing, no doubt, to themselves, but which Jack and Tom cut short with their cutlasses, and soon nothing was left of them but their motionless bodies cut in twain.

Hannibal then took Peter in hand, and proceeded to rub his limbs, and roll him about in a very scientific manner, and the result was speedily shown by Peter opening his eyes, and yawning like one awaking from a deep sleep.

"My own brudder, Peter," said Hannibal, tenderly.

"What de debbel de matter wif you?" demanded Peter, in return. " What's dis de matter? Bits ob snake! Who cut up my lilly ones?"

Jack proceeded to explain, but Peter mourned, and refused to be comforted.

"Dey berry good friends," he said; "and it berry cruel to kill 'em. Oh, Massa Jack! how could you do it?"

"But it saved your life," urged Jack.

"No, no, Massa Jack!—you break dis heart ob old Peter, but dat not mend him body!"

"The Hemperor," said Jim, with remarkable emphasis, "is a hass in some pints, although he can see through a deal board on a dark night; and, the next time, he may get all his pockets full of corberers and boa-constructors if he likes, but I'm darned if I scrape rosin to bring 'em out!"

"Who axed you?" demanded Peter. "You precious fond ob dat ole fiddle! T'ank you for nothin'!"

The fact was, Peter was more annoyed at finding a rival charmer in Jim, than at anything else, and he would almost rather have died than have been saved by his rival. But the fit was not lasting.

He soon came round, and apologising, freely thanked them, with a speech interlarded with such long words as are never found out of a dictionary, and very seldom in it, and, by this means, general good-feeling was restored.

This disposed of, Jack proceeded to examine the huts, and found, to his horror, heaps of human bones, and fragments of sailors' clothing.

This revealed the awful fact that the wild men were cannibals.

"I will exterminate these wretches," he said. "To-night they will return to their huts. Who volunteers for the service?"

Everybody, as might be expected, held up their hands; but, as all were not required, and could not be spared from the ship, Jack chose Hannibal, Peter, and half a score of the men, and sent Tom Warren and Jim Swaby back with the rest.

"As soon as you hear firing, throw up lights," he said, "so that we may see what we are at. I will spare none but the women and children. The children may grow up wiser and better."

"Let us hope so," replied Tom, and went away.

Happy Jack then stowed himself and his men in one of the boats to wait for night, which, as the sun was far away in the west, was now close at hand.

———

CHAPTER XXIX.

A FIGHT WITH DEMONS.

"I MUST trust to your care for the first signs of the enemy's approach," said Jack, addressing his faithful blacks.

"Yes, Massa Jack," said Peter; "you trust dis chile's ears, and you be all right."

"Ole Hannibal's worf ten ob 'em," said Hannibal.

A wrangle being imminent, Jack quickly shut them up by saying that the first who heard anything was to give warning.

Then, stipulating for complete silence from the rest, the two brothers stretched themselves at full length upon the ground.

The sun sank rapidly, dipped into the sea, and disappeared.

Then darkness came down upon them like a cloud, and silence, broken only by the occasional cry of a nocturnal bird, reigned around.

Not a man moved a muscle, and the twin negroes might have been made of stone, so motionless were they.

Both were by the opening to the hut, which was without a door, and so, in addition to hearing, they were able to see.

There was a dead calm, and the forest was motionless. The sky was without a cloud, and full of stars, which were perfectly reflected in the glassy sea.

All on board the "Swallow" was quiet, for Jack had strictly commanded that it should be so, and therefore there was nothing to impede the two watching and listening brothers.

Suddenly, both spoke in a whisper at once—

"Comin' now, Massa Jack!"

"How far away?"

"Half-mile, or tharabouts," both speaking as before.

"Draw up closer," whispered Jack to the men.

They crept up cautiously, and crawling down, waited for the approach of the wild men.

Another silence of a minute or so, and then Peter was the first to speak—

"Me see 'em, Massa Jack!"

"Me see 'em, too," said Hannibal, quickly.

"Whar?" asked Peter.

Hannibal paused a little, and then replied—

"Jes' by the rock, thar."

"Dem's bushes," said Peter, with a low, scornful laugh. "Ole Hannibal's eyes like holes in a cocoa-nut!"

This comparison seemed to exasperate Hannibal exceedingly, and he raised his huge fist with the deliberate intention of smiting his brother, but Jack called him to order, and bade both think of what they were doing.

"Now dey come across de open, whar we sat dis morning," continued Peter.

Hannibal, too, could see them now, but he refused to say anything.

"How are they coming, Peter?" asked Jack.

"All de men in front, and de women a long way behind," replied Peter, craning his neck.

"Tell me when they are within fifty yards of us."

Another pause, and a very impressive silence, which was soon broken by a crunching sound not far away, which Jack knew to be caused by the footsteps of the wild men and women.

"Near now, Massa Jack!" whispered Peter.

"Up, every man of you!" said Jack, in a low tone, "and draw your cutlasses quietly. When I fire, rush out and attack."

He drew a pistol from his belt, then walking quickly forth, fired it in the air.

Two lights were thrown up by the "Swallow" instanter.

A row of startled savages stood within a few feet of him, and their faces, under the glare of the lights, were hideous.

With a shout Jack rushed upon them, and twenty knives in the bony hands of foes flashed forth.

The women and children turned and fled, uttering the most fearful yells.

There was no lack of courage in the cannibals, for they fought like furies, and finding their short knives no match for the cutlass, sought to close with the sailors, and rend them with their teeth and nails.

They clutched hold of the cutlasses, and ignoring the wounds they received, sought to wrench them away.

A brawny wretch held Jack's weapon thus with one hand, and grasped the hilt with the other.

The strength of fifty men seemed to be his, for with a quick movement, he lifted Jack high in the air, and sought to dash him to the ground.

It was a point with our hero never to yield his weapon to any man, and although lifted in the way we have described, he kept his presence of mind, and launching out his foot, dealt the cannibal a terrific blow in his chest.

The wretch reeled and fell, and the two fell upon the ground together.

The next moment, Jack felt the teeth of his antagonist close upon his shoulder.

It was not fighting a man, but a beast, and the sickly sensation men feel when the paw of a lion or tiger descend upon them was felt by Jack, and he feared his senses would leave him.

Fortunately, the feeling was but momentary, and recovering his nerve, he drew a pistol from his belt, and shot the cannibal through the breast.

Then leaping to his feet, Jack looked around him for other foes.

The fight was raging furiously, but as before, the better weapons and superior discipline were gaining the day; but some of the men of the "Swallow" were in trouble.

There was one poor fellow who had fallen on the ground, with three foes upon him, who, forgetting even the rude weapons they carried, were tearing at him like wild dogs.

With a shout of rage and execration, Jack rushed upon them, and at the same moment, Hannibal bore down upon them, too.

The penalty of their atrocity was speedily paid, and they rolled over lifeless; and now, heated with excitement, our hero dashed hither and thither, followed by his servitors, dealing death right and left.

All this time, lights were kept burning, and another boatload of men was despatched towards the shore; but by the time they touched land all was over, and every man of that wild band of strange savages had breathed his last.

They had fought courageously enough, for that matter; but the wolf and tiger has courage, too, and they are not spared by the hunter.

One of the men of the "Swallow" was dead, so cruelly torn by the monsters that he had bled to death.

I care not to dwell upon such scenes as these, but they will serve to show how low a man can fall when he lives a debased life.

The contrast between the honest tars and their savage enemies will suffice to show this to our readers.

Let us shift the glass, and move on to brighter things.

———

CHAPTER XXX.

TWO YEARS LATER.

IT was a gorgeous night in midsummer, and the moon shone upon a región where all that is delightful in climate was combined with the magnificence of civilisation.

On the banks of a small river, stood what the owner was pleased to call a villa, but which was in reality a magnificent mansion.

There was nothing wanting.

All that taste and a lavish outlay of wealth could command was there, and the splendid abode seemed to partake of the character of a fairy palace.

Stone walls, marble terraces, and windows, revealing the richest furniture and objects of art, and tables spread for guests, with such a profusion of viands and rich wines, that a king dropping down suddenly upon it would have had no cause to grumble with his fare.

The owner of this place was a certain Guillelmo Riaz, a Mexican, it was believed; but this point was only a matter of belief, and not of real knowledge; for who he was, or what he was, or wherever he came, he never took the trouble to reveal.

That he was wealthy, nobody could dispute, for he had everything of the best, and paid for the same in good coin, and he was at once the envy and admiration of the surrounding people.

Some of them were rich, too, and owned large tracts of country, which they cultivated by means of slavery; and the produce, in the form of tobacco and sugar, finding ready market in Europe, brought them in good returns.

At first they had sought the society of Riaz, but he repelled them all, and lived in solitary grandeur for more than a year, when suddenly his home became alive with guests.

These men were strangers, too, and had also plenty of money, which they threw about as a thing of no value; and oft in the midnight hour the sounds of revelry or brawling were heard by those who passed along the high road, about three hundred yards from the villa.

In the deep piazza before the house there one night assembled a numerous party, who arranged themselves about in every position indicative of ease and abandonment, and seemed, in different degrees, to enjoy the delicious balm and freshness of the air.

Their ages varied from twenty to sixty, and all were of the so-called sterner sex—that is, men.

The gentler portion of our race were conspicuous in their absence.

A great many of the loungers were in naval dress, but scattered among them were a few caballeros attired in the costume of the Caraccas, with gorgeous scarf and drooping plume, lending additional beauty to the scene.

But not only were they under the piazza, but down in the gardens; some of the same class strolled lightly and easily about, some talking in undertones, as if they feared to break the delicious calm, while others silently lounged against the trees, enjoying a fragrant weed.

But farthest away from the villa, and close by a fountain, sat a party of four—two Frenchmen and two Spaniards—whose heads were held close together in secret conference—men of about forty years of age, and villainous countenances all.

"So," said one, a Spaniard, "he has fallen into the trap."

"Yes, Riaz," returned another Frenchman. "He has taken the bait, and is as good as our prisoner."

"Thanks to your cunning, Pierre," said Riaz, who was the owner of the villa. "This English boy has been a pest to our gallant fellows for years, and now he madly puts his head into the lion's jaws."

"Taking that lion for a lamb," said one of the other men, with a low laugh, in which the rest joined.

"But hearken," said Riaz, with an uneasy smile, "will no evil come out of this? The British flag is not to be insulted with impunity."

"Have I not told you," replied Pierre, with an impatient gesture, "that the little viper is an outlaw in his own land, that there is a price upon his head?"

"Granted; but we must not forget that he is British born, and that nation is jealously watchful over its subjects. May it not be asked by what right we put him to death?"

"Has he not sunk, captured, or destoyed at least twenty of our good fleet?" demanded the other Spaniard. "Have we not lost hundreds of our noblest and bravest fellows, who now lie at the bottom of the deep?"

"Sacre! It is true!" muttered the Frenchman, savagely twirling his moustache. "Was I not myself blown into the water, when he sent a shot into the magazine af the 'Raven, and did I not spend two accursed days clinging to a hen-scoop, and but for the good ship 'Serpent,' must have perished? Oh! I owe a long account to this daring devil of the seas, and I will pay him ere the sun rises again!"

"He is bold beyond all boldness," said Riaz. "He comes and anchors in our waters, knowing pretty well what we are."

"Not what *we* are," interposed Pierre, "but what our fleet is. He does not think that we are naval men."

"So; and he comes to-night?"

"Aye, aye—the Lion Gate."

"Alone?"

"No; his friend and lieutenant comes with him. We shall have both birds, and then we may do what we like with the rest."

"And how did you decoy him here, my good Pierre?"

"By writing in a lady's hand to bid him come to a native dance," grinned Pierre.

"Aye, then he shall dance—upon nothing. What is the hour appointed?"

"Eleven."

"It is near that now."

"The avenue is full of men. Once he passes through the gate, he cannot escape."

"Let us go and watch him come up the road."

The foregoing conversation was in Spanish, which we translate for the benefit of our readers.

As it concluded, the four men rose, and diving into a grove of trees, wended their way to the Lion Gate, which looked upon the public road.

An avenue of trees led from the gate to the house, and as the four men passed through a portion of this, Pierre, the Frenchman, exchanged several words with some men in ambush, whose glittering arms could be faintly seen.

Great preparations were, indeed, made for the capture of that obnoxious young Englishman, who was no other than our hero, Happy Jack.

———

CHAHTER XXXI.

THE RESULT OF THE AMBUSCADE.

WHEN the four conspirators reached the Lion Gate, they saw three figures approaching—two in the naval costume generally worn by English officers, and the third in very little costume at all, being no other than Pitchpot,

the nigger, bearing upon his back a parcel of gifts for the "lady of the house" who had honoured our hero with an invitation.

Happy Jack had, indeed, fallen into the trap, and without a suspicion of what was taking place ahead, chatted with Tom Warren about the beauty of the scenery around them, and the prospect of a little fun.

Two years had made a great change in them, and both were now well grown and as good-looking as any fellow could wish to be.

On any other expedition, Peter the Great and Hannibal, who were still alive, and very little the worse for two years' travelling about, would have been with them; but Jack was averse to burdening his hostess with them, and so, much to their indignation, left them on board the "Swallow."

A prophetic spirit came over Peter, when he heard our hero's decision.

"Massa Jack," he said, "you neber leabe Peter behind before, and no good come ob it."

"Nonsense!" said Jack. "You fellows think I cannot live without you."

"Massa Jack, it not dat," said Peter, earnestly. "You lib berry well widout us—but we no lib widout you. Do take us, Massa Jack."

But Jack would not.

"No," he said. "I shall have to leave you kicking about in the servants' hall, while I kick about the ball-room. You will be just as well here as there, so I shall leave you behind, taking only Pitchpot to carry a box of Indian shawls for the lady."

And so it was that Pitchpot was with them, the bearer of the burden, and much he groaned beneath it, for a lazier rascal never trod this earth than that same Pitchpot.

"I wish you would move a little faster," said Jack, turning upon him as they neared the gate. "You crawl like a snail."

"Dis box cut berry big hole in Pitchpot's sholler," replied that worthy nigger. "Gib me a lilly rest, sare, or, p'raps, I jest roll on my back, and gib up de ghose."

"If you try anything of that sort," replied Jack, significantly, "I will undertake to bring you to life again."

"But do, Massa Jack, gib dis nigger a lilly rest."

"Sit down, then," said Jack, "and follow us presently. Mind you bring the box to the house, and do not part with it until you see me."

"I'll hold on to him, sare, like sticking-plaster, as soon as I recubber my strenf by a lilly rest," replied Pitchpot, and, without further ado, sank down by the side of the box, like one utterly exhausted.

"A lazy brute," said Tom Warren, as they moved on. "I would tan his hide, if I had my way!"

"No use bothering," replied Jack. "He is a real nigger, and you will never make him anything else."

Now they reached the gate, and opened it.

The avenue lay before them, silent and empty.

"We are late, I suppose," said Jack. "All the guests have arrived. At home, they are not so punctual."

"I can hear music and voices," returned Tom. "The dance has begun."

They entered, and quickening their steps, walked up the avenue.

"A quiet night," said Tom.

"Not a breath of air," replied Jack.

"And yet the leaves are moving."

"Where?"

"Just by us. What is that? Look out, Jack! Sharks ashore!"

Jack turned and put his hand upon his cutlass, but it was too late. A hundred men, at least, pounced out upon him and his friend, ropes were thrown around them, and they were secured.

"Oh, bitter folly!" groaned Tom. "We have fallen into the hands of the Phillistines!"

"I fear so," returned Jack. "But be of good heart. For the present, our enemies prevail; but we may yet escape."

CHAPTER XXXII.

THE SENTENCE.

THE men bound their captives, hurried them up the avenue, entered by a side door of the villa, and carried them into a long room, furnished like a council chamber.

In the centre was a long table, with chairs ranged on either side, and at the top was a raised daïs, with a seat upon it for the President, and this was now occupied by Riaz.

The other seats were filled by a number of men, all of whom were in the uniform of the Mexican Navy, but both the President and those with him wore masks.

As the men bearing Jack and Tom entered the room, Riaz, in deep tones, said—

"Place the prisoners at the foot of the table, and leave them."

All their arms being removed, the bonds were cut asunder, and our hero and his chum were told to stand at the foot of the table.

The men who had brought them in then left, and the four masked officers at the end of the table rose up and took a position on either side of the prisoners, two and two.

All four were armed, and held pistols ready for use.

Jack smiled at these preparations, the more so as he was inclined to look upon the whole thing as a joke.

"Prisoners," said Riaz, "you will do well to abstain from all levity for the present, until we have arrived at a decision with regard to your crimes."

"Of what are we charged?" demanded Jack.

"Piracy upon the high seas," was the reply.

"That's a cool charge," muttered Tom, "considering from whence it proceeds."

"Perhaps I may be permitted to learn the name of my accuser?" said Jack.

"You are charged by the Secret Council of the Kingdom of Mexico," replied Riaz.

"That which is secret is seldom honest," said Jack.

"You are not called upon to criticise the Council," was the dry response, "but to defend yourself. We have the power to order your execution at once; but we have no desire but to do that which is right and just, and after that you will either be acquitted or condemned."

"You know that I am condemned already," said Jack, contemptuously; "but that you seek by the quibble of this poor pretence of justice to ease your consciences."

"Do you know so much?" sneered Riaz.

"And more," said Jack. "I know you to be a set of villains, and your navy to be a pretence for piracy on a large scale. You assert that you fight only with your acknowledged foes; but a hundred sunken ships, and thousands of victims, and the plunder you have amassed, bear record of your deeds, and give you all a lie."

"Bravo, Jack!" cried Tom. "True—every word of it"

"You put a bold front upon it," sneered Riaz; "but a rat in a corner will turn."

"And a lion will die, when stung to

death by vermin, without a groan," said Jack. "Go on. Let us have this farce of a trial over, and then do your worst!"

"The trial had better begin at once. I agree with you, prisoner," said the President. "Stand forward, Marum."

One of the masks near him rose, and stood ready to be questioned.

"You were commander of the vessel 'Esmeralda,' sloop of war?" said the President.

"I was."

"What became of her?"

"She fell in with the 'Swallow,' commanded by the prisoners, and was attacked. All her rigging was cut away, and then we were boarded, and after a sharp fight, every man was slain or captured."

"Prisoner," asked Riaz, "is this true?"

"It is," replied Jack; "but if I had treated that man and his crew as pirates are wont to do, he would not now be alive to tell the tale."

"Then you admit?"

"I do."

"Henry Barton, stand forth."

A second mask arose, and the President proceeded to question him.

"You were second officer of the 'Thrush,'?"

"I was."

"She was captured on the high seas?"

"Yes."

"By whom?"

"The prisoners, who surprised us in the night, as we were bringing home a prize."

"He sank her?"

"Yes, and took the prize away. I was turned adrift with my crew. The captain was slain in the fight."

"With twenty-one days' rations," put in Jack.

"You do not deny this?"

"No," said Jack.

"Have you any questions to ask?"

"Not of a man who has forgotten every tie of country and of kindred," said Jack. "What could I ask of you, renegade? If a man lies to his country, he will lie to all the world."

"Again I must warn you to make no comment of this description," said Riaz. "They will not offend us, nor will they serve you."

"I am glad that to find they caused that dog to hang his head," said Jack, pointing to the witness.

"The next witness," cried Riaz.

"Pardon me," interrupted Jack. "Read out the list of the vessels, and I will not deny anything that is true."

"The 'Palm,' said Riaz, "is missing."

"I have her safe in custody," said Jack, "Go on."

"The 'Cobra' sailed a year ago, and has not been heard of since."

"I captured her off the Cape, and finding her too much riddled with my shot to be of much service, allowed her to sink," said Jack.

"What became of the crew?"

"Such as were spared thankfully joined my service."

"You lie!" cried a dozen of the Council, together.

"I speak the truth," returned Jack, coolly; "but I cannot call them to bear witness to it, for they are far away in my island home, taking care of my prizes."

"The next is the 'Rock Ahead,' said Riaz, "She was burnt by you?"

"She was."

"And why?"

"Because she was a pirate, and in full chase of an English schooner when I came up with her."

"It would be folly to contradict you."

"It would. You know as well as I do that the calling of this gang of pirates a navy is a farce."

"I have other vessels here," continued Riaz. "The 'Marie,' the Juarez,' the 'Lightning,' the 'Avalanche,' and the 'Fair Luna.'"

"All of which, I have either captured or destroyed!" cried Jack, triumphantly; "and if I have not the chance of doing any more work on earth, I have done well."

"And all of them were mine!" cried Riaz, rising wrathfully. "Mine!—fitted out at my expense, and set afloat by means of my hard, solid gold. Diabolo, you dog! you shall pay heavy for this!"

"So," said Jack, "this is your Mexican Navy—this is the armament which only fights with its known foes! I see all now. I have been capturing the chicks, but I have fallen upon the old hen at last. What is your name, villain?"

"If you would have a fair trial," cried the President, "be more moderate in your speech."

"Moderate to you?" cried Jack, with inexpressible scorn in his voice. "Moderate to a man who fits out ships and speculates in the proceeds of murder and rapine upon the deep! Moderate to you, who dishonours his country, and puts a stain of infamy upon his nation which centuries will not wipe away! No; kill me, if you will; torture me, if you please, and my last word will be that of scorn and contempt for loathsome wretches as you and all who fight under your flag are!"

"Hurrah!" cried Tom, tossing up his cap. "Give it to the skunks!"

An angry fire of oaths ran round the table, and several started to their feet; but the President waved them down.

"I will deal with these gentlemen as they deserve," he said.

"Make the death a speedy one," cried Jack.

"I will make it such a death as will pay the penalty you have earned to the full. What says the Council? Guilty or not guilty?"

"Guilty!" shouted the masks, together.

"Oh, wonderful unanimity!" said Jack, smiling. "Oh, impartial assembly of noble men! Strip off that uniform," he added, with sudden energy, "and put on the war-paint of the savage. Take tomahawks in your hands, and scalp women and children, then pick their bones like carrion crows!"

"Peace!" cried Riaz.

"Peace in the midst of wolfish men! Impossible!" cried Jack. "Would submission from me bring mercy? No; on the contrary, the poorer and weaker the victim, the greater your dastard cruelty. Such wretches as you dabble in the life-blood of women, and suck the red stream as it flows from dying babes! By land and sea, the spirits of the poor and weak cry out for vengeance, and your hour shall come. You may revel now, but——"

"Hold!" cried Riaz. "I will hear no more."

"You shall hear me!" cried Jack, carrying all before him in the torrent of his wrath. "It is time for the ears of such as you to tingle, and for your hearts to quake. It is well that you have masks to hide the ghastly cheeks which proclaim your lily-livered natures. Stand out any two of you, choose your weapons, and give me a rusty sword, and I will show you who is the better man!"

"And I will fight two more!" shouted Tom, raised to a pitch of excitement by Jack's eloquence. "Close with them!"

But Jack had already fallen upon one of the men near him, and wrested a brace of pistols from his hands, and ere the others could recover from this astonishment, Tom Warren had performed a similar feat.

"Back to the door!" cried Jack, "with your face to the foe. The first man who lifts a hand, or stirs a step, dies! Silence, you dog at the head of the table, or I will stop your tongue for ever!"

All this was the work of a few moments, and the dumbfounded council of knaves sat like figures of stone, and moved not until the noise of the closing door proclaimed the prisoners gone.

Then, with fearful oaths breaking from their lips, they rose up, and dashing in a body to the door, darted forth in pursuit.

CHAPTER XXXIII.

THE FIGHT IN THE VILLA.

OUTSIDE, Jack lost no time in putting as much ground as possible between himself and foes; but, unfortunately for him and Tom, the interior of the villa was strange to them, and instead of taking the turning which led into the grounds, they kept straight along the passage, which terminated in a staircase.

"Back!" cried Jack, "there is no escape this way!"

It was too late to retreat, for their foes were already approaching in a body, and they must either go up the staircase, or stand and fight it out there.

Prudence forbade the latter alternative, and turning, Jack and Tom leaped up the staircase, three stairs at a time, with a dozen bullets from the pistols of their foes pattering about them.

The first landing was reached, but there was no halting there, as no window looked out upon the lawn, so they ran up the next part, with the pirates clattering behind them.

"Let us have a shot at the fellows!" suggested Tom.

"Don't forget," replied Jack, "that we have but four charges. Come on!"

Another step or two brought them to the top of the house, with three doors.

A rapid examination showed that two of them were locked, and the third led into a small room, handsomely furnished, and evidently the private apartment of the owner of the house, who, no doubt, had very excellent reasons at times for absenting himself from the company of his guests.

Closing the door and locking it, the two daring young fellows proceeded to pile up the furniture against it, and the landing outside being now full of their enemies, a brisk fire was opened upon them.

Fortunately, the first few shots missed, and after that, shooting was a mere folly, for our friends succeeded in getting such a pile of furniture and cushions against it, that no pistol-shot could penetrate into the room.

The enemy presently became aware of this, and desisted, a dead silence outside following their futile efforts.

"Well, here we are," said Jack, sitting down, and wiping his face. "Precious hot work, Tom!"

"But rare fun, if we only get out of it."

"Of course it is."

"But there is the 'if,' Jack."

"Oh, dear no! We have got out of worse things than this. Let us have a look at the window. Ah! a stiffish height from the ground, and nothing to cling to! A drop would end in broken bones. Phew!"

A shot was fired at them from the outside, and a bullet struck the sill, not more than two inches from Jack's head.

"A watch set already," he said; "and with such a moon it might as well be day. Now, Tom, what do you propose?"

"We are in a trap," replied Tom. "There is not even a chimney, If there was, we might climb up it and disguise ourselves with the soot."

"There is nothing but the door, or the window Tom. Which is it to be?"

"All seems to be quiet on the landing."

"Weasels asleep, dear boy."

"I am afraid, by the window, we have the agreeable alternative of breaking every bone in our skins, or being potted at like wild geese."

"Let us sit down and think."

They sat down to think, but not for long, for in a few seconds there came a hammering at the door.

"What-ho, within there!"

"Who are you, and what do you want?" cried Jack.

"I am the master of this house, and I call upon you to surrender!" replied the voice of Riaz.

"I shall call upon you for the same thing when I have completed my preparations," said Jack, coolly. "Turn over that case in the corner, Tom, and tell me what is in it."

"Half a dozen pistols—beauties—powder and shot of the primest!" replied Tom.

"That's good," said Jack. "Hallo! you piratical rascal! Are you still outside?"

"I am here," said Riaz.

"Is that anywhere near you?" asked Jack, as he made a slight opening in the barricade, and fired in the direction of the voice.

A deep groan and a howl of rage from a dozen throats was the reply.

The bullet had gone straight to its mark, and Riaz would never send another pirate ship to sea.

"Are there any more of you?" asked Jack.

The others were too prudent to reply, but the little noise they made as they dragged their dead leader away, guided our hero, and he fired again.

"*Sacre!*" cried the voice of Pierre; "it shall be the cursed English pullet in mine leg!"

"It *is* the bullet," said Jack, scoffingly. "Why are you not grammatical?"

Pierre had spoken in English, which he understood as well as the average Frenchman; but he had yet to learn his verbs, which he would now have an opportunity of doing if he lived long enough, for he was lame for life.

Jack closed his barricade again, and it was well he did so, for at least a dozen pistols were fired at the door, and three of the bullets glanced off the leg of the table, and buried themselves in the ceiling.

"A little outburst of very natural rage," said Jack. "Hark! they are retreating!"

"In right earnest this time!" said Tom; "but the door is of no use to us, as they swarm below. We must be patient, Jack, and wait the tide of events."

"We must. And now I hear them coming back again. What is up now?"

Something heavy was thrown down with a tremendous crash, and a chuckle was heard.

"I don't understand this," said Jack, with a puzzled look. "Listen!"

Another crash, like that of furniture pitched indiscriminately upon the landing.

But what were the enemy doing?

"It seems to me," said Jack, "that they are barricading the door outside."

"What use can that be?"

"I cannot tell; but they are certainly doing it."

"So they mean to keep us here; and if we can only wait long enough, our friends will put in an appearance."

"I wonder what became of Pitchpot?"

"I have no idea, Jack; but most likely the rascal came up about an hour after us, and had his throat cut quietly."

"I hope not. I wish nobody but ourselves to suffer. What fools we were!"

"Rather, Jack."

"'Donna Ximena Riaz solicits the honour of the company of Captain Scarborough and Lieutenant Warren.' So ran

"Is that anywhere near you?" asked Jack, as he fired in the direction of the noise.

the note, and it took us in completely. What asses we were!"

"Don't mention it," said Tom. "My very hair curls to think of it. More lumber being piled up outside"

"The move I cannot understand.'

"No more can I: but, perhaps, having shut us up that way, they intend to assault by the window."

"No; the door would be easier, under any circumstances. There is something in this we cannot comprehend."

"And yet the vagabonds are assembling upon the lawn."

"So they are, and are pointing rifles at the window, Tom. Self-preservation is the first law, you know. Stoop down, old fellow!"

Half a dozen bullets came crashing through the window, and brought down a mass of plaster from the ceiling, but did no further harm.

Jack waved his cap defiantly.

"These pistols are no use at this range," he said. "Oh, for a good rifle, to have one pot at them!"

"Jack!" cried Tom, leaping up, "can you not smell something?"

"Yes," replied Jack, sniffing. "Smoke or fire?"

"Fire!" said Tom. "They have barricaded us in, and set the villa ablaze! Hark! Can you not hear the roaring flames below?"

"They are resolved to have our lives at any price," said Jack; "but shall we hide like rats in a hole, and be roasted alive?"

"Never, Jack!"

"Then pass me those table-covers here. rip up the carpet, and we will make a rope. Shout, you villains, if you like! but I am coming, and you shall find that you have not finished with Happy Jack!"

CHAPTER XXXIV.

GOOD AND TRUE.

THE pirates assembled on the lawn were now in high glee.

They had, indeed, fired the villa, after barricading the staircase too effectually for any escape that way; and in case the prisoners should seek egress by the window, twenty men with rifles loaded were told off to bring them down as soon as they should appear.

The villa was a costly affair, and the furniture was magnificent; but now that the owner was dead, it was of little value to the horde of ruffians in his pay, many of whose lives hung upon a thread.

They knew well enough that the escape of our hero would bring further confusion upon their piratical career, the more especially as the secret of their calling was fully divulged.

Nothing less than his death would leave them to carry on their nefarious traffic upon the seas.

So they fired the villa.

The flames ran merrily over the woodwork, and shrivelled up the ornaments and pictures on the walls; then, running up the broad staircase, fired the landings above, and in a few minutes such a mass of flame was leaping and roaring that the escape of the two young heroes imprisoned in the attic seemed impossible.

There was, indeed, no time to be lost, for the smoke crept in under the door, and rapidly filled the room; but, fortunately, the bullets of their enemies did good service by breaking the windows, and thus creating a rough but effectual form of ventilation.

"If you keep near the floor the smoke will not inconvenience us much," said Jack. "Sit down, and do your work upon your haunches, Tom."

"You take it coolly," said Tom, fairly overcome with admiration.

"What will it avail us to take it otherwise?" was Jack's reply. "We can but die once, so let us die like men. How they shriek and yell! I suppose they call that cheering?"

"There are half a dozen strips, Jack; knot them together, old boy."

"Right," said Jack, rapidly performing this part of his work. I think there is enough, Tom. It is time to go. Look at the door!"

The woodwork was now showing signs of dissolution, and several fast-widening cracks revealed the raging flames outside.

There was no alternative but to fly.

Jack fastened their rope to the window-sash, and, without pausing to test it, threw himself outside.

A fearful yell greeted his appearance, and a dozen rifles were fixed at him, the bullets peppering the wall on either side of him; but the aim of his enemies was evidently too hurried.

"Come on, Tom," cried Jack; "it is hot work, but our only chance!"

Tom paused but a second, and then followed his friend.

Another yell greeted him; but ere a

shot could be fired, an honest British shout rang through the night air.

Jack paused in his descent, and looking round, saw about thirty of his gallant "Swallows," led by Jim Swaby, Hannibal, and Peter the Great, who rushed in upon the pirates, cutting and slashing like furies.

With a responding shout, Jack slid down the rough rope, and, with a pistol in either hand, rushed into the fray.

One of his late foes lying, dying, upon the ground, our hero stooped and took his sword from his hand.

Jack, now completely armed, joined his friends, who greeted him with a most tremendous hurrah.

The band of villains were all taken aback; but they had as much pluck as such men can ever hope to possess, and turning like the rat to which Riaz had compared Jack, they fought furiously.

It was night, but there were two lights to show the combatants to each other— the refulgent moon, and the blazing villa, either of which would have been sufficient.

"Follow me, 'Swallows!'" cried Jack, as he dashed into the midst of his foes.

"Follow Massa Jack!" roared Peter the Great, who still bore his favourite gingham, although time and trouble had played sad havoc with its beauty.

"Fight for Massa Jack!" cried Hannibal, slashing about him with a huge cutlass, worthy of the hands of Shaw, the Life Guardsman; and Jim Swaby, without shouting, lent his aid like a man.

The pirates had no heart for shouting, but they fought with great fury, and as their ranks grew thinner under the terrific onslaughts of the gallant tars, they cut about them like madmen.

It was no time to use their rifles, for the whole of the combatants were in a close knot, and pistols, strange to say, they had none.

Thus far they were at a disadvantage with Jack and his men, who were all armed with a brace of pistols each, one of which they fired, and reserved the other for a grand coup, according to their accustomed tactics.

The sounds of this terrible conflict must have been heard, and the light of the fire seen, by the neighbours, but none came near. Our readers will remember that Riaz had held himself aloof from all around, and that, brawling being no uncommon thing in his grounds, he had gained a bad name.

Mexico even now is not in a very good condition, and big brawls are nothing strange. Political adventurers, unscrupulous men, who talk of the "rights of the people," and grow fat upon ruin and misery of the million, are common; and at the time we write of, the land was in a state of anarchy, brought about by rival factions.

Englishmen often open their eyes and wonder how such things can be; but have we nothing of the sort at home? Are there no blind followers of the knaves? Have we no rabid speakers, who prefer to live upon the subscriptions of the starving poor instead of gaining their bread by honest labour?

The land is full of them, and the records of their work is written upon the faces of dying women and starving children. The world is wide enough for any man with energy and brain to do without unionism.

But to return. None came to see the fight, or to aid one party or the other, and so by the light of the moon, and the blazing villa, they fought on, with the tide of victory setting slowly but surely in one direction.

The knot of combatants was suddenly broken, and the remnant of the pirates turned and fled. With a ringing cheer, the "Swallows" followed up in pursuit, popping them off one by one, until but three were left, and these reached the wood and escaped.

Then Jack called his men together and congratulated them upon their gallant conduct, thanking them heartily for coming to the rescue. They cheered him again and again, and none shouted louder than those whose bleeding wounds attested how well they had fought.

"But how did you hear of my danger?" inquired Jack.

"Me find it out, Massa Jack," replied Peter the Great. "Me find it out, sare."

"How was that?"

"Pitchpot come an' tell me, Massa Jack."

"Then Pitchpot must have the credit."

"No, Massa Jack."

"Why not?"

"When Massa Jack gib Peter the sword to clean," replied Peter, with a knowing twinkle in his eye, "and Pitchpot lose dat sword, Massa Jack blame poor old Peter. Now dat Pitchpot do de cleber t'ing, Massa Jack must gib Peter de credit ob it."

"I do not see your logic quite clearly," said Jack; "but, at all events, I thank you for coming, and I must thank Pitchpot, too. Where is he?"

He was not in their midst, nor was he among the slain, and the wounded had all gathered round our hero, ignoring their sufferings for the time. Jack asked where he had last been seen.

"He came up the road with us," said Jim Swaby, "and just as we got near the gate he said he must sit down a moment and rest."

"There, no doubt, we shall find him," said Jack, smiling. "Pitchpot is always taking a rest."

Falling into marching order, and leaving the pirates as they were, the "Swallows," went down to the gate, where, sure enough, they met Pitchpot just coming in with a box upon his shoulders.

"Hallo!" said Jack. "What is this?"

"Dis your box, Massa Jack," replied Pitchpot.

"Have you been carrying it ever since?"

"No, Massa Jack. When me see you hab a lilly turn-up wif de Mex'can chaps, me fro him down, and run to de 'Swaller.' Den me *lead* de men back here, and find de box, but him too heaby to bring up in a hurry."

"Oh! I see. You sat down again to rest?"

"Dat's it, Massa Jack. Pitchpot 'bliged to rest."

"And a good long rest you shall have, if you will," said Jack, heartily; "for you have this night saved my life, and that of Mr. Warren. Never mind that box. Pitch it into the ditch, and fall in with the rest!"

"Massa Jack," asked Pitchpot, "may I hab dis box?"

"Certainly you may," returned Jack, "for you have earned it. Forward!"

The men stepped out, and Pitchpot, now that the box was his own, carried it right away to the boat, and never hinted at being fatigued.

Nor did he part with it until he had stowed it away under his bunk on board the "Swallow."

CHAPTER XXXV.

A CLEAN SHOT.

JEALOUSY is inherent in our natures. Some have it to a very extravagant degree, and find cause for repining in every fancied neglect; and others so far curb their feelings as not to show their emotions; but all have it in their hearts, and when the true spring is touched, it jumps up and reveals itself.

Peter the Great was jealous, and jealous of Pitchpot.

It was a bad day for that unhappy nigger when he carried the message back to the "Swallow," and saved our hero's life, for from that time Peter hated him with a deep and bitter hatred.

"*You* sabe Massa Jack!" he said, one morning, when the "Swallow" had been two days at sea. "You come back wif a message, and get all de honour and glory dat belongs to oder people. Why, skarn your limbs, what do you mean by it?"

"Me mean not'ing," replied Pitchpot, humbly. "Me do de best for Massa Jack, like *any oder nigger*."

"What do you mean by *oder nigger?*" demanded Peter, raising his voice.

"Dere oders in de world 'cept Pitchpot," replied that worthy.

"What oder niggers?"

Pitchpot declined to furnish any answer, and Peter waxed very wroth.

"P'r'aps," he said, taking hold of his gingham firmly by the handle; "p'r'aps you mean *me?*"

This time Pitchpot replied, but not quite so lucidly as he might have done.

"If," he said, "Massa Peter say he am not a nigger, den he not a nigger; but if him say dat he am a nigger, he am. Massa Peter a moniliment of trufe."

This, so far from pacifying the outraged Peter, roused him yet the more, and speaking a little louder still, he uttered the following request—

"You say I am a nigger—jes say it?"

"Pitchpot allers obey him massa," said Pitchpot, edging away. "You *am* a nigger!"

Down came the gingham, and smote him amidships. Pitchpot leaped into the air with a most abominable howl, then fell upon his back, and rolled about as if in the most frightful agony.

His cries bid fair to arouse the whole ship, and Peter was afraid that he had gone too far.

"Get up, ole chap," he said, in a soothing tone.

But the "ole chap" was not going to get up just yet, and did so twist and turn himself about and shriek that a goodly company of the seamen, headed by Jim Swabey and Hannibal, soon assembled.

"What on airth is all the row about?" asked Jim. "You'll have the skipper up directly. What is the row?"

Peter the Great was the man for an emergency, and he promptly replied—

"Pitchpot got de cholic!"

"Dat's a lie!" returned Pitchpot, recovering himself immediately, and sitting up.

"Well, I'm darned if ever I seed a chap come round like that!" said Jim. "It's gammon, that's what's the matter with him. "I'll cure the beggar! Lay hold of him, stem and stern, mates!"

But an eel is a difficult thing to lay hold of in the way mentioned, and Pitchpot was an eel. A series of wriggles kept the sailors alive for a few moments dodging about here and there, until the culprit suddenly sprang to his feet, and ran down below.

Jack now came on deck in company with Tom Warren. The two had been holding a consultation below as to the advisability of sending a letter to England, and it was settled that a record of the "Swallow's" proceedings should be sent to Mr. Scarborough—Jack's uncle—with instructions to forward a copy to the Admiralty.

This epistle was written, and the next question was how to get a messenger. A merchant vessel, homeward bound, was required, and a sharp watch kept for the appearance of a sail.

Towards evening, one appeared in sight, and they bore down upon it. The stranger proved to be a tea vessel, returning from China, and the captain made an effort to get clear off, but the sailing qualities of the "Swallow" proving superior, our friends drew within a quarter of a mile, and then hailed him with a speaking trumpet.

The trader still kept up all sail, mistaking Jack for a pirate, and it was not until a shot was fired over his bows that that he hove to.

A number of men crowded upon her forecastle, seemed to be making preparations for resisting an attack; but our hero, jumping into a boat, unarmed, and taking with him only four men, pulled over, and went on deck.

This pacific mode of boarding calmed the fear of the captain, a bluff, burly man, who came forward and asked Jack what he wanted. Jack gave him the packet, and told him that, on delivering it, Mr. Scarborough would pay him one hundred pounds.

"Mr. Scarborough!" cried the old salt. "You don't mean to say this letter is for the owner of Clifton Grange?"

"It is," said Jack.

"Then I'm bothered if I wouldn't take it double the distance for nothing," replied the old salt. "He was a good friend to me when every other man turned his back upon Bob Grimsby. I lost the 'Martingale' in a storm, and some of the passengers were drowned. Your uncle was aboard, and stood by me when a lot of beggars tried to get my certificate taken away and ruin me. 'Grimsby,' says he, 'did all a seaman could do, and much more than many would do,' and that pulled me through and saved me. Give me that letter, and if it leaves my pocket afore I put it into his hand, may the next gale I come across blow my head off!"

This fervent speech came from the old sailor's heart, and Jack, who was deeply touched, took his hard, horny hand, and grasped it.

"Upon my word," he said, "it is pleasant to meet with a little gratitude in this world. You have heard my story?"

"Only as other men tell it," replied the captain, "and sorely I've grieved over a Scarborough coming to the bad."

"But you do not know my real story," returned Jack; "and, as I have no time to tell it now, just you spend an evening, when you get home, with my uncle, and hear what he has to say."

"That I will," was the hearty reply; "not that I want him to tell me you've got an honest face, and the look of true blood about you. Nothing of the pirate about you, my lad."

"Very little, indeed," said Jack, and then, with another shake of the hand, they parted.

The trader spread her canvas again, and, before night had fallen, was gone.

Jack was rather thoughtful that night, wondering what his message home would bring forth.

"To sustain the charge of my being a pirate," he said, "they must bring the crimes of a pirate against me, and where is the man or woman who can say that *my* hand was ever uplifted unjustly against them?"

The sun set pale that night; but, long after it was down, there was a pale, red light in the sky, and, as the darkness deepened, this light grew stronger.

The phenomenon was so unusual, that fifty speculations were made concerning it, but Jim Swaby was the man to give out the truth.

"That light," he said, "comes from a ship on fire!"

CHAPTER XXXVI.

A CHASE BY NIGHT.

A SHIP on fire!

There is no more awful casualty at sea than this. The "devouring element," as penny-a-liners call it, is terrible at all times, when it gains the upper hand of man; but it is doubly and trebly so when it holds the frail barque in its fatal, fiery embraces.

Sailors have a dread of shipwreck, and when the wind is high, there is much examination of charts, and anxious looking toward the horizon, where land is expected; but, at the worst, there is a chance of escape, until the vessel goes to pieces under the power of the breakers. In the case of *fire*, there is none.

Many anxious eyes were turned towards the red light as the "Swallow," with every stitch of canvas she could carry, bore up towards it; and, as fitful, forked flames arose now and then, exclamations of impatience burst from their lips.

If the "Swallow" had flown that night, the pace would have been too slow for those gallant hearts, anxious to save their fellow-men.

The glare of a fire is deceptive, and the distance between us and the conflagration is often much greater than we imagine.

Thus, it is not to be wondered at, that the "Swallow" kept upon her course for nearly an hour, and seemed to be very little nearer the scene of the disaster.

And now the light began to pale, and a conviction that he was too late to be of any service took possession of Jack; but he kept on, as some of the survivors might be upon the deep.

A little later, and the light disappeared, and then our hero was nonplussed. Nothing more could be done than keeping in the same direction throughout the night, and this he did.

In the morning, just after sunrise, they passed several pieces of floating wreck, in which the experienced eyes of those on board recognised part of a vessel of war—"British," Jim Swaby said, and most of the men agreed with him.

Further on, they saw an unmistakable English tar, clinging to a plank, and a boat was lowered to pick him up.

When it neared him, he dropped off, and swam towards it, as if the night in the sea had done him very little harm.

Indeed, he seemed to care very little about it, and, when he got into the boat, shook himself like a water-dog, and asked if anybody had such a thing as a drop of rum.

This was given him, and he drank it off with great gusto, and thanked them in the following manner—

"It's werry kind o' you, mates, and if ever I meets yer under sm'lar circumstancials, darn me, if I don't return the complerment!"

Then he sat down, and, borrowing a quid of tobacco, chewed it with a thoughtful air.

As he did not seem to be very communicative, nobody troubled him until he got on board, when Happy Jack took him in hand.

"Are you one of the crew of the ship, burnt last night?"

"I ham, your honour," he replied, emphatically; "and about the only one."

"What was she?"

"Frigate."

"And her name?"

"'War Heagle'—Captain Cursly."

"What!" cried Jack. "Here, come below to my cabin."

The man followed him with the same indifferent air which had characterised him throughout, only pausing a moment to borrow a fresh quid of one of the "Swallow's" men, and to rid himself of the old one.

"You have had a rough time of it, my man," said Jack, as they reached the cabin. "Take a seat."

"I will, yer honour," he replied, and took about two inches of a locker, which was a trifle more uncomfortable than nothing at all.

Then, wetting his finger and thumb, he gave his two locks of hair a bit of a twist, and then sat ready to be questioned.

"Tell me how all this happened," said Jack.

"I can't spin a yarn, yer honour," replied the man. "Ax me a few questions."

"What is your name?"

"Coddem—Chris'n name, Dick."

"How did the fire happen?"

"Shot from a henemy upset something in the cap'n's cabin."

"What enemy?"

"Privateer-lookin' chap—Mexican built, I think. Come right on us, and the cap'n showed a funk."

"Nothing new in him. So you had a brush?"

"Not much. We got no orders to get ready, and t'other chaps had it all their own way. We run away, and he peppered us."

"And what did your men say?"

"Cussed and swore like anythink, and the cap'n took down the names o' the worst to try 'em for mutiny."

"And what followed?"

"The henemy, sir, come and gave us half-a-dozen red-hot shot; and afore we knowed where we were, we were on fire."

"Which put Captain Cursly into a greater funk than ever?"

"Jes' so, your honour; and nobody knowed which way to turn, for none of the hofficers gave any orders."

"Why not?"

"'Let the ship burn,' they ses. 'Better sink that way than get taken.' And there weren't a man aboard as wouldn't have rather been burnt alive than struck to the foe."

"Good and brave fellows!" said Jack. "A pity such men were not better commanded."

"So the ship blazed up," continued the seaman, "and the henemy gave it to us right and left, until up springs Mr. Granby—a midshipman, sir—and he ses, 'Let us die fighting! Fire away, my men!' and then we all began to blaze away, but it was too late."

"The fire had got too great a hold?"

"That's it; and, one after the other, all the guns had to be abandoned, and we was all drove forward, when Captain Cursly orders out a boat."

"Did the men obey him?"

"Not at first, your honour; but all of a sudden four men volunteered to take him, and he gets into a boat with 'em; but what do you think they does?"

"Pitch him overboard."

"No, your honour; but they does something cleverer. They pulls right over to the henemy, who wasn't further away than you could shy a biscuit, and they hands him over, and ses, 'Here, take the only chap as have got a white feather amongst us;' and then they pulls away like mad to get back again, but a round shot stove the boat through, and they all sunk."

"Brave fellows!" exclaimed Jack. "Go on; this story is worthy of the British hearts of oak."

"The henemy now come a little nearer, but he holds well away on account of the fire, and shouts out some gibberish which the lieutenant said was a call to surrender. As he was now in command, he shouts something back—French it was, I think—which made the other chap so riled that they fired into the midst of us."

"A set of dastards; so you could not return it?"

CHAPTER XXXVII.

TWO MORE WITNESSES

"NO, your honour, it weren't possible; and just then somebody shouts out that the fire was getting near the magazine: so a sort of natural panic rose, and every man, laying hold of what he could, plunges overboard; and the henemy, fancying the same thing, I suppose, sheered off, and sure enough, in a miuute or two, there was such a blow up as I never seed afore, and never want to see again."

"Awful!"

"Aye, sir, it was awful; and the red-hot spars and bits of timber fell about us like snow flakes, and many a poor fellow, swimming for his life, got a blow that sent him under. I was hit in the back, but not badly hurt."

"Lor', sir," continued the seaman, after a moment's pause, "it was a scene! and to make it worse, the henemy threw up lights, and put out boats."

"To save you?"

"No, your honour, but to take pot shots at us, and I give you my word that I saw Captain Cursly standing and looking on with a very happy face."

"The monster!"

"To give him his due, sir," said Coddem, "I don't think he wanted to see us all slaughtered for the love of blood-spilling; but, you see, he didn't want no witnesses against him, and when he gets home, he can tell his own story! That's how I looked at it."

"Which shows you are not a dunderhead, Coddem."

"Thanky, your honour. Most people think I am."

"Then most people are wrong."

"I see man after man go down," pursued the sailor, resuming his story; "shot away from the hencoops, life-belts, and bits of timber they were clinging to; and how I was overlooked, I do not know; but I was, and the current carried me away until you came across me, and picked me up."

"And do you not think that any of the others were saved?"

"I don't think a man-Jack 'cept myself got clean off.

"That is—you and Captain Cursly?"

"Well, sir, I don't reckon him, for he ain't a man."

"I will not controvert your opinion," said Jack. "Now I think you may go

I shall make notes of this story, as both them and you may be of great service to me."

"If *I* can do anything, I'll do it," replied Coddem, fervently, smiting his thigh; "for your honour has the rig of a true-hearted genelman, if ever there was one in this world."

As soon as Jack was alone, he entered all the minutes of his story, and made a copy of them to send home on the most favourable occasion, just as he had done before; and then Tom Warren came in with the news that more of the wreck was sighted to windward, and that some men, dead or alive, were clinging to it.

* * * * *

A boat was lowered, and Happy Jack took his place in the stern-sheets, and bade the men pull for their lives towards a mass of wreck heaving upon the waves about a mile away.

There was very little need for this injunction, as the gallant tars were ready and willing to go to the help of the poor fellows, whose forms could be distinctly seen lying in various attitudes upon the wreck.

As the boat drew near, Jack could see five figures motionless, as if in death, and a black speck upon one which at first he could not make out, but soon perceived that it was a *vulture*.

"A bad sign," thought Jack, as his heart sank. "Poor fellows! there is no better messenger of death than yon foul bird!"

The wreck was reached, and the bird of prey gorged with human flesh, rose into the air.

One of the hapless men was torn to pieces, and the face was quite gone.

A sickening sight.

Four of the victims upon the raft were men, and the fifth a boy, with just such a face as Jack had called his own in the days of his early service upon the seas.

In one man and this poor lad they found faint signs of life.

First casting off the dead from their resting-place, so as to foil the vulture in his feast, they pulled back to the "Swallow," and efforts to restore the man and boy were immediately made.

Both Peter the Great and Hannibal were of great service here, as they had a deal of African knowledge of such matters, which now proved to be useful.

Dick Coddem recognised both at once. One, he said, was Townsend—a man in his own mess—and the other was young Granby, the midshipman who had proposed to die fighting.

I need not say that Jack heard who they were; for here were two more witnesses to clear his course to a proper recognition in old England of the injuries he had received at the hands of Captain Cursly.

Once get them home, they could do all he required in any court of law.

Young Granby was the first to recover, and once his eyes were opened he shook off the lethargy which exposure and fatigue had wrought upon him, and in a few words thanked Jack for having saved him.

It took another half-hour to bring Townsend round; and when *he* recovered consciousness, and saw Dick Coddem standing near, he asked him "if it was his watch."

"No; it ain't," replied Dick.

"I'm glad o' that," replied the other; "for I'm reg'lar done up, somehow. I feel all over stiff-like."

"Jest you run back a couple o' days in your mind," said Dick, "and see if you can't account for that 'ere stiffness."

Townsend did run back a couple of days in a couple of minutes, and the whole of the late misfortunes of the "War Eagle" came back to him.

A few questions and answers set him right as to where he was, and then he and Dick settled down to have a chat over "White-feather Cursly."

During this a rather merry party was in Jack's cabin, consisting of himself, Tom Warren, Charley Granby the mid, and Hannibal and Peter the Great.

The two latter were waiting at table; but they considered themselves part of the company, and struck into the conversation with a lack of reserve which would have horrified some of the old East Indian majors and captains, who treated their black servants like dogs, and expected them to act like men.

It may be here observed that the service of Peter and Hannibal at the table was purely voluntary.

Jack never desired it, as many others could have been found for the duty; but as his two sable friends were never happy unless in his presence, and as he had a great respect and admiration for their faithfulness, he was only too glad to accede to their wishes, and have them there.

They would not have served the mightiest sovereign upon earth with half the pleasure they waited upon our hero—indeed, I doubt very much if they would have served without compulsion any potentate, be he whom or what he might.

The wretched Pitchpot was their great source of trouble.

This black gentleman attended at dinner, too, but he was kept outside to carry away the dirty plates. But outside he would not keep, and whenever Peter or Hannibal relaxed in their vigilance he stole into the room, and listened to the conversation with a most complacent smile.

A series of wrangles took place in consequence, and the exit of Pitchpot was often accelerated by a kick; but as a little more or less acquaintance with shoe-leather did not matter a straw to that nigger, he was no sooner kicked out than he was in again.

"I tell you what, sare," said Peter the Great, as he turned out Pitchpot for the sixth time, following him into the passage, "you come listening to de conbersation ob genelmen, an' dat am de height ob imperdence."

"Some ob de conbersation am genelmen," replied Pitchpot, "but de oder ain't."

"What oder?" demanded Peter.

"De oder conbersation," said Pitchpot, "it ain't all de conbersation ob genelmen—some berry common stuff in it."

"Dat mine, I s'pose?" said Peter.

"I not say it ain't," said Pitchpot.

A wrathful gleam flashed into Peter's eyes, and he looked about for his gingham. He had placed it by the door when he came in, but now it was gone.

"Whar dat rumblerella ob mine?" he asked.

"How should I know?" asked Pitchpot.

"Peter," called out Jack from within, "bring a bottle of claret."

"Coming, Massa Jack!" replied Peter. Then, shaking his fist at the unmoved Pitchpot, he poured down the following fearful execration upon his head—

"You de berry cussest, blackest nigger dat eber crawl about on two legs like broom-handles! May dat darned hide ob your'n stink like de skunk, and Massa Jack kick you oberboard! It an ebil day for me when I sabe your life—it be an ebil day for you when I kick you clean out ob creation!"

"Now, Peter, that claret!" roared Jack.

"Come out ob de way!" roared Peter, aiming a blow at Pitchpot with his fist.

Pitchpot ducked, and Peter smote his knuckles against the wall, taking the skin off most beautifully.

A roused lion was nothing to Peter now; but as Jack wanted the claret, he was obliged to postpone his vengeance for a more fitting opportunity, a piece of good luck which generally fell upon Pitchpot when he had driven his master to distraction.

"Whatever has made you so long?" asked Jack, as Peter entered with a bottle of claret.

"I t'ink dat Pitchpot drive me into a rheumatic consylum," replied Peter. "He neber do what him told, and allus do dat what he not told!"

"You had better hand him over to Hannibal," said Jack, smiling.

But Peter would not hear of this.

There was a dignity in having a servant, even if there was a little inconvenience.

Dinner was just over, when Jim Swaby came down with the news that the breeze was freshening, and might strengthen into a heavy gale.

Jack went up and shortened sail, and made all snug, and then returned to his friends, who were now smoking, and had become rather hilarious.

"What the news, Jack?" asked Tom.

"Heavy gale brewing."

"Bother the gale, then! Let it blow. Sit down, Jack, and be merry. This Granby is a very good fellow."

"I am sure he is," replied Jack. Granby, your very good health! Peter, another bottle of claret, and put a little whisky on the table!"

"Hannibal!" whispered Peter, as he went out.

"Yes, ole boy!" returned Hannibal.

"I t'ink," replied Peter, "dat if Massa Jack don't mind dis night, dat he get a little obfusticated."

"Dat so, Peter; and me tell you anoder t'ing!"

"Wurra dat?"

"Jes' dis. If you keep on drinking all de lilly drops out ob der bottles dat you get a lilly worse dan Massa Jack!"

"Hannibal, you forget de man you am obdressing," said Peter, drawing himself up, and trying to look very stern; but, nevertheless, showing a great weakness in his legs.

"Get that wine, will you, Peter!" said Jack, and Peter bolted out full tilt against Pitchpot, who had put a dozen plates upon his head, and was just getting ready to march away.

—

CHAPTER XXXVIII.

THE STORM AND THE PHANTOM.

AS Peter and Pitchpot fell together, a peal of thunder rang out, and drowned the minor commotion caused by the fall of master and man, and, at the same moment, a terrific gust of wind laid the "Swallow" upon her beam-ends.

The confusion was terrible. Our hero and his two friends rolled upon the floor, and Hannibal pitched head foremost against the sides of the cabin with such force that if any other part of his anatomy had met the brunt of the fall, he would have been killed outright.

But a nigger's head is the only invulnerable part of his body, and he was only a little confused. As to Peter and Pitchpot, both were so utterly confounded by the sudden attack of the elements, that they forgot their little differences, and made an effort to scramble to their feet, shouting out in alarm.

On deck, all was dismay. One man had gone clean overboard, and the rest of the watch had been shot into the lee-scuppers, where they lay in several feet of water, holding on to the nearest objects within reach.

A wreck seemed imminent.

Jim Swaby was holding on to the wheel with another man; but he, to use his own expressive term, was too "flabbergastered" to do anything, or even to shout out a word of command; but this loss of presence of mind was soon put aside by the old salt, and with a roar worthy of a bull, he gave the order to cut away the masts.

Fortunately, this expedient was not necessary, for the wind for a moment lulled, and the noble little craft righted.

Then came another lull.

The wind had ceased, but the sea rose and fell heavily, and the dark clouds in the heavens still sped upon their course. There was little need to tell an old sailor that the rest was but temporary.

It lasted long enough, however, for Jack and his companions to reach the deck, and to lend a helping hand, if necessary. Our hero at once gave orders to have the hatches battened down.

The sailors ran forward to obey, and at that instant Peter and Hannibal leapt upon the deck; but Pitchpot, who sought to follow them, received the hatches upon the crown of his head, and shot down again like a leaden plummet.

A few rapid orders were given, and with storm-sails only, the "Swallow" was put before the wind—or as near to the point of the compass as they could get her. The lull was not at an end, and with a shriek like that of ten thousand furies pursuing their prey, the hurricane burst again upon the frail ship.

The scene that ensued was fearful.

High rose the waves, with their snowy caps of foam, and the heavy, sack-like clouds sank almost to the sea.

Rain fell in cataracts, the lightning flashed, the thunder bellowed, drowning all sounds save those made by the contention of the elements.

The lightning illuminated everything, and the silent watchers of the storm could see each other as plainly, almost, as if it were day.

By the wheel stood those in command, and the men were scattered here and there, holding on to the stays to prevent themselves from falling, as the "Swallow" pitched and rolled.

Close by Jack, were Peter the Great and Hannibal, clinging most affectionately to the compass-box, but with their eyes upon their leader, ready to follow him over the side, if he were washed away.

It is a saying that, in storms, waves "rise mountains high;" and, indeed, the vast masses of water which rose and fell might justly be compared to the hills on land, and the deep troughs of the waters to valleys.

Suddenly a big ship loomed in sight, with all sails set, and passed them not more than twenty yards away.

Such a strange and awful phenomena, at such a time, put fear into many a heart that would not have quailed at the cannon's mouth, and every face followed this wondrous visitant.

They could see the deck clearly; but not a soul was in sight—not a man at the wheel or elsewhere; but close to the masts was a strange phosphorescent light, which played about in fitful and puny imitation of the lightning.

As the vessel passed, she heeled over, and the topmasts seemed to kiss the storm-sails of the "Swallow;" and so awful was the sight that the stoutest-hearted man on board veiled his eyes.

They knew, every man of them, that this was but a phantom, and when phantoms are seen at sea, evil and misfortune are not far off.

Jack was the first to look up again, and when he did so, the sea was clear.

"Gone!" cried Jack, with a keen sense of relief: but he had barely uttered the word, when the ship loomed up again upon the opposite tack, apparently bent upon mowing them down.

This time Jack did not quail.

"I never wronged any man," he thought, "and I have nothing to fear. Let it come. Avaunt, you ghastly visitant!"

It seemed as if his half-breathed defiance was answered, for the phantom suddenly veered away, and disappeared again in the gloom.

And now, strange to say, the storm lost its power, and the clouds breaking, the moon shone forth like a peaceful harbinger of better things.

The sea still raged, but the first great danger was over, and the "Swallow" was spared.

A little later, and the word of command could be heard; and Jack ordered all but the watch below to rest.

The men, glad of relief, lost no time in obeying

But not to sleep.

Sailors are all superstitious.

Their constant meeting with inexplicable wonders naturally makes them so, and the question in every man's mind was—

"What was the phantom ship?"

What did her coming mean?"

Was it old Vanderdecken at his tricks again, or had some shadow of the past taken to roaming upon the sea?

This was good, debatable ground, and arguments ensued, not only between the men, but with their superiors; and even Pitchpot ventured to give an opinion, which, however, being only a suggestion, that "ebery man was berry drunk, and thought he saw him," was very properly scouted.

That night a joke was played which ended in an uproar.

A couple of the men having descended to the hold for the purpose of enjoying a wee drop of grog on the quiet, were visited by two terrible phantoms.

A door opened, and a ragged and horrible figure entered, beating his breast and groaning in a most blood-curdling fashion.

Then a wicket opened, and the alarmed men saw through the aperture the head of an old man bearded and grizzly. The rum bottles fell to the ground and the men bolted.

Their exit was followed by a loud peal of laughter, and turning back, they saw it was two of their shipmates who had played them the trick.

Something like a battle royal would have ensued, but Jack appeared on the scene, followed by a few picked men, and the culprits, having been severely reprimanded, were sent to their hammocks.

Daylight broke while many were yet arguing, and then there came a cry from Jim Swaby.

"Ship ahead!"

Up sprang every man, and ran upon the deck, and there, in the offing, was the same ship in full sail, and, as before, no signs of anybody upon deck.

"Port, there!" cried Jack. "I'll run up, and see what this means!"

"Don't, sir, if you wally your life," said Jim Swaby, solemnly; "you can't run a risk like that without getting into trouble."

"I cannot see how we can be harmed," said Jack. "Port, there!"

The "Swallow" turned in obedience to the helm, and ran close up to the stranger.

"Ship ahoy!" cried Jack, through the trumpet.

No answer, and with all sails set she kept on.

The deck could now be very plainly seen, and not a man was there; but Jim Swaby's nautical eye detected that the helm had been lashed up, and that the hatchways were open. Everything on board, too, seemed to be nautically perfect, and those to command and those to obey only lacking.

"That is no phantom ship," said Charley Granby, after a careful survey of her. "I know her; she is an East Indiaman—the 'Singapore.' We spoke with her a week ago."

"Then there is something wrong on board," said Jack, "and I will know what it is."

This was easier said than done; for the craft was a fast sailer, and was going before a stiffish breeze. It was as much as the "Swallow" could do to keep up with her.

Jack crowded on every stitch of canvas he could, but he seemed to gain very little ground, and the chase promised to be a long one, especially as it now assumed the position of a stern chase.

The men of the "Swallow" did not half like it. They could not rid themselves of the notion that the stranger was a phantom, luring them to destruction, the more especially as she had been in the storm with a cloud of canvas, which ought in all reason to have sunk her.

Still, they did not venture to cavil at the commands of their leader.

To hear was to obey with them, and behind him they would go to death.

For over three hours they chased this

vessel, and then there fell a calm, and both ships rested idly upon the bosom of the deep.

"Out with the cutter," cried Jack, "and man it with volunteers."

In spite of their superstition, there was no lack of these, and several lost the opportunity of going.

Charley Granby and Tom Warren went in the stern with our hero, and Peter and Hannibal took up a position in the bows, with the laudable intention of being the first to board.

In this, however, they were disappointed.

Jack, fathoming their intention, ordered the men to back in, and was the first to reach the deck.

It was a strange scene—that great vessel without a sign of life, but with so many signs of life having lately been there.

The captain's telescope lay in the scuppers, and close to it a woman's hat and a camp-stool overturned.

The fittings of the ship were intact, and but for the position in which the craft was found, she might have been lying idly in a harbour, and all ashore on the spree.

"I never saw anything like this," said Tom Warren.

"Nor I," said Charley Granby.

"Let us go below, and see if all is as silent and lonely there," said Jack.

So they went below, and some of the men and the twin brothers followed, all involuntarily treading as quietly as if entering the resting-place of the dead.

And it was indeed a tomb.

Throwing open the door of the main saloon, Jack entered, but immediately recoiled in horror, for a most fearful sight met his eyes.

Around, were ranged a number of men and women, each with a cord around their throats, and the eyeballs staring fixedly ahead.

A table was overturned, and a few chairs had been tossed about, and therefore either the struggle had been brief, or the wretches who had committed the atrocities had put the place in order when they ranged out the dead in ghastly mockery of a burying party of people.

All these were passengers, and by their clothes showed signs of wealth.

Their jewellery was all gone, evidently removed by the hands of the pirates.

Some of the women were young, and their faces were the most painful to look upon, for the hellish wretches, who had taken their lives, had left nothing damnable undone.

The men had been simply strangled and robbed.

Jack's face was flushed with anger, and all the hatred he had entertained for the pirates and plunderers of the seas was redoubled.

A life would be too short to devote to the capture and extermination of such monsters.

They found no other signs of humanity in the ship.

All the seamen were gone.

"Walked the plank," as Charley Granby suggested, "with a fifty-pound shot to their feet."

All that was valuable had been taken away, and, in the fore-cabin, was found a heap of rubbish, piled up, and with signs of fire about it.

The pirates had evidently contemplated burning the "Singapore," but had failed.

The next two hours were occupied in a solemn and reverential interment of the dead, and, this done, the sails of the Indiaman were furled, and a consultation held as to what should be done with her.

"I think I shall take command of her myself," said Jack. "She is a noble craft and worth a mint of money. I shall run her into my harbour, with the rest of my prizes. You, Tom, can take command of the 'Swallow,' and we will sail in company. A little rest, although I am loth to lose time, will do none of us any harm."

Charley Granby stayed with Tom, and Jack took the three niggers and twelve men with him—not half or quarter enough to work the ship, but, as they were going under easy sail, he thought he could make shift with these.

And so, he started in the "Singapore," little dreaming what the command of that vessel would bring upon him.

CHAPTER XXXIX.

SAVOURY DISHES.

THE "Singapore" and the "Swallow" turned in a southerly direction, and sailed in company for four days, and then troublesome gales arose again.

The night was particularly stormy, and when it was over, Jack looked over the sides of the "Singapore," and saw nothing but sea on every side around him.

This did not trouble him much, for Tom Warren had his sailing directions, which were to bear up towards the island, and get the "Swallow" stowed away in the lake where the prizes were kept, and there to await the coming of the Indiaman.

"I dare say she will lag a little," said Jack; "but nobody in these latitudes will touch her now. If her old enemies come across her, they will bolt right away, thinking it is her ghost."

He said this, laughingly, and left his own gallant craft with a light heart, full of hope for the future, and joy in the present.

The men he had were few, but they worked well, and, somehow, the "Singapore" was kept under easy sail.

Hannibal took charge of one watch, and Peter the Great the other, and Pitchpot was elevated to the position of cook.

Pitchpot was very proud of this position, as he had only been assistant on board the "Swallow," and inspired by his advancement, he invented several dishes which certainly had the merit of novelty, if nothing else.

At dinner, on the sixth day, Jack sat down to dinner, and the cover being removed, a stew of some sort was revealed to him.

"What is it?" he asked.

Peter, who was waiting, peered into it, and replied that he didn't know.

"I am not mighty particular," said Jack; "but I have an Englishman's wholesome prejudice, and like to know what I am eating. Ask Pitchpot what it is."

Peter sought out Pitchpot, and put the question to him.

Pitchpot replied that the dish was "berry good."

"Dat no answer," said Peter, wrathfully. "What am in the dish."

"Meat and graby," replied Pitchpot.

"Wurra meat is it," insisted Peter, "and what de graby?"

"If Massa Jack eat him and no like him, den I make him up no more," said Pitchpot; "but if he like him, he hab de same to-morrow."

"What am dat dish?" roared Peter.

"Meat and graby," said Pitchpot again.

At this Peter bounced out of the culinary department, and returned to Jack with a full account of the interview.

Jack declined to eat it, and the dish was put aside, contenting himself with some salt junk and biscuits and cheese.

After dinner, Peter and Hannibal missed the dish, and went in search of it.

Pitchpot was just finishing it as they came upon him.

"Dis dish berry good," he said.

"What am him?" asked Hannibal.

"Me find him in dis tin, wif oders, in de cupboard," replied Pitchpot, holding up a tin usually used for potted meats.

The name was on a label, and as Peter could read a little, he sat down, and by dint of great perseverance, read out, "potted partridge."

"Good!" said Peter; "I t'ink it am too good for a nigger like you. A reg'lar cuss like you ought to hab potted cat."

Now, we have said that there was no signs of life on board the "Singapore," but we ought to have excepted an old tom-cat, long past the prime of its existence, and evidently going down the vale of life; and at this moment it came up *apropos*, and rubbed its head against Pitchpot's legs.

"Dat the sort ob food for you," said Peter, and stalked away.

The potted partridge was not the only meat found, and Jack, well assured that all was right, made a very hearty meal off several very desirable things; but what he left was invariably carried away by Pitchpot, and never returned.

Peter and Hannibal had only the usual ship's rations, and a burning desire came over them to have what was left for their own consumption; but so dexterous was Pitchpot that as soon as the dishes were handed outside they disappeared, and the brothers were foiled.

"I t'ink dat you might gib us some ob dat for supper," said Peter, one day, as he handed out a dish, "as Hannibal and me berry tired ob beef and ship biscuit."

"Dat not'ing to me," replied Pitchpot, "Massa Jack grumble if I feed the ship's company on potted parfridge."

All potted meats it is well to mention, were potted partridge to Pitchpot, and as custodian of the larder, he had no right to serve out anything extra without Jack's orders.

Our hero would not have refused the sable twins the dishes left, but as they were too modest to ask him, he thought nothing about it.

The most exasperating part of the business to Hannibal and Peter was that they knew Pitchpot regaled himself like an alderman, and his fast-fattening form bore witness to his gormandising propensities; so after a few consultations they resolved to fall foul of him, and demand a portion of the spoil.

So they sallied into the cooking cabin, and Hannibal, taking Pitchpot round the waist, laid him upon the table, like a pig waiting for the butcher's knife, and Peter stood over him with a pistol cocked.

The terror of the unhappy cook was extreme, for he verily thought his last hour was come, and, opening his mouth, he gave vent to such a howl that the ship rang again.

It was such a vocal effect that only a nigger can produce.

"Anoder word," said Peter, "an I scatter yer brains. Yah! be quiet will yer?"

"What dis chile done?" demanded Pitchpot.

"You goramise ebery'ting," said Peter, w'ile de two officers ob the ship go about widout—widout—a—a bit of parfridge to dere backs. You make de big dish, and Massa Jack eat lilly bit ob him. Whar' am de rest?"

"I put him in de larder," replied Pitchpot.

"Dat's a big lie. You put him *here!*" cried Peter, striking Pitchpot most unfairly below the belt; "dat's whar' you put him."

"Ma-assa — Peter — ha-ab — mercy!" gasped Pitchpot; "me no put him dere ag'in."

"Wurra you do wif him, den?"

"I make a nice lilly dish for Massa Peter an' him brudder," replied Pitchpot.

"When, sare?"

"Dis berry night."

"You sure, sare? No humbug."

"I sw'ar!" said Pitchport; and then they set him free.

Hannibal took the first night watch, and it was arranged that the supper should be ready just before, and the two brothers partake of it upon deck.

Pitchpot was enjoined to make it as savoury as possible, and he promised with all sorts of vows to do so.

As it was just possible that Jack might be on deck at the time, Peter thought it would be better to tell him that a supper was coming on, which he did, but not exactly in the way he should.

"Massa Jack," he said, "Hannibal berry ill."

"Hannibal ill!" replied Jack. "I am very sorry for that. What is the matter with him?"

"He not *berry* ill. P'raps only lilly faint when de night watch is his."

"If that is the case, I will take it for him this time."

"No, Massa Jack, he no want dat, but he going to hab a little bit ob supper just before. Pitchpot make him a stew ob de scraps—only de scraps, Massa Jack!"

"Ah, I see!" said Jack, smiling. "You are going in for a great spread. But why eat scraps? Tell Pitchpot to give you a feed of the best he has."

"Jes' like you, Massa Jack. T'ank you!" said Peter, and hurried away to Pitchpot with the message.

The cook received it with an ugly gleam in his eyes, and promised to give them something "berry good and *quite new.*"

"I invent him to-day," he said. "I make him in my head first, to-night I make him in de pot!"

That night Hannibal and Peter sat under the lee of the compass-box, waiting for the dish, and with marvellous punctuality Pitchpot put in an appearance with a most savoury mess.

"Dat smell de right t'ing?" he said.

"It berry good," replied Peter, sniffing joyously.

Putting down the dish, Pitchpot squatted himself before them in Turkish fashion, surveying them like a benefactor.

"You not wanted now," said Hannibal.

"I like to see gentlemen eat," said Pitchpot, and that compliment secured him permission to remain.

Peter dipped a fork into the dish, and brought forth something like the leg of a hare.

This he put on to Hannibal's plate, and covered it with gravy.

"Eat him while him hot," said Peter, "Golly! what a cleber feller you are, Pitchpot! Anoder leg! I hab him."

So Peter helped himself, and with his brother pegged away merrily.

The contents of the dish sank rapidly, and there was a prospect of reaching the bottom.

"Hab a lilly more, Hannibal, ole boy?" said Peter.

"Jes' a lilly more," replied Hannibal.

Peter filled up his plate with gravy; but this was not enough for Hannibal, who asked for some meat.

"Dere no more meat, I t'ink," replied Peter, groping about. "Stop! What dis?"

He hauled up something about eight inches long, which at first looked like a bit of old rope; but a closer inspection revealed the fact of there being hair upon it

"Golly! what dat?" shrieked Peter.

"Golly!" roared Pitchpot, as he sprang to his feet, "I left in de cat's tail!"

He bolted away, and the two brothers, wheeling round, sat facing each other.

"Hannibal," said Peter.

"Peter," said Hannibal.

"Warra dis we've been eating?"

"I no know, but I guess dat it——"

"Am dat ole tom-cat!"

"You right, Peter."

"Lat me get 'ole ob dat Pitchpot, and I'll lash ebery bit ob life out ob him!"

The most galling part of the affair was that there was a man at the wheel, who had been a spectator of the whole affair.

It could not, therefore, be kept a secret.

Burning with rage, the two gourmands sought out the cook, who prudently kept out of their way until Jack came upon deck, and then, relying upon his protection, came forth.

But the two brothers were too enraged to be baulked of their vengeance, and with a yell of fury they at once pounced upon him; but Jack intervened.

"Have the goodness to tell me what is the matter?" he said.

In a few words Peter told the story of his wrongs, and it was as much as Jack could do to contain himself; but turning to Pitchpot, he asked him, with assumed sternness, what he meant by it.

"Massa Jack," said Pitchpot, "may I ask Massa Peter some questrums?"

"Certainly."

"You tell me to eat dat tom-cat, didn't you?" asked Pitchpot, addressing his lord and master.

"Me did," replied Peter, loftily.

"Den dat's why I made him up for you," rejoined Pitchpot. "*What am good for one nigger, am good for anoder; so you hab de tom-cat!*"

CHAPTER XL.

THE OLD "THUNDERER."

WHAT could be done to Pitchpot after this confession?—literally nothing: for in the first place, Peter and Hannibal had no real authority for ordering all sorts of nick-nacks to eat, and in the second, they had not specified what the dish was to be made of, and was therefore bound to accept whatever the cook provided for them.

"I think," said Jack, "that in future, Peter, you had better stick to the rations of the ship; and you," he added, turning to Pitchpot, "endeavour not to exceed your duty, or play practical jokes upon anybody."

Thereupon he left them, and the twin brothers, burning with wrath, retired for a time, apparently satisfied with the verdict of the court; but that very night Pitchpot was fallen upon in his hammock, gagged, bound and severely cobbed by some person or persons in the dark. In his own heart he had no doubt as to the identity of the perpetrators, but without evidence he could not convict, and so he wisely bore it, and secretly chuckled over the tom-cat episode.

There were a great many allusions to that savoury dish by the ship's company, but Peter and Hannibal prudently abstained from resenting these personal allusions, and in a day or two the event began to die away.

During this time the "Singapore" blundered on, and having lost sight of the "Swallow," the life became dull. It did not suit our hero, who was by far too spirited and active to endure relegation without repining.

"Oh, Peter!" he said one day, "how I pray for a brush with somebody!"

"Wif dis ole ship, Massa Jack?" asked Peter.

"No. She would be worse than useless."

"I t'ink so," said Peter; "but, golly, Massa Jack, it berry dull cruising 'bout wif never a shot nor a clash ob de cutlash."

"A sail!" roared out the man at the mast-head.

"Where away?"

"Right astern, sir."

Jack turned in the direction indicated, and saw a sail just peeping above the horizon. He watched for a few minutes, and the hull appeared. She was coming up hand over hand.

"War or peace, friend or foe?" muttered Jack.

There was nothing to do but to watch and wait, and take his chance. He had no means of resisting an attack. If it was a trader, all was well.

But if it was not?

Aye, there was the risk. If it was a man-of-war, he could only yield, and now he began to feel the folly of leaving the "Swallow" more deeply than ever.

"I have been a fool," he thought. "But what matters? All may yet be well."

In half an hour the stranger was fully revealed, and then there could be no question as to her character.

She was a man-of-war.

The next question was—What was her nation?

"If English," thought Jack, "she will board me to a certainty, and then what

They knew, every man of them, that this was a phantom, and when phantoms are seen at sea, evil and misfortune are not far off.

shall I say? All the papers of this precious craft have been destroyed. Heigho! here is a fix, I am afraid."

"Peter!" he said.

"Yes, Massa Jack."

"You have good eyes. What do you make of that craft? Take my glass."

"See better wifout it, Massa Jack. Dat a man-ob-war."

"Many guns?"

"Two row, Massa Jack."

"What colours does she carry?"

"*De Union Jack.*"

"Done!" muttered Jack, turning way. 'Nothing now but to bear the worst bravely."

He could not but feel gloomy, for here was a threatening end to his wandering life, and, as far as he could see, an end to his hopes of confounding his enemies also.

For mark how the case stood.

Suppose he was captured, taken to England, and tried on a charge of piracy, what could save him?

The facts were too heavy against him.

He had fitted out a craft in a secret manner, and gone afloat without a charter from his Government.

He had fired upon an English vessel.

Tom Warren and such witnesses as he could have called were far away.

They would miss him, but not knowing whither he had gone, would never dream of coming to his rescue.

Or if they did eventually decide upon such a course, their coming might be too late.

Turn which way he might, the prospect seemed to be hopeless.

One thing only gave a ray of hope, and that was flight.

But that was very feeble indeed, with a craft of the small sailing powers of the "Singapore."

It was too much undermanned to be kept going in full sail, and the little charm there was lay in the hope that night might save him.

"But there is a moon," muttered Jack, in despair, "and the sky is without a cloud."

Every minute now brought the ship nearer and nearer into view, and as the rigging began to show in detail, Jack thought that he recognised an old friend.

To the ordinary eye, one ship of a certain make is like another, just as one sheep is like another sheep to a casual observer; but a sailor can easily distinguish one craft from another, as the sheep tells one member of his woolly flock from another.

Anxiously and wonderingly did our hero keep his eyes upon the vessel, until at last the truth burst upon him, and he knew her.

"The old 'Thunderer!'" he cried. "The craft I first set foot upon. Now, is this a good or evil omen for me?"

"Boom!"

A gun of warning for him to haul up.

"Run up the Union Jack," cried our hero. "Perhaps that will suffice!"

Up went the flag, and then there was another moment's suspense.

"Boom!"

"It will not do," said Jack. "Heave-to, then."

The "Singapore" was brought to, and rocked idly upon the waves.

A boat was lowered from the "Thunderer."

"Call the men aft," said Jack, and in a few minutes the whole of the crew were clustered around him."

"My men," he said, "I have resolved not to risk your lives in fighting against our countrymen. It would do no good, as they are by far too heavy for us, and such of us as might escape the fight would be captured and hanged outright.

"We shall be taken as it is," said one of the men.

"True," replied Jack; "but I hope that I shall be the only sufferer. You know me too well to suppose that I yield from fear."

"I should think we do," was the prompt response. "Hurrah for Happy Jack!"

"That is well, and I thank you," returned our hero, with mingled emotions of sorrow and pain. "I thought the matter over when that ship hove in sight, and as we have only our pistols and cutlasses, fighting would be mere bravado. So, to your post, and trust me to exonerate you as far as I can, when we appear at the tribunal of our country. But say nothing—admit nothing."

"Ship ahoy!" sung out a voice, and a boat grazed against the sides of the "Singapore."

CHAPTER XLI.

DEEPER SHADOWS.

"ALL right, here!" cried Jack. "Come on board."

A lieutenant climbed over the

side, and looked about him with an air of curiosity.

"Short manned," he said.

"Very," replied Jack, drily.

"Where have you stowed the rest away?"

"Have no more. The whole of my crew are upon deck."

"Tell that to the horse-marines," replied the officer. "Where are your passengers? They will tell me a different tale, I'll swear."

"I have no passengers."

"But this is a passenger ship."

"I know that; but I have not a passenger on board."

"I don't understand what is going on here," said the officer. "Let me look at your papers."

"I have no papers."

"No papers!"

"None."

"Hallo! What's the name of this craft?"

"You can read it on that bucket there."

"Oh, the 'Singapore!'" said the officer. "She was a passenger ship; but your being here is rather odd. Where's her captain?"

"I am her captain."

"You!—a mere youth! Blarney! There's been mutiny here, I guess. Upon deck, a dozen of you, my lads!"

A number of Jack Tars came rolling up, and stood ready, cutlass in hand.

"Down with your arms, there!" cried the officer.

"We give them up," said Jack, bowing gracefully. "We are neither pirates nor dogs."

"Peaceful traders are not generally armed as you are," was the reply. "I shall take half of you at a time; but don't try any nonsense with me."

"Had I been disposed to resist you," said Jack, coolly, "you would have found me very serious."

"You have a great deal of dash and pluck about you," said the officer, "and there's an honest cut about your face; but I do not understand you."

"I do not suppose you do," said Jack. "Come."

He beckoned to Peter and Hannibal, and both sorrowfully followed him into the boat.

The next moment Pitchpot dropped down, and took up his positon close behind our hero.

"Massa Jack," he said.

"Hush! No names."

"True to de end," whispered Pitchpot. "I say nuffin."

"Thank you. I am sure you will be true."

"Dey make soup ob me fust," said Pitchpot.

And then he nudged Peter, who involuntarily grinned.

He had quite forgiven Pitchpot the trick he had played.

About half the crew were stowed away in the boat, and then they put off, and pulled to the "Thunderer."

A number of men and officers were looking over the side, wondering what was up.

Jack looked at them intently, but they were all strange to him.

The officer went up the companion, and touched his cap to a stout, good-looking man, whose uniform revealed the fact of his being the commander.

"Anything wrong, Anson?"

"Yes, sir; but what it is I can't make out. She's the 'Singapore,' and in very strange hands; but whether part of a mutinous crew or pirates I can't tell. Come up here."

"I will," said Jack, who was addressed, "when you speak a little more politely."

"I will make short work of you if you don't!" growled Anson.

"Hush!" whispered the captain; "that's no common young fellow. He looks a gentleman all over."

"Will you have the goodness to step upon the deck?" said Anson, biting his lips.

"I will," said Jack, and, running up as lightly as a cat, sprang on deck, and faced the captain.

"Now, sir," said the captain, "I am Captain Rowley, and command this vessel. Will you be kind enough to tell me who you are?"

"I would rather not."

"You had better. Your reticence may get you into trouble."

"All you can do is to take me to England, and try me before my countrymen," said Jack.

"You are, then, a British subject?"

"That much I am willing to tell you."

"But more you will not. Very good; you are under arrest."

Two marines, in obedience to a signal, stepped up, one on either side of our hero. Then Peter, Hannibal, and the other men came up, and were placed under arrest. The boat went back, and brought the rest of the crew.

Captain Rowley looked at them keenly,

and then asked them in a body if they would say who and what they were.

"I give you warning," he said, "that a bad construction will be put upon your silence. Are you the regular crew of the 'Singapore?'"

No answer.

"Is this young fellow your leader?"

No answer.

"Remember, he who speaks first will save his life," urged the captain: "the rest, I reckon, will be hanged."

A slight shuffling among the men followed this address; but, as before, none uttered a word.

"Put them all in irons!" said Captain Rowley. "And keep a strong guard over them!"

"I have one thing to say," said Jack, as a strong guard of marines came up. "Have I permission to speak?"

"Yes," curtly returned the captain; "but be brief."

"I wish to say this," replied Jack, "that if there is any culpability in what has been done, it rests entirely upon me. The men have nothing to do with it."

"That remains to be proved," said Captain Rowley. "But will you not tell me what has been done?"

"No. I have nothing to tell here."

"Mere sullenness," returned the captain; "take them away."

"Will you not take our parole?" asked Jack.

"Certainly not."

"I am a gentleman," said our hero, "and you may regret any unnecessary restraint you may put upon me."

"I shall regret nothing which I consider to be my duty."

"At least treat the men more considerately. Do not put them in irons. They are good and true men," urged Jack.

"Take them away!" was all Captain Rowley deigned to reply, and the captives were marched below, where irons were put upon them, and they were thrust into the hold, with a strong body at the door.

CHAPTER XLII.

WHO ARE THEY?

"DIS a precious dark place, Massa—Ahem! Dis a berry dark place—ain't it?" said Peter, as our hero and his friends settled themselves upon the floor.

"Very," replied Jack. "But bear up, and forgive me for bringing you such trouble."

"Forgib you, Massa—"

"I tell you what it am," interrupted Hannibal, "you put your foot into your mowf if you open it so wide. What did Massa—. Golly! I 'bout to do de same t'ing. Peter, my brudder, forgib your Hannibal."

A roar of laughter from the men followed Hannibal's attempt at reproof and disastrous failure. Hannibal perceived his blunder, and clutched his wooly head in despair.

"You have made a pretty hash of it," said Jack.

"I berry big fool," said Hannibal.

"Dat nuffin fresh in the way ob news," growled Peter. "I allus go de right way to work, and cough 'Ahem!' so dat I not speak Massa Jack's name."

Another roar of laughter rang through the hold, and it was now Peter's turn to clutch his top-knot, which he did with an energy that threatened to remove every hair from his head.

"Upon my word," said Jack, "you fellows must be careful, or you will spoil all."

"Oh! I cry for berry shame!" moaned Peter.

"I must take your word," replied Jack, "for I cannot see your face."

The door opened, and a sergeant of the marines, followed by two men, entered.

One bore a lantern, and the other some biscuit and water.

"You seem to be a merry lot," said the sergeant, "laughing and going on as if you'd just got paid off, with a month's furlough."

"Why should we be downcast?" asked Jack. "Honest men have nothing to fear."

"Not if they are honest," returned the sergeant. "Here's some biscuit and water for you. If I leave you a lantern, you can manage to divide the biscuit into rations."

"We will try, thank you," said Jack.

And the sergeant, putting the bag within reach, hung up the lantern, and departed.

Just about this time, Captain Rowley, of the "Thunderer," was meditating.

He was sorely puzzled by the conduct of his prisoners, and being afflicted with rather more than the average amount of curiosity, he could not rest until he had fathomed their secret.

"I'll send for Anson," he said, after a long thought.

And for Anson he sent.

The young lieutenant entered the captain's cabin, and saluting, waited to be questioned.

"Anson," said Captain Rowley, "in your report of the prisoners, you simply state that you found them on board the 'Singapore,' and brought them here."

"That is all I had to report, sir," returned the lieutenant.

"Indeed! Did you find nothing to give you any clue to the prisoners—their previous position, and so on?"

"Nothing, sir."

"You examined her thoroughly?"

"Thoroughly, sir."

"I should like to have run over her myself," said the captain. "Not that I think you have in any way neglected your duty, for I know you to be a careful and efficient officer."

"Thank you, sir."

"But very often two pairs of eyes are better than one."

"True, sir."

"Now, Anson, do you not think that you could screw some information out of them?"

"Obstinate as pigs."

"So they are; but every pig has vulnerable points. Some of the men may be weak."

"I do not think so, sir. They seem to be devoted to their young leader."

"A handsome fellow, and with the look of the service about him. I fancy I have seen him somewhere before."

"His face seems to be familiar to me, sir," said Anson. "Nothing is to be got out of him or the men. The only chance is the niggers."

"A good thought of yours, Anson. Let us try the niggers. An African is generally a very soft subject."

"They seem to be above the common run, sir."

"So they are; but still, they can be no match for *me*."

"Certainly not, sir."

"Knock off their irons, and bring them here," said Captain Rowley. "Put a guard by the door, and keep yourself within hail."

"Aye, aye, sir!"

Anson departed, and executed his mission so promptly that within a quarter of an hour the rattle of muskets was heard, the door was thrust open, and Lieutenant Anson, of H.M.S. "Thunderer," ushered in the three sable heroes—Pitchpot, Hannibal, and Peter the Great.

CHAPTER XLIII.

THREE CHEERFUL NIGGERS.

CAPTAIN ROWLEY looked at the three arrivals and smiled, for he felt he had an easy task before him.

The expression upon the faces of one and all was that of hopeless stupidity.

"Leave us, Anson," he said, and the lieutenant, bowing, departed.

"Now, my fine fellows," continued the captain, "I want to have a few words with you."

"Yes, sare," said Peter.

"Berry glad, sare, to hab a dozen," said Hannibal.

Pitchpot opened his mouth and gasped, but nothing came of it.

Captain Rowley accepted his silence as a cordial assent to the proposition.

"It is a pity to see three such fine fellows as you in this position," said the captain, "for as sure as I am sitting here, and you are standing there, you will all be hanged."

Peter and Hannibal remained immovable, with no more expression upon their faces than one sees in an ordinary Dutch clock.

Pitchpot thoughtfully felt his windpipe, and gasped again.

"I have pointed out this fact," the speaker went on, "but I wish to say that you will be hanged under present conditions—that is, unless you make a clean breast of it."

"Yes, sare," said Peter. "When shall we wash him?"

"You are very stupid!" said the captain, petulantly. "By making a clean breast of it, I mean an open confession—tell who you are and those about you."

"Yes, sare," said Peter.

"Now, then, this is coming to the point. Who are you?"

A dead silence, the trio of sable heroes all with their eyes ahead.

"Come," said the captain, addressing Pitchpot, "you know all about it."

"Me don't, sare," replied Pitchpot.

"Not know who you are! That is absurd!"

"Me berry stupid," said Pitchpot. "Me t'ink I berry clebber when I was lilly boy; but I get changed."

"Don't be a fool, man! Speak the truth."

"I not make myself, sare, and I berry big fool. All niggers fools—common niggers berry bad."

"Come, that won't do for me," said the

captain, persuasively. "Once again, tell us who you are?"

A brilliant idea came to the rescue of Pitchpot, and he answered—

"T'ree niggers, sare."

"This is unbearable. What is your name?" turning to Hannibal.

"Got none, sare."

"Nor you?" turning to Peter.

"No, sare. Fader and moder had none; all berry poor niggers."

"But your master or captain has one? Out with it, sharp."

"You 'member massa's name?" said Peter to Hannibal.

Hannibal went into a fit of meditation, which lasted fully two minutes, and would have lasted much longer if Captain Rowley had not asked him what he was thinking about.

"I am t'inking," he said, "about my massa's name."

"Is it very difficult to remember?"

"It a berry big name, sare."

"Berry long," assented Peter.

"Try, then, to remember it," said Captain Rowley.

"What am dat name?" murmured Hannibal. "Was it Rummytudledum?"

This question so exasperated Captain Rowley, who saw that he was being fooled, that an oath sprang to his lips.

But he checked himself, and swallowing his wrath, spoke in as mild a tone as he could assume.

"It is impossible for a man to have such a name."

"What am de name, den?" said Hannibal, still appealing to Peter.

"I t'ink it sumfin' like Wagglededoralum," replied Peter.

"Once for all," cried Captain Rowley, now losing all patience, "will you tell me his name or not?"

"Once for all," said Peter, "we don't mean to do nuffin ob de sort."

"You defy me?"

"No, sare; but we are not going to peach."

"You will remember that I am commander of this vessel."

"Yes, sare."

"And that I can punish you as I please."

"No, sare."

"What! Not do as I like in my own vessel!"

"No, sare," replied Hannibal. "You British subjeck, me British subjeck. One law for all in dat great country—black and white, all de same. No man condemned until him tried."

"But suppose I choose to hang you, who will know anything, or care a rap about you?"

"De men on board," said Peter, warmly. "De lub ob justice am strong in be heart ob ebery man, and if you forget what am due to us, sare, de men hab you up as soon as you get ashore. You know dat. Take us home and try us. We hab nuffin to do wif you. We bow to de law ob our country, not to ebery man who am lucky enuf to get de command ob a ship."

Peter's harangue might have been a little hazy, but it had sufficient of what was true in it to carry weight, and Captain Rowley felt that he was powerless.

In our country no one is bound to criminate himself.

And wherever a ship of ours is afloat, on board that ship the same law is in force.

Touching a small bell upon the table, he summoned Anson, the officer, and bade him remove the three contumacious niggers.

"They are so stupid that I can make nothing of them," he said. "The fellows are up to their eyes in fat, too. Put them upon short rations."

"We issue the rations in a lump, sir," said Anson, "and the prisoners divide it."

"Give each man his portion, then, in future, and put these niggers upon boys' allowance."

"Aye, aye, sir!"

Pointing to the door, he bade the three prisoners go out, and then followed them. Outside he undertook to reprove them for their obstinacy.

"If you had only told the truth," he said, "you would have gained your liberty at once, and got your rations with the men."

"Hannibal!" said Peter.

"Yes, ole boy."

"Shall I gib dis man the sentiments ob my heart?"

"Do, ole boy," said Hannibal; then added in a whisper, "You let out my name."

Lieutenant Anson heard the name, and marked the whisper, making a mental note of both. Peter, turning to him, said—

"What do you take us for?"

"Niggers," was the reply.

"Dat is, black men," said Peter.

"Just so."

"What am de diff'rence between a black man and a white one?"

"I am not good at conundrums," replied the officer; "but I believe there is a difference."

" Only in de colour," said Peter, warmly. " You jes' cut a lilly hole in de skin, an' you find dat our blood as red as yours; go lilly deeper, an' you find a heart beating jes' in de same way. Now, sare, you lub your country ? "

" I believe so," replied the officer.

" S'pose you in de hand ob the enemy, and asked to gib up that country. Would you do it ? "

" Certainly not."

" Dat jes' de case wif us," replied Peter. " Our massa am our country — we lib and die for him, and when he say, ' Do dis,' we do it; when he say, ' Do *not* do it,' we stan' down on our lilly black feet ike fighting cocks, an' tell you an' dat blessed ole chap inside dat cabin dat we see you rolled in ginger an' b'iled fust."

" Dat sentlement is berry good," put in Hannibal.

" De best sentlement I eber heard," added Pitchpot.

" We will try to shake that sentiment out of you," said the lieutenant. " Here you are! On with those irons again, and put these fellows into the hold ! "

CHAPTER XLIV.

THE "SWALLOW."

WHEN Tom Warren found that he had lost sight of the " Singapore," he was sorely distressed and puzzled, and with a hope of falling in again with her, he cruised about here and there for several days.

" She cannot have outsailed us," he said to Charley Granby. " She was much too heavy a craft for that."

" The ' Singapore ' could carry a pile of sail," returned Charley, " and if she got before a fine wind, there's no knowing what she could do."

" If you call to mind the night we first saw her," remarked Jim Swaby, " you can picter her capable of doing something."

" True," said Tom. " But now she is so under-manned."

" At that time she had no men at all."

" I wish I knew what to do," mused Tom, " for I am in a regular fix! If I cruise about here, and he is gone on, we shall not be doing any good; and, on the other hand, if anything has happened to the ' Singapore,' we shall do wrong by going to the rendezvous."

" It's a sore puzzle," said James Swaby, " and when a chap's in a fix, he ought to trust in luck."

" How can we trust to luck in this case ? "

" Write on one bit of paper, ' Wait here,' and on another, ' Go to the island;' then put 'em in a hat, shake 'em up, and get Mr. Granby to draw one."

" I have not much faith in things of that sort," said Tom, half smiling; " but. really, I do not see what else can be done."

Accordingly, he obtained the pieces of paper, and wrote upon them the words mentioned by Swaby; then, putting them into his cap, he asked Charley Granby to draw one.

" What is it ? " he asked, as the middy pulled out a scrap.

" Go to the island," said Charley.

" That's all right," said Jim Swaby, as if perfectly satisfied with the result. " We shall find 'em there."

So in the direction of the island they sailed, and after a varied voyage, it appeared in sight.

The anchor was dropped outside, and Jim Swaby, with a dozen men, went towards the creek.

They found it closed, and as this was conclusive evidence that no enemy had been there, they returned to the ship.

The other boats were lowered, and preparations made for towing the " Swallow " in.

Our readers will readily remember how the creek was stopped by the felling of a tree, and creepers trained over it, so as to hide the lake from ordinary eyes.

The plan had proved successful in the first instance, and afterwards, on the occasion of other visits to the same place, the manœuvre had been repeated.

The fact of its being now intact proved that the " Singapore " had not arrived: but as it was just possible that the " Swallow," although, perhaps, behind at first, might have outsailed the Indiaman in the long run, Tom Warren was not very much troubled.

He would rather have found Happy Jack there; but as he was not, Tom was prepared to be patient and watchful for a few days before he began to despair.

A couple of pounds of gunpowder cleared the barrier of the creek, and the " Swallow " was towed into the silent lake, whose waters none had yet fathomed.

This place had been found to be very remarkable in many ways.

In the first place, as we have declared. it gave no soundings; in the second, it was intensely cold ; and in the third place, the water, although so near the sea, was fresh.

To a sensitive palate, it was brackish, but to such men as those who fought under the flag of the "Swallow"—men accustomed to the vicissitudes of life, and ready and willing to take the hard bumps of a wandering life—it was all they could desire.

They used it for washing and drank it, but none of the men could ever be induced to bathe in it. Not for a mine of wealth or a world of jewels would one of the seamen strip and trust his body to that mysterious lake.

About a year prior to the present arrival of the "Swallow," our hero had put in for a few days with one of his prizes, and while fixing the "Swallow" in her position, one of the men fell overboard.

Now, drowning men, they say, come up three times to the surface, and, as a rule, those who fall into the water generally manage to come to the surface, whether they can swim or not, twice or thrice ; but this hapless sailor never came up again.

He went down like a plummet, the water closed over him silently, and he appeared no more.

Who can wonder that the men had a superstitious horror of the place ?—and when Tom Warren put in, they asked leave at once to camp ashore.

This was not the first time they had done so, and leave was readily granted, on the condition that a sentry should always be upon the summit of the rocks to keep a good look-out.

The "Swallow" was not the only ship in the lake, for there were a number of prizes—pirate crafts for the most part—moored to the shore, and the masts of every one had been taken out, earth put upon the decks, and creepers twined over the side.

The object of this will be remembered when we recall the tactics pursued by Happy Jack when first he made that lake his home, and so well had it answered that, although several vessels had undoubtedly touched the island, none had marked the presence of his captures.

Even natives had been deceived, for Peter once declared that a large number of them had landed there in their canoes and held high revelry, most probably over the body of their foes, which had in all likelihood been consumed after the fashion of those gentlemen who put Robinson Crusoe into such an unmitigated funk,

and finally furnished him with the faithful, intelligent Friday.

A week passed and the "Singapore" did not arrive. Tom's doubt deepened into anxiety, and anxiety developed into despair. Day and night a look-out was kept, and watch-fires burnt to help the missing ship upon her way, but alas ! vain was the consumption of fuel, for that good and gallant Indiaman was then resting in the dock of Portsmouth waiting the coming of the "Thunderer."

"What shall we do ?" asked Tom, one morning. "I am sure something has happened to our noble leader. Where can we go ? What can we do to help him ?"

"We can only sit here and await his coming," said Jim Swaby, gloomily. "It was a mad thing for him to venture in that old craft."

"Most acts of pluck and daring are looked upon by some as madness," said Charley Granby.

"Suppose he is captured," suggested Tom, "and taken to England ?"

"They'll hang him right away," said Charley.

"The whole job is a puzzle," said Jim Swaby. "Let us wait a little longer. In a day or two we may hear something."

They waited a day or two and finally a week passed, but nothing touched the island.

Once a sail rose above the horizon, but Jim at once declared that it belonged to a schooner, and when it disappeared, there was great sorrow evinced.

"A stranger could not help us," said Tom. He had a good heart, and loved his friend deeply. It was no common sorrow which troubled him now.

The smile so familiar to those around him was gone.

He shunned all society, and lay upon a rock almost from noon till night, with his gaze fixed upon the far-off line of the sea.

No work as weary as that of an earnest watcher, and in time this unwearying vigilance began to tell upon him.

Jim Swaby implored of him to be patient, and take a rest ; and Charley Granby volunteered to keep his post.

"No, no," said Tom ; "I can never rest until I see my dear old friend again. Do you think that I can forget what he risked for me ? Did not this wandering life of his spring out of my misfortune ? Did he not lose honour and rank for me ? How, then, can I, with one spark of love and friendship in my heart, sit down and *rest* while he is away ?"

"The 'Singapore' may yet arrive," suggested Charley Granby.

"I had a dream last night," said Tom Warren, "a dreadful dream! Worn out, I suppose, I fell asleep upon the rock, and a thousand dreadful shadows gathered around me. At first, in misty form, they floated here and there, but soon they began to separate, and assume an individuality—limbs, bodies, faces stood out by degrees, until I saw a thousand awful demons."

"Dreadful!"

"It was indeed terrible; but more was yet to come. These shadows formed into a circle, and, like a tree growing rapidly, a scaffold sprang into their midst, and upon it hung a human form. I knew it at once. Poor Jack was hanging there!"

"It was only a dream," suggested Charley Granby, who saw that Tom Warren was sorely puzzled.

"Only a dream!" cried Tom; "but what is life? Do not the years past and gone hover about us like a dream? And have we not many a vision of our sleep as firmly imprinted upon our minds at things which we call real? A dream!—is may be so—but it was a dream of *what is, or what will be.*"

"Heaven grant it otherwise!" said Charley Granby, fervently.

"Amen!" said Tom; "but who shall order otherwise than what is ordained? Oh, that we were home, Charley!"

"A sail!" cried Charley.

"Where?"

"To the sou'-west. Look!"

"A big craft, too!" cried Tom, in a fever of excitement.

"But not the Indiaman," said Charley, sadly.

"It is not a common trader," returned Tom.

"It is not a trader at all," replied Charley; "it is a British cruiser. Look at her colours. Now can you not see?"

"I can. Let us go down at once."

They leaped lightly down the rock, and ran to where the men were lying under the shade of the tents, smoking.

"Danger at hand!" cried Tom. "Up with every stick, and get on board at once!"

In a moment every man was on his feet, and the tents fell as if by magic. In ten minutes everything was on board.

A boat went back with Tom Warren and Charley Granby to keep a look-out.

By this time the man-of-war was in the offing, and she was undoubtedly British.

There was the Union Jack flying in the breeze, and a blue pennant trailing up.

"An admiral on board, then!" said Tom.

"They are making preparations to come ashore," returned Charley Granby. "Hark! they are piping away the long-boat."

"Botheration!" muttered Tom. "This is the last sad scene of all, which ends our strange eventful history."

"Will you fight?"

"I have strict orders from Jack not to fire upon the British flag."

"Then they will simply come in and take us?"

"That is so, my friend. The creek is open. Come, let us go on board, and surrender as gracefully as we can."

They returned to the "Swallow," and announced the fate in store.

The men heard it in silence, but more than one hand was laid upon the cutlasses.

"No violence, remember," said Tom Warren, authoritatively. "You will be tried by a tribunal of your countrymen, and, if all goes well, you will be acquitted with honour."

"And if it doesn't?" muttered one of the men.

"Then we shall swing," growled another.

"Men of the 'Swallow,'" cried Tom, in a clear voice, "do you mistrust your leader, Happy Jack?"

"No," replied the men; "but he is not here."

"I have his written authority for doing what I have done," said Tom. "Will you obey that?"

There was a moment's pause, and then all answered with one voice—

"We will!"

"Put your arms aside, then, and meet them peaceably. Lay the cutlasses by the capstan, and the pistols here. Here are our friends."

A boat made for the creek with two officers in the stern.

Immediately they saw the "Swallow," one gave the word—

"Easy all!"

The men lay upon their oars, and the officer cried out—

"Ship ahoy!"

"Boat ahoy!" replied Tom.

"Who are you?"

"The 'Swallow.'"

"What nation?"

"England."

"Who's captain?"

"Happy Jack."

"Then you are pirates!" cried the officer; "and, in the name of the King, I command you to lay down your arms, and surrender!"

"Our arms are laid down, and we surrender."

"No tricks, now," said the officer, as the boat drew near, "or you will dearly rue it!"

"You have my word," said Tom, disdainfully. "If you funk boarding us, go back to your ship, and send another man."

The men in the boat laughed, and the officer muttered a curse.

Then the boat grated alongside, and he came upon the deck.

"This is all well," said he, looking at the weapons; "but I do not understand the 'Swallow' fellows giving in like this."

"Do you think we are cowards?" demanded Jack.

"It looks very much like it."

"Indeed!" said Tom, running towards the companion; "then I will show you how little we fear. You that funk being blown up by the magazine clear out at once! Men of the 'Swallow,' stand fast!"

CHAPTER XLV.

THE "THUNDERER" IN PORT.

PORTSMOUTH was in a state of great commotion. Happy Jack had admitted who he was, and the news of the home-bringing of John Scarborough, *alias* Happy Jack, the pirate, spread abroad like wildfire. Everybody rushed down to the dock gates to see the villains landed.

Public opinion was divided with regard to them, for Mr. Scarborough, senior, was rather a popular man, and even those who were partly convinced of Jack's guilt felt a sympathy for the kindly gentleman whose purse had ever been open to help the poor.

That purse, alas! was now closed.

A Government whose sagacity it would be treason to doubt had decided to confiscate that gentleman's estate on the score of his being privy to piracy on the high seas, and Jack's uncle had been reduced to beggary.

He accepted the blow without a murmur, left the house with his hat and stick, as if going for a walk, and had never been seen or heard of since.

The general supposition was that he had committed suicide, and the excitement of his disappearance had barely died out when the "Thunderer" came home, bringing with it the nephew captive.

News from a vessel flies over a town like wildfire, and the vessel had barely dropped its anchor when a crowd was on its way to the gates.

Those who knew the officials, or had passes, got in; those who were not so fortunate hung about in groops outside, and execrated their hard fate.

Opinions, as we have said, were divided. Some believed in the infamy of our hero, others stoutly maintained that he was the victim of a tyrannical captain.

"That's all bosh," said a red-nosed man with an umbrella under his arm; "if the young fellow did not like the service, he was at liberty to leave it, and there was no need for him to turn pirate."

"How do you know he has been a pirate?" asked a seaman.

"How do I know?" replied the red-nosed man; "how do we know anything? Isn't it printed in the papers? Haven't the Government offered a reward for him?"

"But papers and Government may be wrong," said the sailor. "I served under Cursly, and I know him well. He is a tyrant, and a white feather. I don't know this young fellow, but I remember hearing of his being tried for mutiny against Cursly."

"That's something," said the red-nosed man.

"But he was acquitted," returned the sailor; "and when a court sets a man free there ain't much against him."

"Hear, hear!" cried several voices.

"Now, I'll bet that when this young fellow comes to be put on his trial again," pursued the sailor, "that he will get free."

"Unless Captain Cursly is hereabouts," said a voice.

"But he ain't," said the sailor; "and, from all that can be gathered, ain't likely to be. The 'War Eagle' is long overdue, and it's supposed that she's either fallen into the hands of an enemy, or gone down with all hands."

"If he met a henemy," said another man, "Cursly wasn't the man to fight him. He was took right off."

Several persons soon came out of the dockyard, and those who had remained outside crowded around them.

"What news?" they cried.

"They will be brought ashore to-morrow, at eight o'clock," was the reply.

0

"I'll be here," said the red-nosed man, "and give my opinion on the villains pretty strong."

"And so will I," replied the seaman who had argued with him; "and if you open your mouth too wide, I may be tempted to put something into it."

The red-nosed man glanced with an evil eye, and tightened his clutch upon the umbrella; but he said no more, for public opinion was against him, and he prudently walked away.

The next morning, long before the hour named, a port admiral was on his way in full rig towards the dockyard.

A gorgeous sight to see—Admiral Fitz-Gibbons was not in a very good humour, for early rising did not suit him, and to add fuel to the fire, an unlucky street arab, while endeavouring to get out of his way, slipped down, and the admiral fell over him.

This happened near the gate dividing Southsea from Portsmouth, and an unlucky sentinel hard by burst into a roar of laughter.

The Arab, whose nature was eel-like, wriggled from under the admiral and bolted; there was nothing left then but to curse the sentinel, which the old officer did most heartily.

"I ax your honour's pardon," said the sentinel; "but it was ingwoluntary burst of the visible faculties."

"Confound you!" roared the admiral, "I'll have you tried by court-martial. Salute, you beggar!"

The soldier saluted, and the old man passed on frowning. He entered the dockyard, and in five minutes was on board the "Thunderer."

Captain Rowley met him with all honour, and then led the way to his cabin to breakfast.

Everything was of the best, but Admiral Fitz-Gibbons was in the humour to quarrel with everything, and the way he bit his toast was sufficient to keep Captain Rowley silent.

"It's an infernal nuisance dragging me up at this time to see a lot of piratical rascals," said the admiral, worrying an egg. "Why did you not arrange to bring them ashore later?"

"I only obeyed orders, sir," replied Captain Rowley.

"Why, then, did you not hang the rascals right off?"

"That, sir, I imagine, would be exceeding my duty."

"Oh, as for that, Government would not have bothered itself about them," said the admiral. "What have you there?"

"Potted prawns."

"None, thank you. I like them fresh."

"These privateers are no common men," said Captain Rowley, after a pause; "their leader was in the service, and is still very little more than a youth."

"A nephew of Scarborough's, I hear."

"Yes; the whole affair is bad. The others, with the exception of those confounded niggers, are all deserters from the navy. Oh, by the way, the prisoner, John Scarborough, wished to see you."

"To see me?"

"Not you actually; but he expressed a desire to see the first admiral who came on board."

"I do not think that I am bound to say anything to him."

"Certainly not; but something may come out of the interview."

"Oh, very well. As soon as breakfast is over, have him brought here. I have finished."

"And so have I."

A couple of servants speedily cleared away, and then an officer and ten marines were sent to bring Jack into the presence of the admiral.

CHAPTER XLVI.

ASHORE.

WHEN our hero was brought in, the result of his imprisonment was at once apparent.

He was pale and thin, but handsome still—"more interesting," as ladies say, than perhaps he had ever been in his life.

He walked in with a proud step, bowed gracefully, and stood still, awaiting to be spoken to.

"You have something to say to me," said the admiral

"I have," said Jack,

"What you have to say, say quickly," returned the admiral.

"It is only this," replied Jack, "that I am in a position most unfortunate. I have no money, and no friends, and the weight of evidence is against me. My uncle was a gentleman well known to you all, and apart from the trouble I have brought upon him, there is no stain upon his life."

"I admit that he was an honourable

gentleman," said the admiral, in a softened tone.

"But he is gone, ruined," said Jack "cast out for my sin."

"You admit your guilt."

"No, not the guilt I am charged with. I am no pirate."

"Come. You have fired upon a British craft.

"In pure self-defence, and when I was unjustly fired upon. Captain Cursly committed the first breach of the peace."

"Captain Cursly is not here to defend himself," said Captain Rowley. "You will not do wisely if you throw mud at him."

"I have no desire to asperse an absent man."

"Who is, in all probability, dead."

"He is not dead," said Jack.

"What do you know of his fate?"

In a few words Jack gave a rapid outline of what he knew of the fate of the "War Eagle." The admiral and the captain smiled.

"You expect us to believe this?" they said.

"I expect you to take the word of a gentleman," said Jack.

"I have no wish to quarrel with you about titles," returned the admiral. "You *were* a gentleman, I admit; but what of that? Is that all you have to say?"

"No," returned Jack. "I want to ask you, as a Christian gentleman, to do your best to aid me in my defence—to give me as much time to prepare for my trial as can possibly be given."

"The desire to prolong life is only natural," sneered Captain Rowley.

"Be quiet, if you please, for a moment," said the admiral, tartly; "what is your motive, prisoner, for asking this? Have you any hope of evidence in your favour arriving?"

"Yes, a great hope."

"From whom?"

"From my island in the Pacific—the island I have made my home, and where all the vessels I have captured from the ruffians who infest the seas are stowed away."

"What ruffians?"

"The pirates—the so-called Mexican Navy."

"Hum! This island of yours—where is it?"

Jack gave the latitude and longitude, and the admiral referred to the chart.

"There is no such island here," he said.

"In the chart, no," replied Jack; "but on the sea, yes. It it there, and a mighty island it is."

"I do not think this story will assist you much," said the admiral, "and I seriously advise you to pursue another line of defence."

"Enough," said Jack, "I see how it is. I cannot hope to be believed. I have only one more request to make."

"What is that?"

"If all goes against me," said Jack, "let me be shot, and not die a felon's death."

"That must rest with the court," said the admiral, rising. "Captain Rowley, it is time we went ashore."

"So let it be," said Jack, and passed out with his guard.

Outside, and in the dockyard, great crowds had gathered, every man and woman in a ferment to behold those who were charged with a gross outrage upon their country's laws.

True to his promise, the red-nosed man was there; and true to his, the seaman was not far away.

The police were "active" as usual—that is, they walked slowly and solemnly through the crowd, looking very important, and every now and then giving vent to their authority in speech.

"Pass on—pass on there! You must not block the gangway. Make way there, if you please. Pass on—pass on!"

But the crowd only shifted a little, and did not pass on; and upon the ears of those outside there shortly fell a roar of voices.

At first, it was difficult to say whether it was a hoot or a cheer; but soon it drew nearer, and the tone of it was unmistakeable.

It was a cheer.

Nothing is so infectious as a cry.

Even those who come to hoot oft tune their voices to the prominent tone; and scarcely a man in that vast crowd outside but was disposed to give our hero a friendly reception.

Even the red-nosed man repented himself, and took off his hat with the deliberate intention of waving it.

The police suddenly, and expertly, formed two lines, thus leaving a clear course for the egress of the captives.

The gates opened, and a company of marines emerged.

Next came Happy Jack, where he had always been—at the head of his followers —guarded by two marines.

He was not spared any indignity, and his hands were bound with handcuffs.

His handsome face turned what little of popular disfavour there was against him, and such a shout went up, that the police, fearing a rescue, put their hands upon their truncheons.

Jack smiled contemptuously, and, taking advantage of a minute's lull, spoke a few words to those who had given him so kindly a reception.

"I thank you, friends," he said. "I accept this salutation as an omen of my triumph. I am innocent of this foul charge. I love my country, and desire to obey its laws."

"Hurrah for Jack Scarborough!" cried the voice of the red-nosed man. "Hurrah for the bold boy of the 'Swallow'!"

Not only the hat, but the umbrella of that turncoat was thrown into the air. The hat he recovered, but some impartial observer secured the gingham for his own private use and benefit, and it was lost to the red-nosed man for ever. A very just retribution upon him for having vituperised our hero.

Jack passed on, and next came the seamen who had fought under him—every gallant tar walking with dauntless bearing.

What had they to fear? What crime had they committed? What, then, need they fear?

They answered the shout that was given with such a one as they had often given at sea, when the enemy succumbed; and then came Peter the Great, Hannibal, and Pitchpot.

Poor Peter was a sad wreck. His attire, ill-suited to the confinement he had undergone, was soiled, torn, and twisted out of all shape.

No street-nigger ever had a more comical rig-out than his was at that time.

Still, nobody laughed at him, for there was that in his face which told of pluck and daring, of fidelity and love to his master, and the shout for the "three niggers," was as hearty as any that had gone before.

Pitchpot and Hannibal, in their ragged shirts and trousers, looked as well as could be hoped under the circumstances, and if, at any other time, people of fastidious minds might have felt disposed to give them a wide berth, their wan faces and manacled hands sufficed to secure them sympathy.

The police closed behind the *cortege*, and the crowd ran by its side, shouting, and waving their hands.

The red-nosed man was so excited, that he ran against a post, and having, by this involuntary act, knocked all the breath out of his body, was, for the time being, left behind.

The mob gathered as it went, and soon there mingled with the shouts, cries to rescue the prisoners.

"Shame! Shame!—let them go!" cried fifty voices, and the officers of the marines gave the word to close up, and the police drew their truncheons.

"No rescue!" cried Jack. "What is liberty to me, if I am dishonoured? Remember that you are Englishmen, and a law-loving people. No rescue!"

"Massa Jack a bit ob a fool dere," said Peter to Hannibal. "Him much berrer hab him liberty, at any price!"

"Much berrer," muttered Hannibal. "Oh, Peter! s'pose dey hang us!"

"Den dere an end," said Peter.

Jack and his friends were to be taken before the magistrates, and, on reaching the Town Hall, found everything had been prepared for their reception.

The police were in force, and it was whispered that soldiers were not far away.

The prisoners were put into the dock—that is, as many as could be got there, and the rest were ranged in front.

In the course of changing about, Peter managed to get beside Jack.

"Oh, Massa Jack!" whispered Peter, "why you not hab a rescue? De people was quite ready."

"It would have been useless," said Jack, sadly; "and I have yet hope that justice will be done me. Let them send out to my island for witnesses, and I will stand by the laws of my country. If not, then I will—do what I can."

"It all ober," murmured Peter; "'specially as Misser Scarborough gone. Where am he?"

"Dead, perhaps," said Jack, sorrowfully. "My poor uncle, I have been your ruin? But I did my duty, and that will cheer me when death is upon me!"

"Silence in the court!" cried an usher, and the court, now crowded in every available space, became hushed in a moment.

A full report of the proceedings is not needed here, especially as they lasted several days, with intervening days of remand; but we may state that the main evidence was this—

First, then, the identity of Jack and his men was proved.

Then came evidence as to the fitting up the "Swallow," and the secret way the guns were got on board.

Next, Jack's firing upon the "War

Eagle" was proved by a friend of Captain Cursly, who happened to be on board.

Then Captain Rowley and Lieutenant Anson gave an account of the finding our hero on board the "Singapore," and the owners of the vessel brought in the list of passengers and cargo, which had left Bombay with that ill-fated vessel.

So black was the evidence, that the majority of those who had cheered our hero turned once more against him, and the red-nosed man repented himself again, and went about like a roaring lion, bellowing against all pirates, and our hero in particular.

The depositions being complete, John Scarborough, *alias* Happy Jack, and all those who had been arrested with him, were committed for trial, and conveyed away to prison.

CHAPTER XLVII.

AN OLD FACE.

OUR hero, being the principal malcontent—the head and front of the offending party—was honoured with a cell for his own use, a favour he could have dispensed with, as solitude, anything but desirable under the best circumstances, was doubly trying to one in his unfortunate position.

Next to him were our three dark friends —Peter, Hannibal, and Pitchpot—who sang songs of their own composing, after the manner of niggers all the world over, to cheer him up.

The men were all put into a sort of ward.

The songs of the niggers, however comforting, were not strictly poetical, and the rhyme and rhythm might have been better; but what they lacked in composition they made up in good feeling.

The following specimen will suffice to give a notion of the rest:—

"Massa Jack,
We soon go back
To de isle upon de open sea,
And lib for eber by dat sweet, lubly riber,
Which run about among de tree.
So cheer up, Massa Jack,
And den we soon go back.
Golly! golly! golly! we soon go back."

Whenever the song finished, Jack invariably tapped the wall in acknowledgment of the kindly sentences expressed, which made Peter bellow like a bull, and

Hannibal and Pitchpot utilised the collars of their shirts to wipe away their tears.

One day, just as a song ended, the gaoler unlocked the door of Jack's cell, and throwing it open, briefly announced—

"Visitors!"

With a sudden bounding of his pulse, Jack stood up, and faced two men in naval uniform. At the first glance they seemed to be strangers to him, but in a moment more he recognised them; one was Captain Rowley, and the other—surely not his bitter foe?

Yes; it was the author and the cause of Jack's wandering life, and, by that means, the cause of his present imprisonment. It was Captain Cursly.

"You are surprised to see me," he said, smiling in his own sardonic way.

"I am surprised," replied Jack, briefly.

"And pleased?"

"For your own sake I am not sorry," replied Jack; "for mine I have no feeling whatever; your being alive or dead can make no difference to me."

"You will find that it does," replied Captain Cursly. "I shall appear against you at the trial."

"No doubt, if you can be of service to the prosecution," said Jack, coolly; "I am not surprised."

"And yet he is disposed to be a friend to you," put in Captain Rowley, "on conditions, of course."

"And what are those conditions?" asked Jack.

"That you retract the whole story you have circulated about me," said Captain Cursly.

"What is that story?"

"That I refused to fight with the 'War Eagle,' and gave in to a pirate without one effort to save her."

"I'll tell the story as it was told to me," said Jack, calmly.

"The story is a villainous concoction of your own," said Captain Cursly; "you know it is."

"*You* know it is not," returned Jack.

"Come, come," said Captain Rowley, "let us have no holding out if the thing can be done. You are in a bad way, Scarborough, and you will not save yourself by throwing mud at an old and respected officer of the service."

"That he is an old officer I admit," said Jack, "that he is a respected one I emphatically deny. What is your story?"

"The 'War Eagle' was blown up by a red-hot shot from the enemy," replied Captain Cursly. "I alone was picked up by the pirate, and, for some reason or the other, my life was spared. A week later, we fell in with the 'Dreadnaught,' who sank the pirate, saved my life, and strung up every villain on board."

"At your suggestion, I know," said Jack, contemptuously. "I can see it in your face. You feared even their evidence against you, and came home with a lie upon your lips to find me here with the truth."

"It is false, I say," said Captain Cursly.

"If your story is true, what have you to fear?" said Jack. "Your word will be taken against mine, and I shall die, and after that—look out for a great home-coming of men who shall bear me out."

"What men?"

"Charley Granby and several of your crew. You may turn pale, but they will come, and may be even near us now. Look at him, Captain Rowley. Is that man a pitiful coward or not?"

"Rowley," said Captain Cursly, "I will stay no longer to reason with this scoundrel. Let him swing."

"Stay a moment," said Captain Rowley. "Scarborough."

Jack bowed.

"Would you, upon oath, verify this statement?"

"Yes," replied our hero; "and permit me to suggest one thing in favour of my truthfulness. How could I tell that Granby was on board the 'War Eagle,' unless I met him? She was not commissioned until long after I had left the country."

"True," said Captain Rowley, thoughtfully. "That is something in your favour."

"But not much," said Captain Cursly, angrily. "He could have obtained that information from any of our vessels in foreign ports."

"Excuse me," said Jack, "but such a meeting I have studiously avoided."

"For very good reasons," sneered the captain. "You may also have learnt it from a merchantman."

"Merchantmen, as a rule, know nothing of the navy."

"It matters not to me what merchantmen may know," retorted Captain Cursly, very red and very angry; "I only know that you are a base liar."

"I deny it," said Jack.

"I have nothing more to say to you," said our hero's enemy, turning upon his heel. "I leave you to your fate. Whatever befalls you will be upon your own head."

"I am content," said Jack; and the two

officers left the cell, Captain Rowley very quiet and thoughtful.

Outside the prison, the two officers paused, and Captain Rowley seemed in doubt as to which way he should go.

"The fellow is very obstinate," said Captain Cursly, affecting an air of indifference. "I had a hope of being of some service to him."

"Captain Cursly," said the other, stiffly, "there is something in the story of this unhappy youth which you have failed to clear up entirely to my satisfaction. If you are wrongfully accused, I have done you a great wrong; but until the question is settled I should prefer meeting you as a stranger."

"So," muttered Captain Cursly, watching the retreating figure of his brother officer, "the same ill-luck sticks to me. That beggar in prison, and charged with piracy, is believed before I am, still holding the rank of an officer in the service, and with every right to be treated as a gentleman. After that young hound has swung, I will call you to account for this, Captain Rowley. "Curse you!"

A bitter black look settled upon his brow, and as he walked down the street he cut but a poor figure in comparison to that youth who sat in his cell and awaited his coming fate with an unruffled face.

CHAPTER XLVIII.

ON THE ISLAND.

IT requires a bold man to face the blowing up of a magazine, and the prospect of immediate and unexpected death, will raise a qualm in the stoutest heart.

It was, therefore, no wonder that, when Tom Warren uttered his threat, the officer, and some of his men, rushed to the side with the idea of "skedaddling."

Tom Warren laughed, and stepped again upon the deck.

"Where is the coward now?" he asked.

The officer smiled, and held out his hand.

"Forgive me," he said. "I did not understand you."

"With all my heart," replied Tom Warren.

And in a moment they were friends.

"You need fear no violence from my men," said Tom. "They follow their leader implicitly."

"Just like our gallant tars," said the

Chorus :—"Massa Jack, we soon go back
To de isle upon de open sea," etc.

other. "By the way, we have not introduced ourselves. My name is Barnham, and I am second lieutenant of the 'Jupiter.'"

"I am Tom Warren, late midshipman on board the 'Thunderer,' now first lieutenant of the 'Swallow.'"

"A neat little craft," returned Barnham. "You must have had some fun in her?"

"Rather! You can see the vessels around you—pirate crafts, every one."

"We have been strangely misled at home about you," said Lieutenant Barnham. "The papers have been full of accounts of the 'Swallow' plundering here and there, and murdering everywhere."

"All lies!" said Tom.

"I can see it is now. Will you come on board with me? I must introduce you to Captain Marston, one of the old school, but a very good fellow. I shall leave a few of my men in charge, as a matter of form."

"Very good."

"Who is this weather-beaten old fellow?"

"Jim Swaby— a splendid old salt. Here, Swaby, let me introduce you to Mr. Barnham."

"I hope your honour is well?" said Jim, with a scrape and a bow.

"Quite well," was the reply. "Mr. Warren, if you are ready, we will return to the 'Jupiter.'"

A quarter of an hour more brought them to that vessel, and Tom was introduced to Captain Marston, and several other officers, fine-looking men every one.

Captain Marston was one of the old school, and a good disciplinarian. He had been a cabin boy in his youth, and by pluck and daring had worked his way into his present position. In his time, there was plenty of work, and a chance for a man to distinguish himself; very different were those days to our own, when ironclads are masters of the deep, and men fight on scientific principles, with a good two miles of water between them.

The hand-to-hand fighting is almost over, and more's the pity, we say, if we must have fighting at all.

Barnham told briefly the story of the "Swallow's" doings, and it was a pleasure to see the old man's face light up with a glow of satisfaction. Noble and daring deeds are always agreeable to noble and daring men.

He went to the creek in person, and examined the prizes. Their rigs and fittings left no cause for doubt, and he declared himself ready to go to England, to clear our hero's reputation, as far as he could, of the vile inputations against him.

"I shall not take the craft," he said, "for I cannot spare the men, and you and young Granby must come with me. By the way how came he here?"

The story of the "War Eagle" was told, and the indignation of the old salt was a sight to see and wonder at.

"I always knew that Cursly was a bit of a white feather," he said. "I served with him in the 'Orion,' but I never dreamt that he was such a cur as this."

"It will be rather awkward my going away," said Jim, "in case Scarborough should arrive."

"You can leave Swaby and a few of the men here with an account of our coming," said Captain Marston; "but, between you and me, I fear something has happened to the brave lad."

"Such is my opinion," said Tom, sorrowfully. "What would happen to him if he were captured?"

"All depends upon the man who nabs him," replied Captain Marston. "Some would string him up off hand, to save trouble, and some might take him home to be tried."

"Heaven forbid that either should be the case. I think I had better go home with you."

"And those belonging to the 'War Eagle' for evidence."

Jim Swaby and a dozen men were told off to remain on the island, and the rest were shipped on board the "Jupiter" and told off to different messes.

"If I reach England in safety," said Tom Warren, "I will return to you, Swaby; but if Jack turns up, let him set sail at once. Here is a packet containing the depositions of the 'War Eagle' men, signed by Captain Marston. It may be of service to him, in case we are lost, by the way."

"We won't be lost on the way, sir," said Jim, confidently.

"Why not?"

"Because there's a look about you all that speaks of good luck. What a joyful thing it will be, Mr. Warren, if our cap'n clears himself."

"I should think so; and now, good-bye, Jim. Is there anything more that I can do for you?"

"Nothing, sir, 'cept another shake of the fist, for next to Happy Jack, I like you better than any other living creature in the world. Adoo, Mr. Warren, and good luck to you.

"Good-bye, Jim."

And so they parted.

The "Jupiter" spread its sails, and, with a fair wind, left the island behind her. Charley Granby and Tom Warren leant over her sides, and watched the receding land until it looked like mist in the horizon.

"It's a lovely spot," said Charley, sighing, "and a pity to leave it."

"Yes, it is lovely," replied Tom, "and full of dear memories to me. We may return to it again."

"If Jack gets clear, I should like for him to come and settle down upon it," said Charley; "we would make him king."

"Then we should want a queen," returned Tom, smiling; "and you and I can bring subjects, and dutiful followers of his majesty would be bound to have wives also, and then the men would follow us in the same tack, and then what a precious rookery this would shortly be."

"Yes," said Charley, "and no baby-linen."

"No boot and shoe-shops."

"No carpenters, no builders; and when our own clothes were worn out, where should we go for tailors?"

"The sail-makers could make them."

"Who would weave the cloth?"

"Ah, I see," said Charley, sighing again, "it won't work. No; after all, civilisation has a few advantages."

Charley had been told off to the midshipmen's mess, and a very fine reception the youngsters gave him.

But for the allowance of drink being limited, I am afraid that they would have made a night of it.

As it was, they were merry enough, and had to be cautioned twice by the first lieutenant before they would turn into their hammocks, and even then there was so much laughter and noise going forward that the general law and order of the "Jupiter" was quite scandalised.

In a few days they sighted the Cape, where, as usual, rough weather was going on; but they rounded it safely, and bore up towards home.

"In two months," said Tom, we shall be home. It seems a long time. What may not happen in two months!"

He had one instance given him of what a day may bring forth, by a dead calm on the morrow, and towards evening a dense fog settled upon the ship.

It was so thick that they could not see half a dozen feet before their noses, and the men went groping about the vessel like players of the exciting game of blindman's buff with this difference that they were all blind men.

To remain still in the deep ocean is an impossibility.

If there is no wind, there are always the currents, and the "Jupiter" was undoubtedly rapidly shifting.

Captain Marston was continually on deck, and the lead was constansly heaved.

For a long time there was no soundings, and for ten whole days the "Jupiter" drifted on, and the fog clung to her like a garment.

Then came a finding of the bottom.

"Seven fathoms five!" sung out the captain.

"Let go the bow anchor!" sang out the man.

Too late that cry, and the next moment the "Jupiter" struck upon a rock.

All was confusion.

A heavy swell raised the ship for a and then she struck again.

The fog, as if delighting in the calamity, closed more heavily around them, and the confused officers and seamen groped about in despair.

"To the boats!" was the cry.

The "Jupiter" lifted again, and struck so heavily that everything on board was shaken like nuts in a bag.

"Lost!" cried fifty voices.

The men felt about for the boats, and in endeavouring to get into them, several fell overboard.

Their despairing cries, muffled by the mist, rang upon the ears of the listeners, like a death knell.

"Where are we?" cried a voice.

"Steady men, there!" sang out Captain Marston. "Be quiet, and all will be well. The coast may not be far away, and this fog may not last."

Again the vessel upheaved, and with a fearful crash fell once more upon the rocks.

An ominous sound fell upon the seamen's ears.

She was parting amidships.

Still discipline was, in a great manner, maintained.

The men, such as had retained their wits knew that their safety lay in obedience to orders, and they stood mutely at their posts, prepared to obey the word of command; but also ready to meet death should it come.

Tom Warren and Charley Granby wei

side by side on the poop, and close to them was Lieutenant Barnham.

They could just see each other, like dim shadows.

"Can you swim, Charley?" asked Tom.

"Like a leaden plummet," replied Charley. "I shall find the bottom as well as the best man amongst you."

"Poor boy!" said Tom.

"I like that notion," said Charley, "you are a very aged party to do the parental."

"How well you bear it, Charley; but this light-heartedness is assumed."

There was a pause.

"I do not fear to die myself," said Charley, breaking the stillness; but I am sure they will miss me at home."

"Have you many friends?"

"A mother, and a brother and sister. Poor Harry! I know how he will grieve."

"Is he younger than you, Charley?"

"Yes; quite a little fellow. I promised to take him home a lot of shells and a parrot, and I know he is looking for me every day. If you escape, Tom, will you do me a favour?"

"Go to them—my house is at Chislehurst, in Kent; everybody there knows my mother; go to her, and say that I died as bravely as my father did. Will you do that?"

"I will," replied Tom, taking his arm; "but trust me, I shall not leave you. We will sink or swim together. When the breakup comes, keep quiet."

"I will, never fear, Tom. There is not much funk in the Granby family."

"Now she heaves again," Charley. Are you there, Barnham?"

"I am here," said the lieutenant, and the "Jupiter" came down with a noise like the fall of a huge building—and parted.

CHAPTER XLIX.

JACK'S RESOLVE.

THE authorities who rule our prisons are well acquainted with one great fact, and that is, the prisoners *must* have a little air and exercise, if they are to live, and attached to every prison house there is a dreary space of ground known as a prison yard.

This spot is invariably the most uninviting place, except other prison yards, of course, under the sun. The prison on one side, and high brick walls upon the other, without one atom of green to relieve it, makes a hideous spectacle to the prisoners who come out for the benefit of their health.

Not a shrub, not a tree, not even a blade of grass relieves the dull blank, and naught but the prison, and the wall, except a patch of sky, can be seen.

Oh! how many a weary heart has looked up, on a fine summer's day, at the azure space, across which the white, fleecy clouds are sailing, and have thanked God that no ingenuity of man could *shut that out* and yet give air!

How many a wan face, pinched by prison fare, and goaded to madness and despair be the solitude of the gaol, have hailed that strip of Heaven with a cry of joy!

Surely man was made for the light, and surely our Creator never designed us to be shut out from the sight of the sweet infinite space; but if man will sin, he must suffer by the strong arm of the law; but how many an innocent man has languished behind stone walls, and worked out a sentence for the crime of another man!

The prisoners in the place where Jack was confined were brought out in bodies, and having been ranged in a row about six feet apart, were left moving round and round in a silent, solemn procession.

There were men of all classes there, from the boy who had stolen an apple to the wretch who had brutally beaten the woman who gave him birth, and it was not difficult to tell who were the old offenders and who were the new.

For several days, Jack saw nothing of his friends, but on about the sixth, Peter, Hannibal, and Pitchpot were brought out with him.

Peter got next to his master, and as they tramped round and round endeavoured to get a word with him.

"Oh, Massa Jack! me hope you bear up," he whispered.

"Silence, there!" roared one of the officers. "Who is talking?"

The prisoners went round once more, and then Jack whispered back—

"I bear up well. You do the same."

"Massa Jack, dey tell you to be tried alone."

"So I have heard, Peter; but I do not intend to be tried at all."

"How dat, Massa Jack?"

"I have got a friend."

"A friend, Massa Jack?"

"Yes—a file!"

"Who is talking there?" cried another

of the officers, staring indignantly at a fat prisoner, who had been walking as quietly as the "Dumb Man of Manchester." "If you don't shut up, I'll stop your meat!"

"Indeed, sir, I haven't spoken," said the man, humbly.

"You are speaking now, and it is against the rules. Hold your tongue, and close a little up, will you?"

Another round, and Peter took advantage of an opportunity to get in a question.

"How got you him, Massa Jack?"

"The warder brought me a pie, which he said was sent by a friend. I found it in it."

"Who dat friend?"

"I don't know for certain, but I suspect it was Captain Rowley."

"He no friend to you, Massa Jack, and he call us a set ob 'fernal, cussed, bandy-legged niggers."

"I am sure he is a friend to me. I saw him again, alone, the other day, and he told me that he was sorry the evidence was against me, but that he would do all he could to help me."

"Hooroar for Cap'n Rowley!" roared Peter, suddenly, forgetting where he was.

"Oh! it's you, is it?" said the officer, pouncing upon him. "Come out of the ranks, will you?"

"Wurra for?" demanded Peter.

"Talking is against the rules."

"Wurra for you talk, den?" demanded Peter.

"Come out of the rank, will you?" said the officer, jerking him forward by the collar.

Peter muttered something like an oath, but Jack only said "Peter," and he was as quiet as a lamb.

Hannibal now closed up, and the circle went round with Peter in the centre for a pivot. Unmoved by the fate of his brother, Hannibal put in a word.

"Massa Jack—Massa Jack!"

"Yes, Hannibal."

"Will dey not hang Hannibal for you."

"No, Hannibal, thank you—I would not have it if it could be done."

"Shall I knock de officers down, and gib you a back ober the wall? Peter on me, and you on Peter, would do him."

"No, Hannibal—it could not be carried out."

"Golly! I t'ink it could, Massa Jack."

"There's some talking, somewhere," said the warder, looking savagely about him. He was a red-headed man, with a very irritating dyspepsia, and trifles annoyed him acutely. "Who is it?"

"Massa Jack!" whispered Hannibal.

"Oh, it's you, is it?" said the warder, and in a twinkling, Hannibal joined his brother.

"If either of you open your mouths," said the warder, "I will send you to your cell."

Pitchpot was now the next to Jack, and, with a prudence characteristic of the nigger tribe, he soon got himself into the same boat with them. Not being of a very conversational turn, he asked Jack the somewhat unnecessary question "if he did not tink it a berry fine day?"

Before getting an answer, the warder, with a deep oath, had him out, and Pitchpot, having strenuously denied that he had uttered a word, was removed to the cell, where, in about half-an-hour, Peter and Hannibal joined him.

"It berry strange ting in some niggers," said Peter, "dat dey allis make asses ob demselves."

"Dat berry true," replied Pitchpot, "and de biggest ass get de best luck."

The meaning of this retort did not run very clear, but Peter took it as a personal affront, and asked Pitchpot what he meant.

Pitchpot, we know, was rather an evasive youth, and he declined to furnish any meaning to his observation.

"If you want de meaning," he said, "take one ob your own."

"Ob all de——" began Peter.

"Be quiet, can't you, you two cusses?" growled Hannibal. "Tell Pitchpot what Massa Jack whisper when him go by."

"Aye, tell me dat," said Pitchpot. "Was it anyting 'bout me?"

"'Bout you!" replied Peter, scornfully, curling his lip tight up under his nose. "Ob course not. Who the debil take trouble to whisper 'bout you?"

"Massa Jack whisper sumfin."

"He whisper dis—'Look out for me dis night.'"

"Ah! him going to knock agin de wall."

"What a chump ob a head you got!" said Peter. "Put that black lump ob stuff on de top your shoulders closer, and listen. *Massa Jack got a file!*"

"Oh!"

"You know wurra dat for?"

Pitchpot looked very sagacious, but said nothing.

"You know wurra dat for?" repeated Peter.

"To stab de warder wif," said Pitchpot.

"Dat Pitchpot an ass," said Peter, turning away. "Sit in dat corner, and not open your mouf until dark; den, tear, your blanket and rug into lilly strips."

"Dat a good notion," said Pitchpot. "Wurra dis chile to sleep in?"

"You not sleep here to-night!" returned Peter, in a thrilling whisper. "You understand *dat?*"

"Massa Jack comin' through de wall?" said Pitchpot.

"No!" growled Peter; "but when him tap at de window, we take de glass out, and help him to file de bars. Hannibal scrape out be putty ob dat bit ob glass, so dat we be quite ready for Massa Jack."

CHAPTER L.

GONE.

DARKNESS fell upon the prisoners. The day warders went to their homes, and the night warders came upon duty.

The terrible treadmill stopped, and the weary convicts who had been "grinding the air" all day were ushered into their cells.

The governor went his last round, sentinels were posted, and the stillness of night reigned upon that prison-house.

Most of the prisoners, especially the old hands, rolled themselves in their blankets, and endeavoured to lose consciousness in sleep. But some, and these were the new arrivals, sat with bent heads, and watered the floor of their cells with tears of agony and repentance.

In two cells only there was unwonted activity—one occupied by Happy Jack, and the other by his negro friends.

Jack was busy upon the bars with a file, stopping now and then to grease it with a bit of fat which had been sent in the pie, to steady the sound.

Ten minutes, and the first bar was cut through.

There were two upper, two lower, and two on either side to be operated upon—eight in all.

Eight times ten are eighty.

One hundred and twenty minutes before all could be done.

Surely an age to a man who is making an effort for his life!

The great consideration which induced our hero to make an attempt to escape was, that he feared he might not have time to clear himself before justice would take its course—that is, before he would be hanged unjustly.

Coming home, he had relied upon his uncle for help, but that help had failed, and thrown upon his own resources, escape seemed to be hopeless, except in the way he was endeavouring to carry it out.

The second bar cut through, he paused and rested a moment.

It was tiring work, for he had nothing better than his drinking tin to stand upon, and this only gave him hold for one foot.

A low scraping sound from the other side told him that his friends were on the watch.

"Coming, Peter," whispered Jack to himself. "Be patient, old boy, and I shall be with you."

Slowly and steadily, but surely, the file did its work, and the bars lay upon the floor of his cell. First thrusting his bed-linen through, already torn into strips, Jack followed, and stood in the prison yard.

It was a cloudy night, and the moon was hidden. This Jack could not but regard as a fortunate circumstance, for although no warder passed them, it was possible that some of them might be looking from the windows.

The next moment, the frame quietly drawn out, and Peter the Great whispered—

"All right, Massa Jack."

"All right, Peter. Is your bedding ready?"

"Quite ready, Massa Jack."

"Thrust it through, and go on with the filing while I make the rope," said Jack. "Work steadily, or you will be discovered."

Peter passed through his bedding, a considerable quantity now that it was torn, and Jack handed in the file.

"Use the coarse he said. "It works quicker, and here is some fat. Grease it well."

"All right, Massa Jack."

Our hero sat upon the ground, and carefully feeling through every bit of torn bedding, proceeded to twist and knot it into a rope.

It was a task which required much care, and to one less composed than Jack was, would have been simply impossible; but he went on steadily, accompanied by the low and almost inaudible groaning of the file.

The negroes took the work turn and turn about, and being driven to the same use of their drinking vessel to stand upon, it was only natural to them that one of them should fall off.

Pitchpot executed this feat, and the crash he made very nearly spoiled all, and led to a discovery. Jack sprang to his feet and listened, but there was no alarm, probably owing to the thickness of the cell door, and contenting himself with a word of warning to be more cautious, he resumed his work.

"If you're not an ass," growled Peter, in an impressive whisper, "den I'm a ripperpotermy. Get out ob de way."

"It only putting de pan right again," muttered Pitchpot.

"Take down de pot, and kneel dere—me stand upon your ugly back."

Pitchpot demurred a little to this, but both Hannibal and Peter insisted upon it, and he knelt down.

Peter got upon his back, and Pitchpot immediately collapsed, and lay flat upon his stomach. Peter rolled over, and carried Hannibal with him.

"If you fellows are not quiet," said Jack, addressing them through the window, in a low tone, "you will ruin all."

"It dat jammed Pitchpot," said Peter.

"My hands slip on de cold stone floor," pleaded Pitchpot. "Massa Peter berry heaby, too."

"Pass me out the file," said Jack.

It was handed to him, and in a few minutes he completed the severing of the iron bars.

Then the trio inside came forth, Peter first, Hannibal second, and Pitchpot—who, discreetful, came out head first, and dropped upon it—last.

"The rope is completed," said Jack; "now see if you three can walk quietly for once."

"Yes, Massa Jack."

"I have only one regret now," said Jack, "and that is, my other poor fellows are not with me. I have no idea where they are. Have you seen them at any time?"

"No, Massa Jack."

"I have the assurance of Captain Rowley that they will only be tried for desertion, and at the most they will only be confined till I come to clear them. Find me a stone, a large one, Hannibal.

"Here one, Massa Jack."

"Help me to tie it up in the end of the rope. That's it One turn more. Now, who is the strongest?"

"Me," said Peter.

"Me," said Hannibal.

"Dis child," put in Pitchpot.

"You try first," said Jack to Hannibal; "throw it over the wall, there are spikes upon the top, and the rope will catch."

Hannibal took the stone and cast deftly over the wall. It caught.

Jack tried it—hard and fast.

"Now, Peter, up you go," he said.

"No, Massa Jack, you first."

"I come last, Lose no time, but get away."

It was no time to argue the point, so Peter went up hand over hand, and took a seat upon the wall, holding on by the spikes.

In two minutes all were there, and at that moment the moon peeped forth and shone full upon them.

"Lie flat for your lives!" whispered Jack.

Below there was a fort, with a sentinel pacing to and fro with a bayonet fixed. Beyond the fort was the beach and the sea.

"Hush!" whispered Jack, "I hear a marching."

A body of soldiers appeared round a bastion, and a sergeant called a halt. The sentinel saluted and took a place in the rear. Another man went into his place, and the guard passed on.

"Thank Heaven!" murmured Jack; "I was afraid that we had been missed, and they were in search of us."

"But how we to get down, Massa Jack," whispered Peter, "wif dat chap movin', bust him?"

"Let me be for a moment; I must think," said Jack.

He lay quite still for a moment, and then his plans were made.

"Hawl up the rope," he said, "and drop it upon the other side; but, gently, for your lives. Steady, now! Pitchpot, you be quiet—you will only make a mess of it!"

———

CHAPTER LI.

MR. GRUBBIN'S YACHT.

THE sentinel paced to and fro, humming a song, and occasionally looking up at the moon, across which banks of cloud were flying, obscuring her light for brief instants; and, taking advantage of these periods of darkness, Jack hauled up the rope, and lightly dropped it upon the other side.

Then he paused for a moment, and rested to get breath and strength for the effort he was about to make.

From his elevated position, he had a

fine view of the scene beyond—the Isle of Wight, with the lamps of Cowes and Ryde glistening like glow-worms, and the thousand and one vessels, great and small, lying idly in the harbour, or rocking easily upon the water.

"Oh, for one of those good ships," he murmured, "to carry me away from here! But I must not waste time in wishing. Here comes a cloud that will give me a good five minutes for my work."

The cloud touched the moon, and whispering to the others to lie perfectly still until he gave the word, he slid down like a shadow, and touched the earth without the slightest sound.

"Hey, for the life of a soldier!" hummed the soldier. "Aye! hey, for the life of a soldier. I wish the fool who wrote that song was carrying a musket here to-night. He would pitch a different tune."

He paused, and looked out upon the beach for an instant, then resumed his march, humming as before

Close behind him came Jack, stealthily as an Indian upon the war trail.

"Four hours of this precious work," muttered the soldier. "What an ass I was to think my life in the fields a miserable one! I had my freedom there, and the lark's song gave me a bit of cheer whenever I was down. Oh, for one hour by the rabbit warren, with a few snares in my hand! Ah! Help!"

A handkerchief was drawn tightly over his mouth, and he was jerked to the ground, too much astonished to offer any great resistance.

"Silence!" whispered Jack. "You will not be harmed! Resist, and your life will be forfeited."

"Prisoners escaping!" muttered the soldier. "Well, let them go, poor devils. All right, mate."

"Silence, I say!" said Jack.

The man touched his hand, and pressed it kindly, as a signal that he wished to be their friend.

Jack thought he might trust him, and pulled off the handkerchief, at the same time removing his musket.

"All right, whoever you are," said the soldier. "I am not afraid of you, but I wish to see no poor devil shut up in that place. You may go. What's your lay?"

"What have I been up to?"

"Yes."

"I am John Scarborough," replied Jack. "I am accused of piracy, and I have made my escape."

"Bravo! Well done!" said the soldier.

"Ah! I remember you, Master John. I was a labourer on Mr. Scarborough's estate, but I thought my life too hard. Do you remember me, sir—Dan Bunting?"

"I should think I do," said Jack. "We have had some fun together by the rabbit warren. You were the best hand with a snare I ever knew."

"Don't stop to talk to me, Master John, but get away," said Dan.

"I have three friends with me. All right, up there!"

Down came Peter and Hannibal, with Pitchpot last, who was in such a violent hurry that he dropped upon Peter's head, and nearly drove his neck into his shoulders.

Peter struck at him, but he might as well have aimed at a sprite.

The blow fell harmless, but Pitchpot chuckled.

"It's no use talking to them," muttered Jack, "niggers are as irrepressible as kittens. Come, boys, we must be off; but what must we do with you, Bunting? That rope will get you into trouble."

"Of course it will; but not much if you gag and bind me," replied the sentinel.

"Will you come with us?"

"A soldier deserting his post is liable to be shot."

"I forgot. Perhaps it will be better for you to remain here.

"Particularly as I am able to put them on the wrong track," grinned Bunting.

"True—a happy thought. Hannibal, break off about twelve feet of the rope."

Hannibal, with a sudden jerk, brought down about half of it, and with this they bound and gagged the friendly sentinel.

"That's better! Tear open your coat, as if we had had a struggle!" said Jack. "There it is, and now you look as if you had been terribly mauled. And now good-bye, and if ever I return to England alive and in health, I shall not forget you."

They all shook hands with Dan Bunting, and dropping over the fort, which was only an earthwork, and not very high, with a dry ditch below, and with their eyes and ears open, walked down the beach.

"Anything in the form of a boat will suit us!" said Jack.

"What do you intend to do, Massa Jack?" asked Hannibal.

"To pull out to sea and trust to being picked up by some vessel outward bound. Any vessel will do—the further it is going the better, but France will be better than nothing."

"I t'ink I see a boat dere!" said Peter.

"Where?"

"Down by de pier."

"Yes, you are right. Now, Heaven send us a pair of oars."

In the boat they found not only one, but two pairs of those needful accessories, and, after a careful look round, they quickly launched her and pulled out.

Being beyond the harbour, they ran no risk of being hailed, for pleasure boats were no uncommon sight about that part, and quite at his ease, Jack steered out, with Hannibal and Peter pulling.

"A favourable tide will carry us, in a couple of hours, through the Needles," said our hero. "Steady, Peter, and don't pump yourself out. We may have a deal of work before us."

"Lights movin' about de fort," said Hannibal.

Jack turned, and beheld several lanterns dancing about like will-o'-the-wisps, and at the same moment the roll of a drum was heard.

"Yes," he said, "we are missing; and Dan, I hope, will prove a friend. Pull now, for a few minutes, as hard as you like. Keep your eyes upon the beach, and see if there is anything moving there."

"Beach quiet," reported Hannibal, after a pause; "but light goin' towards de town."

"Bunting is true," said Jack. "Bunting has put them upon the wrong scent. I shall not forget him. Steady; ease off a bit. What is this?"

A small yacht, with everything on board quiet as the night itself. A light was burning at the masthead, to warn other vessels from running her down.

A thought occurred to Jack.

Suppose there is nobody on board, is there not enough of us to manage her?

"Pull close up here, boys, for a moment."

The boat swung under her bows, and Jack, seizing an overhanging rope, climbed on board. The deck was quite clear, but a light was burning in the cabin, and shining through a skylight in the deck.

Our hero crept up, and peeped through it. A table, spread with the remnants of a dinner, was in the centre, and, at the head, in an easy-chair, sat a comfortable-looking man of about fifty years of age, sleeping. He was the sole occupant of the cabin.

"Is he alone?" thought Jack. "If so, our course is easy enough."

He went forward to a hatchway and listened. The sound of deep sleepers fell upon his ears.

"That is the crew," he thought; "they can be battened down."

He went to the bows, and whispered to the others to come up.

Three dark figures were by his side in a moment, and a few words sufficed to have the hatches down.

Then steadily they descended to the cabin, with the object of quietly securing the sleeper in the chair: but as Jack entered, he turned uneasily and looked up.

His first look was of sleepy indifference: his second a stare of astonishment and surprise.

"Silence," said Jack, "and give in to us quietly."

"And pray who are you?" asked the gentleman.

"Escaped prisoners! and we want your yacht to take us down Channel."

"A cool request, certainly," replied the other, in no way disturbed. "But it can't be done."

"It must be."

"It can't. My dear wife—whom Heaven long preserve and keep in cheerful nerve—is coming on board to-morrow to go upon a little trip with me."

"She will have to wait your return, I assure you."

"Mrs. Grubbins is not the woman to wait, I assure you," replied Mr. Grubbins—for that was the gentleman's name. "I put it to her myself only to-day, and urged her to wait for a more propitious season; but she said, 'No, Grubbins! if you cannot take me, you shall not go.' I love my wife dearly," added Mr. Grubbins, with a sigh; "but there are times when a man needs repose from connubial bliss."

"Take that rest now," said Jack, smiling: for he saw that he had an easy man to deal with. "Do a generous action, and save four innocent men from injustice."

"I have suffered injustice myself," returned Mr. Grubbins, toying thoughtfully with a desert-knife, "and I can sympathise with a man in the same strait. Who are you, and what is your case?"

"My name is John Scarborough, and I am supposed to be a pirate."

"Bless me! I ought to have known it by those grinning niggers behind you. You a pirate? Lord, it was only this morning that I was saying to Halliday at the Club—Do you know Halliday?"

"I have not that pleasure"

"Halliday is a very good fellow, and perhaps I may have the pleasure of introducing you some day. Halliday put the case in this way—'Young Scarborough,' he said, 'is no doubt a gentleman, and guilty of the little heroism he is accused of; but, hang it; he is a gentleman, and they ought to let him off.' That was Halliday's cue; but I said to him. 'The fellow is not only a gentleman, but innocent.'"

"Thank you for your good opinion," said Jack, gratefully.

"Who can doubt, particularly when one sees you!" said Mr. Grubbins. "I am a gentleman, although my name *is* Grubbins, and being a gentleman, I am not ashamed of it."

"Time flies—excuse me," hinted Jack.

"Of course it does," said the owner of the yacht, springing to his feet. "Where are my fellows."

"Battened down."

"The rascals. As soon as they saw me comfortably asleep, they went to their hammocks. I'll rouse them up. You need not fear me. I shall not betray you."

"I do not fear you," replied Jack. "We will come up with you, and raise the hatches."

Hannibal raised them, and Mr. Grubbins descended, and his voice was soon heard rating his men below.

"Confound you, you lazy lubbers! Come up and hoist anchor, will you?"

"Is it morning, sir?" asked one of the men.

"What's that to you whether it is morning or night? I want the 'Esmeralda' to go down Channel at once."

He returned upon deck, followed by half a dozen men, who stared at the newcomers as if they had suddenly come upon visitants from the other world.

"Never you mind who they are," said their master, before the question was asked. "You do your duty. Who went ashore to-night with the boat?"

"Tomkins and Green, sir," replied one of the men.

"The two laziest of the scoundrels I am afflicted with," said Grubbins. "Let them stop there, and settle with Mrs. Grubbins. Up anchor. Take in that boat first. Let go the fore-sheets. Steady, there—that's it. Now she swings. I say, young Scarborough."

"Yes," said Jack.

"Did you ever see the 'Esmeralda' sail?"

"No.'

"Then you have a treat in store, for she is a real beauty—the fastest of her size hereabouts."

As most men who own a yacht generally declare the same thing with regard to their vessels, Jack was not particularly impressed with this assurance, but he affected to be very much astonished, and congratulated his host on his good fortune in possessing such a craft.

"She is a real beauty," repeated Mr. Grubbins. "How she goes! What do you think of her?"

Jack was, even in his own heart, compelled to admit that the "Esmeralda" was no common craft, and, with an enthusiasm second only to that of Mr. Grubbins, he watched the sea hissing and screaming as her bows cut throught it.

"Mrs. Grubbins dosen't like her," said Mr. Grubbins. "She likes something broader in the beam. A good old canal barge would suit her, but not me. I say, Scarborough, a word with you. If ever you come to England, you must put me right with my dear wife!"

"I will."

"Say," said Grubbins, with a wink, "that you came on board with a dozen men—all pirates, heavily armed with cutlasses and pistols, and every man Jack wearing a red cap and top boots, like the pirates in the pictures, and that you gagged me after a stout resistance."

"I will, most certainly."

"And say further," continued Mr. Grubbins, after a moment's rest, occupied in arranging more deceptions, "say that I implored of you to take my yacht, and let me return to my wife, and that, on being refused, I wept copiously."

"I will do all this, and more, as a return for your kindness," said Jack, with a look of earnest gratitude in his face.

He was inclined to laugh at Mr. Grubbins' proposal, but he understood and appreciated his stirling generosity.

"Without something in that way to support me," continued the other, "I would rather put my head into the mouth of a cannon, about to be fired, than face Mrs. Grubbins. Especially as I know that she has had a yachting-suit made for this trip, and that she has driven half her friends mad with envy by her description of a life at sea.'

"I admire her taste."

"But it is all humbug on her part," said Mr. Grubbins. "She doesn't like it, and never gets into a walking state to come on deck until it is time to go ashore again. But yachting for ladies is all the go now, you know, and she is not a woman to be behind, if she can help it. And yet she is behind now, you know. Ha! ha! That fault, however, is my own."

"Yacht ahoy!" sang out a voice below.

"Who are you?" asked Mr. Grubbins.

"Revenue boat," replied the voice.

"Are you!" said Mr. Grubbins, calmly. "A cold night for you to be pottering about the sea."

"That's nothing to you," returned the voice. "Stand by, and let us come on board."

"All right," said Mr. Grubbins.

"What would you do?" asked Jack, alarmed.

"All right," said the other. "Simmons!"

"Yes, sir."

"Up with the topsails," whispered the master, "and let her run free."

"Now, then," roared out the voice; "stand by, will you? We can't keep pulling by you all night."

"Who said you could," muttered Mr. Grubbins, "or who wants you to? Be quick, Simmons! That's it! Hallo, my Revenue friend!"

"What is it?"

"Good-night."

"Confound you—stand by!"

"We are going round the isle, and shall be back to breakfast."

A string of oaths from the Revenue officer died away in the distance, and a report, as a signal for them in shore, followed.

"We may have some ugly work at the Needles," said Mr. Grubbins, "unless we are pretty smart."

"I have no right to put this upon you," said Jack.

"My dear fellow, I have a right to protect the innocent."

"But you run the risk of getting into trouble."

"I know I do; but I rather like it. Easy, there!"

"You are a man in a thousand."

"Mrs. Grubbins says I am without a rival in the universe. She calls me the biggest brute in creation."

"That is a species of connubial joking."

"If you had a little to do with Mrs. Grubbins, you would find her no joke. Shake out every rag of canvas, Simmons, and put your head into a bucket, for I expect we shall have a shot or two pitched at us."

CHAPTER LII.

MR. GRUBBINS STANDS TO HIS POST.

"YOU must let my men help your crew," said Jack, "they are very good seamen."

"We can manage very well," replied Mr. Grubbins. "Those two fellows—Tomkins and Green—never do any work when on board, and why I keep them I don't know, unless it is because Tomkins ran away from his wife, and Green has taken a solemn oath never to marry. Both sensible men in their way."

"A hail from the shore, sir," said Simmons.

"Bother the shore!"

"And two boats coming out."

"Run straight through them, and chuck out half-a-dozen life-belts for the swimmers."

"All right, sir," said Simmons, a keen-eyed, taciturn old seaman, who would have obeyed his master even if he had told him to puff peas at a duke of royal blood—a heinous offence, as we all know.

The Needles were now hard by, and the boats named by Simmons drew nearer. As before, a voice from them hailed the yacht.

"Yacht ahoy!"

"What do you want?" roared Mr. Grubbins.

"Who are you?"

"The 'Esmeralda;' owner, Enoch Grubbins, of the Pier Club."

"Can't be the man signalled," said another voice. "I know Mr. Grubbins well, and that's his voice."

"It's a thundering shame," roared that much ill-used gentleman, "that I can't take a run round the isle at night without having a lot of you fellows about me."

"Beg pardon, sir," replied the man; "but some prisoners have escaped, and we were signalled to stop a craft."

"Then you have stopped the wrong one, Good-night."

"Good-night, sir."

"If these fellows had eyes in their heads, they would have seen that nigger peeping over the bulwarks," said Mr. Grubbins, pointing at Pitchpot; "but they haven't; and so it's all right."

Jack sent the niggers all below at once, when Pitchpot received a most unmerciful bastinadoing from his fellow-prisoners, who had been enjoying the moonlight run, and after it Peter gave him a lecture on prudence, which may be looked upon as sweetness wasted upon the desert air —Pitchpot being very unfruitful soil.

Daylight found the "Esmeralda" well down the Channel, and out of sight of land. Jack was sleeping on the deck, overcome with fatigue, and Mr. Grubbins sat by his side smoking a mighty cheroot.

"On my word," he said, "he is a handsome chap. Hang stringing up one like him. 'Hanged by the neck until you are dead,' says the judge. Pshaw! monstrous in the extreme. Grubbins, you have done well, even if you never succeed in restoring your connubial relations with Mrs. Grubbins, which would be an overwhelming misfortune. Simmons!"

"Aye, sir."

"Where are the niggers?"

"All asleep."

"Keep them below, for the present."

"Aye, aye, sir!"

"How much provisions have we on board?"

"Biscuit for three months, and hextras for about two."

"Hum! With short rations, we could make the biscuit last a good four. Eh, Simmons, a good four?"

"All depends on how short you make the rations, sir," replied Simmons, who did not hail the prospect of short commons with any exuberent delight.

"You fellows are overfed," said Mr. Grubbins; "unless I tone you down, you won't get into your Jersies."

"Then we'll get bigger ones, sir," said Simmons.

"Simmons!" said Mr. Grubbins, sternly.

"Yes, sir."

"Have the goodness to leave all jokes to me."

"Aye, aye, sir!"

"I asked you about the grub because I've got a notion in my head. You hear that, Simmons?"

"You've allers got——" began Simmons, bent upon saying something sarcastic; but remembering the admonition lately received, he stopped short, and added, "I'm glad to hear it, sir."

"Are you? You look so. Haul the mainsail a little closer to the wind, and stand by for further orders."

"Aye, aye, sir!"

A little later, Jack woke up, and Mr. Grubbins offered him a cigar.

Jack took one, and lighted it.

"Now," said Mr. Grubbins, "I've a word or two to say to you."

"Go on," said Jack, "nothing would give me more pleasure than to listen to you."

"You are kind enough to say so. You were telling me, last night, about your island home in the Pacific."

"Yes; my dear island home."

"It's a fact, I suppose?"

"Do you doubt my word."

"No; but I thought you might be dreaming. Excitement, and so on, you know, often disturbs a man."

"It is true, every word."

"Then I am going to it;" said Mr. Grubbins.

"Yes?"

"Yes. What of it?"

"But how?"

"In the 'Esmeralda.'"

"Have you any idea of the distance?"

"Pretty fair; and I know the risk; but I mean to try it! I shall be able to sit upon all the club after it."

"But you will encounter heavy seas"

"Where ships can live, the 'Esmeralda' will ride."

"You want provisions?"

"I have got enough to last us to St. Helena, and my credit is good enough there for anything I may want."

"But is not this too much for you to do for a stranger?"

"My dear Scarborough, I do it for myself; as for looking upon you as a stranger, I feel as if I had known you for years. Besides," he added, lowering his voice, "I have a little dislike to meeting Mrs. Grubbins, and the longer that interesting event is put off the better I shall like it. If ever you get married, you will understand my meaning."

"I hope to be married some day," said Jack, laughing. "But will not your wife be anxious?"

"She will, no doubt, I verily believe," returned Mr. Grubbins; "but that will be in my favour. A longer absence than usual may teach her my value. At present she holds me cheap—very cheap."

He turned away and sighed, but the next moment he was as cheerful as ever; and lighting up another cigar, declared himself to be in a perfect state of happiness.

Pitchpot, who had been appointed to the post as cook, now appeared, and announced that dinner was ready.

This was welcome news, for pure air gives us a relish for food, and the pair adjourned to the cabin, leaving the deck in charge of Simmons.

Mr. Simmons was a faithful follower of his master, but he scorned to own allegiance to any other man. He was also very particular about the company he kept, and he professed to have a hearty contempt for niggers. He looked down upon Peter the Great and Hannibal, and as they remained on deck after Jack had disappeared, he ordered them at once below.

"Wurra dat you say?" demanded Peter, every hair of his woolly head bristling with rage.

"Go down," growled Simmons; "I hate a lot of cursed niggers fossicking about."

"You am a berry great ass," growled Peter; "I berry good mind to pull your nose.

Simmons now bristled up. A nigger pull his nose! What next would a nigger think of doing?

"Pull it!" he said.

With a promptitude which left Simmons no time for reflection, Peter laid hold of his nose and pulled it until his eyes watered.

"I'm darned," cried Simmons, dashing his red cap upon the deck, and rolling up his sleeves; "come on!"

"Go on, Peter, ole boy," said Hannibal. "I hold dat hat ob yours."

Peter parted with his hat, and pulled off his coat.

Then he and Simmons faced each other.

I have no wish to depreciate our old friend Peter in any way, but I am bound to admit that he was no pugilist.

Give him a sword and pistols, and he could do his work as well as most men; but with the fist he was very much abroad —in this he was on a level with the general run of niggers.

Fortunately for Peter, the knowledge of the fistic art was almost unknown to Simmons, too.

His great and sole idea of fighting was that the left elbow ought to be kept on a level with the left eye as a defence, and the right fist used for purposes of assault.

This might not be an objectionable thing, provided your enemy pursued the same tactics; but in case he should prove to be more experienced, or pursues an equally novel but different line of attack and defence, the idea of Mr. Simmons would prove a failure.

It decidedly failed with Peter.

The pair performed several circles round about the deck, to the unlimited delight of the crew, and the admiration of Hannibal, who looked upon the display as something passing the common run, more particularly on Peter's part, who moved his arms about in such a manner as to quite confuse the one eye, which Simmon's mode of defence had left serviceable.

"Give it him, Mister Simmins!" said one of the men.

"Wait till I get into quarters with him," growled Simmons, with his right arm drawn back, and fist ready to deal confusion to the enemy.

Suddenly Peter stooped and rushed in head-first.

He caught Simmons under his line of defence, knocked every particle of breath out of his body, and shot him down the hatchway, just as Mr. Enoch Grubbins was coming up to know what all that treading was about.

Master and man rolled together in a heap, and Jack, rushing out of the cabin in alarm, promptly extricated Grubbins from under Simmons.

"This is a pretty go!" he said. "Get up, you vagabond."

Simmons gasped and made an effort to rise, but fell back like one exhausted.

"Is this a fit?" said his master. "Give me a drop of brandy, Scarborough."

Jack brought a little in a tumbler, and Simmons, having swallowed it, was able to articulate.

"Now," said Grubbins, "will you tell me what you mean by coming down the gangway head first? Speak up!"

"Had a turn up with a nigger," said Simmons, surlily.

"And he licked you?"

"With his head, sir," said Simmons. "Never once did he come forrard like a man and let me double him up."

"Of course not," said Grubbins. "Go back to your post, and take my advice, and leave that nigger alone. He is more than a match for you."

"Is he!" muttered Simmons, as he departed. "I'm busted if I don't hev another go in at him!"

The next day they sighted St. Helena, and the "Esmeralda," put in for stores sufficient to last for several months.

Simmons was too busy to have a second bout with Peter, and Peter had forgotten all about it. So peace reigned on board the yacht, although stormy times for all were not far away.

CHAPTER LIII.

TOM WARREN.

DUTY calls us back to Tom Warren and Charley Granby, both of whom we left in the midst of the surging sea.

The terrible fog which had brought

about the destruction of the "Jupiter" now rose, as if satisfied with the mischief it had done, like a curtain, and Tom could see a hundred heads bobbing about like corks in the midst of the foam.

It was not many moments ere the number grew less, for all were not strong swimmers, and the turbid waters quickly bore the weakest under.

As their despairing shrieks rang out, those who were fighting with the deep increased their efforts to reach a rockbound shore stretched out before them.

And now, as if to finish the awful work, the wind swept down upon them, and the sea, lashed into fury, hissed, and bubbled, and roared, and those who were swimming for dear life quailed.

Tom held Charley Granby by the collar, and exhorted him now and then to keep quiet and trust to his God, swam strongly and steadily, making for a gap in the line of breakers which fringed the beach, hoping to get through it and effect a landing.

Many other men turned in the same direction, but one by one they fell behind until he was alone.

It was no time to wonder and look back.

Every man for himself and God for them all, was the only thing now, and keeping his eyes steadfast before him, Tom kept on.

"All right, Charley?" he said, as they sank into the trough of a huge wave.

"I am almost exhausted," replied Charley, panting. "But why not leave me and go on? You will never save yourself and me."

"Sink or swim together," replied Tom.

A mighty wave curled over them at this moment and descended.

As it fell, they were for an instant under a huge canopy of water, and then came darkness.

Charley thought all was over, but with Tom's injunction in his mind, he kept perfectly still.

The friendly grasp did not relax, and they rose to the surface again, breathless and panting.

"You will lose your life," said Charley, as soon as he could speak.

"Sink or swim together," was all Tom replied.

The gap in the line of breakers now widened to the view, and through it they could see comparatively smooth water. Hope lent Tom Warren strength, and with a mighty effort he fought his way through it and glided into the haven.

There was, however, still some distance to go. The shore lay nearly a quarter of a mile away.

"I cannot do it," gasped Tom, "I am utterly exhausted."

"What did you see, Tom?"

"Nothing."

"You did; you are worn out, burdened with me. Let me go."

"Sink or swim together," said Tom for the third time.

"I will not have it," cried the brave middy, struggling to get free.

"Be quiet, Charley, you will only make matters worse. I will not let you go."

Now Charley kept quiet again, and Tom, with despairing eyes and fast-failing limbs, struggled another twenty yards. This was his final effort, and his arms sank to his side.

"Good-bye, Charley!" he said.

"Good-bye, Tom!" replied Charley. "God bless and help them at home."

Then they went down, and the waters for an instant closed over them. The next moment Tom was on the surface again, still holding Charley, who was ghastly pale and apparently insensible.

"Hurrah!" cried Tom.

"What is it?" asked Charley. "Am I still alive?"

"Alive, of course. I've got a foothold upon the sand."

"Oh! Tom, let us thank God for his mercy," cried the boy.

It was no time for long prayers, but a few words spoke volumes at such a time, and the two young fellows breathed their hearty thanks.

They stood up to their armpits in water, and exhausted as Tom was he had some difficulty in keeping an upright position; but the waves and current were both weak, and he held his own.

Charley could stand, too, and he insisted upon being left to himself for a time, so as to give his companion a rest.

Then they both looked around them.

Outside the breakers the sea was running high, and on the rocks were piled several masses of the ill-fated "Jupiter," but neither outside nor in was there a sign of man.

All but themselves had gone to their last account.

"Oh, Tom!" cried Charley, bursting into tears, "this is an awful thing!"

"Aye, it is," replied Tom. "But yesterday, and that noble vessel carried hundreds of brave men, full of life and hope, and now they lie under the cruel sea!"

"It is awful! I cannot understand why it should be so."

"It is not for us to pry into these things," replied Tom. "Man is but a created being, and he knows nothing of the real springs of life. I am sad when I think of the fate of those poor fellows, but I should be sadder still if I thought that that was the ending of their existence."

"I do not think that, Tom."

"I am glad you can believe so, Charley. The lot of man is a mystery, but that he lives beyond the grave is certain. What the new life may be we cannot tell. That question must rest until we pass the gloomy portal of death. Now, Charley, I feel that I have gathered a little more strength, and we will start for the shore."

He made a step forward, and went up to his neck.

Drawing back hastily, he advanced a few paces to the right, and tried again with the same result.

Then he went to the left, and encountered the same obstacle to their progress.

"We are upon a belt of sand, Charley!" he said, "thrown up by some current running close in shore."

"Can you not swim the rest?" asked Charley.

"No," Tom replied, sadly; "all the swim is out of me."

He did not say that he could have swam alone, and that he did not intend to leave Charley to die, but Charley understood very well what sacrifice he had made, and a deep feeling of love and gratitude sprang into his breast.

"What can be done?" asked Charley, "we cannot stay here much longer."

"I do not know," replied Tom, who felt each moment that he was getting weaker.

"What if the tide should rise?"

"Then Heaven help us!" replied Tom, and linking their arms together, they stood still to await their fate.

A quarter of an hour passed, and then Charley spoke again.

"Tom," he said, "the tide is rising."

"Heaven help us!" replied Tom, and bowed his head.

———

CHAPTER LIV.

MR. GRUBBINS MAKES A TRIP IN THE "ESMERALDA" TO JACK'S ISLAND.

HAVING secured her provisions and stores, the "Esmeralda" left St. Helena behind, and with a favourable wind went on her way.

Mr. Enoch Grubbins was in high feather, the novel and exciting journey he had undertaken kept him in a constant state of excitement, and the way he laughed and talked would have astonished Mrs. Grubbins, could that respected and much-injured lady have looked upon him.

"Upon my word, Scarborough," he said to Jack, "I never knew the sweets of real liberty before. Fancy being a good two thousand miles away from the partner of my bosom!"

"I hope that she does not keenly feel the separation," said Jack.

"My dear Scarborough," replied Grubbins, "that woman has a strong mind, and she can bear a deal more than most of her sex. If she suffers at all, it is from doubt. A doubt is harder to bear than a certain evil, and I am fully convinced that she suffers, if she suffers at all, from uncertainty. Bless you, Mrs. Grubbins! Have a cigar, Scarborough?"

Jack took one, and they walked up and down the deck together for awhile.

By-and-bye, Simmons pessed them.

"Hallo, Simmons!" said Grubbins. "What is the matter with your eye?"

"It's black," replied Simmons, shortly.

"Can't I see that for myself, you fool? How came it?"

"I ran agin something, sir."

"Against what?"

"A cussed nigger's fist."

Grubbins and Jack involuntarily burst into a roar of laughter.

Simmons looked at them with an expression generally associated with sour gooseberries.

"What are you laughing at?" he asked.

"Why don't you leave the darkies alone?" said Grubbins.

"I can't; it ain't in my natur'," replied Simmons. "I hate 'em."

"But you always get the worst of it."

"I don't know," replied Simmons, thoughtfully. "I have had a go at Peter, and he fo't with his he'd. I tried the Hannibal chap, and he tucked me under his arm, and punched me friteful. I'll have a go in at the Pitchpot next, and if I don't lick him, I'll chuck myself overboard as soon as we sight a shark."

"I should, if I were you," replied Grubbins. "Let a reef out of the mainsail."

"Aye, aye, sir!" replied Simmons, the sailor again in a moment.

The double defeat of Simmons lowered him much in the eyes of the crew, and some of the boldest dropped the Mister, and, as he said, "tuk liberties with him."

The effect of this was that a relaxing

"Steady, Pitchpot," whispered Jack, "pull her up a bit." The next moment Jack and his faithful niggers were on board.

of the discipline was threatened, and unless Simmons did something to retrieve his character, he would lose his power over the men.

But how regain it?

There was only one way.

And that was to give Pitchpot a thrashing.

Now, Pitchpot was the weakest of his brethren. He had neither the muscular power of Peter, nor the big frame of Hannibal; and Simmons, therefore, had a better chance of giving him a thrashing.

But he was, as before, a little out of his reckoning.

Pitchpot might not be strong, but he was cunning and active as an eel. He might not be able to inflict much damage upon a foe, but he was able to keep clear away from danger.

Simmons, with his usual discretion, selected a time for the confusion of Pitchpot when the deck was very lively. The owner was there, Jack, Peter, and Hannibal were there, and five of the yacht's men.

On the bows sat Pitchpot, washing out some old rags in a broken soup tureen. Simmons went forward apparently in search of a rope.

"Get up," he said to Pitchpot.

"Wurra for?" demanded Pitchpot, looking at him with supreme contempt.

"Because I tell you."

"Dat all? Den I not get up," said the nigger, dipping his cloths into the water, and working them about.

"Now just look here," said Simmons; "I've told you to get up; are you going to get up or are you not?"

Pitchpot twisted a cloth and his face at the same time, and made no reply.

"I give you three times," said Simmons. "One."

Pitchpot went on quietly with his work.

"Two."

The cloths were dragged out, and Pitchpot proceeded to wring them.

"Three!" said Simmons.

He paused a minute, and getting no answer, Simmons aimed a fearful kick at the nigger; but Pitchpot sprang up like a harlequin, and the foot of the would-be kicker sent the soup tureen flying up into a hundred pieces.

The next moment Simmons felt a clout across his face, then something like the body of a man glide between his legs, and he rose in the air.

"Murder!" roared Simmons.

Down he came upon his back, having performed a somersault in the air, and lay blinking, with a very imperfect view of a number of laughing faces, and Pitchpot capering about like a dervish.

His confused thoughts soon settled into their normal condition, and the true state of the case burst upon him.

"Darned if I'm not licked again!" he thought. "These can't be common niggers."

"Now, Simmons, don't skulk there!" cried out his master.

"No, sir," replied Simmons getting upon his feet. "Any orders, sir?"

"Yes; that you let these niggers alone in the future, and stick to your work."

"I didn't want no orders for that," muttered Simmons; "for I'm busted if ever I tackle one of them again!"

"There's a shark over the counter,' continued Grubbins, winking at Jack. "Come, Simmons, now's your time."

Simmons went to the side, and peeped over.

There, sure enough, was a black, ominous-looking fin darting to and fro.

"You don't call that a shark, do you?" said Simmons.

"Yes, I do. What is it?"

"He ain't 'arf growed," replied Simmons; "and I'm not sich an ass as to chuck myself away on *him*. Ease off the jib, there!"

And Simmons went to his duties, for the time abandoning all thoughts of giving himself up to the "pirate of the ocean"— a very prudent step, most people will admit.

The limited accommodation of the "Esmeralda" gave rise to many inconveniences, the most serious of them being the water supply.

Men can wash in salt water, but they must have fresh to drink and to cook with, and a vessel of such small tonnage could only carry a limited supply.

This necessitated their keeping as near as possible to the coast, so as to make the "run in" as short as they could, and in a measure cramped their freedom of action.

Twice they stopped on the coast of Brazil for a supply, and in the next halt they made run upon a barren-looking coast without a sign of man.

It is always a relief to get ashore after some time at sea, and all that could be spared were generally permitted to go to look up a water supply.

Jack took command of the expedition upon this occasion, and the three darkies went with him.

The land had an air of richness, but within a mile of the sea there was no tree.

A few pools of water there were, but as these were rather brackish, Jack resolved to go further inland.

Climbing over a belt of rock, they came into view of the most beautiful country.

Trees, flowers, and birds in profusion, but no sign of man.

"What a paradise!" exclaimed Jack, as he looked at the magnificent ocean.

"Dis berry pretty," said Peter the Great; "but it not like my ole home, Massa Jack."

"Where you were born?"

"Yes, Massa Jack; and when dat ole rogue of a farder sell us to the Yankee—"

"Hush, Peter! no matter what your father was, speak well of him. Remember that he is your father."

"Massa Jack, you berry right; but how can a man lub a farder like him?"

They walked on for some distance, and despite the luxuriance of the country, found no springs.

"There must be water," said Jack; "or why is everything so luxurious?"

"Perhaps dere am a riber which overflows," suggested Hannibal.

"It is either that, or heavy rains," said Jack; "but I am inclined to think that a river is near."

They reached the forest, and stepped beneath its shade.

Noble trees which had withstood the storms of centuries, formed a canopy overhead, and luxuriant moss deadened the sound of their footsteps.

Hares, rabbits, and deer, in great numbers, flitted across the path every moment.

The wood was not very wide, for in half an hour they came to the open country again, but they could see that the trees formed a tiny line—a perfect belt between the country and the coast.

The view now was very charming—sloping hills, with little groves of trees upon their summits, great banks of flowers, and trailing vines.

One thing only was lacking, and that was water. Making a point as a place of rendezvous, Jack scattered his party in every direction, warning them not to go more than a mile or so away, and failing in their search, to return.

Each man went alone, and Peter the Great, whom we will follow, struck out for a hill crowned with trees, about a mile away.

His keen eyesight had detected something glistening there, and he hoped to discover water.

Although the ground looked tolerably even, there were so many undulations in it that the searchers soon lost sight of each other.

Peter was not troubled by any feeling of fear, and he walked along communing with himself in a very cheerful spirit.

"Dis sumfin' like de life," he said. "Oh, golly! de sunshine and de flowers am berry beautiful; better dan big cities and brick houses. Massa Jack better lib about here dan go home eber again. Jimmy! what dis?"

He stooped and looked at the turf.

To the ordinary eye, there was nothing but a slight bending of a few blades of coarse grass, but to Peter it was a sign of the presence of human beings.

"Dat a foot," he said. "Dere de heel and dere the toe. Naked foot mean black man. Here anoder and anoder. Two men 'bout here somewhere."

Peter had come without his usual weapons, an act of folly he was not often guilty of.

What if the men should be near and prove hostile? Would it not be better for him to turn tail and run away?

The thought just crossed his mind, but he dismissed it in a moment.

He would not, so, stooping down and eyeing the ground carefully, he followed up the track.

"P'raps," he thought, "dese men goin' after water."

There was reason in this, and the possibility of their being friendly was not very remote.

All tribes are not savage and hostile.

The footsteps led round the base of a small hill to a clump of trees, and were then lost in what was undoubtedly an old water-course.

Hope rose in Peter's breast. Where water had once been, water might be again.

He crossed the gully, and stood upon the other side.

As he did so, the breaking of a twig fell upon his ear.

"Somebody comin' dis way," he muttered. "Golly! dis chile in for it now!"

A tree was near, and acting upon the prompting of the moment, he climbed into it, and stretched himself at full length upon a branch.

He had barely done so, when two men hove in sight.

They were savages, something after the South Sea Island type, with feathers on their heads, paint on their faces, and no more clothing than was absolutely necessary to save them from utter nakedness.

Each man was armed with bow, arrows, and spear.

They were talking to each other in a low tone, and advanced in a confident manner, the eyes of both, nevertheless, being turned rapidly in every direction.

Peter knew that he must be discovered, and discovered he was as soon as they came near him. One glance at the tree, and his presence was made known.

The two men poised their spears, but Peter made a sign of peace, and they dropped them again.

"Wolla! wolla!" said the foremost.

Peter shook his head, to show that he did not understand.

Then the men exchanged a few words in an undertone.

Peter could read faces well, and he understood pretty clearly what they were saying.

"Dey wondering weffer it best not to kill dis child," he thought; and kept up a series of signs indicative of his desire for peace.

Their conference ended, they signalled for him to come down.

"Come down," said Peter, rather doubtful about doing so.

"Nana curra!" said one of the savages, imperatively, and up went his spear again.

Peter saw that all was up with him. The savages had resolved upon murdering him, but they wished to make sure of doing it by getting him down first.

"Wurra dis chile to do?" thought Peter, pretending to make preparations for a descent. "Dey make cold meat ob me soon enuf."

"Nana curra!" cried the savage again.

He was just under the place where Peter lay, and his spear was within a foot of Peter's chest. A chance of escape opened out, and our sable friend took advantage of it.

Stooping, he seized the spear a little below the point, turned it aside, and fell bodily upon the savage.

Peter was a heavy man, and his fall was fatal to the foe. With a broken neck, the other rolled upon the ground. His companion, startled out of his composure, lost his presence of mind for a moment, and that loss was fatal to him, too.

Quick as a flash of light, Peter dragged the spear from the dead man's hand, and thrust it through the body of the other.

"Lalu! lalu!" shrieked the savage as he fell, and his dark eyes flashed forth lightnings of rage. He made an effort, strong as the last effort of a dying man generally is; but the arm that would have struck the blow fell powerless by his side, and, with another shriek, he gave up his life.

Death is always an impressive sight, and Peter could not but feel for the two men who had lost their lives by their own folly.

"If," he muttered, "you two chiles hab had lilly bit of brudderly feelin', we might now be walkin' down togedder, arm-and-arm, to see brave Massa Jack; but since you berry great bloodthirsty fools, you lie there dead. It not Peter's fault, so it no use your ghosts comin'. boddering him."

Peter armed himself with bow and arrows and spear, and, drawing the bodies aside, covered them with a few branches.

It was the best interment he could give them, and no man can do better than his best.

The sharp crack of the rifle now aroused Peter, and running to a bit of high ground, he beheld a sight which made him quail.

Jack was in an open piece of ground, fighting half-a-dozen savages hand-to-hand, and to the right and left were the forms of Hannibal and the others, running to help him.

This was terrible enough, but not all, for between Peter and his friends was a long line of savages advancing stealthily and rapidly towards our hero.

So close were the savages, that Peter felt himself cut off from offering any assistance, and if he should succeed in saving his own life, it was as much as he could hope to do.

CHAPTER LVI.

THE TIDE-BOUND FRIENDS.

"TOM, the tide has risen to my throat."

It was Charley Granby who spoke, and his voice sounded like one on the point of choking.

"Bear up," was all Tom could say.

"I will," replied the boy, "but will you not leave me now?"

I cannot leave you," replied Tom.

He looked towards the coast, and wondered if, by one great final effort, he could reach it. But no; the little strength he had left was only sufficient to keep him standing there, and it could not be done.

The thought of going alone came to him more than once; but he dismissed it instantly. How could he desert that boy and bear his own life afterwards?

"The tide is near my lips," said Charley. "Good-bye again, Tom!"

Tom made no reply, but pressed his arm, and for a few minutes they stood still. Death seemed inevitable, but the water came no higher. With his eyes fixed upon his companion's face, Tom waited for it to flow into his mouth. Then, indeed, all would be over.

But no; it paused there, and a great hope dawned upon him.

"Keep your head still, Charley, and do not speak until I speak again to you," he said.

Charley turned upon him a look full of resolution. There was a pallor like that of death in his face; but to the end he kept his pluck.

Still and silent as two rocks fixed in the sea they stood while Old Time ticked off two hundred moments from the roll of the passing hour, and then Tom spoke again with a voice full of joy.

"Charlie, we are saved!" he cried. "The tide is falling!"

"Oh, Tom! do not give me a false hope! I am prepared to die!"

"Hold up, old fellow! Believe me, I speak the truth. How rapidly it falls! We shall live through this, and see them we love again! Do not give way now Charley."

The reaction was almost too much for the boy, and his eyes closed as if he were about to swoon, but he did not. The pallor died out, and a flush of joy and new strength gathered in his face.

Rapidly the tide fell, and soon the water was no higher than their waists. Then it was necessary for them to sit down, and with weary bodies but thankful hearts they sank upon the sands, and sat there until the waters ran off and left them high and dry.

Now, around them on every side were knolls of sand and little piles of rock, and, wading here and swimming there, they stepped from one to the other, until the main land was reached, and then, with a glad shout, they sank upon the earth.

Nature, borne up so long by excitement, gave way, and they were as powerless as new-born babes.

They cared not for this, for they knew that strength would come again, and sleep falling upon them, they lost their troubles in the oblivion of sound and unbroken repose.

Charley was the first to wake, and when he opened his eyes it was night.

High above him were the heavens, spangled with stars—such brilliant stars as we, in this cold clime, never see.

He was in an easy, delicious state of mind, such as we enjoy after a fever, and he lay listening to the thunder of the breakers, made musical by the distance, until Tom turned over and sat up.

"Is it my watch?' he asked.

"If you like to take it," replied Charley, laughing.

"Oh! I forgot the 'Jupiter.' I say, Charley, it was a sudden and an awful fate for the poor fellows."

"I wonder why we were spared, Tom?"

"Wonder will not tell us, Charley. All that must be left. I'm horribly hungry."

"So am I, Tom."

"How I should enjoy a cold round of beef."

"And pickles, Tom."

"Don't mention them."

"With a bottle of stout."

"Hold off, Charley. I cannot bear to think of it."

"And a batter-pudding to follow."

"I must walk up and down, Charley. Don't talk of food."

"I will not, to oblige you."

"How are your legs, Charley?"

"I have none; they are stilts."

"Give me your hand—up. Now walk briskly to and fro, and get your joints into play."

They walked up and down for awhile, and then the dawn appeared, rapidly and powerfully lighting up the land and sea.

A great number of pieces of the wreck had come in with the morning tide, among them several biscuit-tubs, one of which they broke open with stones.

Part of the biscuits were wet, but the inside was dry and wholesome, and like two wolves they fell upon them.

With renewed strength came renewed spirit, and as grieving in idleness is folly, they did not mourn as some people do.

Their late comrades were gone, and all the tears and exclamations in the world could not bring them back to life.

"We are upon a very unpromising coast," said Tom; "pretty enough in an artistic sense, but very much like an uninhabited spot."

"What shall we do, Tom?"

"I think we had better remain here, if

we can find water, and build some place of shelter. We shall be able to get no end of provender from the wreck, and some ship may pass this way."

"A very remote hope, I fear, Tom."

"It is the only one. We might tramp for weeks and only get deeper into the desolation of this land. Now, if we only had a boat!"

"I think I see something like one upon the rocks."

"Where?"

"There, by that curious hump like a camel's back."

"I see it, and I'm off as soon as the tide falls, Charley. You stay here."

"All right, Tom. There is no danger is there?"

"None."

"I can hardly bear to part with you."

"You do not like the idea of a life alone?"

"It is not that, Tom, indeed it is not. I could not bear to part from you."

"I believe you, Charley."

About noon the tide run down, and Tom waded out to the rocks, swimming in the deeper patches of water. Charley sat down and watched as he went from rock to rock.

Several times he stopped, and held up something which looked like an oar, and when he reached the object, which Charley imagined to be a boat, he stood up, and waving his cap, shouted like a madman."

"It is a boat," thought Charley, and returned Tom's hurrah.

A little signalling now passed between them, and from it Charley gathered that the boat was staved in, but not irretrievably hurt, and that it could be repaired as soon as it could be got ashore.

"I'll go out to him," thought Charley; but as soon as he stepped upon the sands, Tom waved him back so imperatively that he had no choice but to obey.

"I am sure I could reach him," thought Charley.

Tom was now engaged in hauling over the boat, which Charley soon recognised as the captain's cutter.

It was hard work for one, but Tom got through his work at last, and ran it into a pool of water.

It immediately sank to the rowlocks, and he dragged it up again.

"She's got a stiffish leak," thought Charley.

Let us go and join Tom upon the rocks. The cutter had indeed a tremendous hole in her side, and was utterly useless for the present.

A bit of board and a few nails would have put all right; but where was the board and nails to come from?

There was no end of chests and boxes upon the rocks; but, as usual, the thing he wanted—the carpenter's chest—could not be found.

Some pieces of the wreck had nails in them, but all were so rusty and firmly fixed that without tools it would be impossible to get them out.

Strange to say, there were no bodies to be seen.

Neither officer nor man had been given up by the deep.

This was a problem, for in many great wrecks some are cast up by the tide.

In this case, there were none.

The water was very clear, and Tom could see some distance under.

Getting in a line with the wreck, he could see a shadowy outline of the two halves of the ill-fated " Jupiter " lying on their sides.

Now that the tide was down, not more than twenty feet of water covered them, and the possibility of diving, and seeking the carpenter's chest, struck Tom.

"I might not succeed the first, second, or third time," he thought; "but I can keep under water longer than most men, and in the end I may do it."

He stood looking at the wreck, weighing the chances, until he saw a number of dark forms gliding to and fro.

He knew them at once.

They were sharks.

The presence of these voracious creatures at once shattered his diving hopes, and explained the fate of the men of the " Jupiter."

With a sickening sensation at his heart, he turned away.

"No," he said; "our only hope lies in what the sea gives up."

He walked slowly over the rocks, waving a hand now and then to Charley, and, by-and-bye, reached the open spot where he had swam through with Charley.

The tide was coming in, and a strong current was running through the opening —a current of water clear as crystal.

Going with it were a number of the same ghastly forms which were hovering about the wreck.

The sharks were retiring to the calmer waters for a rest after their feast.

One, as it passed turned upon its back, and flashed its white belly and gleaming teeth in the eyes of Tom.

It seemed like an act of triumph, and appeared to say—

"See, I am ready for you! Your turn will come!"

"Not if I know it! replied Tom, involuntarily answering the brute's action. "No, my friend, I will be getting towards him."

But alas! he had delayed too long. The sands were covered, and there was nothing to guide him from the deep parts of the water.

"I've done it," said Tom; "what a fool I am! How shall I keep my footing here when the waves break over like ten thousand furies; and, if I attempt to swim through them, why, exit Tom Warren down one of the beggars' throats. However, I am not going to funk. Let me send as much as I can to Charley while the tide is running in."

Charley's voice now reached his ear, and it was evident that the boy was getting anxious about his fate.

Tom waved a hand encouragingly, and proceeded to pitch all the boxes and bales he could lift over the rocks, and the tide bore them towards the shore.

The cutter was on the shore side of the breakers, and out of all danger of being carried away, for if washed off, as it probably would be, it would be driven towards the shore or sunk. In either case it could be removed at low tide.

"It's a very bad thing to despair," thought Tom, as the first wave broke over him; "especially as I have been so often mercifully spared; but I really think that I'm settled at last."

He looked towards the shore and saw Charley running to and fro, waving a handkerchief. Then he looked at the water, and beheld it positively alive with fins. He cast a glance behind him, and saw a rapidly-rising sea.

"A cheerful prospect," he thought; "but I bow my head to my fate. If it is so laid out for me, then let me say amen."

CHAPTER LVII.

PETER GOES UPON A LITTLE EXCURSION.

FROM the rising ground, Peter the Great stood and looked down upon the fight. He saw his young master, brave Jack Scarborough, cut down savage after savage, as if they had been wooden images, and the rest quail before him.

Then he saw Hannibal join the young hero, and the pair charge quite a host of the howling redskins, whom they scattered like water, and the other men coming up, fire-arms and cutlasses were used pretty freely.

Fire-arms seemed to be new to the natives, for as soon as the first was fired, many of them ran, and before half-a-dozen pistols were empty, the whole turned tail, and came running towards Peter in a broken line.

This was very good in its way, but it involved Peter in a little difficulty.

The fact of their being defeated by Jack and his party would not improve the temper of the savages, and if they came upon Peter, it was possible that they might avenge their defeat by making mincemeat of him.

Hiding was his next thought; but, in reality, there was no place where he really could hide; and his third and last thought was to run before the foe, until he could get an opportunity of making a circuit back to his friends, and this thought he acted upon.

Peter could run, and if ever he ran in his life, he ran that day through valley and over hills, followed by the crashing of the feet of the foe, and their occasional shouts of horror and dismay.

The fact was that they did not find out for a long time that Jack and his men were not following; and when they did so, as ill-luck would have it, they espied Peter.

Now, having been chivied themselves, it was only in accordance with human nature that they should wish to chivy others, and, with a great shout, they went in pursuit of our dark friend.

He heard their cries, and, putting on a spurt, increased the distance between them; but spurts are not good things when the race is to be a long one, and Peter felt that his wind was going.

To add to his dismay, the track now led to an ugly rough plain, with rocks scattered about, and chasms here and there—probably the scene of some great volcanic eruption centuries before.

Stumbling and staggering, Peter rushed on, falling occasionally by way of variety, but getting up again with the celerity of an india-rubber ball, and speeding onwards.

His boots were a great check. With naked feet he would have covered double the quantity of ground, and in this his pursuers had the advantage. Their feet were naked and hardened by exposure, and they thought nothing of the pebbles and rocks in their path.

"Pit-a-pat, pit-a-pat," came louder and louder upon Peter, and "pit-a-pat, pit-a-pat," went his heart in response.

"'Bout ten hundred ob dese beggars," he thought. "Oh, massa Jack! whar am you?"

"Pit-a-pat, pit-a-pat," came the feet; and Peter, coming to a gully, made an effort to leap over it.

It was too much for him, and he fell upon his stomach on the other side—an ugly fall, and enough to kill an ordinary man; but Peter was not an ordinary man, and springing up, he was off again.

As he left the spot, three spears struck the earth, and remained quivering there.

Well aimed, and would have been fatal but for the activity of Peter.

A huge boulder of rock now fronted him, and flying round it, he found himself in a sort of Stonehenge.

Piles of rocks lay one upon another, in a circle of about four hundred yards in diameter.

In the centre was a rough-looking building with a dark portal.

Any shelter was better than none, and he made towards it.

The savages came bounding after him, shrieking like demons.

He was in their sacred ground, and that was their idol house.

Peter knew pretty well what it was, but it was no time for him to stand upon ceremony, and he plunged in.

Turning, he used his spear against the foremost savage. Thrusting it through him, and leaving it sticking there, he rushed further into the darkness.

About ten steps forward the ground seemed to give way under him, and he sank into a deep and terrible gulf, from whence arose a horrible roaring.

CHAPTER LVIII.

A CHECK TO THE "ESMERALDA."

THE savages had come most unexpectedly upon Happy Jack.

Relying on the sagacity of Peter and Hannibal, he had been walking along, wrapped in thought, thinking of no danger, until, with a wild whoop, a body of them sprang up, and closed around him.

Men accustomed to peril are generally ready to meet it, and undaunted by this sudden assault, Jack drew his cutlass, and with a pistol in the other hand, showed a bold front to the foe.

The battle we need not describe, as we know the issue, and when it was over, a rapid roll was called, and it was found that only one man was wounded and another missing.

That missing one was Peter the Great.

This was the second time that that most unfortunate nigger had got into trouble in a contest with wild tribes; but, unlike the previous occasion, he had not been seen in the thick of the fight, but had simply disappeared.

The savages were pursued by the whites, but only as far as the spot where the two savages slain by Peter lay.

These were discovered by Hannibal, who, at the same time, marked footsteps indicative of the presence of his twin brother.

"These fellows did not fight with the rest," said Jack, "for there has been no time to cover them up. Peter must have encountered them before."

"But how could ole Peter kill dem?" asked Hannibal. "He hab no sword, for he leab him at home."

"This fellow has a broken neck."

"But dis one hab been run froo wif a spear," said Hannibal. "Golly! I see Peter been up dat tree. See de moss rubbed off, Massa Jack? Peter jump on dis chap and break him neck; den he skewer de oder."

"It matters very little, but I think that you are right. Do you think that you can take up Peter's trail?"

"Me try, Massa Jack."

He tried and tried his best, but it was no easy task. What with the hard ground and the footsteps of others, there was little left to guide him, and their progress was so slow that guesswork would have been almost as good.

"I can't make him out," said Hannibal, despairing. "You see, Massa Jack, dat so many tings cubber Peter's foot dat you no know if him been here."

"Shout!" cried Jack.

They shouted their loudest, but they might as well have shouted to the dead, for Peter at that moment lay still in the dark recess of the savages' idol house.

Jack knew not what to do. To stay there without provisions, or more than a very limited amount of ammunition, was impossible; so he hastened back to the "Esmeralda," to consult Mr. Enoch Grubbins.

It was the opinion of that gentleman

that Peter would never be found again, and he was for moving on.

"Not for my sake," he said, "but for yours. The longer we are upon the road, and the longer going home, the better I shall like it; but your business requires attention I think we had better go on. I am sincerely sorry for this poor fellow, but I do not think that we shall do any good by lingering here."

"If you insist, I must be guided by you," said Jack, uneasily; "but I must confess that I do not feel disposed to leave an old and faithful servant without making considerable effort to help him."

"If that be the case," said Grubbins, "let us stay."

"You will not think me imposing at all?"

"On my word, no. Have a cigar?"

Jack took one, although he was in no humour for smoking, and as they burnt the fragrant tobacco together, Jack laid before his friend the plan of his operations.

"I shall live on shore," he said, "and make excursions towards different points of the compass until I find some trace of him. Should I fail in all, I will return on board, and we will proceed."

"That's a good notion of yours, living ashore," said Grubbins. "I have an excellent tent below. It shall be pitched, and I will come to live with you."

"You will find exploring hard work, I am sure."

"I do not intend to explore," replied Grubbins. "While you roam the country through, I shall sit under the shade of the tent, and do the fragrant weed and meditate."

"There are a number of savages about."

"Blow the savages!" said Grubbins. "Look you here, Scarborough. I may be a man who loves his ease and enjoys good things; but I do not live for eating and smoking alone; and, furthermore, if it comes to the point, I am not afraid to die. At the same time, I give you my honour that if any man comes to take my life, he will have to take it at the risk of his own. Did you ever see me shoot?"

"No, never.'

"Then look here. You see Simmons?"

"Yes."

"And you see his pipe?"

"I do."

"Now, how far is he away?"

"A good twelve paces."

"Nearer fourteen; but no matter," said Grubbins. "Now, watch this."

"Surely, you would not shoot him!"

"Of course not; but I'll stop his 'bacca."

Bang! went the pistol, and Simmons' pipe was sent away in a hundred pieces.

Simmons turned coolly upon his master.

"That's your old trick," he said. "Darn it! that was the best pipe I had on board."

"Never mind, Simmons. Take one of these weeds. I was only showing Mr. Scarborough what I could do."

"I hope he enjoyed it," growled Simmons, helping himself to a cigar; "but p'raps he'd like to have *his* weed shot away."

"No, thank you," replied Jack.

"I'll do it with pleasure," said Grubbins, eagerly.

"Another time," said Jack. "Now, let us get ashore at once."

The tent was got out, and, with provisions, Jack, Hannibal, Pitchpot, and Grubbins went ashore. Jack declined to have any of the men, as the "Esmeralda" was rather short-handed.

"If it must come to a question of open warfare, he said, "what is done, if anything, must be effected by strategy."

So they pitched their tent under the shade of some broad trees, and Jack, with his negro followers, set out in search of Peter.

Mr. Grubbins passed the day in smoking and reading a novel, varied with a little light reflection upon the anxiety of Mrs. Grubbins, who by that time, perchance, had been measured for her widow's weeds. He extracted much amusement from this line of thought, and enjoyed himself amazingly.

At sunset, Jack and his followers came back, without a clue, and having partaken of supper, went to sleep, utterly worn out. Grubbins smoked half the night, and then fell asleep also.

The next day, the search was resumed with the same result.

No trace of Peter could be found.

The third came and went, without letting any light upon their errand; and also the fourth, fifth, and sixth bore no fruit.

No guide to the whereabouts of Peter could be discovered.

"I know not what to think," said Jack, as he sat in the tent upon the sixth eve. "Peter has been in so many scrapes, that I am loth to think that anything serious can have happened to him."

"And yet where is he?" asked Grubbins.

"That's the point," said Jack. "If he

is alive and free, he would not be away; but if dead or captive, how can we help him?"

"I wish I could give you assistance."

"I will go out once more," said Jack, "and if I do not find him then, I shall consider all lost; and the 'Esmeralda' shall spread her sails again."

"Take your own time," said Grubbins; "but do not waste that valuable commodity in useless search."

CHAPTER LIX.

ANOTHER PEEP AT DEATH.

WE left Tom Warren upon the rocks in no very pleasant predicament, with breakers behind and sharks before him, and a prospect, if even he had the power to stand his ground, of being twelve hours upon the slippery foothold.

Choosing the highest rock he could find, he crouched in the shore side of it, with his feet against a projection to assist him in overcoming the attack of the waves when they should rise high enough to pour over upon him.

Time, we all know, travels always at the same pace, but imagination often makes it seem to fly or crawl.

To the man who knows that he has but a few hours to live, it runs away on the wings of the wind; but it goes at a sluggard's pace for the man who is awaiting some long-expected blessing.

As Tom crouched, awaiting his apparently inevitable doom, it passed quickly enough, and when the tide was approaching the full, a huge wave ran up the rock, and rising in the air, fell upon him like an avalanche. It was the herald of perils to come.

Lying flat, he clung like a limpet, and resisted the rush of the water; but it left him breathless, and with a sense that half his life was beaten out of him. His fingers were bleeding, too, for the rocks were almost as sharp as knives.

"A little more of this," he gasped, "and I am done."

He heard the thud of a second wave, and saw its crest rise over him. With a cry of despair, he bent down to receive the shock.

It came, but lighter than the last, and, although half-blinded and stunned, he kept his ground, and, clearing his eyes, took a look about him.

What a scene it was!

Right and left the water was pouring over the rocks, beating the surface of the calmer sea within, and raising a thousand turbid eddies for a hundred yards or so. Beyond that, all was smooth as a quiet inland lake.

Nay, what is that moving to and fro? The ugly fin of the monster of the deep. Poor Tom knew it well, and, fascinated by it, he followed the black, razor-like object with his eyes until another wave broke over him.

He was taken by surprise, and his hold being lost, was washed from the rocks, and the next moment was fighting with the hissing water.

The shock was terrible, and he almost lost his presence of mind; but shaking off fear, he struck out for the rocks again.

Turning his head, he looked towards his dreaded foe.

The black fin was coming in pursuit of him.

About fifty feet separated the pursuer and pursued, and the rocks were about the same distance away.

With rapid calculation Tom estimated his chances of escape, and considered the relative speed of travelling of the monster and himself.

The shark had undoubtedly the best of it.

Unless something intervened, Tom was lost.

This he knew, and with a fervent prayer for himself and that lone boy upon the coast, he prepared for the ghastly grip which should take away his life.

Nearer and nearer came the dark fin.

Then it suddenly disappeared, and Tom knew that the monster had dived to strike.

"Have mercy upon me, oh, Lord!" he cried, and as if in answer to that prayer (who shall say it was not?), a huge mass of wreck was washed over the rocks, and fell into the sea, close to Tom.

He saw his chance, and with renewed strength struck out twice and reached it.

One hand upon a rope, and another upon a broken mast, and he clambered up, just as the shark turned and rose to strike, leaping out of the water in his impetuosity, and revealing his ghastly jaws glistening with teeth.

"Saved!" cried Tom, and for awhile he closed his eyes.

When he looked again, the wreck was much nearer to the shore, going in with the tide, and Charley was standing upon a sand-hill, frantically waving his hat.

"Hurrah!" came his cry, faintly borne upon the wind.

Tom tried to answer, but his voice was gone. The late excitement, added to the exhaustion of an already weakened frame, and taken all his strength away.

Nor was the danger over yet.

Round and round the wreck the ugly monster sailed, with his body but a few inches under the water, and his evil eyes fixed upon Tom.

The wreck was rather ricketty, and in a rough sea would have tumbled about in a very inconvenient manner.

But now it was in smooth water, and if Tom could only keep still, he might reach the coast in safety ere the tide returned.

Twice did the rough craft scrape upon the sand, but the current carried it safely over, and soon it was near enough for Tom and Charley to exchange a few words.

"Oh, Tom! I thought you were lost!"

"So did I; but, after this, who would show any fear? Can you see my friend?" pointing to the shark.

"I have watched him throughout, and my blood boiled as I thought of the possibility of his getting at you."

"He begins to despair, I think," said Tom. "A few minutes ago there was hope in his eye, but disappointed malice is coming in its place."

"The brute!"

"He is snapping at everything within reach; all the stray bits of rope he has cut off and swallowed. Good-bye old fellow!"

The shark had turned away, and the raft grated upon the sand.

Tom sprang out, and Charley held him in his arms.

"Come, come," said Tom; "don't pipe your eye."

"It's all joy, Tom. Oh; what should I have done without you?"

"What others have. Cheer up, Charley! Look what a friend the sea is to us. Here comes the old boat, and I can see at least three oars washed up, and as for barrels of pork and biscuit, we might have a dozen with us, and fare no worse for a twelvemonth."

CHAPTER LX.

TROUBLE FOR JACK.

THE tent erected by Mr. Enoch Grubbins was a very comfortable habitation.

That gentleman liked comfort, and he did not scruple to say so; soft cushions, good food and wine, and prime cigars, were things entirely after his own heart.

"So you have had no better luck to-day, Scarborough?" he said, as he cut up a preserved tongue for dinner.

"No," replied Jack. "I have spent my last day in search of poor Peter, and there is not the slightest trace of him to be found."

"Strange. Hannibal I thought, was clever at that style of thing."

"So he is, and more than once he was under the impression that he had found marks of Peter's presence, but the ground was so rocky that he could not be certain."

"Where was this?"

"In a very strange place—an open plain, with huge stones piled up after the fashion of the Druidical remains at home. In the centre was a sort of temple, but the pile had been overthrown, and one part, which looked as if there had been a doorway once, was blocked up."

"Some old fetish place of worship."

"Hannibal was certain that the stones had been recently overthrown, and pointed out some with moss underneath, and some above, as proof of his assertion."

"Could that have had anything to do with Peter?"

"I cannot conceive how it could; but Hannibal seemed to have a fancy for lingering there. He told me that he had heard a groan—and Pitchpot was equally certain too."

"Wonderful hearing these niggers have. What did you do?"

"We waited for a long time, shouting occasionally, but as we heard nothing more, I concluded that both were mistaken, and came away."

"Could you not remove the stones?"

"It would have taken a mighty engine to do it. Hannibal told me that they had been poised upon each other in case of emergency, and that the slightest push, properly directed, was sufficient to send them toppling down."

"How do them fellows get those stones together?"

"That's a puzzle," said Jack, "nobody knows how it was done. That you, Hannibal?"

"Yes, Massa Jack," replied Hannibal, coming in, followed by Pitchpot.

Both sat down with a weary air, and Hannibal heaved a deep sigh.

"Won't you have something to eat?" asked Jack.

"I eat berry small," replied Hannibal, "lilly piece ob bread—pore ole Peter."

"You must not give way," said Grubbins, "he may turn up yet."

"He must turn up soon, sare," said Hannibal, "er I die. Peter and me born togedder, and we die togedder."

"Which is a strong argument in favour of Peter being still alive. If Peter were dead now, so would you be."

"Golly, sare, dat a good idea," cried Hannibal, "we find Peter yet. Massa Jack, please gib me lilly meat wif my bread."

"With pleasure," replied Jack. "Pitchpot, what will you have?"

"I'm berry bad," said Pitchpot; "but de worse I am de more I eat—I have a big bit ob bread and meat."

"Where are the men?" asked Jack.

"Gone down to de boat. Oh, golly, dis tongue am berry good—me certain dat Peter are alibe, and I hab lilly more."

"And me certain dat him dead," said Pitchpot, going upon the opposite tack, "and dat increase my consumption ob de food. T'ank you, sare, gib me a lilly fat."

"Massa Jack," whispered Hannibal, suddenly, "be quiet."

"What is it?"

"Quiet, Massa Jack, if you please."

They sat like statues for a minute or more, and Hannibal, with dilated nostrils, and fixed eyes, seemed intent upon discovering some sound without.

"It is so, Massa Jack," he said, speaking in a very low whisper, "dere am de enemy outside."

"Those fellows we met the other day?"

"Yes, Massa Jack; but more ob dem."

"More."

"One, two, three times more—dey come like locusts."

"Gad!" said Enoch Grubbins, dropping his knife and fork, "it is time that we went out of this. Give me my pistols, Scarborough."

Jack passed them, and drew his cutlass. Hannibal signed to them to be all quiet.

"A rush may save us;" said Jack.

"It de only way," replied Hannibal; "dere too many ob dem for fair fight. Dere berry numbers crush us down."

"Stand ready!" whispered Jack, advancing to the door of the tent.

"All ready, sare?"

"All ready," said Grubbins. "Stay one moment, I cannot leave this lovely bit of tongue."

He put it into his mouth, and then all were prepared.

"Are they close, Hannibal?" asked Jack.

"All round, 'cept jes' in front ob de opening," was the reply.

Unfortunately, the opening of the tent looked inland, and the rush for escape must take a circuitous form; but to weigh the danger was to lose time, and, holding up his cutlass, as a signal, Jack rushed out with a shout.

It is no figure of speech to declare that the place was swarming with savages. There were hundreds, and how they could have gathered at the spot without being discovered before was a startling mystery.

The yell they uttered, as our friends darted forth, would have appalled more feeble hearts. Pitchpot alone quailed for a moment, but the example of Hannibal roused him, and to his credit be it said, that he dealt the first mortal blow to the foe by cutting down a very enterprising savage, with his entire head and face painted a brilliant red.

He was a hideous-looking man, and, no doubt, was best out of the way. The others were scarcely less horrible to look upon, and, as they leaped and yelled, it seemed as if a horde of demons from the lower world had been let loose.

"Forward," cried Jack, "close up; back to back, here."

Back to back they stood, and, with their strong arms, dealt out deadly blows; but numbers were against them; and, although the dead lay thick around them, those behind pressed the foremost on.

Over one of the prostrate figures Jack fell; a savage, whose amiable countenance was streaked with red and blue, aimed a blow at our hero's head.

Jack drew his pistol and fired.

The flame which followed was startling.

The long, rank grass, dry as tinder from the lack of rain, and the hot sun, leaped into a blaze, and like a sudden eruption from the earth, the fire spread around.

The savages, knowing the dread foe which had arisen against him, and, for the most part, believing that Jack had raised it by some power of magic, ran shrieking and yelling off.

The wind was blowing inland, and the fire followed them.

"To the sea!" cried Jack, and he, with his party, tramped through the first line of fire to a better ground.

The conflagration worked against the wind but slowly, and this gave them the opportunity to get clear.

"Can't we save the tent?" cried out Grubbins.

"No," said Jack, "the flames have reached it."

"There is a lovely box of cigars there. I'll have a shot at them."

"Do not be so foolish."

Grubbins, however, was not to be driven off, and diving in through a sheet of flame, he came out with a rush on the other side, with the box under his arm.

"Saved!" he cried. "Now for the sea, my boys!"

"Look there!" cried Jack; "pause, a moment and look upon this awful scene."

Right and left the fire had spread, and, with a mighty rushing down, was going inland—trees, bushes, and grass, all caught with the same fatal facility, and the hapless savages had no chance of escape.

With treble the pace they could move, it rushed upon them, and the shrieking wretches could be seen dancing in the flames for awhile, as they were overtaken, and then falling in the agonies of a dreadful death.

To add to their misery, most of the pigments they had used for colouring their bodies were made from oily clays, and these catching fire, lent vigour to the flames around them.

Some rushed towards our friends, who were backing slowly towards the sea, and with flames high above their heads, shrieked for mercy.

Poor wretches! They thought that Jack had raised the fire with a power of his own, and that he could allay it.

Onward, onward, spread the flames in an awful line, rising here and there as it met the hills, going on with a stately, dreadful march such as no tongue can describe or pen portray.

Not one of them who had come down like wolves upon the tent, escaped, and ere the fire was a mile away, the last had gone through his grim dance of death, and lay smouldering with the ashes of the great fire.

CHAPTER LXI.

AFTER THE FIRE.

WITH the terrible conflagration ended all hopes of saving the lost Peter the Great. None of his friends for a moment doubted that he had perished by the hands of his foes or by the terrible fire which had so unexpectedly arisen and swept over the country.

How far it went Jack never knew, but for hours after it had devasted the country round about, they could see huge columns of smoke hovering in the air, and when the "Esmeralda" spread her sails and left the spot, the horizon was still clouded.

For many days she went south, and half the life, and all the fun, had deserted the little yacht. Who could be merry with Peter dead? Hannibal pined, Jack mourned, Pitchpot was silent, and his eyes were red as if he wept in secret.

Enoch Grubbins was sorry because Jack was sad, and even Simmons got up a look of commiseration suitable for the occasion.

"I've had sundry tittups with him," he said, "and got the worst of it, but I don't bear him no malice now that he's dead."

"I should think not," said his master. "If you did, I would kick you overboard."

"He valleys a nigger more nor I do," growled Simmons, as he walked forward.

The loss of Peter was the first great gap in the little circle which had surrounded Jack through all his varied adventures. Men had fallen, but they had been strangers compared to Peter, who had carried our hero in his childhood on his back, and loved him with a love passing that of a most faithful servant.

He tried to cheer Hannibal, but Hannibal mourned like Rachel, and refused to be comforted. He had lost his twin brother, who had been through life part and parcel of himself.

"He wasn't a brudder, Massa Jack," said Hannibal, "he was me. We was born togedder, farder sold us togedder, we run away togedder, we serve Mister Scarborough togedder, and we fight for you togedder. Peter dead and Hannibal dead too."

Jack did not endeavour to persuade him to the contrary, and let him mourn, hoping that time would heal his grief, and the "Esmeralda," with its mournful burden, skimmed lightly over the sea.

Grubbins took refuge in smoke, and the fragrant Havannah was seldom out of his mouth. He, too, like Jack, hoped that time would bring matters round a bit.

One morning the man on the look-out cried, "Land on the lee-bow!" and sail was shortened to see what sort of place they had come upon.

It looked ugly enough as they approached it.

Long lines of breakers lifted their crested heads, and although there was an appearance of smooth water beyond, it was not the open sea, but only a narrow channel of water between the breakers and the land.

I think we had better sheer off here," said Mr. Grubbins. "Eh, Scarborough?"

"I think so, too. It seems to be uninhabited."

"No, Massa Jack," said Hannibal; "dere seberal people about. I see on de p'int ob dat rock, waving handkercher."

"What eyesight you have!" exclaimed Jack. "Pass me the glass."

"It's the figure of a youngster," he said: "and another, that of a man, is close to him."

"Dere more below."

Jack turned his glass in the direction pointed out by Hannibal and uttered an exclamation of surprise.

"Naval officers and men," he said, "and the coast strewn with wreck. They have been cast away. We cannot leave them."

"Certainly not," said Enoch Grubbins; "but will you tell me how to get inside those breakers?"

"There must be a a way," said Jack, "or they would not be there."

"True; but where a man can get through a boat may stick."

"That may be; but run her in under short sail close to the breakers, and take soundings as we go."

"All right; and a Union Jack at the masthead might cheer 'em."

"A good thought. Up with it!"

They were now near enough to see the figures ashore pretty clearly.

All had clambered to the summit of the rock, and stood waving their hands in an ecstacy of delight.

The "Esmeralda" answered with a shout.

"Here is an opening!" cried Jack.

"Is that wide enough?" asked Grubbins, doubtfully.

"Quite."

"And deep enough?"

"Yes: you may tell that by the blue water. Once inside, nothing will harm you."

"All right. Would you mind taking the helm, Scarborough?"

"With pleasure; and will you kindly stand forward, to let me know if I am running her too close?"

"Of course."

Enoch Grubbins could do nothing without his cheroot, and with one in his mouth, he took a seat upon the bowsprit, dangling his legs over the water.

"Port a little!" he cried out, suddenly.

Jack turned the wheel, and the "Esmeralda," slightly grating upon something, got into deep water again.

"What was that?" cried out Jack.

"A rock like a church spire," replied Grubbins, coolly.

"Ticklish work," muttered Jack.

They were now near the opening in the breakers, and the utmost caution became necessary.

Grubbins took the cigar from his mouth, and kept his eyes upon the water.

She glided between the rocks like a thing of life, and entered the deep water.

"Beautiful!" said Grubbins, "Not another craft, steered by another man, could have done it."

Jack was now at liberty, for the anchor was dropped in about five fathoms of water, and the "Esmeralda" was at rest.

The men on shore descended from the rocks, and were running frantically about cheering.

Something in the run of some of them struck him, and he raised his glass again, but Hannibal was before him.

"Massa Tom thar," he said.

"Impossible!" said Jack.

"It am true," returned Hannibal. "Massa Tom and Massa Charley dere, and de two sailors dat we pick up."

"The boat is ready!" sung out Enoch Grubbins.

Puzzled, and half-inclined to think the whole a dream, Jack dropped into the boat, and in company with Grubbins Hannibal, and two seamen pulling, made for the shore.

All doubts and fears were speedily set at rest. The boat touched the shore.

"Tom!"

"Jack!"

These exclamations of surprise over, they clasped hands, and stood still.

"What good fortune brought you here?" said Tom, at last.

"I cannot tell," replied Jack. "But how came you here?"

"I say, Jack, haven't you a hand for me?" said a boyish voice. "Come, Tom, you have had him long enough."

"Charley, I am glad to see you; but who are these strangers?"

"Allow me to introduce you," said Tom. "This is Captain Marston, of the 'Jupiter, and this, Mr. Barnham, lieutenant of the same, the five men are all that are left of the crew. Two of them you know."

"Coddem and Martin, of the 'War Eagle'?"

"Yes; the others you do not know. Hannibal, how are you? Where is Peter?"

"Oh, Massa Tom!" exclaimed Hannibal, "don't 'ee ax me 'bout Peter—him dead and gone!"

"Dead?"

"Yes, him lost up country dere."

"Oh! only lost. Then, take my word for it, Peter is not dead; he will turn up again."

"You t'ink so, Massa Tom?" said Hannibal, eagerly. "Oh, bless you, Massa Tom, for dat!"

CHAPTER LXII.

AN EXCHANGE OF STORIES.

IT was agreed that the best course would be for the whole party to get on board the "Esmeralda" at once, and go back to England, as there were witnesses enough now to clear Jack, and confound his enemies.

"The 'Esmeralda,'" said Enoch Grubbins, "is small, but she can carry the lot, if you don't mind being stowed away. My berth will do for you, Captain Marston."

"But where will you sleep?"

"On the deck. Nay, no refusal. I love the deck ten times more than my bed, and you will not deprive me of that comfort, surely? The steward's snuggery will do for Mr. Barnham, and, as for the men, they can settle with Simmons where they are to go. Simmons will at once declare that he cannot possibly have you; but say that *I* shall not put up with any nonsense, and he will cave in."

"We will reserve all story-telling until we are afloat," said Jack.

"Just my idea," returned Tom. "I have had enough of this spot, I can tell you. It is much too lively for a man of my sober temperament."

"It is a beautiful country and a charming sea."

"The country is good enough," replied Tom, "but the sea—only look at it now, you will find a dozen sharks staring you in the face. They have eaten everything else, and are now living upon each other."

"The best thing they can do."

In two journeys the boat conveyed the whole party to the "Esmeralda," where they were stowed away with some difficulty. Simmons was very fractious, and took a solemn oath, which he emphasized by smiting the compass-box with his fist, 'that he warn't a-goin' to hev a lot o' man-o'-war's men shovin' their noses into private craft;" and that "if they had any sense of decency, they wudden't ha' done it." But a few words from his master, conveying an intimation that he must and should have them, and that if he did not like it he had better go ashore, altered his tone, and hammocks were swung for the men.

The night was beautifully clear, and a broad, full moon lit up the sea. Jack and his old chum, Tom Warren, sat aft smoking and comparing notes of what had passed since last they met.

Both stories were of interest, but as much of each, as our readers know, need not be repeated, we will, therefore, take up the thread of their conversation at the point, where Charley and Tom were left together.

"You must have felt lonely, Tom."

"Aye, although I had a companion,' replied Tom, "and Charley is a dear fellow. But the sense of being so far away, as I thought, from my fellow-men, distracted me. What, if one fell ill, I thought, would be the end of it?"

"It must have cheered you when you met with Captain Marston and the others."

"It did; and it happened in this way. Charley and I ran up our shanty, and made it as waterproof as possible. Then we stowed our biscuit and so on away, and took it in turns to watch by day upon the hill. Occasionally I went inland in search of fresh food, but I found nothing for some time. At last something like a wild cat ran across my path, and I fired at it. I missed the cat, but I unearthed Captain Marston and his friends from a little cave which had been concealed from me by the trees and ferns before it."

"That was a welcome cat."

"To both of us. Oh! how I hailed them, and how gladly they received me! We made fools of ourselves, and wept at first like children. There are times when tears will not keep back, and then their falling is a relief."

"How did Marston escape?"

"He got into a current, clinging to a bit of the wreck with the others, and was carried down the coast several miles, when they succeeded in effecting a landing. The coast was barren, and there was nothing to eat. This drove them inland, where they found the bread-fruit growing, upon which they lived."

"Did they not watch for a sail?"

"Yes; as Charley and I did, in turns; but their point was some distance from us, and so it happened that we never saw each other. I told them of the store of ship biscuit in my possession, and they came down to live with me."

Peter ran—he seemed to fly; but the cannibals were after him—"Golly! neber was in such a 'dicament afore! all up wid Peter, for suah!"

"How long have you been together?"

"A little more than a month, and, taking all things as they are, the time has not passed badly. When you came upon us we were fitting a boat to run with."

"Rather a risky game in these seas."

"It was, Jack; but there seemed no possibility of a sail coming this way, and how you came in here is a puzzle to me."

"We dare not go very far from the shore, as we can carry but a very little water," replied Jack. "That's how it was."

"Well, here we are together," said Tom, with a satisfied sigh, "and I trust that all our troubles are over."

"I hope so, Tom."

"You will go home straight?"

"Certainly—wind and weather permitting."

"What course will you pursue to clear yourself?"

"I shall give myself up for trial, and call you and the others as witnesses."

"I see," said Tom; "and won't it be a burst up for Cursly. I think I can see the cowardly beggar white as a ghost."

"It will be a sore blow to him," said Jack, "especially as I heard he expected to get promotion."

"Surely they will not make an admiral of him."

"They surely will. Family connection and the proper patronage will do anything and everything. It is not a solitary case."

"No," said Tom. "How merry those fellows are below!"

"Grubbins is a capital host," replied Jack; "a rough jewel, but a good one. He has done me a service I can never repay."

"Mrs. Grubbins hangs a little heavy upon him."

"I think she is a tartar," said Jack; "but he says that if he gets a warm welcome he will remain at home; but if it is a *hot* one he will make one more clear run for it, and never return."

"Massa Jack and Massa Tom," said Hannibal, coming forward, "you wanted berry much below."

"Thank you, Hannibal," returned Jack. "Come, Tom, let us go."

"Eberbody but me berry cheerful agin," said Hannibal, looking after them; "and my poor heart broken."

Then he followed his nigger instincts, and composed a small piece of poetry, which he sang in a low tone :—

"Oh, my brudder!
Nebber get anudder
Friend like de Peter de Great.
Allers pipe my eye
Till I'm sure to die,
And pass tro de great dark gate.
Oh, my brudder!
Nebber get anuder
Like you, ole boy—
You was my only joy."

"I be berry lonely now," sighed Hannibal; "not a soul in de world to care for you."

"Don't say dat," whispered a voice near him, and Pitchpot stood before him.

"Dat you, Pitchpot?"

"Yes, Massa Hannibal."

"You berry sorry dat Peter gone?"

"Berry."

"What you sorry for? He orfen give you lickin'."

"Pitchpot no lub Massa Peter unless he gib him lickins. Lickins do dis chile good. I berry sorry dat I make dat soup!"

"De cat soup?"

"Yes, Massa Hannibal."

"It a berry mean and dirty trick."

"Shall I tell you somet'ing, Massa Hanbull?"

"Yes."

"You 'member dat soup?"

"Ob course I do!"

"It not made ob cat."

"Not made ob cat?" said Hannibal. "Don't lie, Pitchpot!"

"I tells de trufe," returned Pitchpot, earnestly; "I make dat soup ob preserve beef, and I wash de tail berry clean and put him in for fun."

"Now, am dat true?" asked Hannibal, solemnly.

"Yes, I swear it!" replied Pitchpot.

"Den gib me your hand," said Hannibal, "you my friend from dis hour. You can nebber fill up de hole in my heart which de loss ob Peter make, but you can be my fren'."

"I follow you tro all t'ings," said Pitchpot, and their strong black hands clasped tightly together.

CHAPTER LXIII.

HANNIBAL HAS A DREAM.

IT was early dawn, and the sea was tinged with the cold grey light which precedes the warmer hues of the sun, as Jack rose up from a pile of canvas on which he had been sleeping.

Not more than three paces away lay

Enoch Grubbins, snoring prodigiously, and in the other was Tom Warren, sleeping with the quietude and ease of a baby.

As Jack passed forward he stumbled over Hannibal's feet and awoke him. The faithful fellow was upon his feet in a moment.

"You want me, Massa Jack?"

"No, Hannibal. What is the matter with you? You look scared."

"I've had a dream, Massa Jack," said Hannibal; "*I've seen Peter!*"

"You dreamt you saw him?"

"No, Massa Jack, I saw him. It might have been a dream, but he come to me and say, 'Hannibal, we shall meet again!'"

"Of course you will," said Jack, "in a brighter world than this."

"Peter meant dis world," returned Hannibal, shaking his head, "He says, 'Hannibal, my brudder, we shall meet again!' den he go away and come back again."

"Came twice?"

"Yes, Massa Jack; and he say, 'Look hard for de big hill wif four trees on de top.' Den he go away and come again."

"A third time?"

"Yes, Massa Jack."

"And what did he say then?"

"He open his mouf, Massa Jack, but jes' den you fall ober my feet and I wake."

"I am very sorry, Hannibal," said Jack, half inclined to smile, "my coming was very *mal apropos.*"

Jack had not much faith in dreams, but he had no desire to hurt Hannibal's feelings by laughing outright or saying anything of a sarcastic tendency.

"Dat my dream," said Hannibal, with a hopeful look, "and I keep my lilly eye open for dat hill day and night."

"We will all help you," said Jack; "but suppose we come upon one with four trees and no Peter?"

"You set me down thar," replied Hannibal firmly; "I can wait. Peter come one day."

To humour him, a watch was kept for the hill with four trees, and many hills were passed with trees on their summits. Some had more and some had less, and one was discovered which, at a distance, appeared to have only four, but as they drew nearer six were revealed. So the days passed, and Hannibal's dream had not come true.

"It no matter Massa Jack," he said, softly, "I find dat one day."

And found it was, early on the third day of the watch; Hannibal was the first to see it, and as the "Esmeralda" was turned in, the four trees stood out in bold relief about half a mile from the shore.

"Massa Jack," cried Hannibal, "my dream come true."

"My poor fellow," said Jack, "hills with four trees are not very scarce; Peter may not be there."

"Put me ashore, Massa Jack, and I find him."

"We will go with you," replied our hero; "there is a small river running into the sea, I perceive, and as it seems to go round the hill, we will go up it if we can."

"Massa Jack, you berry good," said Hannibal; "I find Peter dere."

"I hope we shall. Have you any objection to heave to, Grubbins?"

Mr. Grubbins declared that he had not; on the contrary, anything which delayed his return to England seemed to give him unlimited satisfaction. They ran the "Esmeralda" close in and anchored on a good sandy bottom.

The boat was lowered, and Hannibal, accompanied by Jack and Tom Warren, rowed down to the mouth of the river.

It was a narrow river, as rivers go in this part of the world, and the tide being at the full, there was little stream to contend against. They pulled easily up until they came in view of the hill, and then a strange but not entirely novel scene presented itself.

Out from the very bowe's of the hill came the river, and they rowed to the very mouth of the cave and sought to fathom its gloom.

It was a terrible place to look at; the river, now that the tide was high, was not more than four feet from the roof, and the sound of the rushing water was answered by ten thousand echoes which rolled like distant thunder.

"I know of no phenomena of Nature so awful as this," said Jack; through what strange caves and hiding places of unknown monsters must this water run! See how it rushes out and sparkles gladly in the light of day!"

"Fearful caves and fearful regions lie hidden from the eye of man," returned Tom; "but this is not seeking Peter. Let us mount the hill and take a look round."

They climbed the hill and on the summit obtained an excellent view of the country. It was very barren and full of undulating ground, but at no point that they could see did the river re-appear.

"This reminds me of that mysterious river upon my island," said Jack, "only here it runs *to* the sea, and mine ran *from* it."

"Incomprehensible and fearful to think upon," said Tom. "It would require a stout heart to risk the exploration of either."

"No Peter! no Peter!" moaned Hannibal.

"No, my poor fellow," said Jack. "Your dream was false."

"No, no; it berry true," replied Hannibal. "I find Peter here. You go, Massa Jack, and leab me."

"I could never do that, Hannibal."

"You must, Massa Jack. Peter may not come for days, weeks, or mumfs; but he come one day, and make my dream true."

"We will stay here three or four days," said Jack, "and then, if Peter doesn't appear, you must come away with us."

"No, no, Massa Jack! neber widout Peter."

"But this is mere folly. You will throw away your life.'

"I dream, Massa Jack, and dat dream come true.'

He was firm, and they were sorely perplexed."

What could they do?

If he remained firm, as he showed every promise of doing, how could they risk everything by keeping his company?

On the other hand, how could they leave him?

"We had better leave him ashore," said Tom, "and come back to-morrow"

"Suppose he runs away?"

"No, Massa Jack," broke in Hannibal, his quick ears catching the reply. "I keep about *here* until Peter come. I hab brought some biskit for de day, as I did not 'speck to find Peter at once."

"Promise me one thing," said Jack.

"What am it, Massa Jack?"

"That you will never go from here, without my leave."

"I will not, Massa Jack.

Having this assurance, they left him, and went back to the "Esmeralda," and passed the night there.

In the morning, they returned, and found him sitting quietly upon the banks of the river.

"Me dream again, Massa Jack," was the first words he said.

"About Peter?"

"Yes, massa. He come again, and tank me. He comin' soon, now."

"We have brought you some more grub," said Tom Warren.

"Tank you, Massa Tom."

"Don't you find it lonely, here? Would you not like to have one of the men with you?"

"No, sare. I like much berrer to be alone."

"I wonder if there is anything in his dream?" said Tom, as he and our hero walked aside. "It seems odd, doesn't it?"

"There is a curious affinity in twins." said Jack, "which is not shown in other people. I have read some wonderful stories concerning them."

"So have I, and, up to this time, have thought them all bosh; but now I begin to have a notion of something different."

For three days, Jack and Tom came to the shore, and spent some time with Hannibal.

He was quiet, but confident: and yet Peter did not come.

On the fourth morning, Jack felt that he could stay no longer.

With extra hands on board the rations would soon give out, and starvation come upon them.

He endeavoured to urge Hannibal to leave, but the black would not.

"Peter come soon," he said; "but you, Massa Jack, had berrer go. I stay here wid Peter."

"But you will starve!"

"No black man starve anywhere," replied Hannibal. "I be all right, Massa Jack. You go to England."

"You must go," added Tom, "unless you want to starve us all."

"I know not what to do," said Jack, uneasily. "Hannibal!"

"Yes, Massa Jack."

"If I leave you here, will you be in this spot three months hence?"

"Yes, Massa Jack; me and Peter, too."

"Aye, you and Peter," returned Jack. "Go I must. Come with me?"

"Oh, Massa Jack! don't tink dat I'm unfaithful to you, but I *dare* not go away, when de dream say 'Stop,' but we meet again, Massa Jack."

"I hope so. Good-bye, and remember, three months hence, I will be here again."

"Good-bye!" said Tom.

They shook hands, and Jack and Tom turned sorrowfully away.

Hannibal sat upon the ground, and covered his face with his hands.

He was sitting this way when Jack

turned and took a last look at him, and thus they left him,

———

CHAPTER LXIV.

THE DREAM COME TRUE.

" DEY gone away," muttered Hannibal. "Oh, good-bye, Massa Jack! I hear de rowlocks ob de boat, and, in a few minutes, I be alone. What dat?"

He knelt down upon the ground, and listened with his eyes intent upon the cavern from whence the waters came.

"Peter's voice!" he shrieked, springing to his feet. "Massa Jack, come back!"

They were too far away to hear, but he could see Jack and Tom clambering over the side.

"Oh! Massa Jack," he shrieked, "I hear him voice!"

The boat was hoisted in, and the anchor began to rise.

Hannibal knelt again, half mad with excitement, and listened.

There was a voice coming from the cave, saying—

"Hannibal, my brudder!"

"Massa Jack! Massa Jack!" shouted Hannibal. "Peter coming. Oh, stop, Massa Jack!"

He ran to and fro like a madman—loth to leave the vicinity of the cave, and yet wanting to rush down to the shore.

"The canvas of the "Esmeralda" filled out, and she fell off before the wind.

She was leaving.

"Massa Jack, don't go!" yelled Hannibal.

And whilst his words were yet ringing in the air, there glided from the dark cavern a rude structure—half boat, half raft—with Peter the Great upon it.

"Hannibal!"

"Peter!"

This was their cry, and with a mighty bound, Hannibal cleared the intervening space, and lighting on the raft, held his brother in his arms.

Locked thus, they glided down the river, and into the sea.

The rocking of the frail structure brought them to themselves, and Hannibal pointed out to sea, where the "Esmeralda" was far away.

"You come a little late," said Hannibal. "Massa Jack not dere."

"I berry late," said Peter; "but I come along a bad road, and I come berry slow. Massa Jack gone? I berry sorry.

"No," cried Hannibal; "him see us!"

"De 'Esmeralda' drop her sail."

"A boat lowered, Peter!"

"And Massa Jack get in. Hooroar!"

They became so excited that they upset their raft, and for a moment disappeared under the deep; but they were up like corks, and clung to the raft until the boat, propelled by four seamen, and Jack in the stern, came up.

"Is it Peter?" asked Jack, as he approached.

"It am dat berry chile," replied Peter.

"Come in," said Jack, giving him a hand. "Oh! what good fortune has brought you hither?"

"I come on dat raft," replied Peter, "tro de ugliest riber in the wide world."

"Under that mountain?"

"Ah, Massa Jack! and tro worse t'ings dan dat."

"But here you are safe and sound. You will get a rare welcome when you go on board."

"I should purfer a little bit ob meat and bread first," said Peter. "I hab not'ing for two, t'ree days."

When the boat touched the side, everybody, especially Pitchpot, made a rush at Peter to ask him questions, but Jack waved them off.

"He must have something to eat first," he said.

Pitchpot plunged head-first below, and reappeared like a sprite, with a quantity of meat and bread, and a bottle of ale.

"Where will you have it?" asked Jack.

"Here," said Peter, sitting down upon the deck, and forthwith begun the attack.

"You may have all you like," said Mr. Enoch Grubbins; "but take my advice, and limit your first cargo."

"Or you'll bust," put in Simmons, from the rear.

Peter took this advice, and made a fairly moderate meal of about a pound of bread and double that quantity of meat. Then he declared himself ready to tell his story.

Niggers like all effects, and nothing would do for Peter but that his listeners should sit in a half circle and he stand in front like an orator.

They yielded to him. Grubbins and the other gentlemen lighted up cigars; Simmons, Pitchpot, and Hannibal all fitted their mouths with a short pipe, and Peter began his story.

He told first how he had encountered

the two natives, and fled from them to the idol-house, where he shot into a gulph and shook the very life out of himself.

With the particulars thus far our readers are acquainted, and from this we will take up his story, not in his own vernacular, but in the best English we can give, so as to make the story clear.

Peter awoke from his insensibility to find himself in semi-darkness and with the noise of falling masses of stone over his head.

He could hear men's voices, too, uttering savage, vengeful shouts, and he came to the conclusion, which was the right one, that they were pulling the idol-house above his ears so as to bury him alive and avenge the sacrilege he had been guilty of.

Soon their work was done, and no light came from above.

Still he was not in darkness.

This gave him hope, and rising to his feet, he shook off the feeling of numbness which had followed his fall, and took a survey of the place about him.

Gradually his eyes pierced the gloom, and he saw that it was a fairly arched room cut out of the solid rock, and graven with strange figures and cabalistic letters.

On one side was a dark recess, which, on approaching, proved to be a passage leading into a darkness so terrible that Peter's heart quailed.

But it was the only outlet.

He searched all round the cavern, but found no other means of exit, and as to stay there was death, he resolved to avail himself of it.

He passed into it, walking with extreme caution, having a lively recollection of his last feat in the tumbling way. But nothing impeded his progress for a distance which he calculated to be at least four hundred yards, and then he came to a rough wooden door.

This was fastened after a fashion, but one thrust from his sturdy shoulder put it down, and he found himself in another chamber, more wonderful than the last.

It was of enormous size, and lighted up by means of a thousand intersections in the roof, evidently very near the earth's surface. These intersections were artificial narrow slits, such as one sees in the old castles, but carefully concealed by a vegetable growth. The floor was of sand, and covered with innumerable serpents, great and little. Through the centre a river ran.

Peter had no fear of the noisome creatures which slid round about him,

more than one of whom lifted their heads to hiss at him; but once a snake charmer always a snake charmer, and none attempted to touch him.

The prospect, however novel, was scarcely inviting. There was no apparent outlet from the cavern except by the river, which ran out of darkness into darkness as far as Peter could see.

While peering into the cavern from where the river emerged, Peter caught sight of the outline of the rude structure in which he appeared before his brother. This was sufficient evidence of the occasional, if not frequent, presence of man; and Peter, plunging in boldly, took possession of the craft, and, cutting it adrift, gave himself up to the mercy of the current.

His serpent friends hissed at him violently as he departed; but this did not trouble him, and bowing politely, he drifted into darkness.

The journey was a short one; in five minutes he was out into daylight in the midst of a beautiful wood. The current was very rapid, and, thinking that it would take him to the sea, Peter allowed his barque to drift on, until at a bend it stuck fast.

There he went ashore, and gathered a little bread fruit. While thus occupied, he heard a dreadful roaring, and, through an opening in the forest, he beheld an enormous lion approaching him.

One thing only could be done—take to the raft again, for he had no weapons. Even those he had taken from the savages had been left behind in the cave.

Seizing a fallen branch, he sprang upon the raft, and pushed it off, just in time to disappoint the furious beast.

For hours it accompanied him on his way, bellowing and tearing up the earth, and hoping, perhaps, that the raft would ground again; but Peter managed to keep it in the full swing of the current, and the lion at last left him.

The next few days he drifted on, not knowing whither he was going, but hoping each day to catch a sight of the sea. One night he heard a murmuring, such as the deep waters make, and his heart beat with hope.

But he was soon undeceived.

A bright glare rose up in the air, and all the signs of a dreadful fire became apparent. This was the conflagration which had arisen when Jack fired, and it was coming towards Peter, marching in great strides.

He could hear the dreadful roaring,

and the hissing of fiery branches as they fell into the river; and death, indeed, seemed near at hand.

But no; when the flames were within two hundred yards of him, the wind suddenly veered, and a great storm arose; the rain fell in cataracts, and, great as the fire was, it succumbed.

Thus was his life saved, but it brought another peril; the river rose high, and dashed upon its course at a fearful rate. The raft was whirled and spun about most terribly, and at last wedged between two fallen trees, where it remained hard and fast.

The waters rise and fall rapidly in these parts, and by the morrow the river was quiet again. The raft fell with it, and Peter continued his strange journey.

The next morning a swarm of savages swam out and boarded him. Resistance would have been absurd, so he allowed himself to be taken quietly ashore.

His captors kept him many days, singing, dancing, and howling over him. What they said he could not tell; but, in the end, they bound him on the raft and set him afloat again.

Tied firmly, he thought he would have starved to death; but, after a mighty struggle, he got one arm free, and the rest soon followed.

Just as he succeeded, the raft slid under a huge mountain into subterranean waters.

The terrors of this part of the journey, Peter never fully explained, but he told many tales of awful slimy monsters clinging to rugged rocks, and ghastly, fulsome vegetation hanging from the roof.

The river ran miles through the mountain, and he must have been there more than a day when he saw the end was near.

Once a serpent, dangling from the roof, struck his face, and fell upon the raft. Peter gave himself up for lost, but the monster rolled off into the river with a splash, and appeared no more.

Sometimes he heard a shouting as of men's voices with a thousand power, with awful echoes that made his blood run cold. At other times, shrieks, as of those in torment, resounded along the roof, but what they were and whence they came, he never knew.

He saw Hannibal, long before he came into the daylight, and shouted out his name.

This was the shout that Hannibal heard, and then they met as we have recorded.

So ended Peter's story.

A strange and wondrous narrative, but told without any exaggeration in desire to make a hero of himself.

In all things, great or little, Peter was simple and guileless as a child.

CHAPTER LXV.

A SENSATION TRIAL.

THERE was great commotion in our little island, all the public were interested in one man—John Scarborough—the so-called pirate.

His story had been told again and again as it was known. He had gone to sea as a pirate, had been arrested, and had succeeded in making his escape; but, more marvellous to relate, he had given himself up again.

Where he came from none of the public knew, but this much was certain, that one morning he and the three negroes who had escaped with him surrendered themselves to the magistrates and desired to be tried.

How they came the reader may readily guess. The "Esmeralda" had returned to port in the night, and when boarded by the Custom-house officers, nothing contraband was found upon her, nothing but Mr. Grubbins and a knot of his own private friends, apparently. Jack and his dark friends had been put ashore previously.

Certain arrangements were made with regard to the "Esmeralda" by Mr. Grubbins, which seemed to be harsh and strange, but nobody grumbled. They were as follows:

For a time, nobody but Enoch Grubbins himself was to go ashore, and nobody from the shore to come aboard.

"I'm man enough to pull a boat," he said, "and I will do it."

He went ashore, and, after a few inquiries, ascertained that Mrs. Grubbins was staying a few miles out with a friend, and that, it being believed that the "Esmeralda," with all hands, had gone down long ago, she had put on widow's weeds.

"I'll spoil her joke," said Enoch Grubbins, grimly; "I'll run down and see her."

Before going he paid a visit to a celebrated lawyer of his acquaintance, and laid before him the facts connected with Jack's history, at the same time empowering him to engage the best counsel, and spend money *ad libitum.*

Then he engaged a vehicle and drove down to startle his would-be widow.

The house where she was staying was just over the Portsdown Hills, and stood in the midst of an orchard—a very pretty place, very suitable for the retirement of one in sorrow.

" I won't knock," thought Grubbins, " but I will go in and give her a shock, she has given me one many a time."

The front door was open, and he walked in. Stooping down by a door and peeping through the keyhole, he beheld a stout, matronly woman in black, with widow's weeds.

" That's her," he muttered; " now for the shock!"

Opening the door he entered.

" Mrs. Grubbins," he said.

She turned, and stared at him with all her might.

" Enoch!" she cried, " is it you?"

" It is, and nobody else," he replied.

" Oh! dear Enoch, how glad I am to see you."

She folded him in her arms with unfeigned joy, and she kissed him again and again.

" Dash it!" he muttered. " I did not expect this. Are you really glad to see me, my dear?"

" I am indeed, Enoch," she replied. " Oh! how sorry I have been for my unkindness. You have no idea how bitterly I regretted my cruelty after I thought you were dead."

" Oh! you never did much, Martha," he said; " a little scolding, and so on."

" It is kind of you, Enoch, to say but I am a changed woman."

" You will never drop upon me again

" Never," she said, and then he kissed her again.

" I owe Scarborough something for this," said Mr. Grubbins, as he strolled up and down the lawn with his wife, and smoking a cigar; " it comes a little late, but connubial bliss is worth having at any time, if it is real."

It may be here remarked that he had lighted that same cigar with the widow's weeds of Mrs. Grubbins, and that the joke was enjoyed by that lady amazingly.

Let us pass over the next few days, and come to the trial of Jack. The excitement was immense, for the trial of the men he had left behind had been put off from time to time, until Jack should be captured, and now all were arranged.

But Jack, as the head and front of the offending, was to be tried separately.

So great was the excitement, that the general public had no chance of obtaining admission, and only such as could obtain orders from the judge, could get into the court.

The ladies were there in great force, and when our hero—manly, handsome, and well-dressed—appeared in the dock, a low murmur of admiration ran round the court; but, as the newspapers remarked at the time, was promptly suppressed by the ushers.

The prosecution was opened by the Solicitor-General, who appeared on behalf of the Admiralty, and he, being a learned man, with brilliant abilities, gathered up the sympathies of the court and listeners, by describing in harrowing details the doings of a pirate at sea. He likened Jack unto a fair serpent, a tiger in a lamb's skin, to a demon in the garb of an angel, and then proceeded to call witnesses.

First, Captain Cursly, who glibly told his old story, and was permitted by Jack's counsel to sit down without cross-examination. Thus far all went well with him, and he took a seat at the solicitor's table to enjoy the rest of the trial.

Next Captain Rowley appeared, and told what he had to tell, and other evidence was given with regard to the " Singapore," which changed the tide of feeling against Jack, and all the listeners set him down as a fiend incarnate.

His counsel, Serjeant Wollopem, cross-examined very little. A few questions he did ask, but nothing of seeming importance; and so the trial proceeded, and all the evidence that could be scraped against our hero was given.

Then his counsel rose to reply.

He began by quietly reminding the jury that every man was innocent until he was proved guilty, and that however black the prisoner might appear at that moment, he (the counsel) was in a position to wash him white. He forebore to asperse the character of any of the witnesses, except Captain Cursly, whom he stigmatised as a " pitiful cur," and " white-feathered bird of the navy." The rest, he said, were simply mistaken, but Captain Cursly knew he was a liar.

The prosecution was under an impression that he had no witnesses to call, and resting in this belief, Captain Cursly smiled at the scathing words of the counsel. He could afford to laugh at such rubbish, for who would believe? But he changed colour when Serjeant Wollopem shouted out—

"Call Thomas Warren!"

Tom stepped lightly into the box, and exchanged a smile with our hero.

"Your name is Thomas Warren?"

"Yes."

"You were an officer of the 'Thunderer'?"

"I was, under Captain Cursly."

"Just so. You were left on the coast of Africa?"

"Yes."

"Will you relate the circumstances?"

Tom told the story of his captivity and rescue as briefly as possible, and long ere it was finished a coming change in the feeling of the audience was visible.

When the story was done—

"Since your captivity, where have you been?" asked the counsel.

"Round the world with my friend there," replied Tom, pointing to Jack, "hunting down pirates and rascals. Under his skilful guidance, we sunk a fleet of them.

"Did you never attack a trading vessel?"

"Never," replied Tom; "but we protected scores."

"That will do. You may sit down, unless my learned friend wishes to examine you?"

"I have not a word to say about such a farrago of nonsense," replied the Solicitor-General.

"Very good," said the Sergeant. "Charles Granby."

Captain Cursly turned deadly white, and clutched the table with his hands as he strove to hide his emotion.

The young mid took his place in the witness-box, and kissed the Book.

"Your name is Charles Granby?"

"Yes."

"What are you?"

"Midshipman in the Royal Navy."

"Where did you last serve?"

"In the 'War Eagle.'"

"Under whom?"

"Captain Cursly."

"You were in her when she was lost?"

"I was."

"Relate how it happened."

"I must object to this," said the Solicitor-General; "it does not bear upon the question."

"It does, indeed," replied Sergeant Wollopem, "I am leading up to the 'Singapore.'"

The court ruled that the examination was correct.

Jack's counsel proceeded.

"What caused the loss of the 'War Eagle'?"

"We fell in with a third-rate pirate craft, and Captain Cursly refused to fight her. She set fire to us with red-hot shot, and blew up our magazine."

A murmur of execration arose; but, as before, the ushers were at their posts, and it was promptly suppressed.

"You were blown into the sea?"

"I was."

"With the others?"

"With some, but most of our gallant fellows were killed at once."

"Was this the first time Captain Cursly refused to fight?"

"No; he funked everybody and everything. Once he ran away from a Dutch lugger."

A roar of laughter followed this reply, and the judge, after a little private choking, sternly reproved such levity.

The examination proceeded.

"When you were in the sea, did you notice anything?"

"Yes, I saw Captain Cursly taken on board the pirate, and when the captain held out his hand, Captain Cursly took it."

"Would you have done so?"

"I would rather have died a hundred times."

"Bravo, youngster!" shouted out a seafaring man, who, for his temerity, was turned out, and lost the rest of the trial.

"You were picked up?"

"Yes, by the 'Swallow.'"

"And treated kindly?"

"I was, indeed. Jack Scarborough is kindness itself."

"You remember the 'Singapore'?"

"Yes. We found her adrift with her helm lashed up. We boarded her, and found that her crew and passengers had been brutally murdered."

"The 'Swallow' had no hand in this?"

"Certainly not."

"Now, since you have known the prisoner, have you seen anything of a criminal nature in his conduct?"

"No; he is honest, noble, upright, and brave at all times," replied Charley. "In my opinion, he has no equal in the wide world."

"You say he is brave," the counsel said.

"Aye, that he is," the lad returned. "We came upon him once bound to a rock. A dozen pirates were aiming at him, but he did not flinch."

The Solicitor-General declined to cross-examine this witness also.

He was young and enthusiastic, and evidently grateful for having his life spared, and, therefore, he "took his evidence for what it was worth," he said, and Charley retired."

But why dwell upon the details of the scene ?

Blow after blow was dealt at the prosecution, until it was shivered to atoms, and Captain Cursly was a ruined man.

Coddem's evidence was as clear as that of Charley Granby; and Captain Marston, of the ill-fated "Jupiter," told the story of the island in the southern sea, with its store of piratical prize craft.

_____

CHAPTER LXVI.

AFTER THE RELEASE.

HIS lieutenant, Barnham, supported him, and Enoch Grubbins, with his now attached and devoted wife seated immediately behind him, added the last item of refuting evidence.

The Solicitor-General threw up his brief; he had no reply, and the jury, in one minute, returned a verdict of "Not Guilty."

The shout which followed could not be suppressed, and it was currently reported afterwards, that the ushers themselves joined in it, and even the judge rattled his feet in a dignified way.

One man was certainly silent, and that was Captain Cursly.

With his head upon the table he sat, and nobody heeded him. Silence was restored, and he sat there still.

Then Peter, Hannibal, and Pitchpot, and the seamen were ushered into the court, and no evidence being offered against them, they were declared free.

Jack had waited for them, and, in a body, he and his men went forth.

The shout which met them outside made the old court ring again.

Captain Cursly raised his head, and found judge, jury, counsel, ushers, all gone. He was alone.

"I am ruined and degraded for life," he said, and then he burst out sobbing like a child.

*   *   *   *   *

The release of Happy Jack and his comrades was hailed with joy by the public, more particularly by those who had been witness of his gallant bearing before the judges on the two occasions.

His hotel was besieged by mobs of people, who insisted upon his coming out periodically, to receive their cheers, and one glimpse of the black muzzles of either Peter, Hannibal, or Pitchpot, was sufficient to secure a general roar.

Jack wanted quiet, and, with a view of diverting the crowd, sent the niggers out for a walk, and desired his men, who were stowed away below, to go with them.

Nothing could be more congenial to the feelings of either the negroes or the sailors, and, in a body, they sallied forth from the hotel.

A shriek of gladness, I know no other term so fitting to describe the cry which uprose from the thousand throats, hailed their appearance, and, forthwith, a procession was organised, and with the niggers and seamen at the head, marched in fours through the town.

Somehow, nobody knew how, a band got at the head, and proceeded to play every tune it could think of, from "See, the Conquering Hero Comes," to "A Frog He would a Wooing Go," which gave a very lively effect to the whole arrangement.

But all was not yet done that an enthusiastic public could do. One man knew of a banner, and another knew of a banner stowed away in the places that were passed, and these were promptly dragged forth and unfurled, until many hundred yards of bunting were flaunting in the breeze.

Many of these banners were not exactly *apropos* to the event, but what did that matter? They *were* banners, and that was enough for the general public. The following mottoes, selected from the gayest, will suffice to give an idea of the whole—

"The Widows' and Orphans' Fund."

"Give and Take."

"Magna Charta, and our Rights."

"Vote for Bones, the Friend of the People."

"Cheap Bread and Dear Labour."

"The Griddle Building Society."

"Up, Guards, at 'em."

"Cripper and Liberty."

"Shall we die like Slaves ? "

And one had a fancy picture of a beadle making soup out of old boots for the poor, being a sarcastic reflection on a very unpopular functionary at the workhouse.

It need not be stated that these banners had been used on previous occasions, and many of them being old friends, had been hailed with joy, that of the beadle being particularly popular.

In addition to them, the procession was ornamented in other ways.

A cartload of butchers' assistants formed a very conspicuous object, and their enthusiasm in the cause of the released prisoners was undoubted.

They sang and danced, and shouted, and cheered in a way which placed their heartiness beyond all suspicion.

There was a brewer's van, also, which having naught but empty casks upon it, offered a fine means of conveyance, which the public availed itself of largely, and those who rode upon the barrels gave alternate cheers for the brewers and the seamen of the " Swallow."

Many other carts and vehicles of various descriptions also fell in, and great was the uproar.

Suddenly there was a cry for Cursly.

Who raised it was never ascertained, but it was taken up readily, and his residence being one well known, the crowd turned towards it.

Peter the Great and his brother knew that this would be distasteful to our hero, and would fain have returned, but the crowd forced them on.

Captain Cursly's house was in an open square, which was filled by the excited mob, and cries were raised for him to " Come out ! "

The unhappy, fallen man was at home, and he only wanted such a thing as this to entirely crush him.

He heard the shouts, knew their purport, and fled to the cellar for safety.

A shower of stones shattered every window in front of his house, and then strong shoulders were thrust against his door.

It had only the ordinary latch up, and it quickly yielded.

There is nothing more dangerous than a mob, be that mob made up of rich or poor.

The love of destruction is in us all, and give an example and opportunity, and terrible things are done.

In ten minutes, the house was wrecked. Captain Cursly was found, dragged from his hiding-place, and hoisted upon the shoulders of some sturdy men.

His pale, terrified face only excited laughter, and cries of " Stone him " were heard ; but suddenly he disappeared from the shoulders of those who bore him, and fell into a little circle of friends.

And who were those friends ?

Happy Jack and his brave followers.

Our hero had heard of the uproar, and came forth in search of his followers.

He found them just as his enemy was dragged from his house, and threatened with death.

He made a stirring appeal to his followers.

"He is but one man," he said, "and shall the world say that it took all of us to kill him ? We are his accusers, but we are not his judges, or his executioners."

They listened to him, and formed a circle round the wretched man, who now saw his own baseness as he had never seen it before : and he bowed his body for very shame, as if he would have grovelled in the dust.

"If you fall," said Jack " I cannot save you. Stand erect, man ! "

"Stone the coward and liar ! "Death ! " shouted fifty voices.

" Hoist me up," said Jack, to Peter and Hannibal.

And they had him upon their shoulders in a moment.

"Men of England," cried Jack, " shall it be said that you killed a man before his trial ? The best and worst of us have alike a right to be condemned by the law, and by the law only."

" He is a coward ! " they shouted.

" I know it," said Jack ; " but let him go. He will suffer more living than dead. You have shown me much goodwill to-day, for my sake let him go."

They listened to him, and a cheer arose, " Hurrah for Happy Jack ! " and the temper of the crowd being turned, the life of Captain Cursly was saved. The people paraded a little longer and then quietly dispersed.

" Captain Cursly," said Jack, " I will leave you now. For the present I think you are safe, but turn your back upon this place as soon as you can."

" Thank you for nothing," said the captain, curtly. " Have you anything more to say ? "

" No," replied Jack, " except this, that a cur you have lived and a cur you will die. Farewell ! "

The captain turned upon his heel biting his lips, and his house being a wreck he went to his club. The porter stopped him at the door.

" I have orders not to admit you, sir," he said.

" Why not ? " asked the captain, savagely.

" Your name is struck off the books."

With a bitter execration, the disgraced man strode away, and came to an hotel. As he entered the door the host met him.

" I cannot take you in, sir."

"Why not?"

"My house would not be safe. The people might serve mine as they have served yours."

"There is no longer any danger," pleaded the captain.

"I cannot take you in," was the decided reply, as he turned from the door.

He tried another hotel with a similar result, and then the feeling of being utterly an outcast took possession of him.

"I have no home, and no friends," he muttered. "Who so lonely in this wide world as I?"

Still, his pity was all for himself, and in his sorrow there no real repentance.

He was in a terrible fix—he knew not whither to turn; and after a little thought, he went to the police-station.

He asked for an escort—and obtained one—to guard him out of the city.

Four policemen saw him two miles out on the road, and then he hired a chaise and pair, and was driven away.

It will be as well to dispose of him at once, and for all.

He was summoned to attend a court-martial, but he never came, and the court sentenced him to a dismissal from the service, and a forfeiture of all the rights and emoluments proceeding from his office.

This act disgraced him, and he was never seen in English society again.

At first it was reported that he had committed suicide; but he was too great a coward even for that coward's act; and, under a fictitious name he wandered about the continent for many years, lived unfriended and alone, until he was shot accidentally in a gambling brawl in which he had no concern, and died in hospital, with naught but strangers round him.

CHAPTER LXVII.

10 THE ISLAND ONCE MORE.

IT will be recollected by the careful reader, that when Tom Warren and Charley Granby left the wonderful Pacific isle where Jack had taken up his headquarters, Jim Swaby and about a dozen men were told off to remain in the snug retreat to take care of the "Swallow" and her prizes.

Now that Jack's innocence had been so conclusively established, and that he was free to do as he chose, his first thought was of the faithful fellow who had passed through so many adventures under his command.

He would have been only too well pleased to have remained at home for a time and taken things easy after the few years of excitement and turmoil upon the ocean; but his conscience told him that his first duty was to his old friend, and we know that Jack never shirked a call. Through the whole of the time during which we have been following his fortunes, his character has been that of the brave, daring, and resolute English lad who follows the dictates of the inward monitor in all things, and thus he had become the idol of every true heart with which he had come in contact. Therefore, it is not to be wondered at that we find him looking about for the means by which to charter a vessel that would carry him safely to his island home.

He had not to wait long, however. The irrepressible Mr. Enoch Grubbins, emerging for a time from the realms of connubial bliss in which he had now ensconced himself, came to the rescue like the jolly, good old fellow he was.

Jack had some qualms as to accepting the gentleman's generosity. He was much beholden to him already in the matter of the "Esmeralda," and he feared to trespass on his bounty.

"Fudge!" ejaculated the owner of the yacht; "you know what a splendid craft she is, and there is no one in the world who can sail her better than yourself; so take her, my boy, and welcome. You have done me the greatest favour in life by placing Mrs. Grubbins and myself on that amicable footing which husband and wife should always occupy, and I must make some return."

"You have already done so fourfold," replied our hero.

"Not a bit of it. Our trip was the most enjoyable portion of my life."

"But you have borne all the expense of the trial, my dear sir."

"That was done for my own gratification. I wanted to silence the carping fellows in the club, and I think I have succeeded."

"Quite true," returned Jack; "but if I go back on the 'Esmeralda,' will you not, at least, accompany me?"

Mr. Grubbins took his cigar from his mouth, and gazed at our hero with an expression of blank astonishment.

"Accompany you, my dear boy!" he

exclaimed. "Why, what are you thinking about? Mrs. Grubbins has announced to all her friends and acquaintances that she will never trust me out of her sight again, and I have passed my word never to go as far even as the Isle of Wight without her. She has also openly confessed her horror of the sea, so you understand that the very idea of my going on such a voyage is preposterous."

Jack smiled, for he thought of the small amount of persuasion that was requisite to tempt the yacht-owner on the previous occasion, and the smile was noted by his companion.

"Ah, you may laugh," said Mr. Grubbins, "but let those laugh who win. I have at last won Mrs. Grubbins sincere regard, and I mean to keep it, Master Jack. Now, if you will have the 'Esmeralda' say so, and I will at once get her overhauled and put in proper trim for the voyage."

"I will take her on one condition," answered Jack.

"What is that?"

"That you will allow me to buy her right out on my return."

"Bah! I make her a present to you."

"But I will have more money than I can ever need when I have sold my prizes, even after I have shared with my former companions and crew."

"I will never take a penny for her from you. I owe you more than I can repay, so don't let me hear another word. When do you intend to sail?"

"As soon as possible," returned our hero.

"Then I will have the vessel seen to at once. By the way," the kind hearted fellow hesitated for a moment—"if you should be—ah—temporarily embarrassed, my purse is at your service to any amount."

"How can I ever thank you for all that you have done?" observed Jack. "But the fact is, I have quite sufficient for my daily needs, though not enough to charter a vessel for a long voyage. Besides, I hope my uncle's estates will be restored to him now, that is, if the dear old boy be still alive, but I can scarcely think he is, else he would certainly have come forward at the trial."

"Just so! the reparation is due to him along with an ample apology. I don't believe he's dead, though," said Grubbins, more gravely. "He was not a man to take his own life under any circumstances, and my idea is that he has hidden himself away under the burden of wrong and seeming disgrace. In that case he may not have heard of all that has been going on."

"Poor old uncle!" sighed our hero, "I only wish he was with me now to share in our joy and thankfulness."

"Cheer up, Scarborough! Things have turned out all right up till now, and you may bet that your uncle will put in an appearance when you least expect it."

The brightness of Grubbins's smile, and his buoyancy of spirits, had their natural effect upon Jack, and imparted a lightness of heart to our hero which he seldom now felt when thinking of his uncle. The mysterious disappearance was the one thing which troubled him, and proved the drop of aloes in his cup of happiness.

"It is kind of you to speak so hopefully," he said to his companion, "and we will try to think of the matter from your point of view."

"Do, my boy. And now I must say *au revoir*, for Mrs. Grubbins will be impatient for my return. Never knew a woman so fond of her husband's society, and upon my word I enjoy it. I'll have the 'Esmeralda' docked this very night, and you may rely upon her being gone over thoroughly. Have a weed? ta ta!"

He was off like a shot, and Jack stood lighting his cigar, as he gazed after him down the street.

"The best hearted old chap in the universe," he muttered to himself. "The yacht is the very thing to suit me, though how I'm to get all the prizes to England for sale is a matter for much consideration."

His reflections were interrupted by a hail from three pairs of lungs at once: "Massa Jack, ahoy!"

He turned to behold his three coloured followers bearing down upon him full sail, with grappling irons all fixed; or, in other words, with arms closely linked together.

CHAPTER LXVIII.

AFLOAT AGAIN.

BEHIND the three trusty negroes followed the rag tag and bobtail of Portsmouth town, who ever and anon sent up a lusty shout which filled the proud heart of Peter, the Great, with unbounded joy. It was evident that the attentions of well-meaning persons towards the ebony heroes had placed them in that condition which nautical persons designate by the term "three sheets in the wind." Pitchpot in particular seemed to labour rather heavily in the breeze, and as he had the central position between his two more burly companions, he seemed like a little merchant-man under convoy of two huge men-of-war.

"Now den, you disruly members ob de immunity," shouted Peter, as he suddenly wheeled round, almost flinging the unsteady Pitchpot on his beam ends. "I'be got to gib you a piece ob dis chile's mind. Dar's Massa Jack Sparbellow enjoyin' ob de calomel ob pieces, an' if any ob you white dirt dare to reproach widin two hundred yards an' a half ob his sakreed pusson, you look out fur squallses, dat's all."

Peter brandished his gingham with the air of a commander-in-chief, and the crowd responded with a cheer which shook the glass in the window frames of all the houses within a reasonable distance.

This seemed to arouse a spirit of emulation within the bosom of Pitchpot. He suddenly withdrew his arms from the supporting elbows of his friends, and drew himself up with much dignity.

"Friends, feller-citterzens, an'—an' udder pussons!" he cried, in somewhat husky tones. "Allow me to t'ank you fur dis heart-breakin' debbilstration—"

Peter here broke in with a laugh.

"You laugh at me?" enquired Pitchpot, stopping short in his harangue.

"Yes, you iggurant nigger."

"No more nigger dan you," retorted the other, rendered somewhat pot-valiant.

"Yes, you am. You no pernounce de English langwidge."

"What I say?" demanded Pitchpot, slightly crestfallen.

"What him say, Hannibal?" asked Peter, turning to his brother.

Now Hannibal had heard the word, and he knew that something had been wrong but what it was had entirely slipped his memory during the conversation that ensued, and so he stood scratching his head, and seeking to recover his ideas from the far away heavens, if one might judge from the direction of his gaze.

"What him say?" demanded Peter, who had himself forgotten the word.

"It wasn't railway-station," his brother answered, in the tone of a man who was making a bad guess.

"Ob corse it wasn't! You as iggurant as de udder nigger. Him say debbil-station, when him mean demonstation."

"Well, it all de same," shouted Pitchpot, triumphantly. "Ain't de demon an' de debbil de same pusson. You iggurant nigger dis time, Massa Peter," and the coloured gentleman's gentleman attempted to indulge in one of those wild gyrations to which his friends had got accustomed. Unluckily, however, for the would-be orator his potations had been rather too deep to permit of saltatory effects, and he came a severe cropper on that portion of his anatomy which Peter used to treat with the affectionate attentions of the lion's tail.

The crowd burst into a roar of laughter, in which Jack could not refrain from joining as he sauntered slowly up.

"Hulloh, Peter! what's the matter with our friend?" he asked.

"Ah, Massa Jack!" replied the dark potentate, as he shook his head, "me 'fraid him head lighter dan him udder part."

"Him drunk," remarked Hannibal, sententiously.

"You all drunk, me sober," Pitchpot affirmed, as he picked himself up with some difficulty. "You no consult dis chile."

"Who's consultin' you?" enquired Peter, with rising wrath.

"Hannibal am."

Jack saw that the waters, or we might rather say, the *liquors* were about to become troubled, so he quickly proceeded to throw oil upon them by changing the subject.

"Well, my brave boys," he said, "what would you think if I proposed another voyage?"

"Hooroar!" bellowed Hannibal, with the voice of a festive lion. "Anudder v'y'ge wid Happy Jack!"

"Hooroar!" echoed his two companions. "Three cheers fur Happy Jack!"

The crowd that had collected, and were standing in enjoyment of the scene we have just described, took up the infectious cry; and "Three cheers for Happy Jack!" went round in one vast, tumultuous roar.

"Come with me, lads!" cried our hero, quietly; and amidst the confusion that ensued, he and his followers made their way to his hotel. The twin brethren dragging their less sober compatriot after them by main force.

When he had got them all seated in a private room, he dispatched a waiter to find Tom Warren, who was putting up at the same place. Luckily Tom was in, and was overjoyed to meet the three sons of Ham.

"Now then, Tom," said Jack, "I have just given a hint to our old friends here that I am likely to go to sea again."

"Of course you are!" Tom Warren interrupted. "Whoever heard of a young fellow turning his back upon the sea once he placed his foot upon the companion ladder."

"Yes, yes!" our hero returned, somewhat impatiently. "But what I meant to say was that I am likely to go to sea again very shortly in my own boat."

"In de ' Swallow?'" enquired Peter, opening his eyes very wide.

"Well, I might if I were really a swallow to be able to fly to the island," Jack replied, with a smile. "No, but I hope to be able to be aboard my dear old craft before many months are over my head. What do you say to a trip on the 'Esmeralda?'"

"But you said your own vessel," Tom observed.

"And she is my own vessel. Grubbins, who is the noblest fellow alive, present company excepted, of course, has made me a present of her, and is having her fitted out for another cruise. Now, what do you think of it, Tom?"

"I am with you," exclaimed his old messmate, enthusiastically. "What a brick old Grubbins is to be sure!"

"An' so say all ob us!" chorused Peter, Hannibal, and Pitchpot.

"Then it's agreed?" cried Jack, standing up, his face all aglow with excitement.

"Agreed!" shouted all, with one accord.

Pitchpot in his exuberance tried to jump on his chair, but only succeeded in upsetting it, overthrowing Peter in his downfall.

The inevitable exchange of compliments succeeded, from which Hannibal stood aloft in a contemptuous manner.

"Dem bofe drunk," he remarked.

When the prostrate pair had picked themselves up, Jack proceeded to lay before them his plans to which Tom Warren bent a willing ear.

"If I can get Charley Granby and the old hands to join," he concluded, "we'll all feel at home again."

"No take Simmons," Pitchpot observed enquiringly.

"I think we can do without him," the captain returned, with a sly chuckle.

So all matters were arranged, and in three weeks, Jack and his friends were once again outward bound for his Island Home.

———

CHAPTER LXIX.

JIM SWABY'S SEARCH.

A GOOD many events have happened in the course of this veracious history since we left Jim Swaby ensconced as Viceroy on the island, if island it were, which Jack had, so far as he was aware, discovered, and which he had converted into a sort of dockyard for his prizes.

The honest old boatswain was now monarch of all he surveyed, and with his twelve trusty subjects set about the affairs of the kingdom in good earnest.

In the first place Jim, being a loyal subject, erected a tall flagstaff on the rocks oposite the camp on which he hoisted the invincible Union Jack, while below it fluttered the pure white ensign of his commander. That being done, he proceeded to strengthen the fort at its foot, where four guns, taken from the least serviceable of the pirate vessels, guarded in grim dignity the entrance to the creek.

The position thus formed was almost impregnable, as by boring a short distance down amongst the crevices of the rock, they came upon a spring of clear water as cool and limpid as if it sprang from an icy bed. The only danger in case of attack was starvation, and that Jim strove to obviate as far as possible, by laying in a store of salted provisions, and biscuit. He had also picked a large quantity of the fruits which grew on the island, and dried them in the sun, thus adding largely to his stock of provisions, and establishing a sure preventive against scurvy.

The fort or battery, the lines of which had been laid down previously by Jack, but which had never been completed, was situated on the top of the precipitous

"A boat! a boat!" they shouted, running and jumping and going on more like madmen than true British tars.

crags which skirted one side of the entrance to the natural harbour, where the "Swallow" and the captured craft lay so cunningly concealed. Between the cliffs and the mainland lay a hollow, which looked as if the sea had at one time rushed between, but which was now filled with a light, grass-grown alluvial deposit, which Jim found no difficulty in cutting through.

Thus Fort Scarborough, as it was christened by the old sailor, became an island, the only accessible methods of ascent being by the rope ladder from the pool, or a winding and craggy pathway from the moat, as they designated the cut through the narrow neck of land.

The thick stockade and earthwork which they erected on the landward side along the edge of the moat was another sure protection against assault, and, when all these works of defence had been completed, Jim Swaby felt tolerably safe in his retreat. The camp was then moved from the low-lying side of the pool to the heights of Fort Scarborough, in the inside of which four strong huts had been built.

It is needless to say that all these precautions for security took many days to perform with only thirteen men working, but they were all strong, willing fellows, who proceeded with their labour in no half-hearted fashion. Thus it was that everything was complete in less time than might have been expected, and then, having replaced the barrier at the mouth of the harbour, the men laid by their toil for a time, and resolved to abandon themselves to a well-earned rest.

The weather was delightful during this time, for a cool sea-breeze counteracted the powerful rays of the sun, and the result was what may be described as a perfect climate.

"Now," said Jim on the first day of their merited idleness, "you've all been right down good lads, and obeyed me just as if I'd ha' been your skipper himself; but there's summat more to be done if we're agoin' to have proper discipline aboard this 'ere fort. Ye knows as how no wessel can sail without bein' properly officered, as well as manned. So you see, if we're to rule this 'ere island, or wotever it is, we must 'ave everything in trim. Now I was appointed captain before Mr. Warren and Mr. Granby left, therefore, that bein' all square, I bein' the senior officer, it devolves upon you yerselves to elect who's to be second and third in command."

After this tremendously long flight of oratory, for Jim was generally a man of few words, he lay flat upon his back upon the top of an earthwork, whence he had addressed the men, as if exhausted, and awaited their reply.

None of them had held any rank whatever previously, except Bob Richley, who had been ship's carpenter, and therefore it was unanimously resolved that he should be appointed first lieutenant, while Ben Kirby, a true old salt, took the third place in command.

Thus they are to be found a gallant little band, commanded by Jim Swaby, with Bob Richley and Ben Kirby as his first and second officers. These appointments seemed to give satisfaction to all, but there were a couple of the men, good fellows enough in their way, into whose hearts the demon of envy had crept. They had coveted the honour of being officers, and the elevation of Bob Richley and Ben Kirby to their new posts rankled bitterly in their minds.

However, they did not openly exhibit their feelings on the point, and so none of the others were the wiser.

Jim Swaby made a note of the appointments in his log, and the two officers took up their abode in the principal hut, while the ten others occupied two of the remainder, the fourth being set aside as a store-room. The magazine had been constructed right in the centre, where the men had, with infinite pains, excavated a huge pit, lining the sides with closely-set slabs, and roofing it in the same manner, placing over the whole a thick covering of earth. The entrance was by a sloping, covered way, and was blocked by a great, revolving block of stone. Into this receptacle had been carried all the ammunition found on the pirates, leaving the "Swallow" alone in a fit and ready state to attack or oppose an enemy.

After the third or fourth day of repose, Jim Swaby called his little crew together.

"Look here, lads," he said, "you must have had plenty of time now to rest yerselves, an' it strikes me there's no use o' remainin' in idleness any longer. I've been thinking that the best way o' ockipyin' ourselves would be to perform a sort' o' survey o' the island. Yer see Mr. Jack, when he set out with Mr. Warren an' the two niggers, was forced to return, an' a blessed good thing it was for us too, so, instead o' sittin' here a smokin' ourselves dry, we might just as well make an exploration."

" Aye, aye, sir ! very good !" exclaimed the men of one accord.

" Well, that bein' agreed on, I propose that our old messmate here, Ben Kirby, an' two men with him remain behind in the fort here as a garrison, while the rest of us proceed on a reg'lar search."

He looked round for a reply, and one was speedily made by Ben Kirby.

" In coorse," responded the old man, " I'm allus ready to obey commands, but I'd rayther be excused from stayin' behind."

" I know, Ben, I know !" returned the captain, " the old flesh is still willin', an' so's the sperrit ; but somebody must stay behind, an' there must be an officer in command, so as you're the oldest among us, and the most experienced, there's nobody else to do the duty."

This seemed conclusive, and Ben grumblingly assented to the arrangement.

Of all the rest of the men there were only two who seemed at all inclined to take the life of ease which was promised by remaining behind, and these two were the jealous members, whose names were Collins and Hearne.

By an early hour on the morrow, the expedition was ready to start, and Jim Swaby, giving strict injunctions to Ben as to signals in case of attack, placed himself at the head of his adventurous party.

CHAPTER LXX.

ON BOARD OF THE " ESMERALDA."

IN fitting out the yacht for our hero, Happy Jack, the generous but eccentric owner had had a few alterations designed in her, which made her more seaworthy than she had been before, and had placed a couple of swivel guns aboard, one in the bow, and the other in the stern. Thus she was, in a certain measure, capable of defence, if attacked by a foe not too much her superior. Her sailing capabilities excellent as they had been, were even improved upon, and there were very few craft about, which could beat her in a fair match.

All went well with the merry party aboard as they bowled along before a favouring breeze, till they reached the Canaries. Here they put in for water and supplies, and our hero, Tom, and Charley, with their escort of the three blacks went ashore to explore the famous Peak of Teneriffe. In those days it was not quite such an easy matter to make the ascent of the Peak as it is now, yet our hero and his friends were not of that class who would stick at trifles, and they performed the journey to the top of the huge cone, where they looked down upon a world of cloud, and back again without any casualty. The time, however, taken up in performing this feat gave the wind an opportunity to change, and when they reached the " Esmeralda " once again, she was dancing impatiently on her hawser, as if anxious to be off.

We know Happy Jack to be a fearless navigator, but he cast his eye at the heavens with a somewhat anxious gaze before he gave the order to heave the anchor.

" What do you think of it, Tom ?" he asked. " Shall we remain where we are, or make a run for it ?"

" Well, you know the capabilities of the yacht, as well as I do ; but, since you ask me, I should say run."

" Then run it shall be," returned our hero.

The order was at once given, and before an hour was over the " Esmeralda " was scudding before the freshening gale in rare style.

" I don't half like the look of things," said Charley Granby, as he stood beside his captain watching the spray as it flew past them in a drenching shower.

" Nor do I," said Jack ; " but the yacht is staunch enough, and if it doesn't increase, this gale can't do much damage."

" If it don't increase," echoed a voice behind them, and turning, they beheld the form of the indomitable Peter the Great, hat, coat, and never-failing " rumble-reller " complete.

" Why do you think it will ?" asked the captain.

" Me sure ob it, Massa Jack. Him squall dreff'ul bimeby."

" What makes you think so ?"

" Las' night new moon. Me see de ghose ob de ole moon in de lilly moon arms."

" They say that is a sure sign of bad weather," returned Charley Granby, with a serious face, " though why it should be so I'm sure I can't tell."

"Nor I," said our hero; "but it is generally accepted as an ominous portent, but why do you call it the ghost of the old moon. You know it is only our shadow cast upon the orb which causes the obscurity of the greater portion."

"Dunno' nuffin' 'bout Bob Skoority, Massa Jack. Nebber hear ob him afore; but I know dis, when de ole moon 'die, him ghose come sometimes in de new moon arms, an' dar ain't no luck in ghoseses."

This seemed quite conclusive to Peter's mind, and also to the mind of Mr. Pitchpot, whose lanky form stood just behind that of his former master. At the mention of ghosts Pitchpot's eyes began to increase in size till they reached an abnormal extent, and seemed to be all white; while his huge mouth expanded until it looked like a mighty cavern in his head.

"Oh golly, golly, Massa Peter!" he exclaimed, as soon as he could find speech; "for de land's sake doan't 'ee talk ob ghoseses."

"Why not?" enquired Charley Granby, with a suspicious twinkle in his eye.

"'Cos I—'cos I—see'd un oncet myself."

"You once saw a ghost, Pitchpot?" said Jack. "Nonsense! you must be dreaming."

"No, Massa Jack, me see'd him, just as suah as you stan' dar."

"Was he a brack or a white ghose, Pitchpot?" asked Peter, trembling all over.

"Him wasn't brack nor w'ite. Him was a blue ghose."

"You must have been drinking, then, Pitchpot," said Jack, with a laugh.

"Come tell us all about it," cried Charley, while Peter drew nearer to listen, though he was quaking in every limb.

"I was aboard ob de pirut at de time," began Pitchpot, "an' it *was* a time, Massa Jack! Dey was a drinkin', an' a sw'arin', an' a cussin' from de mellumcolly morn to de eberlastin' ebe; an' den dey did it all ober ag'in. Well, dar was a pirut, him not so bad as de res', come to me one night when dey was a drinkin' orful, an' him sez to me, he sez: 'Cookee!' 'Yes, massa pirut,' sez I. 'Me berry bad,' sez he. 'Sorry to hear dat,' sez I. 'You suah you sorry?' sez he. 'Sartain suah,' sez I. 'Den you make some broff,' sez he. 'Broff?' sez I. 'Yes, broff!' sez he. 'Got nuffin' to make broff of,' sez I. 'Dar's turtle aboard,' sez he. 'Turtle soop?' sez I. 'Turtle soop,'' sez he. Den me kill um turtle for de capting's dinnah, an' keep back nice lilly basin ob soop an' nice lilly bit ob fin for de sick pirut. Dat night him come an' hab de soop an' de fin, an' him bring me one, two bottle ob rum. Me drink one bottle, den don' know nuffin' more. In de middle ob de night me was awaked by sumfin drefful in de galley. Dar warn't no noise—dar warn't no breavin'; but me knew dar war a sumfin' sumperlateral. Presumly I looks up an' den my hairs stan's upon eend like um squills upon de dirty perky pines. Dar, right in front ob me, a stan'in' on him fins war de ghose ob a blue turtle."

The burst of laughter which followed Pitchpot's yarn, from Jack and Charley Granby, nearly threw the two negroes into fits. The superstitions of their race were strong upon them, and both Peter and the other saw nothing to laugh at in the idea of a turtle's apparition. On the other hand the two English lads were convulsed with merriment, which only subsided when the "Esmeralda" heeled suddenly over, struck by a terrible gust of wind, which had come upon them without warning.

Jack was alive to the situation in a moment. His clear voice rang out above the roaring of the tempest, and scurrying feet were at once rushing in all directions to obey his necessary commands.

Before many minutes had passed the yacht was under bare poles, and officers and crew were on the alert for further developments.

The "Esmeralda" answered her helm like a thing of life, and in spite of the fury of the wind there seemed to be no immediate danger.

"I am afraid," said Tom Warren, shouting in the ear of the captain, "that we won't be able to keep her to her course."

"That won't matter so much," was the reply, "for we have an open sea before us, and we are not particularly pressed for time."

The words were scarcely spoken when there came a shout from the look-out.

"Large vessel right ahead!"

"Port! Port!" yelled Jack, as a great object boomed up beside them.

Every man held his breath; but in another instant the danger was past.

CHAPTER LXXI.

THE EXPLORATION PARTY.

DOWN the zig-zag pathway from Fort Scarborough to the moat marched Jim Swaby, Bob Richley and the eight men under them. Sturdy, strapping fellows they looked in the morning sunlight, fit for any deed of daring, and able to stand any amount of fatigue or privation.

Arrived at the moat, they pulled themselves over by means of a boat on a running line rove through a block on the opposite bank, which could be pulled backwards and forwards at pleasure from either side by the inhabitants of the fort; but which in time of danger could be detached and drawn into a little boathouse, Jim had caused to be erected for it.

On the opposite side they paused, and gave a parting cheer to the companions they left behind, and immediately began to climb the heights on the mainland. By so doing they got on the top of the crags, which gradually heightening as they went inland, formed the precipice which Jack and his friends had found so difficult of access on the occasion of their visit to the interior.

Every one of the party was thoroughly well-armed with carbine and cutlass, and a couple of navy pistols. They were all in the highest spirits, and laughed and joked as they pursued their way. Four of the men, under the immediate direction of Bob Richley, also carried axes, which they presently found to be very useful in cutting a way through the dense undergrowth and trailing vines which intercepted their path. Yet in spite of these obstacles they went merrily onward, till towards noon they called a halt near the spot where the lion had been killed; but, of course, many feet above, for the precipice lay between.

Wild bananas grew in abundance. with oranges, shaddocks, and bread fruit and of these the party made a wholesome luncheon. They were gathering their belongings together to go onwards again, when Jim Swaby uttered an exclamation of surprise, and shading his eyes with his hand, gazed fixedly towards the east.

From the point where they had rested a long view could be obtained in that direction, over a great slope which seemed to tend towards the ocean, although the sea itself was hidden by a range of hills which appeared to girdle in the slope at the further side. They rose precipitously from a wide river, and it was on that which Jim had fixed his eyes.

"Come here," he said, presently, to the others, "and tell me what you see on yonder water."

"By the powers!" exclaimed an Irishman, named McCarthy, "there's a boat on the sthrame!"

"You're right," returned Bob Richley, "and it's an uncommon long one, too."

"That's no boat," broke in Arthur Guy, a queer fellow who had sailed in many waters, and who had been one of the men on board the pirate "Viper," when she was captured, "that's a war canoe crammed full of savages."

All the others turned towards Guy. He had proved a most trustworthy messmate, notwithstanding the evil company in which he had been found, and they knew that he would say nothing without full knowledge of what he stated.

"Yes," he continued, "you'll find I'm quite right. I've seen the same kind of gentlemen before now, and where there's one there's likely to be more."

"Be jabers! ye're spakin' the truth!" cried Pat McCarthy, "for here comes another an' another. Whirroo! let's make haste an' be down upon the divils! Egorra! I'm sp'ilin' for a row."

"Quiet there, Pat!" said Jim Swaby, seriously. "I rather think we ought to give them a wide berth. If these savages be the original inhabitants of this country, I'm afeard they'll feel inclined to dispute our right to take possession of it."

"That's well spoken, Mr. Swaby," observed Arthur Guy, who, whatever his antecedents might have been, was occasionally apt to betray by speech and bearing, a higher education and a more gentle birth than his companions.

"What do you say, Richley?" enquired Jim, turning to his first lieutenant.

"Well, my idea would be to carefully reconnoitre and find out what we can about them."

"That seems reasonable," returned the captain. "What's your opinion, boys?"

The men consulted together for a few

minutes, and then Guy turned to the leader.

"We think Mr. Richley's suggestion ought to be followed," he said, "at the same time we advise the utmost caution."

"The divil a bit of it!" cried Pat, excitedly. "I'm for a scrimmage to oncet."

"In that case, McCarthy," remarked Jim, severely, "you'll either have to wait our return in this spot, or get back to the fort, whichever you may choose."

"Faix then, Mr. Swaby, I'll be as cautious as a crapin' sarpint," answered Pat, brought up with a round turn, "Though, by the same token," he added, "I wish St. Pathrick had put his fut down somewhere here about, for the varmints come to closer quarters than a son of the Emerald Isle is accustomed to."

In this Pat was perfectly right, for the quantity of snakes they had already encountered was enormous. The men did not know whether they were harmless or poisonous, so they had given them as wide a berth as possible; and, sooth to say, the snakes had done the same by them.

"Well, we are quite decided upon ascertaining the position, and strength, and all the rest of it of the savages, eh?" enquired Jim.

"Aye, aye, Mr. Swaby!"

"Then we had better fall in at once, for it's a good two miles to the river yonder."

The men needed no second bidding. Shouldering their carbines and buckling on their belts they set out on their journey once more.

This portion of their march, though easier of accomplishment, was by no means as lightly entered upon as the start. They knew now that there was what might prove a deadly enemy within an appreciable distance, and the cheery song or lively sally which evoked a burst of laughter on the earlier tramp was not renewed.

The ground was more open on the descent towards the river, and there was little axe work required, which was just as well, for there might be hidden anywhere amongst the trees a savage camp, or at least a prowling band of warriors.

So on and on they went, becoming even more circumspect as they proceeded, even the jovial Pat assumed a solemn countenance, and stepped as softly as the others.

It was a good hour since their luncheon, but their progress, by reason of their extreme caution, had been slow, so now Jim Swaby thought they must be very near the stream, and he called a halt.

"I propose," he said, "that we here separate, and steal forth singly through the belt of trees which I fancy must conceal the river from our sight. On no account act rashly, in any emergency, but if so be as you are attacked, fire your carbine, and the rest of us will be on the scene in a few seconds. If nothing should be met with, return to this spot within half-an-hour, and we will compare notes."

They understood him and departed, Bob Richley taking the post on the extreme left while he himself took the right.

Not ten minutes had elapsed when the short, sharp crack of a carbine was heard, and each member of the party rushed in the direction of the sound.

The scene which met their eyes almost beggars description.

In the centre of a little glade stood Pat McCarthy, laughing as if he would split his sides, while round about him were gathered a score or two of savage women gaping at him in open-mouthed astonishment.

<h2 style="text-align:center">CHAPTER LXXII.</h2>

THE SAVAGES.

IT need not be said that the rest of the party were quite as much astounded as the women seemed to be when they perceived Pat's predicament.

"Och, mother o' Moses!" shouted the son of Erin, "just look at that now! Isn't it an illigant situation to be in entirely, wid five and fifty ladies all makin' eyes at yez to oncet? Shure an' I'm the luckiest blagyard unhanged!"

"What did you fire that shot for!" demanded Jim Swaby, bursting through the ring of women; it may be our ruin."

"What did I fire the shot for!" echoed Pat. "Faix, I'm thinkin' you'd 'a' done the same thing yersilf. I'd hardly started out a squintin' t'roo the bushes a lookin for savages, when shure, I finds myself surrounded by nigh three score o' the craythurs! wurra, wurra! sez I, 'Pat ye're in a foine pickle now!'"

"But why did you fire your carbine ? you do not seem to have been in danger."

"That's just it, bedad ! I'm comin' to't. 'Well,' sez I, 'my beauties, what are ye goin' to do with me, at all ? shure I can't marry the lot of ye, wid that they hustles me into this bare place, an' they all begins to dance around me, as if I was a Kerry fiddler. Then they came so close foreninst me that, egorra, I didn't know whither they were goin' to hug me or ate me, so I let drive wid the gun in the air, just to skear 'em a bit ; but, bless your heart, they only stopped their dancin', an' glowered at me as if I'd been a ghost. So, what could I do but laugh at the fun an' divarshun ? "

"Your fun and diversion may be the death of the whole of us," said Richley.

"Och, divil a bit !" exclaimed Pat. "The craythurs are perfectly harmless. See here now ! I'll just spake to one o' thim in good ould Irish, an' I'll bet she'll answer me right off the reel."

So saying, Mr. McCarthy without more ado, stepped up to the tallest and handsomest of the ladies, and addressed some compliment to her in the tongue of his forefathers.

The beauty smiled, showing a double row of the pearliest of teeth.

"_T Lalma Koween_," she replied.

"There, now ! What do ye think o' that ?" cried Pat, turning round triumphantly. "I axed her what her purty name was, an' she sez it's Tlalma, an' she's the Queen."

Jim Swaby, being an ignorant man, was somewhat impressed by this little episode, as were many of the others, so Pat was permitted to sail in after his own fashion.

Again he put some question to the lady in the ancient Irish tongue, and again the lady smiled sweetly upon him as she answered :

"Rawalloa Kee-ing."

The glance of triumph which now flashed forth from the eyes of Pat was that which might have illumined the orb of the ancient Greek, when he exclaimed:

"Eureka !"

"Whirroo !" he shouted, as he executed an impromptu Irish jig. "Didn't I tell ye as how the lady understood the language of Brian Boru. Shure, an' I just axed her if she was the Queen who her husband might be, an' she tells me as how Rawalloa's the King."

How long this farce might have con-tinued no one can tell, but just at this time Arthur Guy stepped up to the leader and whispered :

"I beg your pardon, Mr. Swaby, but it strikes me that the woman understands a few words of English, and if she belongs to one of the Pacific tribes of whose language I have a slight smattering, we may arrive at something tangible."

"Very good, Guy !" returned Jim, "you see what you can do about it. Shall I call off that fool, Pat ?"

"If you please, though I am almost sorry to spoil the fun."

"McCarthy, come here ! " called the leader.

"Och, whirasthroo ! won't ye let me just ax her if she's got a dhrop of Irish whisky anywheres handy ? I'm shure a taste of potheen won't do any of us a bit o' harrum."

Jim, however, was obdurate, and Pat came away muttering :

"May I nivver see Kerry ag'in, if I don't think it is too bad. Shure, it's another injustice to Ireland intoirely !"

Guy's method of attacking the dusky beauty was altogether different from that of McCarthy. He approached her with much ceremony, and then spoke a few words in that low, mellifluous tongue which is common to so many of the South Sea Islands.

It was evident that she understood him at once, for her face, which was of a dark olive tint, and by no means unpleasant to look upon, was lit up by a beam of joy, and she replied to him in the same soft accents.

The conversation thus begun was carried on for some time, and then the man returned to Swaby.

"As far as I can make out," he said, "they do not belong to this island, but have come over here in three big canoes with their men, who have gone on to make war against a tribe who occupy the upper waters of the river, and who are noted thieves and plunderers in these parts. She is the queen of her people, as she tried to explain to Pat, and her husband is leading his tribe. Her friends are peaceable, and will offer no harm—will, indeed, help us, if need be, against the others, so that we may consider ourselves lucky in having fallen in with them rather than with the plundering tribe."

"But if they are peaceable, why do they come here on a warlike expedition ?" asked Jim, with much reason.

"Reprisals, that is all," replied Guy. "Their island, a small one, has been frequently ravaged by the rascals they have now gone to pay out, and they have been goaded into this expedition by a long system of persecution."

"Ah, poor fellows, I can understand it now," Jim replied; "and look here, lads, if this tribe should need our help, we'll give it 'em, won't we?"

There was a shout of approval of these sentiments, and Guy was sent back to inform the queen of the resolve that had been made.

She seemed overjoyed at the intelligence, and her women and she immediately commenced a graceful dance to a song, chanted in a somewhat melancholy minor key.

"Just look at that, now!" cried Pat. "What sort o' music do ye call that for a dance at all, at all? If I had only my fiddle here now, I'd play ye up Rory O'More in a shtyle would make ye take the floor in a different fashion altogether."

Suddenly the dance was interrupted by a sound of savage yelling and shouting in the distance, and with a loud, wailing cry the women rushed off quickly, followed by the band of Englishmen.

The river was reached in a few minutes, and then the cause of the hubbub was apparent.

Three great canoes were being frantically paddled down the stream, with a number of others following in hot pursuit. Clouds of arrows were pursuing the larger craft, and it was evident that the visitors were beaten.

"Stand by, lads!" cried Jim Swaby. "Have your carbines ready for the thieves!"

CHAPTER LXXIII.

THE HUNT FOR THE SLAVER.

THE danger of the collision was past, but in that hurried moment when the yacht was so near her doom, Peter the Great and his brother, Hannibal, saw a sight which made their negro blood boil. The vessel they had so narrowly shaved was labouring heavily, as if she had sprung a leak, and the hands on board were busy consigning the cargo to the deep—the cargo of black ivory—in other words, of human slaves.

To what terrible depths of depravity must numbers of our race have sank, when in cold blood they can throw overboard a living freight of immortal souls! What had the teaching of eighteen hundred years done for humanity when such an awful iniquity could be practised? And yet it is not so very many years ago since England was foremost in the execrable traffic. Let us go down on our bended knees and thank our Creator that the stain has been wiped from our name, and that Britain no longer can have the infamy and disgrace of such a trade cast into her teeth. We have heard a great deal of braggadocio about Britons never, never, never being slaves; but they did not hesitate at one time to make slaves of others, and even the strong feeling of sympathy held by many towards the South in the great American Civil War, shows that, until quite recently, the criminal passion still lingered amongst us. The present writer speaks with a terrible shame upon him while he pens these lines, for his own father was a holder of slaves, and bought and sold human flesh at his will.

Peter the Great and his twin brother knew all too well what these black masses were which went down into the seething waves with such a horrible plunge, and they did not hesitate to lay the case before our hero.

Jack had been too busy attending to his vessel to note anything peculiar about the ship he had flown past at such terrific speed. The "Esmeralda" was in danger, and that was sufficient for him; but scarcely had they cleared the slaver when the black twin brethren were by his side.

"Massa Jack! Massa Jack!" screeched Peter, "for de lub of de world, listen to me!"

Jack turned to him in surprise.

"What's the matter, Peter? Anything wrong?" enquired Jack, in a loud voice.

"Eberyting wrong, Massa Jack. De ship we see'd just now—him slaver running to Cuba. Hannibal and me see him frow black man overboard."

"Yes, Massa Jack," the brother confirmed. "Me see him frow lot into de sea."

"But I can do nothing now," explained our hero. "All my energies are required in looking after the yacht. If the gale should subside, I'll see what can be done."

"Me berry sorry," exclaimed Peter, who had seen Jack come triumphantly through so many trials and troubles that he began to credit him with almost supernatural powers. "Me berry sorry. Me thought you'd go help brack brudder.'

"And so I would, Peter, but I can attempt nothing of the sort in this weather. Keep up a good heart, and let us hope that Providence will yet give us a chance to rescue the poor creatures."

T'ank you, Massa Jack, t'ank you!" exclaimed the tender hearted negro. "Come, Hannibal, we go find Pitchpot, an' all pray to Providence to deliber de poor brack men out of de han' ob de oppressor."

The two went cautiously along the vessel, holding on to whatever came in their way, for the fury of the storm had in no way abated, and the little "Esmeralda" danced and leaped like a cork upon the boiling waters. Finding their compatriot, they quickly betook themselves to the little cabin allotted to the three, and there, kneeling down, they lifted up their hearts in a fervent prayer for the delivery of their African brothers from the peril and misery which beset them.

Who shall say that such an appeal coming from these poor ignorant negroes was not listened to on high as readily as if it had come from the mouth of prelate or pope?

Strangely enough, as if in answer to their supplications, the wind began to subside, and before long, the sea which had raged so fiercely, was comparatively calm.

"De Great Master hab heard our prayer, Hannibal," said Peter, reverently, as he rose from his knees. "De storm am ober, an' Massa Jack will go in search ob de willain slave-dealer."

Pitchpot and Hannibal also rose, and then all three went on deck to importune the captain to proceed at once upon the course they wished to take.

Little damage had been done to the yacht during the storm, save a gap in the bulwarks where a sea had broken over her, and as this was only a trivial matter which the carpenter could set right in a day or two, Jack's humanity would not allow him to delay his hunt for the Cuban vessel.

It was nearly morning, and the crew had not had a moment's rest since the storm burst upon them the previous day, so now he ordered all hands below, save the regular watch, and prepared to stand with them himself, giving Tom Warren and Charley a spell of that needful repose which they lacked. Tom would have demurred, as it was actually his duty to be on deck; but Jack compelled him to follow his wishes.

By-and-bye day began to break, and Captain Scarborough kept an eager look out, but no vessel appeared on the horizon.

"At all events I'll make a big circuit in search of her," he said to himself, "and then, if no signs of her appear I must abandon the poor wretches to their doom."

Peter, Hannibal, and Pitchpot all remained staunchly by his side; but though their eyes were trained almost to see in the dark, there was nothing for them to fix their gaze upon—nothing breaking the monotony of the wild waste of waters either near or far.

"We wait till de sun get up, massa Jack, we see him den, suah enuff," said Pitchpot, with a grin. "Golly, won't we give him beans."

"I'm not quite so sure of that," replied Jack; "but we'll try our best at all events."

Jack now gave orders that the first lieutenant should be roused, as he felt that if the slaver were to be fought, a rest before hand would do him no harm.

Tom Warren was on deck in a trice, and, Jack, giving him all the necessary instructions retired to his cabin.

The three negroes still remained indefatigably at their post, though Jack, before going below, tried to prevail upon them to turn in for a time.

"No, Massa Jack," was Peter's emphatic reply. "We no rest nor sleep till we rescue de brack man from de cruelty ob his brudder man."

So there they stood earnestly scanning the waves in every direction, like three black marble statues on the deck of the yacht.

Time passed on, and the sun rose in all his glory over the broad expanse of ocean, which had so recently been lashed into fury by the kindless wind. Gulls were floating lazily over the surface, seeking for their unwary prey, and every now and again a cormorant on his jet black wing would dash rapidly past, flying close above the crests of the uneasy waves. Still no sign of the black hull which had so nearly sent them to destruction, broke upon the vision of the watchers, and the hopes of the negroes sank low in their hearts.

All at once a wild cry from Hannibal, brought every one on deck around him.

"Dar him is!" he shouted. "Dar him is! Call up Massa Jack, for Providence hab set de niggah free!"

CHAPTER LXXIV.

A SHARP TUSSLE, AND WHAT FOLLOWED.

WHEN the islanders in the great canoes caught sight of Jim Swaby and his men on the bank of the river, they gave themselves up for lost, and wavered in their flight; but T'Lalma, the queen, stepped instantly to the water's edge, and waved them onwards, making signs that the whites were friends. Thus, reassured, they redoubled their efforts, and soon were nearly abreast of the explorers.

"Now, then," cried Jim Swaby, as cool as if he had stood on the deck of the "Swallow" to resist a boarding party, "take good aim, boys, at the fellows, you see standing up in the bows of the canoes. There are about a score of them, if we pick off ten the others will get in a blue funk."

Coolly our friends awaited, amid a shower of arrows, which passed harmlessly overhead, the approach of the yelling savages.

They allowed the three friendly craft to pass, and then they calmly potted the ten foremost men of the pursuers, who, killed or wounded, threw up their arms, and fell headlong into the water.

"Bravo!" shouted Jim. "See! the others have ceased paddling, and are giving us time to reload. Quick, lads, get ready for 'em!"

The carbines were reloaded as quickly as possible—there were no breech-loaders in those days—and then the whites waited for the rest of the canoes to come on. They did not appear to be very anxious, however, to again test the effect of the leaden messengers, which the strange men had sent amongst them. Ten of their chiefs had fallen, and though three had been recovered, the wounds they exhibited did not encourage the others to resume hostilities.

In the meantime the three large war canoes had been drawn up just below the point where the whites stood. A peninsula here ran out into the river, and the little party of ten had ranged themselves shoulder to shoulder along it.

"Don't fire unless they attack us," said Jim Swaby; "but, if they do, don't waste a shot."

It was apparent now that some movement was afoot on the part of the enemy, for a hubbub was heard to the rear of the canoes belonging to them.

Presently an extraordinary sight was presented to the view of the explorers.

The small craft in the river parted, and a great thing shaped like a serpent slowly descended.

The figure-head, if it may be called so, was raised from the stream, and was rudely carved in the resemblance of the head of a snake, while the body seemed to be formed of a series of rafts, crowded with men, and joined together by ropes of woven withies.

As it came on these rafts undulated from side to side, like the motion of a serpent, and seemed to strike awe to the women of the friendly tribe, for they fled, shrieking from the spot where they had taken their stand.

"Bless my stars!" exclaimed Jim Swaby, when he saw the strange craft. "What in the name of thunder have we here?"

"Shure," cried Pat, "the darned haythens have got hoult of the mother of all the sarpints, an', faix, they're takin' a sail on her back."

"Guy," said the leader, calling to the man who had spoken to the queen, "we have not a moment to lose. These wretches will be swarming about us like ants before many minutes are over. Call to the king, Rawalloa, and tell him to come here."

Arthur Guy immediately shouted the name of the chief, and a tall and handsome islander stood up in the nearest canoe.

"Ask him to let us come aboard his boats, and we'll drive these rascals back or perish in the attempt."

The sailor put the question, and the king signified his assent. Then three whites got into each canoe, leaving Jim to make a fourth beside the king. Arthur Guy was also there.

"Tell him to direct the flotilla to draw right across the stream," said the leader, using his interpreter; and the monarch implicitly obeyed the instructions. In less than five minutes the three immense canoes formed a cordon across the river which the enemy might find very difficult to break when defended by a band of resolute Britons with firearms in their possession.

These tactics, however, did not deter the descent of the snake raft. Slowly it came, borne down by the stream, while the sky was almost darkened by the arrows which were shot from it.

It seemed to Jim Swaby and the rest that these arrows were intended to frighten rather than to hurt, and he expressed himself in that manner to Guy, who stood close to his shoulder.

"You may depend upon it that is the case," returned the seaman. "These fellows are cannibals, and intend to take us alive that they may keep and feed on us at their leisure."

"Thunder!" ejaculated Jim, but he said no more just then.

The serpent-raft with its load of yelling savages, brandishing their spears, and making horrible contortions, was now within pistol shot.

"Now let 'em have it!" commanded Jim. "Carbines fust, and pistols arter!"

In his excitement he dropped into his fo'c'sle lingo.

Simultaneously there were ten shots, followed by twenty more in rapid succession.

The cries from the floating serpent were deafening, but on and on it came till the hideous prow struck the central canoe right amidships. The other two were quickly brought alongside the raft, by signals which the friendlies seemed to understand, and then a horrible hand to hand conflict ensued.

The savages fought like veritable fiends, their long sharp spears being thrust hither and thither with marvellous velocity, and every stab meant an ugly wound, or death.

Hitherto the whites were safe, while their dexterous play of cutlass bewildered those with whom they came in contact.

Their allies, seeing the valorous deeds they performed, were also nerved to victory, and in less than a quarter of an hour the fight was over, the tide of battle having been entirely turned in favour of the friendly tribe through the intervention of the Englishmen.

Those of the natives who remained upon the raft refused to surrender, and many of them ran upon their own spear points rather than submit, which conclusively proved to the minds of the explorers, that they dreaded the treatment they might receive as captives. How then would they have treated our friends had they been unfortunate enough to fall into their hands?

Of the smaller craft which had pursued the friendlies when Jim Swaby and his band first appeared, nothing now was seen. They had fled in consternation up the river, leaving the passage free to friend or foe, as the case might be.

"Come, boys!" cried the white leader, as he wiped his reeking brow. "Let's get ashore for roll-call."

CHAPTER LXXV.

A SLAP AT A SLAVER.

HANNIBAL'S shout brought everybody to the side at once, and Jack and the others sprang up on deck in a jiffy.

There was no mistake about Hannibal's accuracy, when a glass was brought to bear upon the slaver. The long black hull was easily distinguishable amongst the short, white-capped, hummocky waves which the storm had left behind, and to all appearances she was bearing down athwart the present course of the yacht.

Jack took a long survey of the vessel through the splendid binocular he held to his eyes—a present from Captain Markham—then he turned to Tom Warren who stood by his elbow.

"What do you think of her?" he enquired, passing the glass to his first officer.

"She's rather big for us to tackle single-handed, I'm afraid," Tom replied.

"That is my opinion, too," our hero rejoined; "but I suppose it must be done."

"Oh, yes, Maasa Jack," cried Peter, mournfully. "T'ink ob de pore brack niggahs in dat hold. Hundreds ob dem may be dar, all crammed togedder like sardines in a box."

"It is quite true, Peter," observed Jack, in a determined tone. "They *shall* be set free, though the yacht should be blown to atoms in the attempt."

"Bravo, Massa Jack," shouted Hannibal, in his most stentorian tones, " now you speaks like de ole cap'n dat we lub."

" Three cheers for Massa Jack," shouted Pitchpot, leading off with a wild " Hip, hip, hip, hooray !" which was taken up by every throat on board.

The course of the " Esmeralda " was then altered, so that she should intercept the slaver, and everything was cleared for action.

Tom Warren and Charley Granby shook their heads over Jack's decision, but they could not deny the fact that he had taken a righteous course in thus endeavouring to carry out the humane dictates of his manly heart.

Anxious eyes measured the ever shortening distance between themselves and the black-hulled craft, and anxious hearts leapt and bounded as the vessels drew nearer and nearer to each other.

" Run up the flags !" commanded Jack, and in a trice the Union Jack surmounting the stainless banner of our hero fluttered from the fore peak.

The slaver must have seen the well known ensign of the seas, for she changed her course, and stood off; but no answering flag announced her nationality.

" She is going to make a bolt for it," said Charley Granby, as he watched the vessel attentively.

" We can soon show her what sailing means if she does," returned Jack. Then he gave the order to chase, and soon the " Esmeralda " was scudding after the sinister-looking craft like a greyhound slipped from the leash.

It is proverbial that " a stern chase is a long chase," but the captain of the yacht cared nothing for that. His blood was now up, and, win or lose, he was resolved to run down the slaver.

With his strong, square jaw firmly set, as it ever was when he had made up his mind upon a point, Jack stood grimly watching the flying vessel. She was a good sailer, built for the inhuman trade which she carried on, but those on board of her were not aware of the capabilities of that little wasp-like yacht which pursued. Though she crowded on all the canvas at her command, she could not get away, and soon her crew saw that she was being overhauled.

Gradually the distance between pursuer and pursued was lessened till Jack with an immovable countenance, turned and ordered his men to load the two brass guns.

" I'll make yonder fellow acknowledge what he is before long," he said to Charley Granby, who happened to be beside him, " or I'll never step on board a ship again."

" I'm afraid he'll be obdurate," returned the young fellow.

" Then, if he is, he'll have to pay for his obstinacy."

Another five minutes passed, and then Jack, stepping along to the bow, sighted the gun himself.

" I'll only try what he's made of this time," he remarked, " the next shot will be more serious."

As he spoke he pulled the line, and a shot went skipping along in the slaver's wake without doing any harm.

But as Charley had prophesied, the vessel was obdurate, and no flag was hoisted to indicate what country she belonged to.

" She's a Cuban, I know, Massa Jack," observed Pitchpot, who had had some experience of such craft when aboard the pirate. " I can tell dat by her build, an' by de rumfluction ob her masts."

As our readers have already been made aware, Pitchpot had a habit of coining words for himself when there were no others handy which he might use.

" I don't care what she is," Jack replied, as the gun was quickly reloaded. " I mean to let her have it in earnest this time."

Once more he sighted the gun, but he was more careful and deliberate on this occasion.

Then came the mighty boom of the discharge, and down came the slaver's top-mast, bearing with it a mass of tangled rigging.

A cheer from the crew of the " Esmeralda " announced the success of the shot, and now the enemy began to show her teeth. While some hacked at the fallen cordage to clear away the shattered spar, others manned the guns which Jack Scarborough could see the ugly muzzles of, grimly peeping out of the opened ports. There were six of them to a broadside, and they were not long in replying to the " Esmeralda's " challenge.

Veering suddenly round, the slaver fired her starboard complement full at the yacht, but either from recklessness of aim, or because of the very diminutiveness of the object at which they were discharged, not one of the six struck the mark.

"Bravo!" cried Jack, in derision, "you can do that again, Mr. What's-your-name; but I don't think I'll give you the chance. Ready for boarding!" he added, in a voice that rang throughout the tiny vessel like a bell.

Each man was provided with pistols of the latest pattern and cutlass, while Hannibal, Peter, and Pitchpot had their own particular weapons which they knew best how to handle. The gigantic first-named had provided himself with a heavy capstan bar, in addition to the cutlass at his belt, Peter seemed to rely solely upon his trusty umbrella, and Pitchpot on the poker belonging to the galley, the point of his chosen weapon being worn down to a sharp spear-like extremity, which made it a very formidable article indeed in the hands of anyone who knew how to use it.

That the coming struggle was likely to be a desperate one, each of our friends was fully aware, from humble Pitchpot up to the fearless commander. The hideous cruelty and recklessness of their own lives, as well as of the lives of their human cargo, were characteristics of a slaver's crew which were familiar to all. They played a terrible game in which death stared them in the face, and they must either vanquish or die.

Jack knew that well, as he looked to his pistols, and tried the edge of his sword. He knew that he must either kill or be killed himself. There would be no quarter once he set foot upon the deck of that floating hell, and he thought he might as well say a word to his crew before the slaughter began.

He signed for them to gather round him, and then he cleared his throat, and commenced:

"Boys!" he said, "I think you all know and understand me. My friends call me ' Happy Jack, the Rover;' but my enemies have a different epithet to apply to me. They call me 'Young Vengeance,' and not without reason; for my life up till now has been passed in avenging the wrongs of the oppressed, and espousing the cause of the weak against the strong. I am now about to undertake a desperate task. That of thrashing yon sailing horror into splinters, and setting free the cargo of slaves she carries. I need not say that I expect you to do your duty, because I know you will without a word of encouragement from me; but what I have to do is to warn you that the issue is life or death. Not one of yon sea-wolves is there who would show an atom of pity. They will hack wounded men to pieces without compunction, and torture us without remorse. Then so lightly do they hold their own lives, that they will not hesitate to fire the magazine, and blow every living thing on board into eternity at a flash. Now, lads, for the glory of old England, and the honour of ourselves, follow me!"

A wild cheer burst from the throats of the men, as they held their cutlasses aloft and swore to do or die for Happy Jack, their bold commander.

Then the "Esmeralda" dashed in under the guns of the slaver—a pigmy attacking a giant.

The grappling irons were at once thrown upwards, and they caught in the shrouds of the enemy with a firm and clinging grip.

With his sword between his teeth, Jack clambered up in advance of the others with cat-like agility, followed closely by Tom Warren, Charley Granby, and the rest. As he stood for a moment on the taffrail, a dark, beetle-browed man rushed at him with a long rapier, but our hero bounded clear over the point of the deadly weapon, and dashed the pommel of his sword with a sickening crash right into the face of his foe. The villain went down on the deck with a dull thud, and Jack stood over him, slashing right and left at the swarming crowd of slavers, who had leapt to the rescue of their captain.

Tom and Charley were by his side in an instant, while the men followed swiftly against the almost overwhelming odds.

The swarthy crew of the enemy fought like demons. Daggers and rapiers gleamed and flashed in the eyes of the "Esmeralda's" lads, but there was no flinching. Cutlasses were swung by brawny arms, and with each descending stroke a foeman fell.

Towering over the others in the very thickest of the melée, stood Hannibal with his terrible capstan-bar. There was a clear ring round the gigantic negro, choked with dead and dying, and as he stood grasping the mighty club, his opponents held back, and paused for a time.

"Come on, you abominable scum ob de ocean!" he roared. "Come on, you brack-hearted dirt ob de sea! Dis chile ain't afeard ob de hull lot on ye!"

Then, leaping over the bodies in front

of him, he swept his bar round like a scythe and mowed down half-a-dozen heads at a single sweep.

Meanwhile Jack and his two seconds were hard pressed. They had performed prodigies of valour with their swords, and many fallen Cubans around them bore testimony to their prowess; but mortal strength has its limits, and they began to feel exhaustion creeping over them despite the excitement which nerved their hands. Peter the Great, and Pitchpot were close behind them, working wonders with their peculiar weapons.

As Jack still pressed forward, a wounded Cuban rose from the deck, dagger in hand, and, raising it, was within an ace of plunging it into the back of our hero, whose life would that instant have been ended; but Pitchpot in the nick of time brought down the nob of his poker upon the dastard's head, and, as the dark-faced villain sank upon the deck again, he plunged the sharp-pointed fire-iron into the Cuban's body with such force that the weapon went right through and stuck in the planking underneath.

"Hooray for Pitchpot!" shouted Peter. "Hooray for de boys ob de poker an' de rumblerella!"

The latter instrument of warfare was now reduced to a skeleton, but it was none the less effective. Used as a lance, the tip made frightful wounds on the faces of the enemy, and in many instances a thrust in the eye had put an end to the existence of a swarthy foe.

Never, perhaps, had Jack known such a stubborn resistance as was made by the Cubans. They sought no quarter, but fought to the death. Their shrieks and imprecations were awful, and their fury was demoniacal. At last, however, they began to flag, just as our hero's arm grew tired. Their signs of weakness gave him renewed strength then, and in a final magnificent burst of enthusiasm, he cheered his men on, and dashed himself upon the slavers with redoubled energy.

Both sets of combatants were now in the death-struggle, as it were; and it became a silent one. Inch by inch the Cubans retreated on the slippery deck, and inch by inch the Englishmen advanced.

It was now that Hannibal, whose head, high above the others, gave him an advantage in observation, saw a Cuban steal away silently from the close body of the rest with a drawn pistol in his hand. The negro, who had heard Jack's remark about firing the magazine, divined the miscreant's intention, and shouted to his commander:

"Look out, Massa Jack! Dey're gwine to blow up de vessel!"

The words reached our hero in their full significance, and with almost supernatural power, he cleft a way through the retreating mass of foeman, and, drawing a pistol, which up till now he had had no opportunity of doing, shot the fellow through the skull as he was disappearing into the magazine.

As he turned he found himself face to face with four of the enemy, and his passage to rejoin his men entirely cut off. He had still five shots in the bull-dog revolver in his hand, and six in the other at his belt. Quick as lightning he passed his dripping sword from his left hand to his teeth, and with a revolver in each hand, stood calmly at bay.

The Cubans paused in the rush they had made upon him.

"Now," he cried, with difficulty, because of the weapon in his mouth, "you dogs! Will you yield, or meet the fate at once which will ultimately reach you?"

He had scarcely concluded when they made a simultaneous dash at him.

"Crack! crack!" went the bull-dog in his right, followed on the instant by an echo from his left hand, and the four Cubans went down—two dead—and two desperately wounded.

This seemed to turn the tide entirely in favour of our friends, who at once charged the remaining Cubans with a determination and courage which drove the villains helter skelter into the forecastle. There they were battened down in the meantime, until it should be decided what their destination should be.

Then Jack Scarborough called his men around him.

All answered to their names save one; and his comrades pointed to him lying on the deck with a Cuban dagger still buried in his back; but his own right hand in the death-clutch grasped his cutlass, the blade of which remained imbedded in the skull which it had cleft.

Charley Granby had a rapier-thrust through the fleshy part of the thigh, and was also slightly wounded in the sword-arm. Jack himself had a nasty cut on the wrist, and a sword point had ploughed an ugly furrow in his scalp. Tom Warren was unscathed; but many of the crew had more or less serious wounds about them. Strange to say the three blacks were unharmed.

When our hero had examined all the injuries with a critical eye, he directed the three worst cases to be placed at once on board the yacht under the care of Peter, who professed some skill in the treatment of wounds.

"Now," he said, " we will see to the poor wretches in the hold."

CHAPTER LXXVI.

JIM SWABY'S ISLAND FRIENDS.

NOT one of the Englishmen had received a scratch during the encounter with the savages, and they congratulated themselves upon their immunity from injury.

"Faith !" said Pat, "the divils could foight like daymons wid their spares an' their bows an' arrers, but the cutlash was a weepun that they didn't undherstan', at all, at all."

The friendly islanders now came crowding round the handful of whites in a curious, but respectful manner. It seemed as if they were not quite sure whether to fall down and worship them or not. Rawalloa, the chief, at last after a long scrutiny addressed himself to Arthur Guy, and the seamen replied in a manner which appeared to give great satisfaction.

Upon inquiry by Jim Swaby it was elicited that the chief was anxious lest the sailors, having assisted in vanquishing the cannibals, would turn their arms against their allies, and slay them with their thunder-makers, as they called the firearms. Guy, however, had assured them that there was nothing to fear, and this assurance had given great pleasure to the friendlies, who now offered to render service to the white men in any way which lay in their power.

They were a good looking set of fellows these dark friends, straight limbed, and broad shouldered, with regular features and long black hair parted down the middle. They were almost destitute of clothes, save for a white cloth round the loins, and a kind of coarse blankets which depended from the left shoulder, and was kept in place by a woven grass rope across the body. Taken altogether they were about as handsome a lot of savages as ever Jim Swaby had seen, and he was very favourably impressed by them.

By and bye the women came in from the shelter of the neighbouring wood in a shy and decorous manner. Taking a second look at the ladies Jim was even more favourably impressed by them than by the men. They wore a short skirt which reached below the knee, and above it a sort of loose tunic.

" By the holy poker !" exclaimed Pat, " they're a purty lot o' darlints altogether. I wondher if they're all married."

"Why, do you contemplate matrimony with a dusky beauty, Pat ?" enquired Arthur Guy.

"Faith, an' I might do worse than that same, only that I'm promised to Biddy O'Brannigan, if iver I see Kerry again, an' I dunno what she'd say."

The women were all dressed in white except T'Lalma who wore a yellow skirt and a scarlet jacket. Round the neck they had many rows of iridescent shells, pierced and strung, and their hair was decked in the same style.

The queen signed to Guy to approach, as she took her place beside her husband with a quiet dignity which became her well, and in her mellifluous language asked him many questions. Who they were, and whence they came ; what they were doing in these parts, and if they intended to leave soon ; which of them was king or chief, and whether they were cannibals or not. To all of which the sailor answered in a respectful and straightforward manner, which satisfied the lady and her partner in no small degree. This having been interpreted to the leader, Jim instructed his subordinate to put a series of interrogatories of the same class to the queen, who answered everything simply and without hesitation.

As she had already informed them, her tribe came from a neighbouring island, being goaded into reprisals by the constant persecution of the cannibals. Now that they had beaten them by the aid of the white men they intended to return to their own homes unless by remaining for a time they could render a service to their white friends in return for the great assistance they had received against their enemies.

"Hanibal, my lubly brudder!" "Sabed! Sabed!" shouted Hanibal. "Come back, Massa
Jack! Peter am cum!"

This latter offer set Jim Swaby thinking.

There was a chance that the fierce aborigines might descend upon Fort Scarborough and give him infinite trouble, therefore he debated whether it would not be politic to carry the war right into the enemies' country, and by giving them a salutary thrashing, teach them a lesson which would put a wholesome dread of the white man into their minds.

After pondering these matters he intimated to his lieutenant and Arthur Guy that he wished to speak with them apart, and moving a little way aside he laid the proposal before them. Richley was for following the victory at once, but Guy took some time to consider the pros and cons of the suggestion.

At length the latter spoke.

"Mr. Swaby," he said, "it is hardly for me to advise my captain, but in the present instance I think we would be running a great risk in ascending the river. We are scarcely free agents in the matter, you know, as we are only left in charge of the prizes, and the "Swallow," during the absence of our commander, Happy Jack. In this case, if we pursue the cannibalistic savages to their strongholds in the upper reaches of the river, we may all be wiped out, and what would our brave young captain say to such a catastrophe on his return ?"

"He would avenge us at all events," burst in Bob Richley.

"I have no doubt about that," returned the sailor ; "but it would be a sorry consolation for the loss of his men. Of course, however, there is another side to the question. If you really believe that the fort might be endangered by leaving these savages alone, I will bow to your decision, but it is not my opinion. By turning one of the heavy guns upon them the cannibals would be scattered in all directions at the first ball, and they would take good care to leave us alone in the future."

There was much sound common sense in Guy's words, and Jim Swaby felt that there was ; but the old war-dog's blood was up and he itched to be at the black fellows up amongst the hills.

"What is your opinion, Bob?" he asked, glancing at Richley.

There was little need to ask. The ex-carpenter was full of fight, and Jim knew it. There were no considerations of prudence about the lieutenant. He had been at sea all his life, and through many wars in that time, therefore he gave his opinion in the following way :

"What ? Sing small to a set o' darned niggers that ain't got a hatom o' respeck for the flag wot braves the battle an' the breeze ! I'd see 'em squashed fust ! Let's go ahead an' hexterminate the warmints. We ain't safe if we don't, an' it's the honly coorse wot's proper to an Englishman as respecks hisself an' his country."

Now these were the exact sentiments which held sway in Jim Swaby's own breast, and though he made a slight effort to check the enthusiasm of his lieutenant for appearance sake, yet he decided in the end to ask the aid of his new friends in carrying on a short raid of extermination against the cannibals.

To this end he commissiond Guy, who sorrowfully gave in to the superior vote for war, to interview Rawalloa on the subject.

The king was not averse to the proposal, but the queen was emphatic against it, and sent a message to the white chief imploring him to think twice before engaging in a conflict which might be disastrous not only to himself but to the kind hearted people who considered the offer of assistance they had made binding upon them in all things.

To this Jim replied that if Rawalloa withdrew from the expedition which had been resolved upon, he would consider the dark chieftain a man whose word was not to be relied on.

This turned the scale in favour of the white men, and T'Lalma as a sign of mourning took off her shell ornaments, and let down her jet black hair before her eyes like a veil that fell to her knees. All her women followed her example, though they would do nothing to dissuade the men, their plighted word having been passed to the whites.

It was now decided that nothing should be done until the following morning, when after a night's rest they should all start invigorated in the morning.

The serpent-raft still remained in the river where their savage enemies had left it when they took to flight in the smaller and more wieldy craft.

The allies of course could make use of it if they thought fit, and Jim Swaby went over to inspect the strange affair.

He found that it was merely a series of canoes, two abreast, connected by bamboo platforms, and joined stem and stern to each other by withies. There were thirty canoes in all, thus giving the length of the flotilla to be that of fifteen canoes, each about fourteen feet in length. The great serpent-head of the prow was of rudely carved wood, painted red, green and black, and Guy suggested that the cannibals were snake-worshippers, of which there are many savage nations in various parts of the world.

On putting the question to Rawalloa he found that he was correct in his surmise, and found also that their friends were sun-worshippers, like the Parsees of India, a highly intelligent and cultivated race. Serpent-worship is one of the lowest, and fire-worship one of the highest forms of paganism, so it raised their allies in Guy's educated estimation to a considerable degree.

A conclave was now held between the white men and the chiefs of the tribe, Rawalloa and Jim Swaby presiding jointly.

A great fire had been lit, and round this they all gathered, Rawalloa had his chiefs on his right and Jim Swaby's men sat on his left. Between the two leaders Arthur Guy was given a place as interpreter. This formed the inner ring. Immediately outside it came the minor warriors, and beyond these again were the women, silent and sad, with their hair-veiled faces bent upon the ground.

The first to speak was the dark-skinned king, and he rose from the ground with stately majesty.

His words, as interpreted by Guy, were as follows :

"White brothers, I have promised on behalf of my people to give you aid in whatever you may ask as a return for the service you have rendered unto us. Rawalloa keeps his word, though T'Lalma, his queen, grieves over the service which our white brother desires. Rawalloa knows the Mallobutos, the cannibal serpent-worshippers; his white brothers do not. They dwell in dark caves of the mountain, where deeds too horrible for the light of day are perpetrated. Serpents live amongst them and protect them against the advance of foes that may seek them in their rocky strongholds. Their arrows and spears are poisoned with the poison of the snakes they dwell amidst, and the smallest scratch is agonizing death to the strongest of men. Rawalloa has told you of the Mallobutos. Rawalloa has done."

Then the chief drew his blanket around him and sat down.

A buzz of approval from the minor chiefs greeted the speech of the king, and Jim Swaby was half-inclined to join in with them, not that he wavered for a moment in his intention of attacking the Mallobutos, as they were called, but because of the quiet dignity and repose which Rawalloa had displayed.

"What shall I say to him in reply ?" asked Arthur Guy.

"Say that we are not frightened by the difficulties he has mentioned, and ask him how it was he attempted to storm their caves in spite of them all."

The sailor-interpreter put the question, and the chief rose again. His words were few this time, and more sorrowful than before.

"Rawalloa knows that his white brother's heart has no fear, and that nothing the king can say will silence the sound of his white brother's thunder-maker; but let his brother understand that when Rawalloa sought the strongholds of the Mallobutos, he was driven thither by the moaning of his people who had lost their children, by the weeping of the children who had lost their mothers. The white man has not listened to these."

There were tears in the eyes of the chief as he took his seat upon the grass, and a low wail burst from the lips of his followers.

"But the white men will avenge the wrongs of his friends," said Jim Swaby.

Arthur Guy translated the words, but Rawalloa only shook his head.

Then a younger chief arose, a brave warrior, whose conduct in the battle had evoked the praise of the Englishmen. He was a more impetuous speaker than the king, and his sentences were thundered forth with much gesticulation.

"White brothers," he began, "you have fought to-day by the side of the dark warriors, and have vanquished their enemies. Kavaloko of the flying arrow marked the strong arm of his white brother. The blood of his murdered babes, devoured by the Mallobutos, cries aloud for vengeance. The tears of their grief-stricken mother bid him seek revenge. Kavaloko will go with you. Kavaloko of the flying arrow will lead you to the stronghold of the serpent-worshippers."

The young chief bent his bow and shot

an arrow high into the air. Every eye was raised to mark its flight. As it descended the point came down in a slanting direction, inclined towards the upper portion of the stream.

A cry of gladness escaped from the lips of the warrior, and all the others sprang lightly to their feet. It was an omen that the sun-god wished them to pursue their enemies to the stronghold up the river.

Neither man nor woman now dared gainsay the order of the sun-god, and preparations were at once commenced for the serious work of the morrow. A war dance was the first ceremony inaugurated, and for this the men immediately began to clear the ground. A wide open space having been obtained, they cast off their blankets, and stood in a circle with nothing on but their loin-cloths. They were neither painted nor tattooed, and their shapely brown limbs and muscular bodies were pictures to the Englishmen who delighted in a display of manly activity.

Proceedings were begun by the king himself, who, entering the ring with a slow step, commenced an undulatory movement of the body to the low chanting of the women, who stood outside the circle. Gradually the song quickened, and as the music grew faster, so the speed of the dancer increased. One by one now his warriors joined him, but he ever held his place in the centre. Wilder and wilder grew the music, and wilder the dancing of the warriors. Spears were hurled aloft, and whirled in close proximity to the dancers' heads. All seemed confusion and mad excitement, till suddenly at a word from the chief the women stopped their singing, and each warrior stood stock still upon the spot where he had been capering like a tarantula-bitten harlequin.

The dance was now at an end, and was to be followed by a great feast. Half-a-dozen of the warriors were dispatched to the forest to bring in provisions, and by request Arthur Guy and Bob Richley were permitted to accompany them. In less than half-an-hour they returned. Two of them were laden with ripe fruits, sweet potatoes and yams, while the others brought in five kids and some wild pigs which had been slaughtered. These were given to the women to dress and cook, and by night-fall they were all seated round three blazing fires, devouring the food. When they were satisfied they stretched themselves on the ground after placing sentinels to give warning of danger. The Englishmen lay a little apart from their uncivilized friends, and soon all were dreaming of the encounter which was to take place on the morrow

---

CHAPTER LXXVII.

PETER AND HANNIBAL RECOGNIZE SOMEBODY.

THE name of the slaver was now discovered to be the "Pluto" of Havana, and Jack's first duty was to get the poor cramped creatures in the hold upon deck. They had been battened down before the fight commenced, and when the hatches were taken off, the stench that arose from below was sickening. Under the hatches was a grating which admitted a certain amount of air and light, and this our hero at once ordered to be removed.

It was too much to ask any of the "Esmeralda's" men to go down amongst the filth and foetid atmosphere of the noisome prison, but Hannibal and Pitchpot volunteered for the service of setting their black brethren free. Armed with hammers to knock off the shackles from the ankles of those who were chained down, they descended the ricketty ladder, and presently the bewildered beings began to make their appearance on deck.

Old men, and old women, young men and young women, boys and girls came slowly and painfully up, gazing about them in a dazed and stupefied way. Some of the women carried babies in their arms, and many of them sank down upon the deck unable to stand after their long and weary sojourn in one position.

Last of all came a patriarchal looking negro with a white fringe of wool around a bare, black scalp. His eyes were sunken in his head, and he was almost blind. On reaching the open air he tottered and nearly fell, but one of the young men caught him, and led him to a barrel upon which he seated himself. Then Hannibal and Pitchpot clambered up, and paused at the top to inhale a deep draught of the precious breeze which blew across the vessel.

The brawny fellow who had done such execution with the capstan-bar looked around upon the coloured people whom he had released till his eyes rested upon the figure of the old man seated on the barrel. He went up to him, and passing a hand under the chin raised the patriarch's face that he might obtain a good view of it. The countenance was not a pleasant one. There were craft, and cunning, and duplicity in it, and it was disfigured by a deep scar down one cheek from the temple to the angle of the jaw. Hannibal scrutinized the features long and earnestly. At length he glanced at the captain.

"Send for Peter, Massa Jack," he said, in a strangely quiet voice for one who was generally loud in his expressions.

"He is attending to the seriously wounded," replied our hero.

"Somebody else will do dat, an' let Peter come here. He *must* come."

"I will go," said Tom Warren, good-naturedly.

"T'ank you, Massa Tom. Tell Peter to come dis precious minute."

Tom went away, and in a few moments Peter presented himself.

"What's de mattah, Hannibal?" he asked.

"See here, d'ye know dis old niggah?"

Peter looked at him as earnestly as Hannibal had done.

"Yes, brudder," he answered, after his scrutiny, "I do know de ole niggah."

"Who is he den?" enquired the brother.

"Our fader."

"You're right, Peter, dat's de ole reprobeast wot sold us when we was lilly boys."

"What!" exclaimed Jack, who had been looking on with much interest. "Do you mean to say that old man is your father?"

"Dat's him, Massa Jack," Peter replied, dolefully. "Dat's de ole lump o' brack dirt as sold my dear brudder Hannibal an' me to de slave captain."

"But how can you recognize him at this distant date? Surely your boyish memories cannot be so distinct as that?"

"Dat's him, sure enough," returned Hannibal, "I knowed him by de cut on his cheek. He got dat wid a knife from a young chief when tryin' to steal his wife for de slave captain."

"Why don't you test him, and see if he remembers you," said Jack.

"It so long ago," replied Peter, "him forget all about it."

"Never mind, try him; perhaps he will recall the circumstance."

Peter then approached the old man.

"Fader!" he cried, in a loud voice. "You remember your piccannnies you sell to de slaver."

The old negro stared at him blankly out of his dim eyes, but made no reply.

"Does he understand English?" asked Jack, after a pause.

"Oh, yes, him understan' English berry well," Peter answered. "Fader!" he shouted again. "What you do wid your two lilly boys?"

"Sole'em—sole'em to de slave cap'n." The voice was very weak and tremulous, but it was sufficient to establish his identity.

"You hear dat, Massa Jack?" exclaimed Hannibal. "De ole reprobeast owns dat he sold us."

Then the rascally patriarch spoke again in the same quavering tones.

"Long ago—long ago," he muttered. "Dey was big strong boys, an' de slave cap'n pay well for 'em. Deir fader was rich man den, but all de money gone now. 'Nudder slave cap'n come an' take away ole man. What he take ole man for? Him too weak to work, him berry near dead. Slave cap'n want gold an' ivory, but ole man got none now, all gone —all gone!"

"But you're free now, fader. Massa Jack set you free," explained Hannibal.

"Who call me 'fader'?" enquired the ancient black. "Me got no boys, got no nobody."

"Yes, fader, dis am Hannibal, an' dat chile am lilly Peter."

"No, no! I sole 'em, I say—I sole 'em to slave cap'n."

"Yes, we know you gone done dat," said Peter, "but we am free men now. We am Englishmen;" and Peter drew himself up with as pompous an air as if he had been a true native-born Briton.

"What you say? My boys free! Den de ole man die in peace. Nebber hab no peace since him sole his boys. Where am you, Peter? Hannibal, where am you?"

"We am here, fader."

"Den you hab an ole man's bressin'. Dere's gold an' ivory in de groun' before de hut, boys. Slave cap'n no find it— ole man no tell. Slave cap'n t'ink he make him tell at Havana; but ole man cheat him yet."

"De slave captain am dead, fader.

Massa Jack kill him an' capture de ship. You am free again like Hannibal an' me. We all go back home bimeby an' get de gold an' ivory, den we go to England, an' live wid Massa Jack."

It was plain now to our hero and Charley Granby, who in spite of his wounds had limped along to witness the peculiar meeting, that the father of the two faithful followers of the captain, was fast losing strength. His hands were wandering about in a vague, uncertain way and his voice grew weaker when he spoke.

"I am afraid he cannot last long," said Jack. "The confinement below has done its work."

"Peter! Hannibal!" moaned the old man. "I'm a gwine on a long v'y'ge, but it ain't wid de slave cap'n. Don't forget de gold an' de ivory, boys, dere's plenty ob it dar an' it's all yours. It's a-growin berry dark, an' dis ole nigger can't see his way. Good-bye, boys, don't forget de——"

The father's head fell forward on his breast, and he was no more.

"De ole reprobeast am dead," said Hannibal, with a tear in his eye. "May de Lord hab mussy on him soul."

"Amen!" responded Peter.

Then they took up the body and carried it to the stern sheets, where they laid it down reverently and straightened the limbs.

The next hour or two was devoted to consigning the dead Cubans to the deep ; and afterwards, with a little more ceremony the father of the two servitors was also buried, with a round shot at his feet.

Jack's attention was now turned to securing the prisoners in the forecastle, and after some considerable trouble this was accomplished.

There were over a hundred and twenty blacks on board, and with these Jack resolved to make his way to Jamaica, placing sufficient men on board the "Pluto" to work her to the port of Kingston.

Both vessels arrived there in due time without any adventure worth recording, and Jack was tremendously complimented upon his daring in having captured a vessel so much superior to the "Esmeralda" in complement of men and arms. His fame was well known in the island, and there he remained for some days till the "Pluto" was repaired ; for he had decided to fit her out, and with a large number

of spare hands aboard to set sail with her for his own haunt in the ocean. The spare hands were to work home the prizes which lay there, and which he knew would bring him a large and well-earned fortune.

When all was ready he took his departure amidst the hearty farewells of the West Indians.

––––––––

CHAPTER LXXVIII.

STORMING A STRONGHOLD.

THE morning broke beautifully over the hills which girdled in the other side of the river bank from that on which Jim Swaby and his lads, together with the friendly tribe of islanders were encamped. As the sun's rays reached them, everyone was stirring, and the dusky people had a simple religious ceremony to perform in honour of the god of day.

This over they set about preparing breakfast from the remains of the feast of the previous evening. There was sufficient meat left for the men to regale themselves upon, but the ladies declined such strong fare, and contented themselves with the luscious fruits procured from the woods hard by.

After the meal a discussion took place between Rawalloa, Kavaloko, Jim Swaby, Bob Richley, and Arthur Guy. Since the unmistakable revelation of the will of the sun god not a dissentient voice had been raised against the expedition. Whatever Guy may have thought he said nothing, and so Jim Swaby and he were back again on their old footing, a slight coolness having been previously observable. It was now proposed by Kavaloko that the attacking party should be divided into two, one force to proceed by water, and the other by land, Rawalloa and Jim Swaby, with half of the warriors and sailors, were to make the river attack, and Kavaloko with Bob Richley and Arthur Guy would head the other. Jim Swaby would have preferred Arthur Guy to be with him, as there was no denying his usefulness, both as interpreter and adviser in time of need ; but Kavaloko had specially asked for him to be on that side, so out of courtesy Jim was compelled to accede to the young chief's request.

The plan to be adopted was a very simple one. The river force was to make their way right up to the stronghold, and make a demonstration in front of it. This it was believed would draw out all the fighting men of the Mallobutos from their cave dwellings. They would probably take to their boats to drive back the intruders from their sacred precincts, upon which the land force would descend the precipitous heights as best they could and cut off the retreat of the cannibals. Such a proceeding would place the man-eaters between two fires, and both parties attacking them boldly in front and rear would totally annihilate the flower of the tribe.

The rocks on both sides of the river below the stronghold were said to rise sheer from the water to a great height, so that the Mallobutos would have no chance of escaping from the attacking foes; and the thunder-makers of the white men, which had already wrought such havoc amongst the savages, would totally paralyize them and render them an easy prey.

This was the whole scheme, and on the face of it, it looked decidedly feasible.

There was one thing which Kavaloko impressed upon the minds of his white allies, the descent to the bottom of the stronghold was covered by creepers and vines amongst the stems and leaves of which lurked the terribly poisonous serpents which the Mallobutos worshipped, and on which they greatly relied as a defence.

Arthur Guy thought he saw a way out of this difficulty, but he resolved to say nothing till time would prove whether he was right or not.

About seven o'clock in the morning the land party started, as they would require a longer time to reach the scene of operations than the others.

Kavaloko and Guy marched at the head, followed closely by Richley and the sailors, while the strong body of warriors brought up the rear.

A considerable detour had to be made because of the nature of the ground, and it was fully half-past ten before the division reached the heights above the stronghold. Here they kept as close within the forest as possible, lest the Mallobutos should gain an inkling of their presence. Arthur Guy and Kavaloko alone ventured forth to reconnoitre.

As the former had anticipated, the trailing plants which were the home of the snakes, depended from the top of the cliffs, and covered the face of them. His idea was that they should be hacked off close by the roots above and thrown over into the river below, and now that he saw them he perceived no difficulty in carrying out the notion.

It was necessary, however, to allow the attacking party from below to begin their demonstration first, otherwise the noise of the axes would alarm the fiends underneath.

Presently shouts and cries from the river announced that operations had commenced, and the leaders made their way to the top of the cliffs, whence they could see what was going on.

As was imagined from the first the Mallobutos swarmed out of their caves at the bottom of the rocks, and prepared to resent the intrusion, but the enemy was beyond the range of their arrows, so it behoved them to take to their canoes in pursuit.

This was exactly what those on the heights were waiting for.

Whack! whack! went the axes at the creepers, and one by one the great festoons went down into the river below.

The number of snakes about them had not been exaggerated, for there they were, coiling and twisting amongst the closely-woven withes like the runners themselves. In a few minutes the whole front of the rock was bare, and a sort of zig-zag pathway was discovered leading down, which the creepers before had hidden.

Down this break-neck descent dashed Kavaloko, with Arthur Guy at his heels, leading the sailors, while behind them came the yelling and whooping pack of friendly savages.

The Mallobutos saw them too late.

The women, children, and old men were the only persons left in the stronghold, and they were of no avail to drive these fresh comers into the water.

With cries of vengeance, the river division now attacked the canoes of the cannibals, while the land force prevented them from retreating up the stream.

As was foreseen, the Mallobutos were completely demoralized, dashing hither and thither in their small craft, unable to land, and impotent between the two fires.

There is this to be said of a few of them who retained their heads that they fought desperately, but it was without the least hope of victory.

Hundreds of them leapt into the river to be drowned amongst the writhing snakes that they worshipped; others of them stabbed themselves, while a few flung themselves upon the deadly weapons of their enemies, there to meet the death of warriors.

In half-an-hour every male Mallobuto of full age was dead, and only the old men, women, and children remained of a once terror-inspiring tribe.

The land force now got into the canoes of the vanquished, as well as the great war canoes of their own tribe, and a victorious procession was formed back to the point where they had left the queen and her women.

Great were the rejoicings on their arrivals, and Jim Swaby and the sailors were made much of by their friends, for to the deadly power of the thunder-makers was attributed the signal success of the day.

The rejoicings were kept up all that night, and the whole of the day following. Dancing and games of a mysterious order were greatly indulged in, and occasional feasts of flesh or fruit gave a variety to the proceedings.

The Englishmen took part in all that went on as far as they were able, and enjoyed themselves thoroughly. Pat, however, nearly got them into disgrace, for he would make love in his Irish fashion to a pretty young attendant of the queen, whom he believed to be single; but the husband became aware of his attentions, and there was very nearly bloodshed before either party could be made to understand that no offence was meant.

At the beginning of the third day Jim Swaby announced that he and his friends must say adieu; but nothing would satisfy the grateful islanders save permitting them to escort the little party to their home at Fort Scarborough.

This, after some hesitation, Jim Swaby allowed, and the astonishment of the garrison of three when they saw the exploring party return at the head of a small army of natives was beyond description.

Their first impulse was to fire upon the dusky train, but Jim held up his hand as a signal that they were to be unmolested, and then he had them conducted across the moat and up to the fort, which they overran in all directions. Their curiosity was intense, but it was principally exhibited by the women, who are of the same nature all the world over.

Rawalloa, Kavaloko, and the warriors were deeply interested in the big guns, which they couldn't understand at all till Jim Swaby had one loaded and fired for their special delectation.

The result was something unexpected.

Every man of the tribe fell flat upon his face as if he had been shot.

Arthur Guy ran to the king to raise him, but the monarch positively refused to get up, and it was so with all the others.

They did not appear to be afraid, only they had made up their minds to grovel on their stomachs for a time, and nobody could prevent them.

At last Rawalloa condescended to pick himself up, and all the others followed suit.

Jim Swaby, who had been exploding with laughter at this novel experience, called Arthur Guy, and instructed him to inquire if his majesty and his friends were better.

"It is nothing," was the monarch's calm reply, as translated by Arthur, "we occasionally have an earthquake at home ourselves, and we find the safest plan is to lie upon the ground."

"Then you are not surprised," continued Arthur, on a hint from Jim.

"No, only that you should be able to produce one. What do you call your earthquake maker?"

"It goes by different names," Guy answered, "cannon, gun, or piece of ordnance."

"Rawalloa would be glad to have one on his island. He would like to make earthquakes."

"No doubt, but I am afraid our chief could not spare you one. Besides, if he should agree to give you a gun, you would not be able to carry it away."

Rawalloa looked somewhat crestfallen, but did not suggest such a gift again.

"The earthquake maker of the white man is the father of the thunder maker," said the king in a self-satisfied tone.

"I suppose so," replied the sailor.

As they spoke together in the tongue of the Pacific islands, the boom of a heavy gun was heard at sea.

The warriors did not fall down on this occasion.

"That earthquake is far away," observed Kavaloko.

"Yes," said the king, "it will not harm us here."

But the gun attracted the attention of Jim Swaby, and the rest of the garrison.

The old boatswain went for his glass and swept the horizon.

"There are two vessels out there," he exclaimed, as a glow of excitement overspread his face. "From the signal I should say it's Happy Jack. Give 'em a shot in return, Richley."

The gun was loaded again.

"You needn't fall on your stomachs now," Jim added. "The earthquake maker, as you call it isn't dangerous unless it's pointed at you."

Guy interpreted this speech as well as he could, and then the discharge of the gun took place. Only two or three went down this time, from force of habit.

All this time the women had disappeared, and were nowhere to be seen about the fort. Bob Richley, however, having occasion to enter one of the huts found them all there packed as tightly as possible.

He couldn't make out the mystery; but after watching them quietly for a few minutes he understood it all. They were taking it in turns to stand before a small ship's mirror and admire themselves in the glass for a few seconds at a time.

Bob gave vent to a wild shriek of laughter, and dashed from the building with the whole bevy of beauties following close at his heels.

Round the fort he ran pursued by the ladies, till he sought refuge behind the handsome figure of the monarch himself.

The ladies were laughing, too, and the queen herself was the merriest of the throng. In a few words she explained to the king what had taken place, and Rawalloa grew as mirthful as the rest. Arthur Guy was soon let into the secret, and guffawed loudly. Poor Richley looked abashed; but when he was told that the penalty for catching the fair islanders admiring themselves, was a kiss all round, he jumped at the idea, and when the ceremony was over, it is stated that he was heard to smack his lips.

In the meanwhile the two vessels were gradually drawing nearer to the island, and by this time the garrison were pretty well assured it was Jack, for at the peak of each floated a couple of flags, the Union Jack and the pure white ensign of the young commander.

When that was properly ascertained, the fort gave forth a grand royal salute of twenty-one guns. This was returned from the yacht, and by-and-bye the garrison was pleased to see the two vessels named the " Esmeralda " and the " Pluto" come into the natural harbour at the foot of the rocks.

It was Jack in reality, hale and hearty, and loud were the hurrahs that welcomed him.

His astonishment was great at finding visitors in the fort; but when he heard the story of the Mallobutos, he held out the right hand of fellowship to the islanders, and told them he was pleased to see them.

Arthur Guy translated his words, and then Rawalloa made a long speech which was interpreted in turn to Jack, and all went as merry as a marriage bell.

Soon the islanders left, laden with many presents, and then Jack took the garrison down into the cabin of the " Esmeralda," and told of all that had befallen him since he left the island.

Jim Swaby congratulated him in the name of the others, and presented Arthur Guy to him for promotion.

Jack did not intend to stay long at the old haunt, so he got everything in order as soon as possible and then set sail with all the prizes for the old country.

A few of the men, however, petitioned to be left behind at the fort, among whom was Pat. He subsequently married a dusky bride, a cousin of Rawalloa's, and thus became akin to royalty. His numerous progeny grew up on the island, and for all we know may be living there still, for it is not so long ago since these events happened.

A prosperous voyage to Portsmouth succeeded the departure from the Pacific seas, and Jack soon found himself in London town a happier and a wiser man than ever he was before.

CHAPTER LXXIX.

JACK IN LOVE.

JACK SCARBOROUGH'S life had been far too busy up till now for the tender passion to have had any part in it. In all his wanderings, although he had been wounded in many parts of the body, his heart had always remained unscathed. Perhaps it was that he had never seen any young lady who could inspire in him that peculiar feeling which poets and such strange creatures designate by the name of "love." Yet so far, at all events, it was so; and though at times he could be as sentimental as most folk, especially when he thought of his poor missing unc'e, the latent spark of affection for the opposite sex had still to be aroused in him.

He was now at that age, however, when most youths become susceptible, and when Don Cupid, that infallible marksman, has his bow strung ready to let fly the winged shaft that pierces through the most invulnerable armour.

Charley Granby, Tom Warren, and himself were now in London, enjoying that well-earned repose which is the due of every one after a season of hard toil.

Amongst other friends whom they had met in the great metropolis was Lieutenant Barnham, who from an enemy had turned round to be a firm comrade, and they were invited to spend their time at the house of his parents, in Kensington. The Barnhams were kindly people, who, though possessing comfortable means, made no great display, but lived in a quiet and secluded manner. Mr. Barnham was a scientific gentleman, who was mostly engaged in a laboratory which he had had fitted up for himself at the back of his house, and where he conducted experiments in chemistry and other subjects to which he had taken a fancy. Mrs. Barnham was a lively little woman, who idolized her son, the lieutenant, and lived for him and his two sisters, having no thought for herself. To be a friend of her Willie, as the lieutenant was called, was to be a friend of herself, and, indeed, of all the family, so it is not to be wondered at that our hero and his two companions were welcomed into the coterie with open arms.

It has been mentioned that the lieutenant possessed two sisters. Both of them were charming girls, and when the family assembled round the fireside of an evening, Jack was called upon to relate the story of his life. Night after night he was asked, like another Othello, to run through the tale, "even from his boyish days, to the very moment that they bade him tell it," and in his own simple way he obeyed them. He was no Munchausen, and, indeed, his story required no embellishment, it was wonderful enough without exaggeration, and the little circle of listeners opened their hearts to him as he told of "the battles, sieges, fortunes that he had passed."

More eagerly, perhaps, than any of the others, Mary Barnham "devoured up his discourse." She was the younger sister, a sweet girl of seventeen, whose large, fawn-like eyes were fixed upon our hero's face for hour after hour, as he narrated his adventures, and whose colour would come and go in the most enchanting manner as he told of success, or spoke of his infamous persecution.

When it came to that part of the story wherein he had to give an account of his imprisonment and trial, the great brown eyes of the maiden filled with tears to overflowing, and she clenched her little hands at the duplicity of the odious captain, while her heart beat wildly with mixed feelings of commiseration and anger.

It was impossible for the fair creature to conceal her emotion, and Jack saw all and was conquered, as he had never been conquered before. The drawn bowstring was loosed with a twang of music, and the arrow sped swiftly to the mark. Without a single effort at resistance our hero capitulated.

"She loved him for the dangers he had passed,
    And he loved her that she did pity them."

At first it seemed as if true love were to have a smooth course in the wooing of Jack Scarborough and Mary Barnham. The elders looked on approvingly, the lieutenant was delighted, and Charley Granby and Tom Warren signified their appreciation by sundry nods and winks, which were oracular in their hidden meanings.

But after all it happened that the proverb was not to be gainsaid.

There was a certain lanky, redhaired young gentleman, who lived a few doors off the Barnhams' residence, named Solomon Sloeberry. Until Jack's appearance upon the scene, this individual had taken it into his head that Mary Barnham was the very individual whom nature had designed to bear the not particularly euphonious cognomen of Mrs. Solomon Sloeberry. So far had he persuaded himself that such was the case, that he had procured an introduction to Mrs. Barnham, through a mutual friend, and had endeavoured upon every occasion of their meeting to ingratiate himself with the lady and her charming daughters, and many were the tokens of affection in the form of flowers and bon-bons, which the enamoured swain despatched to the house of Barnham.

Mary gave his flowers to a smart young maid, who waited upon herself and sister Belle, and ate his chocolate creams with relish.

Alas that it should be so! but neither flowers nor bon-bons acted in the fashion of love-philtres, and poor Sloeberry's advances were received with a calm indifference.

This state of affairs drove the infatuated youth to the verge of despair.

Then he bethought himself of a scheme by which he would obtain an audience of his loved one alone, and pour into her ear an impassioned poem which he had written, and which, he felt assured, must melt her stony heart.

His scheme was simplicity itself. He would suborn her maid by the present of half-a-sovereign, to arrange a meeting for him, and then he would recite to her his ode. It could not fail. Where flowers and bon-bons had proved ineffectual, the divine muse would undoubtedly win.

To this end Mr. Sloeberry seated himself next day behind the curtains of the dining-room window, whence he could command a good view of the street. He knew it was the habit of Lisette, the maid, to trip out of an afternoon about five of the clock to do sundry little errands for her young mistresses, such as posting letters, or purchasing gloves and knick-knacks at the draper's hard by.

Five o'clock came, and his heart began to flutter in a most uncomfortable fashion, but his hopes were high, and he did not mind. Presently his cardiac organ gave a great leap, and obeying its impulse, Mr. Sloeberry also leapt. Lisette was coming lightly down the street.

Poor Solomon rushed into the hall and seized his hat. He was making for the door in hot haste; but being near-sighted, and having forgotten in his hurry to put on his spectacles, he did not perceive his mother's favourite pussy, which came quietly forward to rub its coat against his legs, as was its wont. In making a dash for the hall door, which stood open, the unfortunate lover tripped over the cat, and dived head first down the steps, where he landed on the pave-ment at the very feet of the astonished Lisette.

"*Mon Dieu!*" shrieked the maid, in the wildest alarm.

"Please, Lisette," said Mr. Sloeberry, in the most piteous accent, "do be quiet. I was coming out to see you when the accident happened."

"*Ah, c'est bien drôle!*" exclaimed the merry maid, as she wiped her eyes on her little lace apron. "Vat do you vish vid me, Monsieur Slobbery?"

"Lisette, I believe you know my secret; you French people are so very clever," said Solomon, after they had gone a little way.

"You have secret, monsieur? You are in lofe."

"Alas, Lisette, you are right! I love your mistress."

"Ah! you lofe Ma'amzelle Marie. *Eh bien?*"

"I would like to speak to her alone," murmured Sloeberry, in a confidential tone.

Lisette shook her head.

"*C'est impossible,*" she answered, discouragingly.

"Here is half-a-sovereign, Lisette. Surely you can manage it for me."

A sparkle of mischief shone in the eyes of the maid as she accepted the coin.

"I vill try, Monsieur Slobbery," she said. "Come to de garden gate at eight o'clock, and I t'ink you vill see her den, perhaps." So saying the maid tripped away, leaving the love-stricken Solomon in the seventh heaven of delight.

Five minutes to the hour appointed Solomon Sloeberry stood at one of the doors. Above him a large tree spread its branches over the lane, and rendered the darkness more intense.

Presently the door opened, and a cautious voice cried: "Hist!"

Solomon sidled closer to the entrance.

"Is it you, my adored Miss Mary?" enquired the poetical lover.

"Hush!" exclaimed a low voice, and a hand was put out towards him.

He seized it and covered it with kisses.

Oh, blissful moment!" he exclaimed. "Now, my darling, although my gifts have not had the desired effect, I will speak to you in the accents of love, and I know that then you cannot resist to admit the little stranger to your heart."

There was a sound as of suppressed laughter, but Mr. Sloeberry heard it not.

He was too transported with the rapture in his soul.

"Listen to this, my sweet one!" he went on. "I composed it for your ears alone, and none other shall ever hear the lines."

Solomon paused for a moment, and then in a voice as if he were repeating a Sunday-school lesson, he proceeded :

"There is a vision I adore
  Beyond the power of praise,
And love consumes me more and more,
  My heart is in a blaze.
My soul with love is all aglow,
  Although my gifts she spurns,
Like all the fires from down below
  My brain with ardour burns."

"Put him out! De man is on fire!" cried a voice with a decided foreign accent, and at the same moment a deluge from above drenched the astounded Solomon to his skin.

"Now then, Slobbery, get home at once!" somebody exclaimed from the branches overhead.

"Is the fire extinguished yet?" demanded another from the same direction.

"Take my advice, and never poke your nose where it isn't wanted," said a third person.

Then Solomon "stood not on the order of his going, but went at once."

It was the last time he ever attempted to force his attentions upon Mary Barnham, and shortly afterwards he left Kensington for good.

Mary was afterwards told of the whole affair, but her tender heart was rather shocked at the punishment of the too ardent lover. However, it made no alteration in her feelings towards Jack, and before that young gentleman left the Barnhams he was an affianced man.

CHAPTER LXXX.

ALL'S WELL THAT ENDS WELL.

WITH Jack's return came an order from Government to restore the forfeited estates to his uncle, Mr. Carter Scarborough, but the Government was not in a position to restore the missing gentleman as well.

Our readers will call to mind the fact that, on the forfeiture of his estates, he had disappeared, and left no clue as to his whereabouts—a matter of sore distress to Jack and his friends.

They tried the newspapers, and every morning the readers of the *Times* read the following in the agony column :—

"Mr. Carter Scarborough is implored to return to his nephew, who has succeeded in establishing his innocence, and restoring the family estates. If the missing gentleman is lying ill anywhere, one hundred pounds will be paid on the receipt of such evidence as shall lead to his restoration to his friends. Mr. Carter Scarborough is about sixty-five years of age, tall, with fine head of grey hair and moustache, walks with a military air."

This brought forth no fruit, and Jack was almost despairing, when one day a navvy appeared at the door.

"Master," he said, holding up a bit of the *Times* newspaper, "I've bought this with a bit of cheese, and I've been reading it. I think I know the man."

"If you do," said Jack, "the hundred pounds is yours."

"Some time ago," continued the man, "a aged party, such as is described here, comes to my house, and axes me if I can give him a room."

"What sort of a room?" says I.

"'Anything,' he said, 'so that it's clean and cheap, for I've got little or no money.'

"I give him a room," continued the man, "such as it is, which clean it is, for my old woman is as neat as a new pin, and there he bides, livin' on what he brought with him, only a few pounds, until it were all gone, then he used to go out in the morning to look for work ; but, bless you, there warn't no work for the likes o' *him*, and every day he gets poorer and poorer, and comes anigh starving."

"Is he ill?" said Jack. "Be quick, if you please."

"He's as well as a man can hope to be," replied the navvy, "when you takes into consideration the 'mount of stone-breaking, and the precious little bread it brings him."

"My uncle stone-breaking!"

"That's it, sir. He wouldn't go on to the parish, and it's the only thing he could do."

"Where do you live?"

"At Chichester."

"Can you come with me at once?"

"I can, sir, if you'll guarantee my loss o' time."

"I'll guarantee you something for life, if my uncle is found."

As they neared the ancient city of

Chichester, the man began to look about him."

" I think we shall find him somewhere here," he said.   " Ah ! there he is, under the hedge, resting a bit.   Is that the gentleman ?"

Harry saw a feeble old man sitting under a hedge, but he could not tell whether it was his uncle or no.

He was yet some distance away, and the wan-like figure was so different to that he had known ; but as he drew nearer he recognised something of the old familiar face ; and, running forward, he called out to his uncle by name.

The old man looked up bewildered, and shaded his eyes with his hand.

" Is it a voice from the dead ?" he cried.

" No," said Jack, " it is the voice of the living."

" Oh ! welcome, my darling boy !" cried the old man, straining Jack passionately to his breast ; " but you must hide, you must hide."

" Hide, and why, dear uncle ?"

" There is a price upon your head, and the gallows is ready."

" No ; all that is a thing of the past."

" Oh, Jack ! is this a dream ?"

" Come back to the old house and you will see.

The old man was still bewildered as he got into the trap, and the navvy who stood by holding the horse's head touched his hat, and said—

" I allers knew he was a gentleman, but he was close, werry close, sir."

" True blood does not care to babble about its troubles," returned Jack. " Here is your reward.   Spend the money wisely and well, and don't forget to come and see me again."

And now our story virtually ends. Wrongs have been righted, evil-doers punished, bravery rewarded, and it only now remains for us to give a sketch of what became of those in whom, we trust, our readers are most interested.

Mr. Carter Scarborough in a great measure recovered his health, but was never again quite the man of old.   There were occasions when he had a tendency to wander in his thoughts, and at such times he would have left the house under the idea that it was no longer his, but for the ever-watchful care of those around him.

As for Jack, he married Mary Burnham, and settled down as a country gentleman, thoroughly satisfied with the experience of his early days, and by his amiable disposition and manly bearing, gained such a host of friends that the great house of the Scarboroughs was seldom without visitors.

Tom Warren and Charley Granby went to sea again, and the former soon became post-captain.

Charley is also in a fair way to a high position, and whenever their ships are in port, off they go at once to visit their old chum, and over a bottle of wine and a box of cigars, fignt their battles o'er again.

Captain Marston is also a very favoured visitor there, and so is Lieutenant Barnham ; in fact, Jack has changed only in years, and not in disposition.

With three or four youngsters around him, he is as jolly and frank as ever.

" Not a bit changed !" his friends say, and not being changed, he holds the same position in their hearts.

The proceeds of the prizes being divided, gave a handsome sum to Tom Warren, Charley Granby, and Jim Swaby, and to each man a small but sufficient annuity for their lives.   Most of the men settled down near their old commander, and in the parlour of the village inn spun their yarns to the rustics, and swore that no man ever lived who could compare with Happy Jack. But some went away ; the love of adventure was too strong within them, and they went to the far West and the far North, and did good service to their country, and these, one and all, swore by our hero, too.

Jim Swaby remained at home, and became the oracle of all sea matters to his mates, and the wonder of the village inn.

There are three more persons to deal with, and we have done—Hannibal, Peter the Great, and Pitchpot—all of whom remained in Jack's service ; that is, they lived in the house, and went about and did as they pleased, within certain bounds, of course.

With a good, kind master and every need supplied, what nigger ever hoped or cared for more ?

THE END.

www.ingramcontent.com/pod-product-compliance
Lightning Source LLC
Chambersburg PA
CBHW080823250626

47160CB00008B/2849